destined for love

THE HUNTINGTON BROTHERS
BOOK 1

SARA MCCLAFLIN

INDEPENDENTLY PUBLISHED

eBook ISBN: 979-8-218-42425-1

Paperback ISBN: 979-8-218-43299-7

Edited by Brandy Gibson

Cover and Interior Formatting by Ivy of Hawthorn & Aster (www.hawthornandaster.com)

To my two loving grandmas, whose love, warmth, wisdom, and enduring grace have inspired this journey, and this book is a tribute to all of the cherished moments shared throughout my life.

FIVE-YEAR-OLD DESTINY WALKED INTO HER KINDERGARTEN class, her small hands clutching the straps of her pink backpack adorned with flowers. She wore her new light blue dress with white polka dots, her curly brown hair was pulled back with a matching blue ribbon. Destiny's hazel eyes darted around the room, taking in the vibrant colors and paintings that decorated the walls. Her heart raced as she looked for an empty chair, her nerves getting the best of her.

"Daddy said it'll be fun," Destiny whispered to herself, trying to muster up some courage. She spotted a little girl in the corner, looking like an angelic princess with her frilly multi-colored dress and sparkling jewelry. The other children gazed at her with awe as she showed off her expensive, fancy clothing. Destiny couldn't help but stare, feeling out of place in her simple dress.

"Hey!" A gentle tap on her shoulder caught Destiny's attention. She turned to see another five-year-old girl standing there with short black hair framing her round face, glasses over bright blue eyes and a bright yellow t-shirt with a smiling sun on it. "Can I sit next to you?" she asked, pointing to the empty spot beside Destiny.

"Sure!" Destiny replied, her nervousness fading slightly as the girl sat down next to her, following Destiny's gaze toward the girl in the corner.

"That's Candy Sullivan," the girl in the yellow shirt said, rolling her eyes. "She thinks she's *so* special because all her stuff is fancy."

Destiny gave the girl a small smile in appreciation. "I'm Destiny," she introduced herself, holding out her hand.

"Hi Destiny! I'm Lila." Lila shook her hand with enthusiasm, and Destiny couldn't help but let her smile grow.

As they continued talking, a boy approached their desks. His brown hair was neatly combed, and his green eyes sparkled with curiosity. He wore a red polo shirt and khaki shorts, making him look like a miniature golfer.

"Hi, I'm Miles. Can I sit with you?" he asked, gesturing to the chair on the other side of Destiny.

"Of course!" Destiny replied, happy to have another friend join their group.

"Hi, Miles! I'm Lila, and this is Destiny," Lila took the lead, while Destiny quietly took everything in. The three of them chatted, discussing their favorite cartoons and what they hoped to learn in kindergarten. Destiny felt her anxiety melt away as she found herself surrounded by new friends.

"Alright, class!" The teacher clapped her hands, getting everyone's attention. "Let's get started!"

As the chatter around them died down, Destiny glanced at Lila and Miles, and grinned ear to ear at her two new friends. Her worries transformed into enthusiasm for the most amazing journey!

She knew that together, they could face anything kindergarten would bring their way.

* * *

The sun shone brightly on the last day of eighth grade, casting a warm glow over the schoolyard as Destiny, Lila, and Miles excitedly gathered their belongings and left the building. The air buzzed with anticipation for the upcoming summer and high school adventures that awaited them.

"Guys, can you believe it? We're finally going to be in high school!" Destiny exclaimed, her blue eyes sparkling.

"I know! I can't wait to try out for the debate team," Lila added, adjusting her glasses. "What about you, Destiny? Any clubs or activities you're planning on joining?"

"Definitely drama club. And maybe even the cooking club if I have time," Destiny replied, already envisioning herself performing on stage and experimenting with new recipes.

Miles leaned over to say, "I'm thinking of trying out for the football team. High school's going to be amazing." He sighed out, smiling at the thought.

"Absolutely!" Lila agreed. "But first, we have an entire summer break ahead of us. What are your plans?"

"Nothing special. Just spending time with my dad and maybe volunteering at the soup kitchen," Destiny said. Her father had fostered a sense of community in her. They spent most holidays working in soup kitchens, making sure to donate to every food drive, and helping anyone that they knew was in need. The family made teddy bear blankets for children who were in the hospital, baked bread for the men at the local jail, and organized food drives to help poverty-stricken families get through the harsh winter weather. They took care of their neighbors as if they were part of their own family.

"That sounds great," Lila smiled. They said their good-byes, and Destiny made her way home. Her excitement at the prospect of joining clubs and going to dances with her favorite people was palpable.

Destiny trekked up the driveway to the house she'd grown up in, and took in the sight of it aging but still standing. She had to smile at the dandelions that had pushed their way through the cracks in the pavement. It was definitely time for a replacement, but at least the flowers were blooming. The pale yellow flowers contrasted with the white trim her dad had added last year. As Destiny stepped up the steps, worn down from years of her and her friends running up and down them, she opened the door—a reminder that this summer they would paint it anew. Comfort washed over her.

Upon entering her house, she was greeted by the familiar scent of her father's cooking. She found him in the kitchen, stirring a pot of homemade spaghetti sauce. Destiny hugged him tightly, her excitement still bubbling inside her.

"Hey, kiddo" her father said, returning her embrace. "Remember when I told you I was looking for a new job?"

Destiny nodded, her heart suddenly heavy with concern. "Yeah, Dad. Did you find one?"

Her father hesitated before answering, "Yes. But there's a catch, Destiny. It's a few hours away, and we're going to have to move."

"Move?! What about high school?" she asked, her eyes widening in shock.

"I'm so sorry, honey. This was the only job I could find, and the pay is really good. I know it's hard, but we need this." He looked at her with apologetic eyes, and Destiny knew he was right.

"Okay, Dad," she sighed, understanding the situation. "I'll tell Miles and Lila."

That evening, after inviting her friends over, Destiny broke the news to them on her living room couch. Their faces fell, they embraced her tightly and assured her that their friendship would remain strong.

"Promise me we'll always stay friends," Miles implored, his green eyes shining with determination.

"Always," Destiny whispered, holding back tears and linking pinkies.

A week later, Destiny found herself surrounded by boxes in her bedroom. The walls, once adorned with posters and memories, now stood bare and empty. With each box she taped shut, the room became more and more unrecognizable. Finally, her father knocked on the doorframe, asking softly, "Are you ready?"

Taking a deep breath, she closed her bedroom door for the last time and followed her father out of the house. The once-cozy home now felt vacant, stripped of all the cherished memories that had filled it.

As they drove through the familiar town, Destiny watched the streets pass by one last time. They drove past Peaches, the local café where she had spent countless afternoons laughing, studying and planning for the future with her friends. Her phone chimed, and she glanced down to see a text from Miles, a picture of the three of them smiling under the big oak tree nestled in the middle of the park. It had been there for generations, a symbol of history and tradition just like the town itself.

MILES

best friends forever

Lila sent a heart emoji, and Destiny's eyes welled up with tears. Clutching her phone tightly to her chest, she knew she was leaving behind a significant chapter of her life. But as they drove further away from the town, she realized that this move would open the door to new beginnings and exciting opportunities. Filled with both anticipation and trepidation, Destiny looked forward to the future, knowing that the bond she shared with her friends could withstand any distance.

* * *

Now settled into her new town, 14-year-old Destiny had started high school two months ago. As Halloween approached, she missed the familiar traditions and excitement that came with celebrating the holiday with her old friends. Wanting to keep the connection alive, she sent a message to Lila and Miles, asking what they were going to be for Halloween.

LILA - 3:30 P.M.

I don't know, girl! Whatever it is, it has to be cute! You?

DESTINY - 3:32 P.M.

I'm at a loss. I wish I was with you guys. Can you imagine how fun it would be?!

LILA - 3:35 P.M.

I know right?! I wish you could come to the Halloween party with us!

DESTINY - 3:38 P.M.

What party?

LILA - 3:40 P.M.

Just the one the school has!

DESTINY - 3:45 P.M.

Cool! Miles, what are you going to be?

LILA - 4:15 P.M.

Miles?! Destiny is asking what you're dressing up as??

MILES - 5:30 P.M.

idk. Don't really care.

DESTINY - 5:35 P.M.

Ok then. Miles? You ok?

MILES - 7:00 P.M.

ya I'm cool.

Destiny couldn't shake the feeling that he was pulling away from her. She didn't know why, and it hurt more than she could express.

As Halloween rolled around, the cool fall day brought with it a sense of nostalgia. Destiny returned home from school after a surprisingly great day, eager to share her experiences with Lila. When Lila mentioned there was a Halloween party happening at their old school, Destiny's heart ached. She called Lila and asked if she had heard from Miles, hoping for some reassurance.

"Um, not really," Lila hesitated, clearly uncomfortable. "He's been hanging out with the football and cheerleading crowd lately."

Disappointed but determined to maintain their friendship, Destiny decided to send Miles a Happy Halloween message anyway. Two hours later, her phone buzzed with a response. It was a photo of Miles and Candy, dressed as Barbie and Ken. Their poses were flirtatious, with Candy clinging to Miles' arm and batting her eyelashes while he grinned.

"Best friends forever! Happy Halloween!" the accompanying message read. The generic tone stung, making

Destiny feel like just another name on a list of people who received the same text.

It hit Destiny like a ton of bricks when she realized that Miles had effortlessly replaced her and found comfort with someone who used to be her biggest bully. Candy always acted friendly towards him, but only when Destiny wasn't present. Miles never saw it. He never understood why she wanted nothing to do with Candy.

The pain was unbearable, and she knew she needed to move forward and focus on her own life without Miles. With a heavy heart, she poured her emotions into a goodbye message, hitting 'send' as tears streamed down her face. She then blocked his number, taking the first step towards healing and embracing the future without one of her two best friends.

one

Miles Huntington strolled into the lobby of Vortex, his confident strides echoing through the impressive space. The building itself was a beautiful blend of old-world charm and cutting-edge technology - a renovated historical structure nestled in the heart of a small town. The exterior boasted intricate brickwork and elegant arches, while inside, sleek glass and steel accents hinted at the high-tech world that thrived within.

A massive, interactive touch screen map adorned one wall, showcasing the global reach of the cybersecurity company. Local artwork hung tastefully around the room, a nod to the town's proud heritage. As Miles approached the security desk, he noticed how perfectly the space captured the essence of Vortex – a seamless fusion of tradition and innovation.

"Morning, Paul," Miles said with a warm smile as he greeted the security man behind the desk.

"Good morning, Mr. Huntington," Paul replied, returning the smile.

Miles flashed his access card before the elevator scanner and stepped inside as the doors whispered shut behind him. The executive floor awaited him above, a hub of activity where the top tech team worked tirelessly to protect their clients from cyber threats.

As the elevator ascended, anticipation bubbled in Miles' chest. He truly loved what he did and the people he was fortunate to employ within his company. The doors glided open, revealing the bustling executive level. The area was a carefully designed balance of open workspaces and private offices, all surrounded by state-of-the-art technology. Monitors flickered with complex data streams, while computer terminals hummed steadily, processing information at lightning speed.

To the left, a large conference room featured floor-to-ceiling windows offering a breathtaking view of the picturesque town below. A long, polished table held an array of digital devices, ready for presentations or video conferences with clients around the globe.

Three offices lined the right side of the floor, each boasting a glass wall that allowed natural light to flow through the space. All of the offices are capable of frosting the glass in order to maintain the privacy that is sometimes needed. Assistant desks sat just outside the offices, where talented individuals like Candy managed the seemingly endless flow of paperwork and coordinated schedules with precision.

Miles approached his office, the sunlight pouring through the glass windows giving the space a warm glow. He spotted Candy, her long blonde hair cascading over her shoulders as she sat at her desk, submerged in a pile of paperwork. Vivienne Huntington, Mile's sister in law, stood beside her, handing over a stack of files.

"Hey, Candy," Miles greeted with a wide smile, his green eyes twinkling. "Busy day ahead?"

Candy looked up from her work and returned his smile, her icy blue eyes sparkling mischievously. "Oh, you know how it is, Miles. The world doesn't stop turning just because we want a break."

"True," he agreed, chuckling. "What's on your plate today?"

"Let's see," she mused, tapping a perfectly manicured nail on her desk. "I've got meetings to schedule, contracts to review, and a never-ending list of emails to respond to. All in a day's work, right?"

"Sounds about right," he said with a knowing nod. "Well, if you need any help, just give me a shout."

"Will do," she replied, her grin unwavering.

Miles strode confidently into his office, leaving the door ajar behind him. He liked to keep an open door policy for people to come in and out unless he was in a private meeting. He straightened his tie and took a seat at his mahogany desk, adorned with a sleek silver nameplate. The room exuded an air of success and professionalism, from the leather chairs to the perfectly arranged bookshelves. As he opened his laptop, he glanced up at the wall lined with framed degrees and awards, highlighting his impressive achievements and dedication. Next to them hung photos of Miles participating in various charity events, a testament to his generous nature and desire to make a positive impact in the world.

Candy appeared in the doorway, notepad in hand, and closed the door behind her before taking a seat opposite Miles. She crossed her legs elegantly, the fabric of her dress rustling softly.

"Alright, boss," she said with a teasing smirk. "What's on the agenda for today?"

Miles leaned back in his chair, steepling his fingers as he contemplated the day ahead. "Well, I've got a meeting with a potential client at ten, so I'll need the latest reports on our current projects to discuss with them. After that, I'd like to catch up with Max and Malcolm about any new developments on the tech front."

"Got it," Candy said, scribbling notes down quickly. "I'll make sure everything is prepared for your meeting, and I'll let Max and Malcolm know you want to chat."

"Perfect," Miles replied, relief washing over him. He knew he could always count on Candy to keep things running smoothly, even on the busiest of days. "Anything else I should be aware of?"

"Nothing pressing," she assured him. "Just the usual daily tasks. But if anything comes up, I'll be sure to let you know."

"Thanks, Candy," he said, offering her a genuine smile. "You're a lifesaver."

"Hey, it's what best friends are for," she replied with a playful wink, before slipping out of his office to tackle the challenges of the day.

Miles watched Candy's retreating figure, her heels clicking on the polished floor as she left his office. No sooner had the door clicked shut than Miles' phone buzzed on his desk – a stark interruption to the brief moment of calm in his day. Glancing at the screen, he saw his mother's name, Caroline, flashing. He hesitated for a fraction of a second before answering with an exasperated breath.

"Hello, Mother," he said, trying to keep the irritation out of his voice.

"Darling, I was just calling to remind you about the family dinner tonight. You're coming, aren't you?" Caroline's voice oozed false sweetness through the speaker.

"Fine," Miles relented, knowing that refusing would only lead to more trouble. "I'll be there."

"Good. And why don't you bring Candy along? Max is bringing Vivienne, after all." Caroline sounded far too pleased with herself for Miles' liking.

"Vivi is Max's wife, Mother," he reminded her, not quite able to keep the edge from his voice.

Caroline muttered something under her breath about Vivienne that Miles couldn't quite catch – and frankly, didn't want to. "Well, Candy is your closest friend," she continued aloud. "She's practically family by now. It'll be nice to have her join us."

"Fine," he repeated, rubbing his temples as if that could alleviate the frustration building within him. "I'll ask her."

"Perfect! I knew you'd see it my way," Caroline gloated, satisfaction evident in her voice. "Goodbye, darling!" The call ended, leaving Miles to stew in silence.

Why does she have to force everything on people? It's her way or she makes my life a living hell. He thought, resisting the urge to throw his phone across the room.

"Hey," Max greeted casually as he walked into the office, closing the door behind him. He sat down in one of the plush leather chairs opposite Miles' desk, his green eyes sparkling. Max's grin grew wider as he playfully posed, finger to his chin. "Let me guess," he said teasingly. "Mother dearest just called?"

"Is it that obvious?" Miles sighed, forcing a strained smile. "Yeah, she called about the family dinner tonight."

"Ah, the joys of family obligations," Max mused, leaning back in his chair. "So, are you going?"

"Unfortunately, yes," Miles admitted, rubbing his temples. "And I have to bring Candy. Apparently, she's 'practically family by now.'"

Max chuckled, shaking his head. "I'm assuming you told Caroline you wouldn't bring her just like you always do."

"Yup," Miles conceded, his smile genuine this time. "I don't want her around our mother... ever. I know Candy can stand up for herself, but part of me just wants to protect her. I told Caroline that I would ask Candy, but she doesn't have to know I never did."

"I get that, Miles. I do. Overall, it's your decision whether you want to bring her or not. I wouldn't want Caroline around my friends either. If Vivi didn't insist, I would keep her away too," Max expressed while putting his hand on Miles' shoulder.

At that moment, Malcolm walked up to the door, his messy brown hair sticking up in every direction as if he had just rolled out of bed. Despite his disheveled appearance, there was no denying the sharp wit and intelligence that lurked behind those mischievous eyes. Leaning against the door jamb, Malcolm crossed his arms over his chest and raised an eyebrow at his brothers.

"Ah, I knew I heard you talking about the lovely family dinner," he drawled, his voice heavy with sarcasm, "We can't forget our stepfather-to-be number seven, Lawrence. Can't wait."

"Unfortunately, you heard right," Max replied, sharing a commiserating look with his younger brother.

"Ah, well," Malcolm said, pushing off from the door frame and sauntering into the office, "better brace ourselves for an evening of exquisite torture, then."

"Exquisite torture" was an apt description for any event involving their mother, and Miles chuckled at Malcolm's phrasing. As the youngest Huntington brother took a seat across from them, Miles leaned forward, resting his elbows on the desk.

"Exactly." Miles agreed, his laughter bubbling forth despite the turmoil inside him. He shook his head, trying to refocus his thoughts and turn them away from the impending family gathering. "Anyway, we have work to do. What's new on the client front, Malcolm?"

"Actually," Malcolm said, his eyes lighting up as he leaned forward, enthusiasm evident in his every movement. "I've been investigating this new lead our team has discovered," his fingers tapping rhythmically on the desk as though to emphasize each point. "The company is requesting top-notch cybersecurity for their upcoming product launch. They're dealing with highly sensitive information and can't afford any breaches or leaks."

"Interesting," Miles mused, leaning forward in his chair, curiosity piqued. He studied his younger brother's animated expression and knew that whatever idea was brewing in Malcolm's mind had promise. "Tell me more."

"Alright," Malcolm began, rubbing his hands together excitedly. "So, I've been analyzing our current process and realized that there are some improvements that I can implement to make the encryption automated based off of the parameters that they give us. For example, when collecting basic information that is not private, that could be updated automatically." He paused for a moment, gauging Miles' reaction.

Miles nodded thoughtfully, intrigued by the concept. "Go on."

"We could take a look at information that the client's flag as needing extra security and our team could update that manually," Malcolm continued, his words tumbling out faster now as he grew more passionate. "We could develop an algorithm that quickly calculates the initial risk profile based on the data provided by the client. This would not only save time but also ensure consistency across all assessments."

"An interesting proposition," Max chimed in, stroking his chin as he mulled over the idea. "But how do you propose we maintain the personal touch and human judgment that our clients value?"

"Good question," Miles agreed, his brow furrowing as he considered the balance between efficiency and personalization.

Malcolm grinned, clearly having anticipated this concern. "I'm glad you asked. The automation would only apply to the first stages of our process. Once we have gathered all necessary information and determined the preliminary risk profile, our team would still review everything manually, allowing us to provide personalized recommendations and maintain that human touch our clients appreciate."

"Excellent," Miles said, his eyes shining with approval. "I like the sound of this, Malcolm. Let's start looking into how we can implement these changes and improve our process."

"Great!" Malcolm replied, practically bouncing in his seat. "I'll start putting together a proposal and get feedback from the rest of the team."

Suddenly, Malcolm stopped, clutching his stomach with an exaggerated grimace. "Ugh, I am starving," he groaned, breaking the intense focus of their conversation.

Max's chuckle cut through the air like a warm breeze on a sunny day, his eyes twinkling with amusement as they rolled. "You're always starving, Malcolm."

"Hey, I'm a growing boy. I need fuel," Malcolm retorted, grinning widely and revealing the dimples that had charmed his way out of trouble countless times in the past.

"Fine," Miles conceded, feigning reluctance. "We'll take a break for lunch. But afterward, we have to get back to our discussion on streamlining the client approval process. The sooner we can improve efficiency, the better."

"Agreed!" said Max, clapping his hands together in mock seriousness. "Now, where shall we find sustenance for our dear, famished brother?"

Malcolm perked up at the mention of food, his stomach growling audibly. "As long as it's not another sad desk salad," he muttered under his breath, making a face at the memory.

"Alright, let's see what we can find," Miles said, pulling out his phone to browse local eateries. His fingers danced across the screen, scrolling through various options and imagining the reactions each choice would elicit from his brothers.

"Wait a minute," Malcolm interjected, leaning over Miles' shoulder to examine the screen. "Is that new taco place still open? I've heard great things about their carne asada."

A sharp knock on the door interrupted their decision process, and Miles glanced up from his phone. "Come in," he called out.

The door swung open to reveal Candy, her blue eyes sparkling with excitement and a triumphant smile curving her painted lips. "Good news, gentlemen! I've ordered lunch from Peaches for all of us. They'll be delivering it shortly."

"Ah, that's fantastic!" Malcolm exclaimed, clapping his hands together as his stomach grumbled loudly in anticipation. "I hope Lila is delivering like usual. She knows exactly what we love."

"Indeed," Miles agreed, nodding appreciatively at

Candy. He felt a swell of gratitude for her thoughtfulness, even if they didn't always see eye to eye.

Suddenly, a commotion erupted outside the office, and Miles heard Candy's indignant voice demanding, "What are you doing here?" His curiosity piqued, Miles stood from his chair and made his way towards the door, just as an achingly familiar voice reached his ears – one he hadn't heard in fifteen long years.

Stepping into the hallway, his heart stuttered when he saw her. Destiny Evans. Her brown hair fell in soft waves around her pale face, framing her wide hazel eyes that were currently filled with disbelief.

"Destiny?" Miles breathed, his voice barely above a whisper.

Her mouth opened and closed several times, like a fish out of water, desperately trying to find the right words. Candy crossed her arms over her chest. "Well, look who's back."

Miles missed the venom in her tone, too entranced by the sight of Destiny standing before him. He took a step closer, his voice gentle and filled with wonder. "I didn't know you were back."

Steeling herself, Destiny raised her chin defiantly. "Now why would you know that? It's not like we're friends, Miles." With that, she turned on her heel and stormed away, leaving Miles feeling as if the wind had been knocked out of him.

He made to follow, but Max's hand on his shoulder stopped him. "Let her go, Miles," he advised softly, a knowing look in his eyes.

"Alright," Miles agreed reluctantly, deflating slightly as he watched Destiny disappear around a corner. Malcolm patted his back reassuringly, a small smile playing on his lips.

"Don't worry, I'll talk to Lila and see when she came back. In the meantime, let's focus on what we can control."

"Sounds like a plan," Miles murmured, forcing a smile and turning back towards his office. But as he sat down at his desk once more, he couldn't help but feel that his world had just shifted on its axis – and he wasn't sure where it would all settle when the dust finally cleared.

two

DESTINY LOOKED UP VORTEX ON HER WAY BACK TO Peaches and discovered that Colter Sullivan had funded the creation of the company. The company was owned by her former best friend, Miles. *He also hired Candy Sullivan.* She thought fuming. She's the girl who tormented her every moment she got throughout their whole childhood. She felt the betrayal to her core. *It's like freaking high school all over again*, she thought as she stormed into the cafe. Her anger was visible in the tight lines of her shoulders and the way her eyes flashed with fury. This place was a haven for her, but today, not even the warmth of the familiar place could quell the storm that brewed within her.

She grabbed her apron off a hook by the door, the fabric adorned with playful peach patterns and ruffles along its edges. As she tied it securely around her waist, Lila waltzed up to her, electric blue eyes alight with excitement. Lila Chen had been there for her since their first day of kindergarten. Even though Destiny moved away, Lila remained her best friend throughout all these years.

"Des, I have a quick question," Lila said, tucking a

strand of jet-black hair behind her ear. "For the weekly menu post for next week, should I do a picture of the food or menu or maybe both?"

Destiny tried to focus on Lila's question while trying to hide the irritation she felt about Miles and Vortex. "Why not do both? Show off our delicious creations and give them a sneak peek at the menu."

"Great idea!" Lila beamed. She did a double take as if she could sense Destiny's agitation and put an arm around her. "What's going on, hon? You look like you're about to explode."

"Vortex," Destiny's voice cracked in barely concealed anger. "I delivered an order there today."

Lila's eyes widened in alarm. "Oh no! I'm so sorry, Des. I must have missed the order when it came in, otherwise I would have delivered it."

Destiny narrowed her eyes, reading her nervousness. "You knew that Miles owns Vortex, didn't you?"

Lila nodded sheepishly. "Desy, I just didn't want to add more onto your plate. I was going to handle it."

"Thanks for that," Destiny replied, forcing a small smile.

"So, how does it feel seeing him again?" Lila asked curiously.

Destiny hesitated, then said softly, "You know how I felt about him. I loved him and he basically abandoned me for Candy. Not to mention him taking money from Colter Sullivan to open Vortex and working with her. They ruined my life. I need to move on, though. Rebuild my life."

Destiny's gaze drifted to the display cases, where colorful pastries and cakes sat like little treasures. She noticed a few empty spots that needed refilling, her thoughts racing with the recent conversation about Miles. Lila was already working on the post for next week's menu when she pushed through the swinging doors into the sanctuary of the kitchen.

The familiar smell of baking bread and spices enveloped her as she thought of her late father. She could almost hear his comforting voice, guiding her through the challenges life had thrown at her. "I wish you were here," Destiny whispered, fighting back tears. "You would have known exactly what to say to make me feel better."

She remembered the warmth of her father's hands as he taught her how to bake and cook, the passion for food that they shared. It was no surprise that she found herself managing Peaches after her previous cafe closed; the luck involved in landing this job felt like a sign from her father.

Determined to find solace in the one thing that always brought her peace, Destiny grabbed a bowl of dough and began kneading it on the counter. The rhythmic motion calmed her nerves as she lost herself in the process.

"Desy, I'm pretty sure you've beat that dough enough," Lila chimed in, leaning against the kitchen doorframe. Her eyes held both concern and a little amusement.

"Sorry," Destiny mumbled, releasing her grip on the dough. "It's just... everything with Miles, it brought up everything that I felt before I left. Then seeing Candy just made me feel fourteen all over again."

Lila crossed the room and squeezed Destiny's shoulder reassuringly. "I get it. He hurt you, but remember that you belong here. You always have. Don't let Miles get you worked up, okay?"

"Okay," Destiny nodded, her hazel eyes shining with determination. "Thanks, Lila."

"Anytime," Lila grinned, heading back towards the front of the cafe. "Now, let's whip up some culinary magic and show the world what Peaches is made of!"

* * *

The afternoon sun streamed through the windows molding the bustling cafe in a golden glow on. Destiny watched as the afternoon crew filed in, their cheerful chatter a welcome distraction from her tumultuous thoughts. Glancing at the clock, she realized she'd been working since 5 AM, and despite the emotional rollercoaster, she couldn't help but feel a sense of pride for her dedication.

"Alright, everyone, gather 'round," Destiny called out, clapping her hands to get their attention. The crew huddled together, eager faces looking to her for guidance. She handed everyone samples of the specials for the day. "Today's specials are our savory spinach and feta quiche, and for those with a sweet tooth, we've got mouthwatering mixed berry scones."

"Ooh, I love those berry scones," piped up Jess, a bubbly barista. "They're absolutely divine!"

"Thanks, Jess," Destiny smiled, pleased with the positive feedback. "I want everyone to make sure they mention these specials to our customers. Let's really sell them today, okay?"

"Absolutely!" the group chorused in unison, their enthusiasm infectious.

"Great," Destiny nodded, satisfied with their response. "Now, let's make this afternoon shift amazing!"

As the crew dispersed to their various duties, Destiny hung her apron on its designated hook, feeling the weight of the day finally catch up to her. She waved goodbye to Lila, who was busy clocking out for the day, and slipped away to her sanctuary.

Climbing the narrow staircase behind the kitchen, Destiny arrived at the second floor of the cafe where a two-bedroom apartment awaited her. Part of being a manager meant being available whenever the cafe needed her, so the owners had kindly converted this space into a home for the previous manager to have. When she left after having a baby, Destiny moved in.

Her hand glided along the well-worn wooden banister, fingers tracing over the grooves left by countless years of use. The worn steps creaked softly beneath her feet, echoing the thoughts that weighed heavily on her mind. With each step, the sounds from the cafe below faded, replaced by gentle whispers of wind through small windows lining the stairwell.

Reaching the top of the stairs, Destiny paused for a moment, gazing at the intricately patterned area rug that welcomed her outside the apartment door. She couldn't help but smile, recalling how Lila had jokingly insisted that it was Destiny's "magic carpet" that would whisk her away to a world of peace and solace whenever she needed it.

Unlocking the door, she stepped inside and was immediately embraced by the comforting atmosphere of her home. Sunlight poured through the large windows, casting a warm glow across the living room. The walls were adorned with lively artwork and an eclectic mix of framed photographs, showcasing cherished memories and stunning landscapes that fueled her wanderlust.

An array of potted plants filled every corner and crevice, in various shades of green and vibrant blooms. The lush foliage transformed the space into an urban oasis, their leaves rustling gently in the breeze from the open windows. A cozy reading nook nestled under one window, piled high with plush cushions and a knit blanket, beckoned her to curl up with a good book and forget her troubles.

The open-concept kitchen boasted colorful mosaic tiles that reflected her adventurous spirit and love for experimenting with flavors. An island stood proudly in the center of the kitchen, where she often spent hours concocting new dishes and perfecting her father's cherished recipes.

Destiny breathed deeply, inhaling the mingling scents of lavender and freshly watered plants that filled her home. For a moment, she allowed herself to be enveloped by the familiar surroundings, letting the vibrant colors and soothing greenery wash away the tension that had been building up inside her all day.

"Home sweet home," she murmured to herself, her heart swelling with gratitude for the refuge this apartment provided from the chaos of life.

She padded over to a side table, lighting a cinnamon and vanilla candle that filled the room with a comforting aroma. Kicking off her shoes, she tucked them away in the closet and slipped into her soft, lavender slippers.

"Ah, much better," she sighed, wiggling her toes in contentment.

She made her way over to the plush couch that occupied the center of the living room, its cheerful floral pattern bringing light to the room. With a relieved groan, she plopped down onto the soft cushions, sinking into their welcoming embrace.

Closing her eyes, she tipped her head back and exhaled slowly, allowing herself a moment to just be. The thoughts she had been skillfully suppressing all day bubbled to the surface, demanding her attention.

"Ugh, Destiny, what are you going to do?" she muttered aloud, her voice tinged with equal parts frustration and amusement. "You can't avoid Miles forever."

"Maybe I can," she argued with herself stubbornly. "I've managed for fifteen years, haven't I?"

"True," she conceded, "but now he's practically next door, and Lila knows. You'll have to face him sooner or later." Destiny chewed on her lower lip, the weight of her emotions threatening to overwhelm her.

"Fine," she huffed, sitting up straighter on the couch. "But not today. Today, I'm just going to enjoy my evening and not think about Miles and his stupid Vortex."

"Deal," she agreed with herself, the corners of her mouth lifting in a small, determined smile.

"Alright then," she said, clapping her hands together. "Let's start with a hot bath and some trashy TV. Maybe one of those reality shows where people argue about the color of their wedding napkins."

"Tomorrow is a new day," Destiny reminded herself, her heart swelling with a sense of hope. "And I'll face whatever it brings head-on, just like I always have."

three

MILES STROLLED BACK INTO HIS OFFICE, STILL SAVORING the lingering taste of his sandwich from Peaches. The conference room had been filled with laughter and spirited banter as he, Max, and Malcolm enjoyed their impromptu lunch together. They headed to their offices. All of their desks took up a large part of the top floor. The offices were split into three. When they need to work together, they opened the large floor to ceiling folding doors that open and close to create the perfect atmosphere for collaboration as well as space when needed.

"Man," he said, sinking into a plush office chair, "that was one delicious sandwich."

"Absolutely," agreed Max, taking a seat in one of the armchairs. "Peaches never disappoints."

Malcolm, on the other hand, was going to his desk lined with monitors. "You know," he mused, setting up his laptop on one of the tables in the corner of Miles' office, "we should make this a regular thing. Lunch at the office? Good for morale."

"Good for morale, terrible for our waistlines," replied

Miles with a chuckle. Despite his jest, he couldn't help but think about the mouthwatering combination of flavors that had made his simple sandwich so extraordinary. The tender turkey, the creaminess of the avocado, the crunch of fresh lettuce—it had all come together in perfect harmony. He made a mental note to himself to return to Peaches sooner rather than later.

"Ah, well," sighed Max, stretching his arms above his head. "Back to the grind, I suppose." He got up to head back to his office right next door, focusing on returning the numerous emails awaiting his reply.

Miles, too, tried to refocus on his work, but found his thoughts wandering back to the sandwich. It reminded him of how life could be both simple and extraordinary at the same time – much like the relationships he held dear. "Hey, Malcolm," he called out, unable to shake the memory of their meal. "Next time we do lunch like this, let's try something different. Maybe sushi or Indian food?"

"Sounds good to me," agreed Malcolm, finally tearing his eyes away from his computer screen for a moment. "As long as it's not one of Caroline's eight-course extravaganzas."

At the mention of their mother, the mood in the room shifted ever so slightly. Miles felt a twinge of unease tugging at him, but he pushed it aside and nodded in agreement. "Yeah, let's leave the over-the-top meals for another day."

"Deal," said Malcolm, flashing a warm smile at his brother.

With their plans in place, the three brothers went back to their tasks. Malcolm was the first one to leave; he required all the resources of his office, not just the simple laptop he was working on at the moment.

Miles' phone buzzed on his desk, interrupting his

thoughts. Glancing at the screen, he saw it was a reminder for an upcoming meeting. As he swiped to dismiss it, another notification caught his eye: dinner at Caroline's. A wave of dread washed over him, tightening his chest like a vice.

"Ugh," he muttered under his breath, raking his fingers through his hair. The thought of facing his mother and soon-to-be stepfather was enough to make him cringe. He could already hear the forced pleasantries and thinly veiled insults that would be exchanged throughout the evening.

"Something wrong?" Candy asked, appearing beside his desk with her usual elegant grace. Her icy blue eyes flickered with curiosity and concern as she regarded him.

"Ah, just a family dinner at my mother's place tonight," Miles replied, trying to sound nonchalant despite the tension building in his shoulders. "Not really looking forward to it."

"Caroline's dinners can be...intense," Candy said, a knowing smile playing on her lips. "Would you like me to come with you? Maybe I could help smooth things over."

Miles hesitated for only a moment before shaking his head. "Thanks, but no. It's important for me to face my mother on my own terms. I appreciate the offer, though."

Candy nodded, seeming to accept his decision. "Alright. Just remember, if you need someone to talk to or vent after, I'm here," she said, her voice laced with a hint of seduction.

"Thanks, Candy," Miles managed to reply, forcing a small smile onto his face. Internally, he sighed, wishing he didn't have to deal with his mother's inevitable drama. In the back of his mind, he wondered why family gatherings always seemed more like battles than anything else.

Miles, while still worrying about dinner, knows that he has more important matters to tackle. Just then, a member of the Human Resources Department came in needing some assistance with a new employee. As Miles worked the problem, the apprehension over dinner faded away as he got back to doing what he does best, running Vortex.

* * *

Later that night, Miles approached his mother's ostentatious mansion with a heavy heart. The grandiose structure loomed before him like a gaudy monument to excess and superficiality. Brightly illuminated fountains adorned the meticulously landscaped front yard, casting a kaleidoscope of colors onto the white marble exterior. The sickly sweet scent of heavily perfumed flowers lingered in the air, making Miles feel slightly nauseated as he walked up the pathway. With each new husband came a bigger and grander house.

"Caroline sure knows how to make a statement," he muttered under his breath, bracing himself for the extravagant meal that was undoubtedly awaiting them inside.

Taking a deep breath, he rang the bell, hoping beyond hope that the evening would pass quickly.

The heavy, ornate door swung open slowly, revealing the butler who stood with impeccable posture, his suit pressed to perfection. His face was stern and unwavering as he greeted Miles, but there was a hint of fatigue in his eyes, as if this was just another in a long line of guests to pass through the grand entrance. Miles couldn't help but wonder how long this butler would last before being replaced by yet another perfectly polished version."Good evening, Mr. Huntington. Please, come in."

As Miles stepped over the threshold, he was immediately assaulted by the cacophony of sensory stimuli that was his mother's home. Rich velvets and gleaming golds adorned every surface, while ornate chandeliers cast harsh shadows across the sprawling foyer. The cloying scent of potpourri mingled with the smell of the impending feast—an olfactory assault that made Miles' head swim.

"Your brothers are in the formal living room," the butler informed him, gesturing down the hall.

Their leisurely stroll was accompanied by the measured clack of their polished shoes on the gleaming marble floor, the sound echoing through the opulent mansion like a foreboding beat of a metronome. Miles, ever curious, broke the silence with his question to the stoic butler at their side. "Excuse me," he piped up, "what is your name?"

The butler, who had been moving with precision and grace, stiffened at the interruption before responding icily. "My name is James, sir," he stated in a crisp tone that matched his immaculate appearance. The air seemed to still around them as they continued their walk, the only sounds coming from their footsteps and the ticking grandfather clock in the corner.

Upon entering the living room, Miles spotted Max and Vivienne sitting side by side on a plush loveseat, exchanging tense glances. Malcolm lounged in an armchair nearby, looking as if he'd rather be anywhere else. Their faces brightened at the sight of Miles, offering a small comfort amidst the opulence. Before Miles could even say hello the butler returned to lead them to the dining room.

"Ah, Mr. Huntington," the butler announced, "dinner is ready. If you would please follow me to the dining room."

As they made their way towards the heart of the evening's battle, a flurry of trepidation and determination surged through Miles. While family dinners happen monthly, this is the first that Miles has attended in a while.

He was confident that his brothers would always support him, just as he would do for them. Together, they were a brilliant team and could handle any challenges thrown their way by their mother, as they had done in the past. The immense doors swung open, revealing the huge formal dining room that looked like it had been ripped straight from the pages of a garish fairytale. Caroline sat at the head of the table, draped in a shimmering emerald gown that glinted beneath the crystalline chandelier. She was positively regal, her posture rigid, and her icy blue eyes surveying her kingdom like a queen.

Miles took a seat opposite his mother, with Lawrence—Caroline's fiancé and soon-to-be husband number seven—seated next to her. He couldn't help but chuckle as he glanced down at the menu, which promised a lavish eight-course meal fit for royalty.

"Amuse-bouche of champagne-poached oysters," he muttered under his breath, "followed by a chilled cucumber and mint soup, seared foie gras with fig compote, pan-roasted lobster tail on a bed of saffron-infused risotto, filet mignon with truffle butter, a salad of exotic greens with aged balsamic vinaigrette, a cheese course showcasing rare and imported selections, and finally, gold leaf-encrusted chocolate soufflé."

"Only the best for my family," Caroline preened, casting a smug glance towards Miles. "Now, Miles, why didn't you bring Candy?"

"This is ridiculous, Mother," he retorted, his voice brimming with irritation as he argued about her request for him to invite Candy to dinner. "This is supposed to be a family dinner."

Caroline scoffed. "Well, if Vivienne is here, then Candy should be too, since Vivienne isn't family."

"Mother, this is my wife," Max interrupted, his face turning a deep shade of red.

"Marriages end all the time, dear," Caroline said flippantly. "Yours will too, sooner or later." Vivienne gasped, hurt flashing across her eyes, and Max's fists clenched in anger.

Miles could hear Lawrence's intake of breath before saying, "Is that how you see our marriage Caroline? As expendable?"

Caroline whipped her head towards him and feigned shock saying, "Absolutely not, Lawrence dear. See, Max married out of his social class while you and I are a perfect match." Lawrence, seemingly believing her, gave her a smile and a kiss on the back of her hand.

Miles resisted the urge to roll his eyes, knowing he couldn't let his mother get to him.

He had to stay level-headed for the sake of his brothers, who were all that mattered to him. Despite his desire to explode, he understood the importance of keeping his emotions in check.

"Vivienne is an invaluable asset to our company, Mother," Miles interjected, trying to diffuse the tension. "Her hard work and dedication have contributed significantly to Vortex's success."

Vivienne smiled her thanks at Miles, grateful for his support. Caroline, however, rolled her eyes and said, "Well, Candy is quite the asset too, you know. And let's not forget who she introduced you to Colter Sullivan. He's been a godsend to you, dear."

Miles couldn't help but feel a twinge of annoyance at his mother's words. Yes, Colter had played a significant role in his early career, but it was as if Caroline was giving him all the credit for Miles' success. He couldn't deny, though, that Colter had indeed been influential in his life.

As the second course was served, Miles found himself thinking back to when he was graduating high school. He had been unsure about his future, but then Colter Sullivan had approached him with an offer he couldn't refuse—mentorship under one of the most successful entrepreneurs in the country. Over the next four years, Colter guided Miles, teaching him everything he needed to know about business, strategy, and the importance of connections.

When the time came for Miles to venture out on his own, Colter had offered him the financial backing he needed to start Vortex. It was a generous investment, and Miles was determined not to let his mentor down. He worked tirelessly, and within just a year, he managed to repay Colter every penny he had borrowed.

"Earth to Miles," Max called out, snapping Miles out of his reverie. "You were zoning out there, little brother."

"Sorry," Miles mumbled, trying to refocus on the present moment.

Caroline noticed how Miles' thoughts had wandered and smirked. "Thinking about how much you owe Colter and Candy, dear?"

"Mother, it's not about owing anyone anything," Miles replied firmly, his patience wearing thin. "I've acknowledged and repaid Colter's support and guidance, but I have built Vortex with my own hands and the help of my incredible team. That includes Vivienne."

Caroline pursed her lips, clearly unhappy with Miles' response. But there was nothing she could say to refute his words. The success of Vortex was undeniable, and Miles had proven time and time again that he was a force to be reckoned with in the business world.

Caroline's voice sliced through the haze of Miles' thoughts like a hot knife. "Lawrence and I are planning our wedding for the fall, and we expect all of you to be there," she announced, her tone as imperious as ever.

Around the table, heads nodded in reluctant agreement —until Caroline added with a malicious glint in her eye, "It's going to be an intimate, family-only event. Vivienne, that means you're not invited."

The clatter of forks hitting fine china plates echoed through the palatial dining room as everyone stopped eating the extravagant eighth course in shock. Vivienne's eyes flashed with hurt and indignation, her usually calm demeanor giving way to a steely resolve.

"Max," she said, her voice low but laced with anger, "I am over this bullshit." With grace and dignity, Vivienne pushed away from the table and stood, her gaze never leaving her husband's.

"See?" Caroline sneered, gesturing at Vivienne.. "She's not a good fit for a family of this caliber. Can't handle a little criticism."

"Caroline, please," Lawrence interjected, attempting to diffuse the tension. "This isn't the time or place for such comments."

Miles thought about Lawrence. Sometimes he forgot that he was even there. After everything his mother had said, how could he stay so quiet? Caroline has a lot of barbs that she throws at people, but there was only so much one can take.

"Save it, Lawrence," Vivienne shot back, her green eyes narrowed. "You can't control her any more than the rest of us can. There is a reason you are number seven." She turned to Max, her expression softening. "I'll be waiting in the car."

As Vivienne strode out of the room, her head held high, Max's face went from shock to anger. He could feel Miles and Malcolm's gazes on him, silently urging him to stand up for his wife. The tense silence hung heavy in the air, punctuated only by the faint sound of Vivienne's footsteps fading down the hallway.

With Vivienne gone, Max's anger simmered to a boil. He rose from his seat, eyes blazing as he addressed the room. "I won't be attending your wedding either, Caroline," he declared, his voice shaking with barely restrained fury. "If my wife isn't welcome, neither am I."

Caroline scoffed, rolling her eyes dismissively. "You always were too sensitive, Max." Her words only served to fuel the fire burning within him.

"Sensitive? No, Mother," Max retorted. "I just know how to treat people with respect." With that, he turned on his heel and stalked out of the dining room.

Malcolm watched the proceedings, his mind racing. As much as he wanted to love his mother and be there for her, he agreed with Max. He couldn't sit idly by while their mother treated Vivienne so cruelly. Pushing back his ornate chair with a loud scrape, he threw his napkin down onto the table. "This is stupid," he growled. "And this is exactly why you never stay married for long, Caroline." He glared at her, daring her to argue. "I won't be attending either." Without waiting for her response, he stormed out of the room, following in Max's footsteps.

Miles hesitated, torn between loyalty to his mother and the fierce protectiveness he felt for his brothers and their loved ones. He knew Candy was important to Caroline and that she wanted her in the wedding, but he also knew that standing by his brothers was essential. They had always been there for each other, through everything their mother had put them through.

With a deep breath, Miles made up his mind. "Mother," he began, his voice firm, "I can't attend your wedding if my brothers and Vivienne aren't welcome." Ignoring the harrumphs coming from Caroline, he got up to leave the dining room.

"Fine," Caroline spat, her voice dripping with venom. "See if I care."

"I hope the wedding is all that you hope it to be. Good luck, Lawrence." With that Miles went through the doorway.

Even though his mother had put him through hell, Miles' heart ached at the thought of disappointing her. In the end, he knew that he had made the right choice. He walked out of the room, each step taking him further away from the toxic atmosphere and closer to the solidarity of his brothers.

As they made their way to the formal entryway, the butler silently handed each of them their coats from the closet. The sound of Caroline's heels clicking against the marble floor echoed through the mansion as she followed her sons with a steely determination in her eyes.

"Vivienne," she called out, making sure her voice carried throughout the foyer. "I hope you enjoy your lonely life when Max finally comes to his senses and leaves you."

A flash of pain crossed Vivienne's face before it was replaced by a mask of resolve. She didn't bother responding to Caroline, instead pushing open the heavy front door and stepping into the night. Max followed close behind, with Malcolm hot on his heels, leaving Miles alone with his mother.

"Come now, Miles" Caroline purred, coming to stand next to him. "Don't you think you should at least consider asking Candy out? She would be so good for you."

Miles felt anger rising within him, bubbling up until he couldn't hold back any longer. He didn't even take a second to consider her suggestion. "Stop, Mother!" he snapped. "Candy is my best friend and nothing more.

Don't try to manipulate me like you do everyone else." His heart raced, but he stood his ground, refusing to let her control him any longer.

Caroline's eyes narrowed, her wrath palpable as she glared at her son. "Very well, Miles," she spat. "But don't come crying to me when you realize what a mistake you've made."

With that, she turned on her heel and stormed back into the depths of her grandiose mansion, leaving Miles standing in the doorway, shaking with a mixture of anger and relief. He stepped outside, the cool night air caressed his face as he breathed deeply, in an attempt to calm himself.

He glanced around at his brothers, who were waiting for him on the driveway. Max offered a small, supportive smile, while Malcolm clapped him on the shoulder.

"Let's go," Miles said quietly, and they all walked to their respective cars without another word, leaving the chaotic, toxic world that was Caroline's mansion behind them.

Miles sighed in relief as he sank into the plush leather seats of his SUV. He re-adjusted the rearview mirror before turning over the engine and letting it hum to life, restoring the calmness that had been absent since he arrived at his mother's house earlier that evening.

He rode home in complete quiet, leaving the radio off. As his car trundled along its usual path, the streetlights shone hazy yellow hues that illuminated his journey back to safety.

As he drove closer to his street, the familiar sight of his home came into view. It was a stark contrast to his mother's house—a charming, two-story structure with white siding, black shutters, and a well-manicured lawn that stretched along the perimeter of the property. He felt a wave of comfort wash over him as he parked in the driveway, something he had never experienced when visiting his mom's home.

Miles got out of his car and walked up the driveway towards the front door. He unlocked the door and stepped into the entryway, immediately feeling enveloped by the cozy atmosphere of his home.

The hardwood floors creaked softly beneath his feet as he walked further in. He went to the fireplace and turned the gas watching it light with a blast of heat hitting his face. He stood back and stared at the flickering flames casting a golden glow across the room, dancing playfully on the walls. The smell brought back memories of cold winter nights spent with his brothers, huddled together in front of the fire.

Miles glanced toward the large kitchen, where stainless steel appliances gleamed under recessed lighting and a rustic wooden table stood proudly in the center. This was the heart of his home, a place where he could imagine himself cooking meals with his future family, laughing and bonding over shared experiences. Caroline had once scoffed at the size of his house, saying it was far too small for someone of his stature. But to Miles, it was perfect—a place filled with love and warmth.

As he moved through the house, he took in the sight of his backyard through the sliding glass doors. A lush green lawn stretched out before him, bordered by trees that whispered softly in the breeze. He could almost hear the laughter of children playing on a warm summer day, their feet sinking into the soft earth as they chased each other around the yard. Someone who could stand on her own with Caroline, just like Vivienne.

He couldn't help but smile as he thought about how different his home was from his mother's excessive mansion. While her house was a cold, soulless display of wealth, his own was a sanctuary filled with warmth and character. It was a place where he could be himself, free from the expectations and manipulations that plagued him whenever he visited Caroline.

Miles walked over to the well-stocked bar in the corner of his cozy living room. He felt the smooth, polished surface of the wooden counter beneath his fingertips as he picked out a cold beer from the mini-fridge hidden beneath it. The satisfying sound of the beer cap popping off echoed through the room as he took a slow, measured sip. The chilled liquid slid down his throat, quenching the thirst that had been building up during his tense evening.

In contrast to his mother's glitzy mansion, Miles' home was inviting and unpretentious, reflecting the man who lived there.

Settling into the plush couch, Miles propped his feet up on the coffee table and stared into the dancing flames of the fireplace. His thoughts drifted back to the disastrous dinner, particularly Caroline's insistence on him being with Candy. It baffled him, as he had always been clear about his platonic relationship with Candy.

"Why the hell does she insist on turning my friendship into a romance? Our families are close exactly how we are." he mumbled to himself, shaking his head. Taking another swig of his beer, he thought about Candy—her stunning features, her confidence, and her ambition. She was an attractive woman, no doubt, but something deep within him knew she wasn't what he truly wanted.

His mind began to wander to Destiny, the beautiful, warm-hearted cafe manager who had captivated him since the moment they'd met all those years ago. "Destiny," he whispered her name, letting it linger in the air like a delicate fragrance. The firelight danced across his face, casting a hopeful glow upon his features. He longed for the opportunity to get to know her better, to delve into the depths of her soul and understand what made her so incredibly special.

"Maybe one day," he mused with a sigh, his thoughts drifting towards a future where he could share his life with someone as genuine and loving as Destiny. A faint smile tugged at the corner of his lips as he took another sip of his beer, comforted by the warmth of his home and the flickering firelight.

four

Destiny stood in front of her mirror, examining herself as she adjusted the band of her running shorts. The faint scent of lavender from her laundry detergent filled her nostrils as she double-checked that her earbuds were securely in place. She glanced at her watch and let out a small sigh. She needed to get going in order to get to work on time.

"Alright, here goes nothing," Destiny murmured to herself, plugging her earbuds into her phone and scrolling through her running playlist.

Across town, Miles was doing his morning stretches in his spacious living room. He could feel the tension in his muscles as he leaned down to touch his toes, his body protesting after countless hours spent behind his desk. He knew he needed this run before a long day at the office.

"Come on, Miles. It's time to clear your head," he told himself, grabbing his water bottle and slipping on his running shoes.

As they both stepped outside their homes and began

jogging, the crisp morning air invigorated their senses, making them feel alive and ready to take on the day.

* * *

Destiny's hazel eyes flickered with determination as she focused on her breathing. "One more day wouldn't hurt," she thought, referencing the conversation she promised Lila she'd have with Miles. After all, it wasn't every day that she got to enjoy the peaceful solitude of her morning run. She shook her head slightly, trying to dispel thoughts of Miles, and instead took in the beauty of the world around her.

Meanwhile, Miles' thoughts raced as quickly as his feet. He couldn't help but ponder over his strained relationship with Destiny, wondering what went wrong and how he could fix it. Now that he knew she was back in town, he longed to reconnect with her. Despite his mind's constant tug of war, he couldn't resist the pull of the present moment—the rhythmic pounding of his sneakers on the pavement, the sun's rays gradually warming the world around him.

* * *

With each step, Destiny's senses were awakened by the vibrant world around her. The crunch of gravel beneath her sneakers served as a satisfying metronome for her pace, while the gentle rustle of leaves overhead provided an almost melodic sound-track. As she entered the park, the sight of ancient oak trees greeted her like old friends. Their branches stretched upward, reaching for the sky, and the sunlight peeked through the leaves, casting dappled shadows on the ground below.

"Hey, there," she whispered to the trees, her voice soft and affectionate. "I missed you guys." The trees seemed to nod in response, their leaves swaying gently in the breeze.

As she continued running, her legs felt strong, her strides confident, and her heart pounded in sync with the music. She was so absorbed in her thoughts and the beat that she didn't notice the sudden obstacle in front of her.

"Oof!" Destiny huffed as she collided with what felt like a brick wall. Stumbling back, she blinked in confusion, only to realize that this particular wall had a warmth to it – a warmth that bricks couldn't possibly possess. Rubbing her nose gingerly, she looked up and found herself staring into the eyes of Miles Huntington.

"Uh, hi," she stammered, her cheeks flushing with embarrassment. "Didn't see you there."

"Clearly," Miles replied, a hint of amusement in his voice. "Are you okay?"

"Feels like I took a hit from a heavyweight champ," Destiny grumbled, still rubbing the offended body part. "What about you? Did I break anything valuable?"

"Nothing that can't be fixed," Miles assured her, a lopsided smile tugging at his lips. "Although I didn't expect my morning run to involve getting tackled by a beautiful woman."

Destiny rolled her eyes but couldn't help smiling back. "Well, don't let me keep you from your workout. You know what they say—no pain, no gain."

"True," he agreed, his green eyes twinkling with mischief. "But somehow, I think running into you is worth the occasional bruise."

Destiny's heartbeat quickened as nerves threatened to get the best of her. She had promised Lila that she would talk to Miles, but she hadn't expected to literally bump into him Her hazel eyes darted around, searching for an escape route.

"Uh, sorry again," she mumbled, taking a step back. "I should really watch where I'm going next time. Have a good run, Miles."

"Wait," he called out, his tone tinged with concern. "Why are you avoiding me?"

"Who says I'm avoiding you?" Destiny retorted, trying to maintain her composure. She closed her eyes and sighed. "Look, now is just not the time, okay? Let's just leave it at that."

Miles' green eyes seemed to bore into Destiny's soul, his voice firm yet gentle. "If not now, then when? I deserve to know why you disappeared from my life with just a goodbye message."

Destiny felt a surge of irritation at his words. She crossed her arms defensively and glared at him. "You really want to talk about this now?" she asked incredulously. "Fine. I thought it would be best to keep our distance from each other, okay? And for the record, I'm not avoiding you."

"Really?" Miles raised an eyebrow, clearly unconvinced. "Because it sure seems like it. Literally, you're running away from me right now."

"Ugh," Destiny huffed in frustration, raking a hand through her hair. "Why does any of this matter to you? If you didn't want to try to be friends when we were younger, why do you care now?"

Miles flinched, taken aback by her accusation. "You think I didn't want to be friends?" he asked quietly, hurt evident in his voice.

"Actions speak louder than words, Miles," Destiny shot back, her own heart aching as she recalled their lost friendship. "And your actions said that you didn't care."

"Destiny, I—" Miles began, but she cut him off with a shake of her head.

"Never mind," she muttered, her anger giving way to weariness. "It's all in the past, anyway. There's no point in rehashing it."

"Isn't there?" he challenged, his gaze never leaving hers. "We can't change the past, but we can learn from it and try to make things better going forward."

For a moment, Destiny hesitated, looking as if she might have more to say. But then she shook her head, a bitter laugh escaping her lips. "You know what? Forget it. This is pointless." Her voice held a steely edge as she added, "Bye, Ken. Hope Barbie was worth it. I hope she made you happy."

And before Miles could utter another word, Destiny turned on her heel and sprinted away down the path, leaving him standing there with a stunned expression on his face.

As she ran, Destiny couldn't help but feel a sense of regret mixed with the anger and betrayal she had carried with her all these years. She thought of how things used to be, when they were inseparable friends, and wondered if they could ever go back to that.

But as the trees whizzed past and her breath came in ragged gasps, she couldn't shake the image of Miles and Candy together—a painful reminder of her own insecurities. *No*, she told herself, swallowing the lump in her throat. Some things were better left in the past.

* * *

Miles stared at Destiny's retreating form, her brown hair swaying gently with each step she took. Shock and confusion marred his face as he tried to make sense of their

48

conversation. He felt a strange sense of longing for something he couldn't quite put his finger on. Shaking his head, he turned on his heel and sprinted back home, knowing full well that he had a long day ahead of him.

Once inside the sanctuary of his house, Miles continued to mull over Destiny's reluctance to talk to him. It gnawed at him, like a puzzle piece that refused to fit no matter how many times you turned it. Deciding that a shower might clear his thoughts, he discarded his clothes and stepped under the warm stream of water. As droplets cascaded down his body, questions swirled around in his mind, unyielding and relentless.

"Destiny, what happened?" he muttered to himself as he lathered soap across his chest, the rich scent of sandalwood filling the air.

Finally pulling himself away from the comforting warmth of the shower, Miles wrapped a towel around his waist before heading to his walk-in closet. He chose a charcoal-gray suit, crisp white dress shirt, and a dark green tie —a color he knew brought out the emerald hues of his eyes. His attire was always immaculate, a testament to the professionalism and attention to detail that had made Vortex the success it was today.

Dressed and ready to face the world, Miles strode out of his house with determination etched into his features. The weight of the conversation with Destiny still heavy on his mind, but he pushed it aside, focusing instead on the tasks that awaited him at work. Despite his lingering confusion, he knew one thing for certain: he needed answers, and he wouldn't stop until he found them.

Stepping off the elevator onto the executive floor, Miles took in the familiar sight of rows upon rows of sleek computers and cubicles housing Malcolm's tech team. Amidst the hum of activity, he spotted Malcolm by the large conference screen, animatedly discussing a project with his team, glasses perched on the tip of his nose and hair even messier than usual. Miles walked down past Malcolm's office, Max stood in his own office, phone pressed to his ear, deep in conversation.

Miles made his way through the bustling workspace towards his own office, situated towards the back of the building. As he moved closer, he caught sight of Candy, already at her desk, impeccably dressed and typing away furiously on her keyboard.

He couldn't help but notice that she seemed to be in earlier than usual. Caroline's words from the previous night echoed in his mind, "Don't you think you should at least consider asking Candy out? She would be so good for you." With this thought in mind, he regarded her workspace with a newfound curiosity.

Candy's desk was a shrine to materialism—a display of her unwavering pursuit of wealth and status. A collection of designer pens, each one more extravagant than the last, sat proudly in a monogrammed holder. A gold-plated stapler sparkled under the fluorescent lights, a symbol of her opulent lifestyle. Even her mousepad was covered in sparkling Swarovski crystals, reflecting her desire for luxury and excess. As Miles surveyed the meticulously organized space, he realized that Candy's want for the finer things in life matched her confidence in herself. He paused to appreciate her resolute belief in him.

Candy had done many things for him, but the most significant was her support. He discovered a strength within himself that he never knew existed and it gave him the courage to pursue his enterprising dreams.

His eyes shifted to Candy herself, taking in her perfectly tailored ensemble. She wore a form-fitting pencil skirt that hugged her curves, paired with a silk blouse that shimmered like liquid gold. Her blonde hair fell around her face in cascading waves, contrasting with the ice-blue sharpness of her eyes. The manicured fingers that flew across the keyboard were tipped with nails painted the color of freshly spilled blood—a fitting metaphor for the ruthlessness with which she pursued her goals.

Miles observed her, he felt a peculiar mix of fascination and wariness. Caroline had suggested that Miles should think of Candy as a potential romantic partner, but he just couldn't seem to feel a spark with her. They had a strong bond, but it was always just friendly. Despite trying to envision them together, Miles couldn't see it happening.

"Hey, Miles," Candy said, her voice cutting through his reverie. "You okay there? You look a little spaced out."

Miles blinked, snapping back to the present. He noticed the glint in her eyes—she knew he had been staring at her. But any thoughts of explaining himself or sharing his concerns about Destiny were quickly quashed; he needed to figure things out on his own first.

"Uh, yeah, I'm fine," he replied, rubbing the back of his neck. "Just lost in thought for a moment. Thanks for asking, though."

"Of course," Candy responded with a shrug, clearly not buying it but also not pressing further. "If you need anything, just let me know."

"I will," Miles assured her, and with that, he entered his office and shut the door behind him.

Unbeknownst to him, Malcolm had finished his meeting and watched the exchange between Miles and Candy, he could sense that something was off with his brother. Curiosity piqued, he followed Miles into his office, dismissing Candy with a wave before closing the door behind him.

"Hey, what's up with you?" Malcolm asked, concern

etched across his face. "You seemed a bit...distracted out there."

Miles hesitated, weighing the pros and cons of opening up to his younger brother. Finally, he sighed and admitted, "I've got some things on my mind, that's all. It's nothing major."

"Nothing major, huh?" Malcolm raised an eyebrow skeptically. "You sure about that? Because you looked a million miles away just now. And don't think I didn't notice you checking out Candy. What's going on?"

"Malcolm, really, it's nothing," Miles insisted, trying to brush it off. "Besides, it's not like I was ogling her or anything. I was just...curious. You know what mother dearest said about social class. Plus seeing Destiny this morning on my run... I'm just so confused on why Destiny hates me."

"Hates you?" Malcolm snorted, his eyes narrowing. "You know, back in high school, you were a real shithead when it came to relationships. An absolute asshole. You've come a long way since then, but old wounds don't always heal. Don't sit down and wallow, talk to her."

Miles watched as Malcolm's retreating form disappeared through the doorway, his brother's words echoing in his mind. He leaned back in his chair, his fingers drumming restlessly on the polished wood of his desk. He knew Malcolm was right; he couldn't risk slipping back into the person he used to be—thoughtless and selfish when it came to all relationships.

He glanced out the window, the town looming around him like a blatant reminder of the past. It was Destiny who had been occupying his thoughts recently, her warm hazel eyes and easy laughter etched into his memories. The conversation they'd had earlier that day, filled with reluctance and unanswered questions, itched at the back of his mind, demanding attention.

"Enough," Miles muttered under his breath, determination settling over him like armor. He needed answers. Needed to understand what was going on with Destiny and why she seemed so hesitant to speak to him let alone open up to him. And he wouldn't get those answers by sitting here, wallowing in speculation and reminiscing about past mistakes.

He stood abruptly, the legs of his chair scraping against the floor with a sharp, decisive sound. Resolute, he strode towards the door, his footsteps firm and purposeful.

"Malcolm!" he called out, catching his brother just as he was about to disappear around a corner. "Wait up!" Miles called as he walked quickly to catch up to him, "I need to talk to Destiny. I need to know what's going on."

"Alright, man." Malcolm raised his hands in surrender, a hint of a smile playing on his lips. "You don't have to convince me. Just make sure you're doing it for the right reasons, alright? Don't mess with her head if you're not willing to be there for her."

Miles nodded, his jaw set with determination. "I won't. I promise."

"Good." Malcolm clapped him on the shoulder, his expression serious but supportive. "Now go get your answers. And remember, Miles—be the man you've become, not the one you left behind."

With a final nod, Miles turned and headed for the elevator, his thoughts focused on Destiny and the conversation that lay ahead of them. It was time to face the unknown, no matter what it might reveal.

five

DESTINY DESCENDED THE STAIRCASE, HER BROWN CURLS still damp from the shower. She wore a simple white blouse with delicate lace trim along the neckline, tucked neatly into a pair of high-waisted denim jeans. Her hazel eyes sparkled as she adjusted her favorite apron—a vintage-inspired piece in a warm shade of buttercup yellow, adorned with dainty flowers and pockets large enough to hold her baking tools.

As she reached the bottom step, the scent of freshly baked pastries filled her nostrils, instantly putting a smile on her face. Rows of golden croissants sat beside trays of flaky danishes filled with sweet raspberry jam. Chocolate chip scones, their chips just beginning to melt, beckoned alongside decadent walnut brownies topped with powdered sugar.

Destiny moved effortlessly through the cafe, filling shelves with the enticing treats. The familiar, comforting action brought her a sense of peace and stability that few things in her life could. With a final dusting off of her hands, she turned to open the cafe for the day. The

sunlight streaming through the window caught her attention, causing her to pause and take a deep breath. She
loved the way the morning light brought the world to life.

Her moment of tranquility was shattered as she spotted
Miles outside the door, waiting patiently. Startled, she
couldn't help but jump. Once she calmed, she couldn't
help but look at him and scowl.

"Hey, Destiny," he called through the glass, his green
eyes alight with an unreadable expression. "Can I
come in?"

Destiny hesitated, her hand on the door handle. She
knew that any conversation with Miles could be unpre-
dictable, but something in his eyes told her that this was
important. Taking a deep breath, she opened the door and
invited him in.

"Come on back to my office," she said, leading him
through the maze of tables and chairs that filled Peaches'
cozy interior. Her office was tucked away in the back
corner, hidden behind a tall bookshelf decorated with an
assortment of colorful knickknacks and vintage
cookbooks.

As they entered the small room, Destiny felt a pang of
self-consciousness. The office was a cluttered mess, but it
was her mess—organized chaos, as she liked to call it.
Stacks of papers and baking supplies littered the desk,
while framed photos and mementos covered the walls,
creating a vibrant collage of memories. A worn armchair
sat in one corner, piled high with blankets and throw
pillows, while a small window let in just enough sunlight to
warm the space.

Miles looked around the room with thinly veiled
disdain, his eyes taking in every detail. "Well, this place is
certainly different than my office," he said, picking up a
small figurine from the shelf beside him. He turned it over

in his hands, studying it for a moment before continuing, "It's...messy."

Annoyance flared within Destiny as she snatched the figurine out of his hands. "Are you here for a reason, or just to insult me?" she snapped, placing the trinket back in its rightful spot.

"Sorry," Miles said, a hint of genuine remorse in his voice. "I didn't mean to offend you. I'm just not used to seeing an office like this."

"Clearly," Destiny muttered, crossing her arms and fixing him with a raised eyebrow "So what do you want to talk about?"

Miles shifted uncomfortably in his chair, his fingers tapping nervously on the armrest. "I, uh... I just wanted to clear the air between us," he began, avoiding her gaze. "Things have been weird since we reconnected, and I'm tired of dancing around it."

"Fine," Destiny said, her annoyance giving way to determination. "You wanted to talk? Here's your chance."

"Alright," Miles took a deep breath. "I want to know why. Why you sent that goodbye message back in high school."

Destiny's eyes widened in shock as the memories came flooding back. She hesitated, suddenly unsure if she wanted to revisit old wounds. "I don't think it's a good idea to go back there, Miles."

"Please, Des," he pleaded using the childhood nickname that he gave her. He hoped that would soften her hard exterior. "I need to understand what happened between us."

With a resigned sigh, Destiny finally relented and revealed the truth. "You started pulling away from me, Miles. Your responses to my messages became distant, like you were barely there." She looked away, trying to hide the hurt in her eyes. "I was okay with that. I mean, it hurt a little, but I understood we were growing up and growing apart."

She paused for a moment, gathering herself before continuing. "But on Halloween, you sent me a message that truly broke my heart. There was a photo of you and Candy standing together, dressed as Barbie and Ken. It was captioned 'best friends forever.'" Destiny glanced at Miles, who wore an expression of confusion. "That's when I knew that you had moved on and that I should too. There, now you know the truth. You can leave."

Without waiting for a response, Destiny marched out of the cramped office, leaving a stunned Miles in her wake. As they reached the door, she held it open for him, clearly eager to end their conversation and put some distance between them. She was done living in the past. All she wanted to do was look forward. It hurt, but it was in the past.

* * *

Miles stood in the morning sunlight, his brows furrowed as he tried to process Destiny's revelations. The memory of that Halloween night flooded back, but he knew he hadn't sent that photo. He was sure of it. Candy had taken it on his phone, but he couldn't imagine her sending it to Destiny from his number. It had to be a misunderstanding.

"Destiny," he called out, turning to face her. She looked at him with guarded hazel eyes, her arms crossed defensively. "Look, we were kids back then. High school changes people. Is it possible that Candy made you jealous and you just... read it the wrong way?"

Her expression shifted from guarded to offended in an instant, her eyes narrowing as she stared at him. "You're kidding, right? That has to be a joke. Damn Miles, I can't believe you would think that for even a second."

"Destiny, I just want to understand why it still bothers you so much," he said, trying to keep his tone calm and level. "It's been fifteen years since that Halloween. Why is it so hard for you to move forward?"

"Move forward?" she scoffed, shaking her head in disbelief. "You have no idea what it was like for me after you left. You were my best friend, Miles. If you just took a second to think back, you had people around you. They made you feel comfortable. I only had my dad and you guys. When I lost you, I was completely alone. You swore you would always be there for me, but chose a girl who tore me down with every breath she took. In just a few short months, I went from being your closest friend to becoming completely irrelevant, Miles."

She took a deep breath, her eyes glistening with unshed tears. "I'm not the same person I was back then, and neither are you. We can't go back to how things were, Miles. It's too late for that."

Miles felt a pang of regret deep within him, realizing how much hurt he had caused her all those years ago. He wished he could turn back time and fix it, but there was no going back now. All he could do was try to make things right, moving forward.

"Destiny, wait!" Miles called out as she turned to leave. But her voice was resolute as she responded without looking back.

"Leave me alone, Miles. It was easy then, and it will be easy now."

Miles watched her walk away, his heart aching with the weight of their unresolved past. He turned to leave Peaches, giving the charming café one last look as the door closed behind him. The exterior of the café, painted in warm hues of peach and cream, seemed to reflect the tender kindness that Destiny had always possessed. The colorful flowers blooming in window boxes contrasted with the gray sidewalks, standing out like a beacon of hope amidst the mundane.

It struck him how much everything had changed—not the café, but his life and Destiny's as well. The once inseparable friendship they shared had become an estranged connection, broken by misunderstandings and the passage of time.

As he stood there, lost in thought, Miles realized that the best advice he could get about mending this fractured bond would come from his older brother Max. After all, Max and Vivienne hadn't always been the picture-perfect couple they turned into. They'd faced their share of challenges, including dealing with their manipulative mother, and Max had fought hard to rebuild their friendship too.

With renewed determination, Miles headed back to Vortex, his mind racing with thoughts about what to say and how to approach the situation. As he walked, he couldn't help but ponder on Destiny's words and actions, trying to decipher what lay beneath the surface. Was it possible that she still harbored feelings for him? Or was it simply the pain of losing a cherished friendship?

THE RHYTHMIC SOUND OF A SPONGE SCRUBBING AGAINST the already spotless countertop filled the medium-sized cafe kitchen. The stainless steel appliances gleamed beneath the overhead fluorescent lights, their surfaces reflecting Destiny's focused expression as she wiped down every inch of the workspace. The faint scent of citrus cleaner mingled with the lingering aromas of freshly baked pastries and rich coffee.

With the lunch rush over, Peaches had quieted down, giving Destiny the opportunity to restock the shelves and whip up more delectable treats for customers. As some of the employees clocked out, Destiny glanced around the clean and organized kitchen, appreciating the calm that settled over the space in the afternoon.

Lost in thought, Destiny didn't even notice Lila slipping into the back entrance. It wasn't until she heard the distinct sound of a bag hitting the floor that Destiny jumped, startled, her heart momentarily pounding in her chest.

"Jeez, Des," Lila said, raising an eyebrow. "Why are you so jumpy?"

She paused and glanced away, trying desperately to keep the turmoil inside her from spilling out. She didn't want anyone, least of all herself, to know how much Miles' sudden appearance had affected her. Taking a deep breath, she slowly looked back at Lila and reluctantly confessed, "Miles was here earlier today."

Lila's eyes widened with curiosity. "Oh? What did he want?"

"Apparently, just to talk," Destiny replied, rolling her eyes and returning to her cleaning.

Lila leaned against the doorway, her arms crossed like she was waiting for Destiny to say something. Destiny took a look at Lila and knew that she wanted to know what Miles and Destiny spoke about.

"Ugh, you should have heard him," Destiny groaned, frustration apparent in her voice. "Miles just doesn't get it, Lila. He can't understand why that stupid picture could hurt me so much. Instead, he told me that I was simply 'jealous' of the ever perfect, divine goddess that is Candy!" She threw her hands up in the air, her anger boiling over as she began to raise her voice.

"Jealous? Of Cry Baby Candy? Can you believe that?" Destiny scoffed, turning to Lila, trying to convince herself more than anyone else. But deep down, the green monster of jealousy was gnawing at her heart.

Her eyes met Lila's calm gaze, and she hesitated for a moment, realizing how worked up she'd become. Taking a deep breath, she tried to steady herself by remembering the words her father always said, "Sweetie Pie, remember that storms may come, but you have the strength to weather them. You're a resilient and brave soul, and I believe in you. Just keep your head high, and you'll emerge from any challenge even stronger." Destiny immediately started to calm.

Lila reached for Destiny's hand, offering support and understanding. "Des," she said softly, her electric blue eyes serious, "do you know why that photo bothers you so much?"

Destiny sighed, rubbing her temples as she considered her friend's question. "I don't know, Lila. I really don't. It's just… seeing Candy all over him like that, it's infuriating."

"Maybe Miles isn't that far off with the jealousy thing," Lila admitted gently, choosing her words carefully, "but he misread it. He sees it as Candy being, well, Candy. You know how he is; he never sees the bad in people, at least not right away. He wants to see the best in everyone, even her. He sees her as driven for success, not conniving and manipulative like we know she is."

Destiny nodded slowly, taking in Lila's words. It was true, Miles had always been more forgiving than most when it came to others' flaws. Still, the thought that he couldn't see through Candy's façade was maddening.

"Because you were hurt so badly back then," Lila continued, her voice soft but unwavering, "you're defensive when it comes to Miles. Maybe that's why the photo stings so much—it's bringing back all of the pain you've experienced."

Destiny blinked back tears, her heart aching at the truth in Lila's words. She had always looked to Miles when seeking his support. But when he started hanging out with Candy and getting all of the attention it brought, he'd left her behind without a second thought.

"Maybe you're right," Destiny admitted, her voice barely above a whisper. "But I just wish he could see how much that picture and his actions hurt me, not because I'm jealous, but because it's a reminder of everything we lost."

Lila squeezed Destiny's hand. "We can't change the past, Des, but we can control how we move forward.

Maybe it's time for both you and Miles to have an open, non-judgmental conversation about everything that happened. It won't be easy, but it's the only way you'll both be able to heal." Lila's face lit up in a wicked grin before she added, "Or leave him to rot and let's go to the bar."

Destiny took a deep breath, realizing that her friend was right. It would take time and effort, but if she wanted to truly rebuild her relationship with Miles, it would start with communication and understanding. And maybe, just maybe, they could finally put the past behind them and forge a stronger bond than ever before.

"Okay," Destiny finally said, determination settling in her chest. "I'll give it a try. Hopefully, we can start to understand each other better. Even though I want to avoid him, I knew it was inevitable if he started coming into the cafe regularly. He was the last person I wanted to see, yet I couldn't just run away whenever he walked through the door."

"Good," Lila smiled warmly, releasing Destiny's hand.

Destiny sighed, feeling a mixture of trepidation and hope at the prospect of a frank discussion with her old friend. She knew it was necessary if they were ever going to move past their issues and rebuild their relationship, but the thought still made her heart race.

"Let's get back to work," Lila suggested, breaking into Destiny's thoughts.

"Right," Destiny agreed, forcing herself to focus on the task at hand. As they moved around the kitchen, restocking ingredients and preparing for the next wave of customers, Destiny couldn't help but let her mind wander back to Miles. She wondered how he would react when she approached him for an honest conversation, and whether he would truly be willing to listen.

Destiny pushed thoughts of Miles aside and allowed

the comforting scents and sounds of the cafe to soothe her. Familiar tasks greeted her each time she turned around, providing a sense of stability that was always there.

* * *

Miles sat in his sleek office chair, his mind a whirlwind of thoughts and emotions. The afternoon light filtered through the blinds, casting a warm glow over the polished mahogany desk and the glass wall that separated him from the rest of the Vortex employees. His green eyes were unfocused as he stared at the office door, waiting for Max to return from his meetings and lunch.

"Are you sure there's nothing I can do for you, Miles?" Candy poked her head into his office for what seemed like the 50th time, her icy blue eyes filled with concern.

Miles sighed, rubbing his temples. "No, Candy, I'm fine. Thank you," he replied, trying to sound reassuring. As she retreated, he couldn't help but glance at her desk through the glass wall, wondering if Destiny's accusations held any truth. The thought gnawed at him, making it difficult to concentrate on anything else.

Just then, he spotted Max striding down the hallway towards his office, his brown hair slightly disheveled from a busy day. Eager for the distraction, Miles stood up and headed to meet him

Miles approached Max's office, noticing the dividers between the offices were closed, which offered some privacy. As he entered, he took in the room that seemed to mirror Max's personality – clean and tidy, yet comfortable and engaging. Family photos of Vivienne adorned the walls, capturing their wedding day, their engagement, and various vacations they'd taken together. Art pieces and other personal touches filled the remaining space, giving the room a warm atmosphere.

"Hey Max, can we talk?" Miles asked, his voice tense with concern.

"Of course," Max replied, motioning for Miles to follow him inside. As they settled into the office, they could hear Malcolm typing away in his tech lair through the thin walls. "Do you need some privacy?"

"Uh, yeah, if you don't mind," Miles said, rubbing the back of his neck anxiously. Max nodded and frosted the glass in front of his office, effectively blocking out any prying eyes.

Miles took a seat in one of the plush armchairs, sighing heavily as he leaned back. Max sat in the chair next to him, waiting patiently for his brother to speak. The silence stretched on, but Max remained patient, knowing that Miles would open up when he was ready.

"Destiny told me something today," Miles began, finally breaking the silence. "She mentioned this photo from Halloween when we were in high school. Candy and I coordinated. We were Barbie and Ken."

"Ah, yes," Max said, nodding in recognition. "The infamous Ken and Barbie photo. I remember that."

Miles looked at him, surprised that Max knew about it. "You do?"

"Well, Candy did send it to everyone," Max admitted with a shrug. "But Destiny made it sound like you sent it to her?"

"Right," Miles said, rubbing his temples. "I didn't ask her to clarify, though. I just... I assumed she was jealous."

"Ouch," Max winced. "You know, you really should try to look at it from Destiny's perspective, Miles."

Miles tried to shake off his confusion, but it clung to him like a stubborn stain. "Max, be honest with me," he implored, looking into his brother's eyes. "What am I missing here? Why can't I understand Destiny's perspective?"

Max hesitated for a moment, clearly weighing his words carefully. "Alright," he finally said. "The truth is that you weren't exactly the best brother or friend back then, Miles. You made some poor choices, and sometimes you still do."

"Like what?" Miles asked, his brows furrowing.

"Like letting Candy dote over you, boosting your ego until you felt invincible," Max continued, his voice steady and resolute. "You liked the attention, so you ditched Destiny and Lila and distanced yourself from our family just to fit in with her and the popular crowd."

Miles' heart sank as he realized the truth in Max's words. He had let the allure of popularity cloud his judgment, ultimately resulting in damaged relationships with those who mattered most. Max made it sound like he was still doing it, but in a different way.

"Look at Candy today," Max went on. "She enjoys all the expensive things and the high life, while you've grown to appreciate simpler pleasures. The two of you are best friends, but you have little in common. It's time to think about rebuilding relationships humbly, without any of the ego that held you back in high school."

Miles sighed, knowing that Max was right. "So, what do I do now?"

"Listen to Destiny," Max advised firmly. "Be open to how you hurt her, even if you don't believe the situation should have caused pain. It is her pain and she feels it deeply, it was never yours. "

As Miles absorbed the weight of his brother's words, he began to see the man he had turned into over the years. Had he been so self-absorbed that he never realized the hurt he had caused others? The thought gnawed at him, making it difficult to breathe.

"Thanks, Max," Miles finally managed to say, his voice thick with emotion. "I needed to hear that."

"Anytime, little brother," Max replied, clapping him on the shoulder. "Just remember, we all make mistakes. What matters most is how we learn from them and make amends."

Miles nodded, determined to do just that. He would listen to Destiny, truly listen, and make sure she knew that he cared about her feelings. It was time to rebuild the bridges he had once burnt and become the man he wanted to be—the man Destiny deserved.

Miles stood up, thanked Max once again for his honesty, and returned to his office. He closed the door behind him, feeling a mixture of guilt and determination. As he sat down in his leather chair, he stared at the various awards and achievements that adorned his walls. They felt hollow now, as if they couldn't make up for the years of damaged relationships and self-absorption.

He took a deep breath and made a silent promise to himself. From now on, he would be more aware of other people and less concerned with what others thought about him. With this newfound resolve, his thoughts drifted towards Destiny. If she gave him a chance, he would put his ego aside and genuinely listen to her.

That evening, as Miles drove home, the street lights danced across the windshield, casting an ethereal glow. The weight of the day's revelations still lingered heavily in his heart, but it was accompanied by a shimmer of hope. As he pulled into the driveway of his home, he knew that he had a long road ahead of him. But he was ready to face it head-on, embracing humility and genuine connection.

Miles stepped out of his car and looked up at the night

sky, taking in the vast expanse of stars. He was overcome by a surge of amazement and humbleness, emotions that had been absent for too many years.In that moment, he vowed to become a better man, not just for Destiny, but for himself and all the people he cared about.

"Here's to a new beginning," he whispered to the cool night air, before stepping inside his house, determined to face whatever challenges lay ahead.

THE MORNING SUN CAST A WARM GLOW OVER MILES' house, bathing the exterior in a gentle golden light. It was easy to see why he loved it so much. His house was adorned with charming shutters framing the windows, while a beautiful porch wrapped around the front, beckoning visitors to sit and stay awhile.

As Miles stepped out of his house, he pulled the door closed behind him, fumbling with his keys in an attempt to lock it. He couldn't help but feel exhausted, the weight of countless sleepless nights heavy on his shoulders. The cause of his lack of rest? Destiny Evans. No matter how hard he tried, his thoughts always seemed to drift back to her.

"Get it together, man," Miles muttered to himself, finally managing to lock the door. "You need to focus."

He shoved the keys into his pocket and took a deep breath, trying to clear his mind as he prepared for another busy day at Vortex. There were meetings to attend, decisions to be made, and a company to run. But despite all that, the image of Destiny's brown hair and hazel eyes lingered in his mind, refusing to be forgotten.

"Maybe I should just talk to her," he mused aloud, shaking his head in amusement at his own internal struggle. He knew that there was more to Destiny than the strong-willed cafe manager who volunteered at soup kitchens and had a heart of gold. And he was determined to find out what it was that drew him to her like a moth to a flame.

With a renewed sense of purpose, Miles headed down the driveway towards his car. And maybe, just maybe, he'd find the right moment to reconnect with Destiny and uncover the mystery that lay beneath the surface.

Miles approached his sleek, black SUV that stood out in the morning sun. The vehicle boasted luxurious upgrades like a state-of-the-art sound system and heated leather seats. As he got in, he couldn't help but notice all of the little extras it had.

"Maybe I can learn something from her," he thought, genuinely intrigued by the woman who occupied his every waking moment. Miles started the engine and took off towards Peaches, the coffee was favored by the Vortex employees and that was why he went there. Well, at least that's what he was telling himself anyway.

Upon arrival at Peaches, Miles quickly placed an order for coffees to-go, feeling the warm aroma of freshly brewed java enveloping him. He couldn't help but smile, reminded of the many mornings he'd spent with Destiny, enjoying the same comforting scent.

"Small world," he muttered as he bumped into none other than Destiny herself, just as he collected the coffees. Her eyes widened in surprise, and he could see a hint of curiosity flicker through them. Seizing the moment, Miles decided to trust his instincts.

"Hey, Destiny. Will you have dinner with me tonight?"

he asked casually, trying to mask the nervousness that bubbled beneath the surface.

She hesitated, and he quickly added, "Not as a date or anything, just a chance for us to talk and get to know each other better. I promise I'll listen without judgment."

Destiny's face gave everything away. She was skeptical about how genuine he was being. He knew that he couldn't convince her to give him a chance. So, he waited until she made the decision to meet him. He hadn't realized that he was holding his breath waiting for a response. Miles sighed in relief when she agreed. Destiny tells him, "Okay. But only if we can go to Bella Trattoria. I want to try it."

Stepping out of Peaches, Miles couldn't help but breathe in the crisp morning air, he was invigorated by his brief encounter with Destiny. The sky above him was a brilliant blue, and he took a moment to appreciate the beauty around him before heading to his SUV.

Arriving at Vortex, he parked in his usual spot and gathered the coffees, making his way up to the executive floor. The elevator doors slid open with a soft ding, revealing the bustling tech floor before him. Workers darted back and forth, focused on their tasks, and the hum of productivity filled the air.

"Morning, Malcolm," Miles greeted his younger brother as he handed him his coffee. Malcolm glanced up from his computer, a grateful smile flashing across his face.

"Thanks, bro," Malcolm replied, taking a sip of the energizing brew. "Couldn't have come at a better time."

Miles continued down the hall, spotting Max on the phone. He waited for a pause in the conversation before handing him his coffee, earning a nod of appreciation from his older brother.

"Thought you could use some caffeine," Miles whispered, patting Max on the shoulder before stepping away to let him continue his call.

As he turned the corner toward his office, he saw Vivienne and Candy in deep conversation. He couldn't quite hear what they were discussing, but he caught Candy rolling her eyes just as Vivienne suggested something. Miles approached them, offering a friendly smile.

"Hello, ladies," he said, handing each of them their respective coffees. Candy's demeanor shifted immediately, her previous irritation replaced by a saccharine smile. Vivienne smiled her thanks and ran off to catch Max before his next meeting.

"Hey, Miles," Candy said, her voice dripping with sweetness. "How are you today? You look like you're in a great mood."

Miles hesitated for a moment, his thoughts drifting to Destiny and the unexpected encounter at Peaches earlier that morning. He wanted to share his excitement with Candy, knowing she'd revel in it with him, but he opted instead to focus on rebuilding their friendship.

"Oh, it's nothing really," he replied, trying to keep his voice casual. "Just had a good morning, that's all."

"Really?" Candy raised an eyebrow, her curiosity piqued. "You seem unusually chipper."

Miles chuckled, running a hand through his brown hair. "Well, I guess I just appreciate the little things in life, like a beautiful morning and a cup of coffee from Peaches."

Candy studied him for a moment, her icy blue eyes narrowed in suspicion, but she didn't press the issue. Instead, she offered a small smile and a nod. "Well, I'm glad to see you in high spirits. It's contagious."

"Thanks, Candy," Miles said sincerely, touched by her

seemingly genuine response. "Now, if you'll excuse me, I have some work to do."

With that, he walked into his office, his heart lighter than it had been in days. As he settled down behind his desk, his gaze drifted to the framed photos that adorned its surface—memories of family, friends, and moments that had shaped his life. He couldn't help but notice the addition of these photos after seeing Destiny's office where memories lined every available surface.

As he worked, his thoughts inevitably wandered back to Destiny, her hazel eyes filled with warmth and understanding. He couldn't wait to see her again, to explore the possibility of starting the friendship that he desired over. But for now, he had a job to do. Everything else could wait until tonight.

* * *

Destiny stood in front of the full-length mirror, her hazel eyes studying her reflection as she smoothed down the light, flowy fabric of her sundress. The dress was a soft shade of lavender that complemented her fair skin and brown hair, which fell in loose waves around her shoulders. A hint of blush graced her cheeks while her lips were painted with a delicate gloss, giving her a fresh, romantic appearance.

She hummed a familiar tune under her breath as she fastened a dainty silver necklace around her neck, the pendant resting just above her collarbone. Slipping on a pair of strappy sandals, Destiny took one last look at her reflection before deciding she was ready for the evening ahead.

"Alright, Destiny," she whispered to herself, taking a deep breath to calm her nerves. "You've got this."

The day had been a rollercoaster of emotions, from the unexpected encounter with Miles in the morning to the anticipation of their dinner together. She couldn't deny that she was drawn to him, but there was still so much they needed to understand about each other. Tonight would be a chance to do just that—to talk openly, listen without judgment, and maybe even start to build something new.

Destiny stepped out of her apartment, closing the door softly behind her. She walked down the hallway and through the back kitchen door of the cafe, where she was greeted by the familiar aroma of freshly brewed coffee and the sound of laughter from the staff. The cafe was still open and finishing up the dinner rush, and Destiny couldn't help but smile at the warm, bustling atmosphere that she had come to love.

As she walked the short distance to the restaurant, the market lights strung overhead flickered on one by one, creating a magical ambiance that seemed to beckon her forward. The intimate Italian restaurant she had chosen for their dinner loomed ahead, its ivy-covered brick facade bathed in the warm light of the setting sun. Checkered tablecloths adorned each table, and the scent of garlic and fresh herbs wafted through the air, making Destiny's stomach rumble in anticipation. Though romantic, the restaurant maintained a casual feel that put her at ease, as if she were stepping into the embrace of an old friend.

Destiny was glad that Miles agreed to her condition to go to Bella Trattoria. She had been dying to try their renowned osso buco—tender braised veal shanks simmered in a rich tomato and red wine sauce, served atop creamy risotto. The thought alone was enough to make her mouth water.

As she approached the entrance, she spotted Miles

already seated at one of the tables outside, his green eyes scanning the menu intently. Her nerves surged, and she took a deep breath to steady herself before walking towards him.

"Hey, Miles," she greeted him with a tentative smile, her hazel eyes meeting his.

"Destiny," he replied warmly, a genuine smile spreading across his face as he stood to greet her. "You look lovely. I'm glad you're here."

"Thanks," she said, feeling her cheeks flush slightly at the compliment. "I've been looking forward to trying this place."

Miles pulled out a chair for her, and Destiny took her seat, trying to ignore the butterflies that danced in her stomach. She couldn't help but wonder what the night would hold and whether it would bring them closer together or reveal insurmountable differences.

"Let's hope the osso buco lives up to your expectations," Miles said, having remembered her earlier mention of the dish. Destiny laughed, appreciating his love of food.

The waiter approached their table almost instantly after Destiny's arrival. "Good evening," he said with a warm smile. "Are you ready to order?"

"Ah, yes," Destiny replied, quickly scanning the menu one last time. "I'd like to try the osso buco, please."

"Excellent choice," the waiter nodded in approval. "And for you, sir?" he asked, turning his attention to Miles.

"I'll have the risotto ai funghi porcini, thank you," Miles responded, handing the menus back to the waiter.

"Of course, your orders will be out shortly," the waiter said before leaving them alone at the table.

A brief, awkward silence ensued, and Destiny found herself fiddling with her napkin, searching for the right words. She took a deep breath, looked up, and decided to dive right in. "So, Miles, why did you want to go to dinner tonight?"

Miles hesitated for a moment, his green eyes meeting her hazel ones. He took a sip of water before responding. "I wanted to apologize, Destiny," he began, his voice sincere. "I, ummm, I know now that I didn't think about your feelings when we spoke about the picture. I'm sorry I didn't pay more attention to your struggles. I regret not being there for you."

His apology was genuine, and Destiny could see the remorse in his eyes. It touched her heart, and she felt a wave of appreciation for his honesty and vulnerability. Just as Destiny opened her mouth to respond, a familiar face from the soup kitchen appeared beside their table. The man had a warm smile and a gentle manner about him. "I'm sorry to interrupt," he said apologetically, his eyes darting between Destiny and Miles. "Destiny, I was just wondering if you'll be at the Veteran Pancake Breakfast on Saturday?"

"Of course!" she exclaimed, her eyes lighting up with excitement. "I wouldn't miss it for the world and it's all for the veterans, you know? Such an important cause."

"Great, we'll see you there then. Enjoy your dinner," the man said, nodding politely to Miles before walking away.

As Destiny turned back to face Miles, she noticed a peculiar expression in his green eyes, like a mixture of curiosity and admiration. She couldn't quite put her finger on what it meant, but it intrigued her. "Hey, Miles?" Destiny asked, a hint of amusement in her voice. "What's that look for?"

Miles blinked, seemingly caught off-guard by her question. He shook his head, offering her a dismissive smile.

"Oh, uh, nothing," he insisted, though she couldn't shake the feeling that the look held more significance than he was willing to admit.

"Alright then" she replied, deciding to let it go for now. They still had plenty to talk about, and getting to know each other better was the main goal of the evening.

eight

As his gaze fell upon her, he couldn't help but be captivated by the warmth and depth in her eyes. They seemed to hold secrets and dreams, and he was determined to uncover them all. The way she looked at him made him feel like he was the only person in the world. He found himself mesmerized, wanting to know everything about this incredible woman—not the girl from his past, but the strong and beautiful person she had become. Her presence lit up the room, and he couldn't stop staring at her, completely enraptured by her unique beauty inside and out.

"Hey, Miles?" Destiny asked, a hint of amusement in her voice. "What's that look for?"

He blinked quickly, trying to shake off his thoughts. "Oh, uh, nothing," he stammered, feeling the heat rise in his cheeks. He knew now was not the time to dwell on his feelings; he had already apologized wholeheartedly for his past mistakes, and all he could do was hope she would accept his sincerity.

"Alright then," she said, still smiling. "So, what are your

plans for the weekend?"

"Actually," Miles began, his curiosity getting the better of him, "I was wondering if you could tell me more about that pancake breakfast you were talking about."

Miles leaned forward, resting his elbows on the table as he listened intently to Destiny. Her excitement was contagious as she described the pancake breakfast for the veterans in vivid detail.

"First, we start by prepping all the ingredients early in the morning," she explained, her hazel eyes sparkling with enthusiasm. "We have a team of volunteers who help us cook and serve the food. It's a lot of fun, and the veterans really appreciate it."

Miles couldn't help but be amazed by Destiny's dedication and organization. "You've got quite the knack for this," he remarked with a smile.

Destiny laughed, the sound light and melodic. "Well, I wouldn't say that, but we try our best! And once the food is served, we sit down and chat with them, listen to their stories, and just make sure they know they're appreciated."

Her face softened as she spoke, a gentle smile gracing her lips. The passion she had for helping others was evident, and Miles found himself wanting to be a part of it, to share in this beautiful side of her life.

"Destiny, I'd love to help out," he said earnestly, meeting her gaze. "Sign me up for the breakfast."

"Really?" She looked genuinely surprised, but then a delighted grin spread across her face. "That's great! I'm sure the other volunteers will be thrilled to have you."

"Anything I can do to support such a fantastic cause," Miles replied. He was thinking about donating money, but thought, *Well, looks like I'll be getting my hands dirty.* He knew that getting involved in something so close to Destiny's heart would give him the opportunity to learn more about the person she had become and strengthen their connection.

"Thank you, Miles," Destiny said sincerely, her eyes shining with gratitude. "Your help means a lot to me, and I know it will mean even more to the veterans."

As the conversation continued, Miles found himself enraptured by Destiny's every word. He was determined to make the most of this opportunity, not only to help those in need but also to get closer to the woman who had inexplicably captured his heart.

The savory aroma of their meals filled the air as the server placed the dishes in front of them. Miles took a bite of his risotto, savoring the tender, juicy flavors that melded together perfectly. However, his attention was quickly stolen by Destiny, who had just taken her first bite of the osso bucco she had ordered.

"Holy shit! This is incredible," she exclaimed, her eyes lighting up with delight. The joy on her face was captivating, and Miles felt an odd warmth in his chest at the sight of it. He couldn't help but watch her every reaction to the food, wondering if he could ever make her feel that way again. His heart pounded at the thought.

As they continued to eat, the conversation flowed easily between them. They shared stories and memories, laughter filled the spaces between bites. It was as if the years they had spent apart had never happened, and for a moment, Miles felt like he was back in elementary school, sitting next to Destiny in the cafeteria.

"Thank you for inviting me to dinner," Destiny said as she wiped her mouth with a napkin. "I really enjoyed myself tonight."

"Of course," Miles replied, his heart swelling with happiness. "I'm glad I could make it up to you after everything that happened." He noticed she relaxed and was not sitting as stiff. His shoulders are slightly hunched and she is giving him a small smile.

When they finished eating, Miles insisted on paying the bill. He knew that he didn't want the night to end just yet, not when he had started to reconnect with Destiny in such a meaningful way.

"Can I walk you home?" he asked as they left the restaurant.

"Sure, but I live above the cafe, so it's not very far," she cautioned him. "What about your car?"

"I can come back for it," Miles assured her, eager to spend a few more minutes with her by his side.

"Alright," Destiny agreed, a soft smile gracing her lips. The cool night air wrapped around them, and the sound of their footsteps echoed on the sidewalk.

As they walked, Miles marveled at how easy it was to fall back into step with Destiny, as if no time had passed at all. The warmth of their earlier conversation still lingered between them, making him feel hopeful for the future.

The short walk came to an end all too soon, and he found himself standing in front of the cafe with Destiny. He couldn't help but feel a pang of sadness at the thought of parting ways, but he knew that he would see her again soon, and that thought brought a sense of comfort.

"Thanks for dinner," Destiny said, her voice soft and sincere. "I really enjoyed myself tonight."

"Me too," Miles replied, smiling down at her. "It was great catching up with you, Destiny"

"Goodnight, Miles," she says softly, her eyes sparkling in the moonlight.

"Goodnight, Destiny," he echoed, watching as she turned and disappeared up the stairs to her apartment above the cafe.

* * *

The first light of dawn filtered through the windows of the soup kitchen, casting a warm glow on the long wooden tables and mismatched chairs. Destiny surveyed the room as she walked in, taking in the colorful hand-made tablecloths, each one a unique patchwork of donated fabrics that told its own story. The scent of fresh coffee already filled the air, mingling with the faintest hint of cleaning supplies left over from the night before.

Bouquets of wildflowers adorned every table, their vibrant colors standing out against the otherwise humble surroundings, and strings of fairy lights were strung across the ceiling, creating an atmosphere that was almost magical. The kitchen bustled with activity as volunteers prepped breakfast ingredients, laughter and chatter filling the space with a sense of camaraderie.

Destiny took a deep breath, feeling her heart swell with pride at the sight of so many people coming together to support a cause so close to her heart. It was moments like these that reminded her why she devoted her time to this cause.

"Good morning, Destiny!" called out one of the volunteers, a friendly older woman with a shock of white hair and twinkling eyes. "Ready for another breakfast?"

"Always," Destiny replied with a smile, rolling up her sleeves and tying her apron around her waist. She felt energized by the palpable excitement in the room and found herself looking forward to working alongside everyone, including Miles.

As if summoned by her thoughts, Miles appeared in the doorway of the soup kitchen, his eyes scanning the room until they landed on Destiny. A grin spread across his face as he caught her gaze, and she couldn't help but smile back, waving him over.

"Hey," she greeted him warmly as he approached. "I have us set up over here."

Leading him to their designated work station, Destiny gestured towards the array of mixing bowls, whisks, and measuring cups awaiting them. "I'll show you how to make the batter. It's pretty easy, trust me."

Miles chuckled and rolled up his sleeves, eager to dive in. "All right, teach me your ways, pancake master."

As they worked side by side, Destiny whisked eggs with practiced ease while Miles carefully measured out flour and other ingredients for the batter. The smell of bacon baking in the oven wafted over to them, making their mouths water in anticipation.

"Did you know," Destiny mused as she cracked another egg, "that my dad used to make pancakes every Saturday morning? It was our little tradition. He'd let me help, even when I was too small to reach the counter without standing on a chair."

Miles glanced at her, a gentle smile touching his lips. "That's really sweet. It must be why you're so passionate about this event."

"Maybe," she conceded, her eyes far away as she remembered those simple, happy times. "I think that's why it means so much to me to see everyone here, working together to support the veterans. They deserve to feel that same warmth and love that I felt growing up. About 10.6% of the population of homelessness is made of veterans and 3.6% of the veteran population is unemployed." Destiny thought about her father and how he was unemployed for a while. She thinks about how they almost suffered from homelessness and how lucky she is now.

As Destiny finished her sentence, she looked at Miles,

who was listening intently. His green eyes seemed to hold an entire universe of understanding, and for a moment, she felt as though he could see straight into her soul. But, before she could dwell on the thought, the sound of laughter snapped her back to reality, and she smiled.

"Come on," she said softly, her eyes shining with determination. "Let's make this the best pancake breakfast they've ever had."

The moment the first veteran walked through the door, it felt like a wave of excitement washed over the soup kitchen. Destiny and Miles stood side by side at the griddle, their fingers deftly flipping pancakes and scrambling eggs as the sizzle of bacon filled the air. The other volunteers buzzed around them, each with their own task — setting tables, refilling coffee cups, and helping the veterans find their seats.

"Good morning!" Destiny greeted one of them warmly, her hazel eyes sparkling with genuine happiness. "I hope you're hungry!"

"Starving," the elderly man replied with a chuckle, his eyes twinkling with amusement. "These pancakes smell divine."

"Thank you!" she beamed, dishing up a fluffy stack onto his plate. "Enjoy!"

As more veterans filed in, the atmosphere became an intoxicating blend of cheerful banter and heartfelt gratitude. One of them that caught Destiny's eye was a man who is not someone a person can easily be approached. He is looking around nervously and walking back and forth. He caught Destiny's eye and smiled. Destiny felt this sense of elation that out of the few people he trusted, she was one. It was a whirlwind of activity, with volunteers racing to keep up with the steady stream of hungry mouths to feed. And yet, amidst the chaos, Destiny found herself completely at ease, thriving on the energy that pulsed through the room.

Finally, the last plate was served, and the volunteers took a collective breath, smiling at one another as they surveyed the room full of satisfied faces. Destiny began gathering empty trays, pausing briefly to chat with some of the veterans who thanked her for the delicious meal. She was going to the kitchen to help the other volunteers start packing up leftovers for people to take with them. Their stories tugged at her heartstrings, and she couldn't help but feel a surge of pride knowing that she had played a small part in bringing them comfort and joy.

"Excuse me, ma'am," one of the attendees said, reaching out to shake Destiny's hand. "This is the best pancake breakfast I've ever been to. You've really outdone yourself."

"Thank you so much," she replied, her cheeks flushing with pleasure. "That means a lot to me."

"Keep up the good work, young lady," he added with a smile before walking away.

Destiny continued her cleanup, her heart swelling with happiness. As she went to take the trays back to the kitchen, she noticed Miles engaged in conversation with a group of veterans. Curiosity piqued, she slowed her pace, trying to catch a glimpse of what they were discussing.

"Listen," she heard Miles say, his voice firm but compassionate, "I understand that you might not have much experience in the tech industry, but your background in strategy and security is invaluable. We can teach you everything else you need to know."

He extended his hand, offering them each a business card. Destiny's eyes widened as she realized what he was doing – he was offering them a job at Vortex. The veterans exchanged glances before accepting the cards, their faces lighting up with gratitude and hope.

"Thank you," one of them said, shaking Miles' hand enthusiastically. "You have no idea how much this means to us."

"Trust me," Miles replied, his green eyes filled with sincerity, "I'm just as grateful for the chance to work with you."

As they parted ways, Destiny couldn't help but feel a newfound respect for Miles. She'd always known him as a successful businessman, but seeing his willingness to lend a helping hand to those in need touched her deeply. Perhaps, she thought, there was more to Miles Huntington than met the eye.

Miles walked over to Destiny, an air of satisfaction lingering around him. She wiped her hands on a towel and leaned against the counter, her hazel eyes filled with curiosity.

"Hey, what was that about?" she asked, nodding toward the veterans he'd just been speaking with.

"Ah, well, they mentioned they were struggling to find employment," Miles explained, rubbing the back of his neck sheepishly. "I figured Vortex could use a few more people in the security division, and their skills in strategy would definitely be an asset."

Destiny's eyes widened, and she couldn't help but feel a swell of admiration for Miles. "That's amazing, Miles. Really generous of you."

He shrugged modestly, a slight blush creeping up his cheeks. "It's the least I can do for people who've served our country. Besides, it's not charity – they're going to be valuable members of the team."

"Still," Destiny insisted, her smile genuine and warm, "it's a wonderful thing you did."

Together, they finished cleaning up the kitchen, chatting easily as they worked side by side. The time flew by, and before they knew it, everything was spotless and in order. As they stepped outside into the crisp evening air, Destiny took a deep breath, feeling lighter than she had in a long time.

"Thanks for inviting me to help out today," Miles said, stretching his arms above his head. "It was a great experience."

"Thank you for coming," Destiny replied, her cheeks tinged pink from the cool breeze. "And for everything you did today. It meant a lot."

They stood there for a moment, looking at each other, the weight of their shared history between them. Destiny's mind wandered to the boy who had hurt her so long ago, a flicker of anger rising within her. But as quickly as it came, she let it go. This was a new beginning, a chance for friendship and healing, and she wouldn't allow her past to hold her back.

"Hey, I would love it if we could hang out more," Miles asked, his voice tentative but hopeful. "You know, as friends."

"Friends," Destiny echoed, feeling the word settle comfortably in her heart. "I'd like that, Miles."

"Great," he replied, his smile lighting up his face. "I'll see you soon, then."

"See you soon."

nine

THE VAST EXPANSE OF THE VORTEX OFFICE WAS A testament to the success and innovation that Miles, Max, and Malcolm had brought to life. With the dividers open, it felt like an infinite playground for their genius minds to collaborate and create. Miles' desk stood on one side, meticulously organized with various reports and documents neatly stacked, while his laptop hummed quietly in the center.

On the other side of the room, Malcolm's tech lair buzzed with energy. It was a wonderland of sleek gadgets, screens, and cutting-edge technology. Malcolm sat at his desk, fingers flying across multiple keyboards as code filled the numerous monitors surrounding him. His brown hair in disarray, he was the epitome of a tech wunderkind on a mission.

In the middle was Max's desk. It was organized with a touch of personality. His office was a reflection of his role as a family man. His brown hair was always neatly trimmed and styled to perfection. He had removed his suit jacket and placed it on the back of his chair, focusing on typing away at his computer.

Between these three areas, a frosted glass partition separated the main workspace from the assistants' desks and the tech team's open area. This provided privacy when needed, without hindering the free flow of ideas.

Miles glanced over at his brothers, a sense of pride washing over him. They were working together on a monumental project, one that could potentially change the landscape of cybersecurity forever. Their focus was on developing advanced measures to protect sensitive data and networks, creating cutting-edge firewalls, intrusion detection systems, and encryption technologies beyond anything currently available.

In addition, the project involved designing and deploying state-of-the-art digital surveillance systems that relied on artificial intelligence and machine learning to detect and prevent security breaches and threats. This would revolutionize the way companies and governments approach cybersecurity, and Miles knew that with his brothers by his side, they could achieve greatness.

Max and Malcolm exchanged a glance, their excitement palpable. As the three brothers delved deeper into their work, they knew that they were on the cusp of something truly groundbreaking. The challenge was daunting, but they were more than ready to rise to the occasion and make their mark on the world of technology and security.

Miles studied the report on his computer screen, analyzing data points with unwavering focus. The faint sounds of Malcolm's fingers flying across his keyboard filled the office space. The scent of coffee lingered in the air, a testament to the long hours they had been working.

"Ugh," Malcolm groaned, breaking Miles' concentration. He looked up to see his younger brother slumped in his desk chair, arms limp at his sides and head thrown back. "I am starving."

Max laughed from his own workspace, eyes crinkling in amusement. "You're always starving, Mal." He mimicked Malcolm's groan with a playful smirk. "*Staaarving*."

"Alright, alright," Miles chuckled, shaking his head at their banter. "How about we take a break and grab some lunch at Peaches?"

"Sounds good to me," Malcolm agreed, sitting up straight and stretching his arms above his head. "I could use a pick-me-up."

"Me too," Max chimed in, getting up from his chair. "A little break should do us some good."

"Hey, you know what they say—all work and no play," Miles teased, eliciting laughs from his brothers.

"True. But I hope you're not suggesting that eating is 'play' for me," Malcolm quipped, feigning offense.

"Wouldn't dream of it," Miles replied with a grin, enjoying their lighthearted camaraderie.

"Speaking of dreams, did I tell you guys about that crazy one I had last night?" Malcolm asked, as they began to gather their belongings. "It involved a giant gorilla and a unicycle – I kid you not."

"Okay, now I have to hear this," Max said, curiosity piqued.

"Save it for lunch, boys," Miles interjected, already looking forward to hearing Malcolm's inevitable wild tale. "Let's get a move on."

The brothers worked together, shutting everything down and lowering the privacy frost on the glass, they got up and went to lunch. When they headed out, they saw Candy at her desk. She stopped typing and looked at them.

"Hey, are you guys grabbing some lunch?" she asked, trying to sound casual.

"Yep, we're off to Peaches," Miles replied with a friendly smile.

"Mind if I join?" Candy asked hopefully, but before Miles could respond, Vivi came up to her, handing over a stack of papers.

"Sorry, Candy, but I need you to handle this task right away before you head off to lunch. It's quite urgent," Vivi said firmly, though not unkindly. As she walked away, she gave Max a subtle wink, which he returned with a knowing smile. Candy gave Miles an annoyed look.

"Maybe next time," Miles offered. But Candy just huffed and turned back to her computer.

Shrugging it off, the boys headed over to the elevator and got in, making their way to Peaches. As they walked over, they chatted about their day and what was going on in their lives. Malcolm shared more details about his bizarre dream.

When they reached the cafe, Max opened the door for everyone. The delicious aromas drifted out, causing Malcolm's stomach to growl loudly. After their order was placed, they took their seats, Miles couldn't help but glance around the café, searching for Destiny. He knew she was working, and he couldn't deny that seeing her bright smile always brought a warmth to his heart.

Miles' eyes scanned the cozy café, finally landing on Destiny as she emerged from the kitchen, a takeout bag in hand. Her hazel eyes sparkled with excitement as she approached a man waiting near the counter. She greeted him with a wide smile that seemed to light up the entire room. Miles couldn't help but notice how her light skin seemed to glow against the backdrop of delicious pastries and warm lighting.

As much as he tried to focus on Max and Malcolm's conversation, he found himself captivated by the interaction between Destiny and the man. He watched as the man leaned in closer, his voice low and intimate, and Destiny's laughter filled the air. The sight of her so at ease with another man stirred something deep within Miles – an unfamiliar heat that spread through his chest.

"Did you see that new software update?" Malcolm asked, pulling Miles back to reality for a moment.

"Uh, yeah," Miles replied, trying to feign interest while his gaze remained locked on Destiny. He knew it was irrational, but he couldn't shake the feeling of jealousy bubbling inside him. Why did it bother him so much to see her flirting with someone else? They were just friends, after all.

Destiny glanced over, catching Miles' eye, and her face lit up even more. She raised her hand, giving him a small wave. His heart skipped a beat as he returned the gesture, forcing a smile onto his face. He could feel Max and Malcolm's eyes on him, their expressions a mixture of amusement and concern.

"Alright, what's going on with you?" Max asked, leaning in and lowering his voice so only they could hear. "You've been staring at Destiny like a lovesick puppy since we got here."

"Nothing's going on," Miles insisted, though he couldn't quite keep the edge out of his voice. "I'm just… curious about who that guy is, that's all."

"Curious, huh?" Malcolm chimed in, an eyebrow raised. "You sure it's not something more than that?"

Miles sighed, rubbing the back of his neck. "I don't know, okay? It's just… seeing her with someone else, it doesn't feel right."

Max and Malcolm exchanged knowing glances before turning their attention back to Miles. "Well," Max began, placing a hand on his shoulder, "maybe it's time you figure out what she really means to you. Friends don't usually get this jealous over each other."

Miles nodded, taking in his brother's words. He had a lot to think about, but for now, he needed to focus on the present. He forced himself to turn away from Destiny and engage in the conversation with Max and Malcolm, laughing at their jokes and sharing stories of their own. But deep down, he knew he couldn't ignore the feelings brewing within him any longer.

* * *

As Destiny handed over the takeout bag to Kyle, she couldn't help but admire the genuine warmth that radiated from him. He was a well-built man with a kind smile and an easy-going manner that put everyone around him at ease.

"Hey, Destiny," he said, "it's been ages since you and Lila came by the bar. We miss seeing you guys there. When are you coming back?" Kyle gave Destiny these puppy dog eyes that make her giggle.

Her face lit up at the thought of spending time at Kyle's cozy bar with her best friend. "We'll definitely come soon! Life has just been so hectic lately, but I can't wait to relax." Kyle makes looking lovesick so real.

"Great!" Kyle exclaimed, his eyes crinkling with happiness. "I'll hold you to that promise."

Destiny turned back toward the cafe and caught Miles' gaze for a moment. She offered him a small smile and a quick wave before being summoned back to the kitchen by the frantic calls of her staff. The lunch rush was in full swing, and they needed all hands on deck.

As she rushed into the kitchen, Destiny tied a pastel-colored apron around her waist. The fabric was adorned

93

with adorable illustrations of cupcakes, hearts, and paw prints - a perfect reflection of her personality. Lila had given it to her as a gift, knowing her love for all things cute and sweet.

As Destiny bustled around the kitchen, chopping vegetables and stirring sauces, she couldn't help but steal glances at Miles through the window. She couldn't quite put her finger on it, but there was something different about him today. His laughter seemed forced, and his eyes kept drifting back to her, as if he was making sure she was still there.

"Focus, Destiny," she chided herself internally, shaking off the distraction and returning her attention to the task at hand. "There's work to be done."

But even as she tried to concentrate on her culinary creations, Destiny couldn't shake the feeling that something important was happening just outside the kitchen doors. And for some reason, it felt like Miles was at the very heart of it.

"Destiny!" one of her coworkers called out, snapping her back to reality. "We need more sandwiches, stat!"

"Right away," she replied with determination, pushing the thoughts of Miles to the back of her mind. For now, all that mattered was getting through the lunch rush and making sure her customers left with full bellies and happy hearts.

Once the last of the lunchtime customers filed out of the cafe, Destiny finally found a moment to catch her breath. She glanced around at the now-empty tables and smiled; another successful day at the cafe. But there was still work to be done, especially with creating the specials for the next day.

Knowing Max, Miles, and Malcolm would be coming in for lunch as they often did, Destiny wanted to make sure she had their favorites ready for them. Max, with his refined palate, would surely enjoy a gourmet turkey club sandwich on freshly-baked sourdough with an avocado-sun-dried tomato aioli and a lemon-blueberry scone. Miles, known for his love of comfort food, would be satisfied with a hearty roast beef sandwich complete with caramelized onions and horseradish sauce on warm ciabatta bread with a classic apple pie. And Malcolm, dessert being the most important, would appreciate a salted caramel-topped chocolate brownie with a light yet flavorful caprese sand-wich – fresh mozzarella, tomatoes, basil, and balsamic glaze on a chewy baguette.

With her decisions made, Destiny grabbed a piece of chalk and began to write the specials on the cafe's elegant chalkboard. Each item was written in flowing cursive, accompanied by colorful illustrations of the sandwiches and pastries. The board came alive with vibrant hues of reds, greens, blues, and yellows, giving the cafe an air of excitement and anticipation for the next day's offerings.

The cafe was quiet now, the customers gone and the last of the employees saying their goodbyes as they left for the night. Destiny took a moment to appreciate the calm atmosphere, the soft glow of the overhead lights casting a warm ambiance over the empty tables. She reached for the switch to turn off the lights, her fingers hovering just above it when she caught a glimpse of Miles standing outside the locked door, his green eyes meeting hers through the glass.

A smile spread across Destiny's face as she unlocked the door and let him in. "Hey, Miles. What brings you here so late?"

"Couldn't resist coming back after those delicious specials," he teased with a grin. "Actually, I was wondering if you had any plans for dinner? I'm starving."

Destiny chuckled. "I was just going to throw something

together upstairs. You're more than welcome to join me if you'd like."

"Sounds perfect," Miles agreed, relief evident in his voice.

They made their way up to Destiny's apartment, Miles settled onto one of the barstools at her kitchen island, watching as Destiny began to gather the ingredients for dinner.

"Alright, let's see what we have here," she mused, rummaging through her fridge and pantry. "How does a creamy sun-dried tomato pasta sound?"

"Amazing, as always," Miles replied, his stomach growling in anticipation.

With a nod, Destiny started pulling out the necessary ingredients: a jar of sun-dried tomatoes, fresh basil, garlic cloves, heavy cream, Parmesan cheese, and a package of fettuccine. She quickly made a mental tally, ensuring she had everything she needed before diving into the cooking process.

As she boiled the pasta and whipped up the sauce, the mouthwatering aroma of garlic and sun-dried tomatoes filled the air. Miles couldn't help but be mesmerized by Destiny's ease in the kitchen, her every movement precise and fluid.

"Here you go," Destiny said as she slid a cold beer across the counter to Miles, the bottle gleaming under the warm kitchen lights. She uncorked a bottle of red wine for herself, pouring a generous glass before joining him at the island.

The pasta was a symphony of flavors, the tangy sun-dried tomatoes melding perfectly with the richness of the cream and the sharpness of the Parmesan. They ate in companionable silence for a few bites, savoring each delicious mouthful, before diving into a conversation that touched on everything from work to their families and shared memories.

Miles raised his glass, clinking it gently against Destiny's. "To good food and even better company," he said, his green eyes warm with affection.

"Cheers to that" Destiny replied, a smile playing at the corners of her lips as she took a sip of her wine. They resumed their conversation, the easy flow of words between them like a dance they had perfected over time.

As they laughed and reminisced, Miles noticed the way Destiny's hazel eyes sparkled when she got excited about something, and how her laughter filled the room with a contagious joy. He couldn't help but feel grateful for the bond they shared, solidified through both triumphs and hardships.

Eventually, the plates were empty and the conversation began to wind down. Destiny rose from her seat, collecting the dishes and silverware. "I'll take care of these, you don't have to—"

"Nonsense," Miles cut her off playfully, standing up and reaching for a plate. "You cooked, so I'll clean. It's only fair."

Destiny smirked, acquiescing with a nod. "Alright, if you insist." Together, they tackled the aftermath of their meal: washing, drying, and neatly putting away every dish and utensil. The counters were wiped down until they gleamed, and the kitchen was returned to its pristine state.

As they worked side by side, Destiny couldn't help but notice how natural it felt – as if this was something they were always meant to do together. A comfortable warmth settled in her chest, and she realized that their friendship had grown into something more profound than before.

"Thanks for your help, Miles," she said sincerely, giving him a soft smile.

"Anytime, Destiny," he replied, returning her smile. With one last glance around the immaculate kitchen, he added, "I should get going. But let's do this again soon, alright?"

"Definitely," Destiny agreed, accompanying him to the door. As he stepped out into the night, she felt a bittersweet pang of longing, quickly followed by a sense of happiness at the possibility of truly having her friend back. She closed the door and leaned against it for a moment, allowing herself to savor the feeling before turning her attention to getting ready for bed.

ime this week.

Al scooted himself closer to me and used his nose to move my hand onto his head. He wasn't an official service dog of any kind, but he always knew when I needed him. Even the first night I had him home and this happened it was like he knew exactly what to do.

The moment my fingertips felt his fur they would start lightly moving back and forth. Soon my heartrate would start to slow. I just needed to take a deep breath and make things slow down.

Inhale 1, 2, 3, 4. Hold it 1, 2, 3, 4. Release 1, 2, 3, 4.

After serval minutes of my breathing exercise my pulse felt slower, and the nervous shaking seemed to be subsiding. The world around me was becoming more focused. I was in my room, Al was next to me, there is nothing scary or dangerous. With one more deep breath I leaned my face down to Al's.

"You are the best guy, Al. Thanks for always being my support," I gave him a little kiss on the top of my head. His tail beat against the bed a couple times in response.

I laid myself down and keeping my hand on Al's fur. His breathing was steady and calming, but I wasn't going to fall asleep any time soon. If I couldn't sleep, then I might as well bake. I could whip something up for the BBQ tomorrow. I pulled my hair up and started digging out flour, sugar, vanilla and every mixing bowl I owned.

By the time I was finally feeling tired my kitchen was a mess. I had started with a batch of my rocky road cookies for the kids. Then decided to make double fudge bourbon caramel brownies. I also made a batch of my lavender shortbread cookies for Mr. and Mrs. Simmons.

After packaging everything and cleaning the kitchen, I collapsed in bed around four in the morning.

When my eyes opened again there was light streaming in from the curtains, I had forgotten to close all the way. I must have thrashed around a couple more times in my sleep because I was turned sideways in the bed and Al was sleeping where my pillow had been. It was now laying with my comforter was on the floor and the sheets were wrapped around me.

"Morning Al," I said with my eyes closed and face still pressed against the mattress. I could hear the swish and soft thump of his tail on the bed. I reached over to pet his fur. He quickly got up and started licking my face.

"Ok ok, I'll get up and let you outside," I laughed pushing myself up.

I glanced at the clock; it was almost noon. I was going to need to a shower and lots of coffee, before I could get ready to spend the afternoon with everyone.

Today was a perfect day for a BBQ. The weather was still warm, but not oppressive. I picked up a couple six packs of beer from the Blue Crab before heading to the Beckett house.

Roger and Julia had bought their two-story house after having their twin girls twelve years ago. Although, after the attack that left Roger confined to a wheelchair, the house had to be renovated.

Fortunately, the master suite had always been on the ground floor. The few modifications downstairs were easy to get taken care of before Roger ever made it out of the hospital.

I went in without knocking, just like I had done a million times before. The Beckett's were family and their home had been my second home for years. The air inside was cool and I could smell the intoxicating aroma of Julia's home cooking. She always cooked with love and made enough to feed an army.

"Hello," I called as I made my way toward the back of the house.

"Kitchen," Julia answered. I found her pulling a cast iron skillet out of the oven.

"It smells amazing in here," I told her putting my food contribution on the counter, then tucked the beer in the fridge.

"Thanks Girl! This is the last bit of my cooking duties. I made potato salad, coleslaw, baked beans, and my skillet cornbread," she listed off everything with a satisfied smile on her face. "What is that?" she asked nodding to the boxes next me.

"Couldn't sleep so I baked," I said.

"Thoughts of your hot date keeping you up?" she wriggled her eyebrows at me.

"It wasn't a date and no I wasn't thinking of JT," I said. It was mostly true.

"Oh, it's JT now. How was your not date?" she smiled at me. There was something in her eyes that was mischievous.

"My dinner at the Blue Crab was fine. Where is everybody?" I asked to ignore the rest of my impending interrogation.

"Roger is in charge of the grill today. He's out on the

deck. The girls are setting up some fun stuff for the kids to do," she said. "We will talk about your date later."

I was already walking to sliding door that led to their deck. As much as I loved Julia, she felt the need to mother me sometimes, when she wasn't trying to play match maker.

"RAE RAE," Roger's giant smile greeted me as soon as I stepped foot outside.

"Hey Partner," I said leaning over to hug him. His arms wrapped around me in a true deep hug. "What's different about you? Did you cut your hair?" I asked with a laugh has a patted his shaved head.

"Funny stuff there Rae Rae. It's my new wheels, got them this week," he said rolling back and forth in a new wheelchair. It was an upgrade from the clunky one he had been using for the past year.

"Pretty sweet ride, my friend," I said watching Roger wheel around balancing on just the larger back tires.

"Easy hotshot, this food isn't going to cook itself," Julia said walked towards the grill carrying a tray of things to grill. Roger stopped showing off as she leaned down to give him a kiss.

I never thought I was the marrying type; it wasn't who I was. But seeing the love between these two always has me feeling like something deep inside was missing. They had loved and fought for years and there was no doubt in the strength of their relationship when you looked at them.

"Auntie Rae Rae!"

I glanced over my shoulder to see the girls. Two beautiful dark-skinned girls with bright eyes and long limbs. At almost thirteen Zara and Zoe were taller than me and soccer playing machines. Nobody stood a chance when the Beckett twins took the field.

"Do I know you?" I called. "I mean you look kind of

like my nieces, but they only come to about here," I put my hand to just above my hips.

"Auntie, you're being ridiculous," Zara said with a laugh.

I had spent the last two years in firm denial that the girls who once slept on my shoulder were now entering their teenage years. I suppose as long as they still laughed at my jokes and like hanging out with me, I could learn to live with them getting older.

Stepping off the deck I made my way across the back-yard to see what mischief they were setting up. While they were twins and played the same sport, their personalities were opposites. Zoe was the girly girl who liked fashion and makeup. Zara liked the natural athletic look. They were the mini version of their parents, and I loved them so much.

"What are you two putting together out here?" I asked looking at the pile of supplies on the ground.

"Water balloon capture the flag," Zara said enthusiastically.

"The hay bales on either side of the yard will act as home base for each team. The flag will be strung up halfway between the bases," Zoe added holding up a black and white checked flag.

"This is impressive," I said examining what they had set up so far. "What if we added something to make it interesting?"

"Like what," they said together.

"Let's spread out a large tarp under the flag, then cover it with dish soap, then put your old blow-up kiddie pool under the flag. We'll fill it with soapy water."

The girls looked at me with wide eyes and I could see the incoming squeal working its way to their mouths.

"Girls, what are you plotting?" Roger called from the deck.

"Nothing," the three of us responded plastering smiles on our faces.

We were always up to something sneaky, and Roger was always watching. It as the game we had all been playing for years.

"Is Dad going to feel left out?" Zoe looked at me with sadness in her eyes and I could see the same look in Zara's eyes.

Roger had always been a very active and athletic guy. He was always running around and taking the twins on adventures. It wasn't lost on anyone that it hurt him to not be the same person anymore.

"Oh Sweetie, your dad wants you to have fun and keep doing things. Don't stop being active because you think it leaves him out. He would hate that even more. You two start filling balloons. Don't worry about your dad, I have a plan."

They both nodded and headed off to fill as many balloons as humanly possible. While I set to work on the center of our flag course.

MILES LEANED BACK ON HIS PLUSH SOFA, A COLD BEER IN hand. His brothers were sprawled across the other seats, their laughter filling the living room. The sun streamed through the floor-to-ceiling windows, casting a glow over them. It was one of those rare moments when the three Huntington brothers could simply relax and enjoy each other's company.

"Alright guys, we need to start planning this year's charity event," Miles said, taking a swig of his beer. "We've got to make it even better than last year."

"Last year's gala was amazing," Max chimed in, his green eyes glittering with enthusiasm. "We raised what, half a million dollars for that children's hospital?"

"Yep, and don't forget about the year before that," Malcolm added, running a hand through his dark hair. "We helped fund that new wing for the homeless shelter. That was pretty incredible too."

"Definitely," Miles agreed, his thoughts racing. "So, any ideas on which charity we should focus on this time around? And where should we dedicate our efforts?"

Max scratched his chin thoughtfully. "Well, we've done healthcare and homelessness… What about something related to education or job training?"

"Great idea, Max," Malcolm nodded. "There are so many people out there who just need a chance, you know? A little push in the right direction."

Miles stared at the beer bottle in his hand, an image suddenly popping into his head. He remembered the veterans from the pancake breakfast Destiny had organized. The ones he gave his business card to all reached out asking for a chance at a job, and they were now thriving in the company. But there were so many others there who could use the support.

"Guys, what about helping veterans?" Miles suggested, looking at his brothers earnestly. "I think we should make the gala in honor of them. They've given so much for our country, and they deserve our support."

Max and Malcolm exchanged glances before nodding in agreement. "That's perfect, Miles," Max said, raising his beer in a toast. "To making a difference in the lives of those who have sacrificed for us."

"To our veterans," Malcolm echoed, clinking his bottle with theirs.

With their decision made, the conversation shifted back to planning the event. "We'll need a caterer for the gala," Malcolm pointed out. "Someone who can understand our theme and create a menu that complements it. The one last year just didn't quite get it."

Miles thought for a moment, and then Destiny's smiling face popped into his mind. "What about Destiny? She's an amazing chef and she understands the importance of supporting veterans."

"Destiny!" Max and Malcolm exclaimed in unison, their faces lighting up with excitement. "That's perfect!"

"Great, we'll ask her," Miles said, grinning at his brothers' enthusiasm. Just as he finished speaking, the game came on the television, and the boys turned their attention to it, their minds already racing with plans for the upcoming charity gala.

A few nights later, Miles and his brothers met up at Kyle's bar, a popular spot in town where they could kick back and relax. The girls were going to dinner beforehand, and Max couldn't help but express his gratitude for Destiny and Lila's friendship with Vivienne.

As they entered the bar, Miles took in the retro ambiance of the place, picking up on the hum of conversation and laughter that filled the room. Neon signs cast a colorful glow over the patrons, while the clinking of glasses and the low thud of bass from the jukebox created an energetic soundtrack for the evening.

"Man, I love this place," Malcolm said, inhaling deeply as if trying to capture the essence of the bar. "It's got that perfect mix of nostalgia and modernity."

"Couldn't agree more," Max chimed in, nodding toward the counter. "Let's grab some drinks before we find a table."

As they approached the bar, Miles caught sight of Kyle, the owner, and chuckled to himself. Miles reflected on the moment Destiny discovered his jealousy towards Kyle. He remembers her expression, a mix of confusion and surprise that he had never seen before. He replays the conversation in his mind, how he asked her if she wanted to be with Kyle because she always seemed to be laughing around him. Miles could feel his vulnerability rising as Destiny giggled with sparkling eyes. Unable to face her, Miles turned away as Destiny reassured him that she was not interested in Kyle. A few days later, Miles met Kyle and his partner, who were now clients of Vortex after facing financial struggles at their bar.

"Hey, Kyle!" Miles greeted, giving him a friendly nod. "Three beers, please."

"Coming right up, Miles," Kyle replied with a grin. "Enjoy your night, guys."

The brothers found a comfortable booth near the back of the bar, sinking into the worn leather seats as they continued to chat about work, family, and their upcoming charity event. Time flew by as they exchanged stories and laughter, the bond between them growing ever stronger.

"Can't wait for the girls to join us," Miles said, glancing at the entrance every now and then, eagerly anticipating Destiny's arrival.

"Same here," Max agreed, sharing a knowing smile with his brothers. "Something tells me tonight is going to be one for the books."

"Definitely," Malcolm chimed in, raising his glass once more. "Here's to an unforgettable night."

"Cheers!" They toasted, excitement filling the air as they awaited the arrival of the women who brought them so much joy.

* * *

Destiny stood in her room, hands on her hips, eyeing the four outfits laid out before her. A sky blue dress with delicate lines caught her attention, while a sleeveless white jumpsuit exuded confidence. An apricot wrap dress with subtle embroidery radiated femininity, and an olive green shift dress promised timeless elegance as she twirled throughout the night.

"Ugh, decisions, decisions," Destiny muttered to herself.

With her lip between her teeth, she scanned the outfits for what must have been the hundredth time.She decided to wait until Lila and Vivienne arrived to get their opinions on what to wear. After all, since her apartment is closest to the bar, they had agreed the night before that they'd get ready together.

As she sat on the edge of her bed, Destiny's thoughts drifted back to wine night the previous evening. Lila and Vivi had each brought their favorite bottles of wine, and they spent hours talking, laughing, and getting to know each other better.

"Seriously, though," Vivi had said at one point, swirling her glass of Pinot Noir, "I need an assistant who's as passionate and hardworking as you two."

"Look no further!" Lila had joked, raising her glass of Riesling. "We're a package deal, though. You'll have to hire both of us!"

"Deal," Vivienne had laughed, clinking glasses with Lila and Destiny. "Now let's make a pact. Tomorrow, we get ready together, go out for dinner, and then join the guys at the bar for a fun night."

"Agreed!" Destiny and Lila had chimed in unison, sealing the pact with another round of clinking glasses and sips of wine.

The doorbell rang, jolting Destiny back to the present. She quickly tied her silk robe around her waist, the deep purple fabric feeling luxurious against her skin. Padding across the living room, she opened the door to find Lila and Vivienne standing there, their arms laden with dresses, shoes, and jewelry.

"Hey, you two! Come in," Destiny greeted them warmly. "I haven't even decided what to wear yet."

"Perfect, we can help!" Lila grinned as they entered Destiny's apartment.

"Let's see the options," Vivienne chimed in, her eyes sparkling with excitement.

"Wow, these are all stunning," Lila commented, examining each option closely.

"Agreed," Vivienne added, running her fingers over the delicate lace on the little black dress. "So, which one do you feel most like yourself in?"

"Help me decide, guys," she implored, her hazel eyes searching their faces for suggestions.

"Of course," Vivienne reassured her, stepping forward to examine the outfits once more.

"Whatever you choose, you'll look amazing," Lila added, her electric blue eyes twinkling with confidence in her friend's decision.

"Okay, I think this one is perfect for you," Vivienne declared, holding up the wrap dress. The dress was cinched at the waist, highlighting Destiny's curves, while the sweetheart neckline added a touch of romance. A pair of floral wedges and rose gold hoop earrings completed the ensemble.

"Wow, I love it!" Destiny exclaimed, beaming at her reflection in the mirror as she imagined herself in the chosen outfit. Lila nodded in agreement.

"Definitely. It's sexy yet sophisticated—just like you," she grinned, winking at Destiny.

As the three women danced and sang to the playlist they set up last night, they began doing their hair and makeup. Destiny opted for loose waves cascading over her shoulders, framing her face beautifully. Her makeup was subtle but striking, with a hint of shimmer on her eyelids and a glossy, pink lip to match her dress.

Lila, ever the edgy fashionista, chose a fitted, burgundy jumpsuit that hugged her figure in all the right places. Paired with black, ankle-strap stilettos and a statement silver necklace, she exuded confidence. Her jet-black hair was styled in a sleek, high ponytail, and her electric blue eyes were accentuated by a dramatic cat-eye.

Vivienne, on the other hand, went for understated elegance. She wore a sophisticated navy-blue midi dress with a tasteful slit, revealing just a glimpse of her toned legs. Her accessories included delicate pearl earrings and a matching bracelet, adding a touch of timeless grace. Her soft brown hair was pulled back into a neat chignon, and her makeup was natural with a hint of blush and a rosy lip.

"Wow, we all look… absolutely perfect! !" Destiny said, admiring the trio in the mirror. "Let's go have some fun."

With excitement bubbling inside them, the girls left Destiny's apartment and made their way to a local hotspot for dinner. The trendy restaurant, illuminated by warm, soft lighting, was an eclectic mix of modern art and vintage charm. Exposed brick walls were adorned with vibrant paintings, while the wooden tables and plush velvet chairs provided a comfortable atmosphere.

After enjoying their delicious meals and paying the bill, the girls headed out to meet the guys at the bar. As they walked in, still chatting and laughing, Destiny glanced towards the back and spotted Max, Miles, and Malcolm sitting in a booth. Max was wearing a crisp white button-down shirt with dark jeans, while Miles had opted for a casual navy blue sweater over a light blue collared shirt and khakis. Malcolm was rocking a black leather jacket with a graphic tee and black jeans, looking effortlessly cool.

The boys noticed them and scooted over to make room for the girls. It was a tight fit and everyone scrunched together. The waiter came by shortly after, and the boys ordered drinks for everyone. Destiny received a lychee martini, Lila got a spicy margarita, and Vivi was given a classic cosmopolitan. Destiny raised her eyebrows in surprise when she saw her drink.

"Wow, Miles, you remembered my favorite?" she asked, impressed.

"Of course," he replied with a grin. "I pay attention to the important things."

The laughter only grew louder as they enjoyed their drinks, the girls sipping on their respective cocktails while the boys enjoyed their beers. The atmosphere was electric, everyone trying to outdo one another with amusing anecdotes and witty remarks.

"Remember when we were kids and thought we could fly if we just jumped high enough?" Lila reminisced, giggling at the memory.

"Of course," Miles chimed in, "You actually convinced me to jump off the garage roof with an umbrella—like Mary Poppins."

"Hey, it worked for her!" Lila defended, causing the entire group to erupt into laughter.

"Speaking of flying," Max said to Vivienne, "How's your drone photography coming along?"

"Slowly but surely," Vivi replied, blushing slightly at the attention. "It's amazing what you can capture from a bird's eye view."

"Destiny," Malcolm began, leaning towards her with a cheeky grin, "I heard you tried bungee jumping last month. Now that's some real flying!"

"More like free falling!" Destiny laughed, recalling the adrenaline rush. "But seriously, it was incredible. I'd do it again in a heartbeat."

As the night progressed, they continued to share stories and experiences, their camaraderie growing stronger with each passing moment. Eventually, they noticed the bar beginning to empty, signaling that it was time to call it a night.

"Alright, everyone," Malcolm announced, standing up and stretching his arms. "I'll drive Lila home. You guys good?"

"Yep, we're all set," Max confirmed, placing a protective arm around Vivi. "See you all soon."

Destiny and Miles scooted out of the booth and get ready to follow everyone out. As they make they're way to the front, Miles grabs her hand when she stumbles. Destiny smiled her thanks, but noticed that he didn't immediately let go.

"Destiny, would you like me to give you a lift home?" Miles offered, his eyes filled with pure happiness.

"Thanks, Miles, I'd appreciate it," Destiny agreed, grateful for the ride since she did not want to trek back home in her heels.

Destiny made them all promise to text when they got home. They all said their goodbyes and headed out into the night. Miles led Destiny to his car, opening the door for her before sliding into the driver's seat. The drive was short but filled with light conversation, both of them still buzzing from the evening's events.

As they pulled up in front of the cafe, Destiny reached for the door handle, eager to get some rest. But before she could exit the car, Miles stopped her.

"Wait, there's something I wanted to ask you," he said, his voice a mix of excitement and nervousness.

"Sure, what is it?" Destiny replied, curious about his sudden change in demeanor.

"Well," Miles began, "Every year, Vortex hosts a charity gala. It's a big event we organize to raise funds for various causes close to our hearts. This year, we were thinking about dedicating it to the veterans—like the ones we met at the pancake breakfast."

"Wow, that's incredible! I'm so glad you remembered them," Destiny said, genuinely touched by his thoughtfulness.

"Actually, that's where you come in," Miles continued, looking directly into her eyes. "We need a caterer for the event, and I couldn't think of anyone better than you. Would you be up for it?"

"Are you serious? I would love to!" Destiny exclaimed, her face lighting up with joy. "I can't believe you're asking me to be part of such an important event."

"Great! And if you don't mind, we'd also like your help planning the gala itself. We really value your creativity and insight," Miles added, his admiration for Destiny evident.

"Of course, I'd be honored," Destiny agreed, feeling both thrilled and humbled by his request.

As they exchanged smiles, Destiny knew this opportunity was not just about catering an event; it was a chance to make a real difference in the lives of those who needed it most. And she couldn't wait to get started.

Destiny walked up the stairs to her apartment, her mind buzzing with ideas for the charity gala. She couldn't help but feel a surge of excitement as she considered different themes and how they would tie in with the menu. She knew that this event could make a real difference for the veterans, and she was determined to create an unforgettable night.

"Maybe a vintage military theme," Destiny mused out loud, as she unlocked her door. "Or perhaps something more elegant and upscale, like a black-tie affair with a touch of patriotism."

Just as she stepped inside, her phone chimed with a text message. It was Miles, already sending her some initial thoughts on the gala's theme. Smiling, Destiny typed back her own suggestions, their conversation flowing with creative energy.

After exchanging a few more messages, Destiny decided it was time to get ready for bed. As she changed into her pajamas, she imagined the various dishes she could prepare for the gala – hors d'oeuvres inspired by classic American cuisine, an entrée with flavors that paid tribute to the veterans' global service, and a dessert that was both indulgent and visually stunning.

"Something savory, something bold, and something sweet," she whispered to herself, mentally bookmarking various recipes and plating techniques. Her heart raced with anticipation, knowing that every detail would matter. This wasn't just any catering job; it was a chance to demonstrate her unwavering support for the men and women who had sacrificed so much for their country, just as her father had all those years ago.

With a final glance at her phone – one last text from Miles, wishing her sweet dreams – Destiny turned off the lights and snuggled under the covers. She closed her eyes, still smiling, as visions of beautifully decorated tables and impeccably dressed guests danced through her head. The thought of working closely with Miles in planning this event filled her with warmth and joy, a feeling she hadn't experienced in a long time.

"Goodnight, Miles," she whispered into the darkness, her heart swelling with gratitude and excitement for the journey ahead. "We're going to make this gala amazing."

MILES STOOD BY HIS DESK, BASKING IN THE WARM SUNLIGHT that shone through the windows. He furrowed his brow as he scanned through the results of the customer satisfaction survey. His lips were pressed together in a tight line, his mind whirring with thoughts on how to improve their services to keep their clients safe and satisfied. Max sat opposite him, one leg crossed over the other, drumming his pen against a pad of paper.

"Okay, so we need to come up with a way to provide better and faster support for our clients," Miles began, green eyes flickering with determination. "We're already stretched thin as it is, but there has to be a way to stream-line this process without compromising on quality."

"Right," Max agreed, nodding his head. "If we could create a more efficient system, maybe even automate some tasks, we'd free up more time for our team to focus on the clients who really need our help."

"Exactly." Miles paused, thoughts racing as he tried to envision a new plan. "But how do we go about it? We've already tried implementing chatbots, but they lack the human touch that our clients crave."

Just then, the office door swung open, and Malcolm strolled in, looking every bit the tech genius with his messy brown hair and confident stride. His keen eyes took in the scene before him, immediately sensing the charged atmosphere.

"Hey, guys," he greeted them, pulling up a chair next to Max. "What's going on?"

"Perfect timing, Malcolm," Miles said, gesturing for his younger brother to join them. "We're trying to come up with a way to streamline our client services without losing that personal connection."

Malcolm's eyes lit up, and he rubbed his hands together. "I've actually been thinking about something like that. What if we developed a system where clients could access a personalized dashboard containing all their relevant information? That way, they can quickly find what they need, and our team can focus on those who require more assistance."

"Interesting," Max mused, scribbling down the idea. "That would certainly cut down on a lot of back-and-forth communication."

"Right, and it would empower our clients to take control of their own accounts," Malcolm added, his voice filled with passion. "We could even incorporate some AI technology that learns from each interaction, so it gets better at helping them over time."

Miles nodded, clearly impressed by his brother's idea. "I like it. It combines the efficiency of automation with the personal touch we're known for. Let's explore this further and see if we can make it a reality."

Just as the brothers were discussing the finer details of their plan, the office door opened with a soft creak. Candy sashayed into the room, her long blonde hair swaying with each calculated step. She was wearing a fitted white blouse tucked into a tight black pencil skirt that accentuated her curves. On her feet were a pair of designer stilettos that clicked against the hardwood floor. Her icy blue eyes scanned the room before settling on Miles.

"Here's that report you asked for, Miles," she purred, extending a perfectly manicured hand holding a sleek black folder. She bent over to move her face closer.

"Thanks, Candy," Miles said, taking the folder from her and placing it on his desk.

Malcolm cleared his throat, drawing everyone's attention to him. "So, did Destiny agree to cater the gala?"

Miles noticed the surprise flicker across Candy's face before she regained her composure. "Destiny Evans?" she asked, a hint of disdain in her voice. Miles was caught off guard by Candy's surprise when she heard about Destiny's return. He realized in that moment that he had been lost in his thoughts and hadn't actually shared anything with Candy.

"Yep," Malcolm confirmed slowly, his gaze fixed on Candy. "She's working at Peaches."

Candy scoffed. "Hmph. I wouldn't expect much from a place like that."

In a desperate attempt to shift the mood, Miles turned to Max with a forced smile. "Let's talk about the gala. This year, it has to be bigger and better than ever before. What are our projected earnings?" His tone was tinged with urgency, knowing that Candy could push people's buttons with her passionate responses, Miles tried to change the subject to something that they can all get behind.

Max glanced down at the figures he'd been working on earlier. "We're hoping to raise at least two million for the charity," he responded confidently. "With guests coming from big cities all over the country, it should be an incredible event."

"Sounds amazing," Miles agreed, his eyes drifting back to Candy. "Will you be available to assist me at the gala, Candy?"

Her eyes lit up at the question, and she beamed, "Of course, Miles! I'll be more than happy to help."

Miles smiled back at her, then glanced at Max and Malcolm. Their expressions seemed to suggest that something was amiss. He couldn't help but think of his mother's attempts to push him and Candy together, wondering if she might have been under the impression that she'd be attending as his date rather than his assistant. He brushed the thought aside, dismissing it as absurd.

"Great," Miles said, returning his focus to the matter at hand. "Now, let's get back to work on streamlining our client services."

"Am I still needed here?" Candy asked, her tone a mixture of sweetness and expectation.

"No, that should be all for now. Thank you, Candy," Miles replied, doing his best to maintain a professional demeanor despite the lingering suspicion that she might have misunderstood his intentions regarding the gala.

With a nod and a swish of her designer skirt, Candy turned on her heel and left the office, closing the door behind her. Malcolm waited until the door clicked shut before turning to his brother with a sly grin.

"Are you going to meet up with Destiny?" He raised his eyebrows, playfully nudged his shoulder, and gestured towards her with a slight lift of his chin.

Miles couldn't help but smile at the suggestion. "You know what? That's a great idea."

As Max and Malcolm returned their attention to discussing ways to streamline customer service, Miles pulled out his phone and typed out a quick text message to Destiny.

MILES - 1:30 P.M.

Hey Destiny. How would you like to discuss the gala menu over dinner tonight? My place?

He hit send and tried to focus on the conversation happening in front of him, but his thoughts were already racing ahead to the prospect of seeing Destiny again. When his phone vibrated with her response, he couldn't help but grin.

DESTINY - 1:45 P.M.

Sounds perfect! What time should I come over?

MILES - 1:46 P.M.

6 P.M. Can't wait to see you!

He slipped his phone back into his pocket and rejoined the conversation with Max and Malcolm. He was getting more excited about the gala, for more than one reason.

* * *

Destiny stood in the café's bustling kitchen, surrounded by the aroma of freshly baked bread and the sizzle of oil in pans. She studied the colorful array of ingredients laid out before her, already brainstorming potential appetizers for the upcoming gala. However, she realized she needed to collaborate with Miles on a theme before making any final decisions.

Her phone chimed from across the counter, causing her to momentarily break her concentration. Drying her hands on a nearby towel, she eagerly picked up her phone, her eyes widening as she read the message from Miles.

A genuine smile brightened her face, her heart fluttering in anticipation. This was not only an opportunity to cook for the highly anticipated event but also a chance for them to reconnect. She couldn't help but let out a giddy little laugh, feeling the thrill of the opportunity at hand. She glanced back at the ingredients spread out before her, her mind racing with ideas for the perfect dishes to complement the yet-to-be-decided theme.

Destiny slipped her phone back into her apron pocket, the corners of her mouth still curled upward in a smile. Just then, Lila burst into the kitchen, her electric blue eyes wide with excitement.

"Hey, guess what?" Destiny couldn't contain her enthusiasm. "Miles asked me to cater the gala!"

"Really?" Lila's face lit up. "That's amazing, Des! Can I help? Please say yes!" She clapped her hands together, practically bouncing on the balls of her feet.

"Of course you can!" Destiny grinned, already envisioning them working side-by-side, creating culinary masterpieces for the event. "We'll make a great team."

Lila leaned against the counter, her eyes twinkling. "So, tell me more about this gala. Who's it for?"

Destiny wiped her hands on a towel, her gaze wandering over the countertop as she thought about how to explain the cause. "It's for veterans, actually. Miles came up with the idea. He wants to give back to those who've served our country."

"Wow, that's really thoughtful of him." Lila nodded approvingly. "And you're going to his house tonight to discuss everything, right?"

"Yep!" Destiny confirmed, her cheeks flushing slightly at the mention of spending an evening with Miles and his brothers. "I'm meeting all three of them there. I can't wait to bounce some ideas off them and get their input on the menu."

"Sounds like fun," Lila teased, nudging her playfully. "Just promise me one thing, okay?"

"Sure, what's that?" Destiny raised an eyebrow, curious about her friend's request.

"Tell me everything later on," Lila winked, grinning. "I want all the juicy details."

"Deal," Destiny laughed, shaking her head at Lila's insatiable curiosity. "Now, let's get back to work. We've got a lot of prep to do!"

With that, the two friends dove into their tasks, filled with anticipation and determination for the upcoming gala. As Destiny chopped vegetables and Lila measured out ingredients, the sounds of their laughter and banter echoed through the kitchen.

* * *

At six that night, Destiny stood before Miles' house, her arms laden with grocery bags filled with fresh ingredients she had picked up after work. Her heart pounded with anticipation as she pressed the doorbell, listening to the chime echoing inside.

Miles swung the door open, his green eyes lighting up when he saw her. "Destiny! You're right on time," he said warmly, his gaze briefly moving to the bags she carried. "Let me help you with those."

"Thanks," she replied, gratefully dropping the load into his strong arms. As he turned and led her inside, Destiny couldn't help but be awed by the opulence of his home. But it was nothing compared to what awaited her in the kitchen.

"Here we are," Miles announced, setting the bags down on the counter.

Destiny gasped, her hazel eyes wide with wonder. The kitchen was a chef's dream come true. Sleek stainless steel appliances gleamed under the soft glow of recessed lighting. An enormous island dominated the center of the space, topped with a beautiful wooden table. Ample storage lined the walls in the form of custom cabinetry, and not a single utensil or gadget seemed out of place.

"Wow, Miles, this is amazing!" she breathed, running her hand over the smooth surface of the counter, excitement coursing through her veins. "I can't wait to start cooking here."

"Go ahead, make yourself at home," Miles encouraged her, his eyes twinkling with delight at her enthusiasm. "Everything you need should be here. If not, just let me know."

"Thank you, really," Destiny replied, already pulling out the ingredients she had brought with her and arranging them neatly on the counter. She felt a surge of inspiration as she began to chop, sauté, and season, her movements fluid and confident in the luxurious space.

Destiny carefully rubbed marinated spices onto the chicken's skin as she preheated the oven. Miles stood next to her, handing her ingredients and cracking jokes, his deep voice rumbling through the kitchen. With each quip, Destiny couldn't help but laugh, feeling completely at ease in his company.

It wasn't long before the doorbell rang again, its sound cutting through their laughter. "I'll get that," Miles said, wiping his hands on a dish towel and leaving the kitchen to answer the door.

Miles returned to the kitchen with Malcolm and Max

following behind, their faces lighting up as they caught sight of Destiny.

"Hey, Destiny!" Malcolm greeted her enthusiastically, his messy brown hair bouncing slightly as he walked over. Max offered her a warm smile, his green eyes shimmering with friendliness.

"Hi, guys! Good to see you both," she responded, smiling back at them. They took seats on the barstools at the counter, making themselves comfortable as they chatted.

"Is Vivi coming?" Destiny asked Max, referencing his wife.

"Unfortunately, no," Max replied, shaking his head. "She had to stay late at the office to figure out how to organize the assistants for the gala."

Destiny nodded in understanding and turned her attention back to the stove, where the aroma of her cooking filled the air. A few minutes later, she announced that dinner was ready, and they couldn't help but be impressed by the feast she had prepared.

The table was laden with dishes that tantalized all the senses. The sight of golden-brown roasted chicken, glistening with herbs and surrounded by colorful vegetables, tempted their eyes. The tender, juicy meat seemed to melt in their mouths, while the crispy skin provided a satisfying crunch. The scent of garlic and rosemary wafted through the air, mingling with the fresh, earthy aroma of a vibrant garden salad. A velvety potato gratin, rich with cream and cheese, beckoned from another dish, its warmth enveloping their taste buds like a cozy blanket. For dessert, a tangy lemon tart, its pastry crust crumbling delicately between their fingers, offered a refreshing balance to the indulgent meal.

As they enjoyed the food, Miles brought up the topic of

the gala's theme. "I was thinking," he said, taking a sip of wine, "black tie with a touch of patriotism."

Destiny listened intently, her hazel eyes reflecting her interest. "That sounds perfect," she agreed. "Elegant, but with a meaningful connection to the charity we're supporting."

"Exactly," Miles nodded, pleased by her enthusiasm.

"Let me throw out some ideas for appetizers and the four-course meal," Destiny suggested, her mind whirring with culinary possibilities. As she described various dishes, incorporating patriotic colors and flavors while maintaining a sophisticated tone, the brothers couldn't help but be captivated by her creativity and passion.

"Wow, Destiny," Malcolm said, overexaggerating a bow. "The food is going to be the talk of the party."

"Agreed," Max chimed in, his admiration evident in his smile. "You truly have a gift, Destiny."

She felt a warm glow spread through her chest at their praise, grateful for their support and the opportunity to contribute to such an important event. Together, they continued to brainstorm and refine their plans for the gala, their conversations filled with laughter, wit, and a shared desire to make a difference in their community.

After a few more minutes of discussing the gala, Max leaned back on his barstool and changed the subject. "Destiny, I've always wondered, what happened when you moved away right before high school?"

Destiny swallowed hard, her fingers tightening around the stem of her wine glass. "Well," she began hesitantly, "it was tough starting over in a new place. We didn't have much money, so we moved into a small house."

"Did you make any friends?" Malcolm asked gently.

"Eventually, yes," Destiny replied with a small smile. "But it took some time. I focused on my studies and worked part-time to help support my father and me. That's when I discovered the technical side of cooking that fueled my passion." She glanced at Miles, appreciating his quiet support as she delved into a difficult chapter of her past. "Over the years, I dabbled in various jobs in the culinary world, eventually becoming a cafe manager."

"Which led you to talking to Lila," Max observed, nodding thoughtfully.

"Exactly," Destiny confirmed. "When I moved back here, she told me about the job at the cafe, and we've been inseparable ever since. It feels like we were never apart."

As they listened to her story, both Malcolm and Max could see the strength and resilience that Destiny had developed during the trials of her life. Destiny noticed Miles' eyebrows drawn together in thought and couldn't help but ask, "What are you thinking about, Miles?"

He hesitated for a moment before asking, "Why did you move back here without your father?"

The question hit Destiny like a punch to the gut, and she struggled to speak past the lump in her throat. "My father... he passed away a few years ago," she managed to choke out, her eyes glistening with unshed tears. "He had cancer, and there was nothing anyone could do."

"Destiny, I'm so sorry," Miles said, reaching out to place a comforting hand on hers.

"Me too," Max and Malcolm echoed, their eyes filled with sympathy.

"Thank you," Destiny whispered. She took a deep breath, willing the tears away as she focused on regaining her composure. The atmosphere in the room shifted, the weight of her story hanging in the air, but the bond between them all somehow grew stronger.

"Alright, enough of the heavy stuff," Malcolm interjected. "How about I share some embarrassing stories of Miles' high school days?"

Destiny couldn't help but snicker at the idea. "Oh, this should be good."

"Hey, now," Miles protested, his cheeks already reddening in anticipation. "Some things are better left in the past."

"Too bad for you, little brother," Max chimed in with a grin.

"Fine," Miles relented, rolling his eyes. "But don't blame me if you regret it later."

"Alright, so picture this," Malcolm began, leaning back in his chair with a mischievous glint in his eye. "Miles had just turned sixteen and was convinced he was going to be the next big skateboarder. You know, the Tony Hawk of our generation."

"Wait," Destiny interrupted, laughing. "Miles? On a skateboard?"

"Hard to believe, I know," Malcolm replied, smirking. "So one day, he decides to show off his 'skills' at the park. He starts speeding down this hill, completely out of control, and ends up crashing into a hot dog stand!"

"Malcolm!" Miles groaned, hiding his face in his hands as Destiny and Max burst into laughter.

"Wait, there's more," Max added, wiping tears from his eyes. "He ended up covered in mustard and sauerkraut. The look on his face... I wish I had taken a picture."

"Alright, that's enough," Miles muttered, trying to maintain some semblance of dignity. But he couldn't help but chuckle along with them, knowing that they all needed the levity.

Later that evening, as Destiny prepared to leave, she took a moment to appreciate the warmth of the living room, the soft glow from the fireplace casting an inviting light on the space. The conversations and laughter still echoed in her ears, making her feel truly at home for the first time in years.

As she glanced around the room one last time, her eyes fell upon the kitchen, and she couldn't help but marvel at how perfectly it aligned with her dream. From the gleaming countertops to the state-of-the-art appliances, it was as if Miles had designed it specifically with her in mind. She briefly wondered if he had remembered her descriptions from junior high and subconsciously incorporated them into his design.

"Thank you again for having me," Destiny said, smiling warmly at Miles as she stepped toward the door.

"Anytime, Destiny," Miles replied sincerely. "We all really enjoyed having you here."

With a final wave goodbye, Destiny climbed into her little car and drove away, her heart feeling lighter than it had in ages.

twelve

MILES WALKED UP THE DIMLY LIT BACK STAIRCASE OF Destiny's apartment, his footsteps echoing on the worn steps. The cafe below was closed for the night and anticipation thrummed through his veins as he remembered the message she had sent him earlier, asking to meet. He couldn't help but feel a rush of excitement surge through him at the thought of spending more time with her.

As Miles continued up the stairs, his thoughts drifted back to the day they had booked the hotel ballroom for the upcoming gala. Destiny had played an integral role in planning the event, and Miles couldn't help but feel a sense of pride for her accomplishments. In his mind's eye, he could see her standing in the center of the opulent ballroom, awestruck by the grandeur of it all. The intricate chandeliers that hung from the high ceilings, the elegant gold accents adorning the walls, and the way the sunlight filtered through the tall windows and danced across the polished marble floors.

"Isn't it amazing?" Destiny had whispered, her hazel eyes wide with wonder.

"Absolutely," Miles had replied, unable to tear his gaze away from her radiant smile. His heart skipped a beat as he watched her, and he realized how much he looked forward to working alongside her to make the gala a resounding success.

Finally reaching the top of the staircase, Miles took a deep breath and knocked on Destiny's door. As he waited for her to answer, he tried to shake off the lingering memories of the ballroom. Instead, he decided to focus his energy on the present.

Miles stood outside Destiny's apartment door, taking in the charming accents he had never noticed before—a tiny sunflower wreath hung above the peephole, and a small doormat with an message that read, "Home is Where the Heart is" accompanied by a heart-shaped cookie. Miles couldn't help but laugh as he looked at Destiny's front door. Every inch of it was hers.

"Hey, Miles!" Destiny welcomed him as she opened the door, stepping aside to let him in. Her brown hair was pulled up into a casual bun, tendrils framing her face, and there was a smudge of flour on her cheek, giving her an endearing, disheveled appearance. She looked so effortlessly beautiful that it took a moment for Miles to regain his composure.

"Hi, Destiny," Miles replied, smiling at her. His days were filled with smiling and helping his employees, so when the night rolled around he was ready for some much needed rest.

"Come on in," Destiny guided him further into her apartment. They headed over to the countertop where they had been doing most of the gala planning. Spread out on the bar were an array of little sweet and savory appetizers, each meticulously crafted and plated.

"Wow, Destiny, these look really great!" Miles

exclaimed as he scanned the assortment. There were bacon-wrapped dates with goat cheese, mini crab cakes topped with homemade creamy horseradish , smoked salmon blinis, caprese skewers drizzled with balsamic glaze, bite-sized beef wellingtons, prosciutto-wrapped asparagus, chocolate-dipped strawberries, mini éclairs filled with vanilla pastry cream, raspberry macarons, and petite fruit tarts garnished with a mint leaf.

Unable to resist, Miles picked up one of the prosciutto-wrapped asparagus and popped it into his mouth. The combination of the salty prosciutto and the tender-crisp asparagus was sublime. "Destiny, this is perfect," he said sincerely, savoring the flavors.

"Thank you! I'm glad you like them," Destiny replied with a smile, her eyes shining with pride. "So, we've got our ten luxury canapés all set then. It's going to be an unforget-table night."

"Absolutely," Miles eagerly nodded, feeling a rush of genuine excitement at the prospect of working alongside Destiny to make the gala a night to remember. His mind raced with images of lavish decorations, mouth-watering cuisine, and an atmosphere filled with laughter and joy. He couldn't wait to see their hard work come to fruition and create a truly unforgettable experience for all in attendance.

"Alright, let's move on to finalizing the plated dinner menu," Miles suggested, picking up the mock-up menu with the courses. His eyes scanned the carefully selected dishes as he read them aloud, "For the first course, we have an arugula and pear salad. Next, a creamy lobster and corn chowder for the soup course," Miles continued.

Destiny's eyes lit up at the mention of the lobster chow-der, and Miles couldn't help but smile at her enthusiasm. "For the main course, we have a choice of a herb-crusted beef tenderloin with garlic mashed potatoes, a pan-seared Chilean sea bass with lemon herb risotto, or a wild mushroom and truffle ravioli for our vegetarian guests."

"Yum, I'm getting hungry just listening to these options!" Destiny admitted with a chuckle.

"Finally, for dessert, we have a rich chocolate mousse cake adorned with gold leaf," Miles concluded, looking up from the menu to see Destiny's happy reaction.

"Okay. I know I wrote the menu, but even I am impressed," she laughed.

"Great! Now, how about table settings and layout?" Miles asked, eager to finalize the last details. Destiny furrowed her brow thoughtfully, tapping her finger on her chin.

"Should we have the waiters passing around the appetizers during the cocktail hour?" she inquired.

"Definitely," Miles replied without hesitation. "We can also set up tables with memorabilia and photos from the charity's past events. It'll add a nice touch and provide some talking points for our guests."

"Perfect!" Destiny exclaimed, her eyes sparkling with excitement.

As they continued discussing the gala preparations, Miles could feel Destiny edging closer towards him. He couldn't help but stare at her beautiful face, lit up with joy and excitement as she talked about her ideas. His admiration for her had grown from just being a friend, to something far more profound. As if on cue they both leaned in closer, their faces mere inches apart. Miles felt his heart skip a beat; it was as if a veil had been lifted and he was seeing Destiny in a way he never imagined before.

Miles' thoughts were interrupted by Destiny's voice, pulling him back to the present. "What do you think about incorporating some gold accents into the table settings? It would tie in nicely with the menu design," she suggested.

Miles struggled to keep his voice steady as he spoke, "Gold accents would be a perfect choice." As much as he fought against it, Miles knew deep down that his heart belonged to Destiny, and the thought both terrified and electrified him. A surge of fear and excitement coursed through him, but it was quickly overwhelmed by the uncontrollable joy and warmth that filled his soul.

* * *

"Speaking of gold accents," Destiny said with a playful smile, "I've noticed you're turning a bit pink. What's got you blushing, Miles?"

Miles felt his cheeks grow even warmer as he tried to come up with an explanation that wouldn't reveal his newfound feelings for her. "Oh, it's just... warm in here," he stammered, avoiding her curious gaze, while rubbing the back of his neck.

"Really?" Destiny teased, raising an eyebrow. "Because I feel perfectly comfortable."

Destiny, noticing Miles' blush deepen, decided it was time to move on. "I've got something else to show you," she said as she went to the closet in the front of her apartment. She emerged with a large vision board tucked under her arm. Bringing it over to the countertop, she propped it up for Miles to see.

"Here's what I was thinking for the linens and table settings." The vision board was covered in fabric swatches, photos, and sketches, all displaying a perfect blend of black tie elegance and patriotic flair. Destiny pointed to a particular set of linens. "These will work perfectly on the tables and with the napkins. They'll match the ones the waiters will use while passing around the appetizers."

Miles examined the board, impressed by Destiny's attention to detail. "I love how you've managed to make everything look so sophisticated while still incorporating the patriotic theme. It's a perfect balance."

"Thank you," Destiny replied, her hazel eyes twinkling with excitement. "Now, imagine this: the guests enter the ballroom and are greeted by beautifully set round tables draped in deep navy blue tablecloths with delicate gold stars scattered across the fabric. Each seat has an elegant gold charger plate topped with a crisp white napkin, folded into a classic bishop's hat shape and held together by a red, white, and blue striped ribbon."

"Sounds amazing," Miles commented, clearly envisioning the scene in his mind.

"Wait, there's more," Destiny continued, her enthusiasm contagious. "In the center of each table, we'll have tall glass vases filled with red and white roses, surrounded by smaller vases of blue flowers. Gold accents will be found throughout the room, from the chair sashes to the candle holders, creating a cohesive and luxurious atmosphere. And, of course, we'll have a large American flag displayed on the stage."

"Destiny, it sounds absolutely perfect. I can't wait to see it all come together in just a few days," Miles said sincerely, his green eyes sparkling with anticipation.

"Me too," a proud smile spread across her face as she raised her chin to admire their creation. "It's going to be incredible."

As they wrapped up their discussion, Destiny walked Miles to the door. "I'll see you at the ballroom for the walk through! Thank you for letting me be part of this," she said as she hugged him goodbye.

He smiled warmly as he looked into her eyes and said, "Destiny, of course. You're the only one I would trust to do this job." She felt a warmth in her chest that made her giddy with their blooming friendship.

One week later, the day of the gala had finally arrived. Destiny and Lila stood in the grand ballroom, ensuring every last detail was perfect. The tables were set up for the black tie event, each adorned with luxurious navy blue tablecloths with gold stars that shimmered under the warm glow of the chandeliers. Destiny took a step back and admired the little personal touches that they'd incorporated into the place settings.

Each setting featured a gleaming gold charger plate, topped with a crisp white linen napkin, held together by a red, white, and blue striped ribbon. The menus and name cards were printed on elegant ivory cardstock, with gold embossed lettering that matched the overall sophistication of the event.

"Wow, Destiny," Lila breathed, her electric blue eyes wide with awe. "You really outdid yourself. It's beyond beautiful."

"Thanks, Lila," Destiny replied, her hazel eyes glistening with pride. "I couldn't have done it without your help, though. We make a great team."

Destiny looked around the room, absorbing the magnificence of the old roman style building. The painted ceilings depicted scenes of angels and cherubs frolicking amongst the clouds, while the crystal chandeliers cast a warm, golden light upon the room. Huge gold accents lined the walls, framing tall windows draped with lush velvet curtains.

As she surveyed the room, tears welled in Destiny's eyes when she thought of her father. She knew he would have been so proud of her and this moment. She could almost feel his presence with her, as if he were standing right beside her, beaming with pride.

"Hey, are you okay?" Lila asked gently, wrapping an arm around Destiny's shoulders.

"Yeah, I'm alright. Just taking a moment to process ... everything," Destiny said as she inhaled deeply and ran her hand down her clothing, smoothing out any imaginary creases. "It just feels like... a new beginning."

Lila smiled warmly and gave her best friend a tight squeeze. "You deserve all of this, Destiny. You've worked so hard, and you're going to make this night one to remember."

The moment Destiny and Lila climbed into the van, Destiny turned to her best friend with a grin. "So, tell me more about these crimes you've been helping the police solve. Any new ones that you can talk about?!"

Lila's eyes sparkled as she launched into the story of her latest case. "Well, there was this one where someone had stolen a priceless painting from a museum. I managed to trace it back to an underground art dealer."

"Wow, that sounds intense!" Destiny replied, clearly impressed. "And who is this guy you've been working with?"

Lila blushed slightly but couldn't help the smile that spread across her face. "His name is Thad. He's been my partner in crime-solving, and he's just... amazing."

"Thad, huh?" Destiny teased, nudging Lila playfully. "Sounds like someone has a bit of a crush."

"Maybe," Lila admitted, her electric blue eyes dancing with mischief. "He's smart, kind, and incredibly handsome. What's not to like?"

"Is he single?" Destiny asked, joining in the playful banter.

"Thankfully, yes," Lila grinned. "We've been spending

a lot of time together outside of work, too. I think there might be something real between us."

"Oh my god! I'm so happy for you, Lila!" Destiny gushed, giving her friend a quick hug. "I can't wait to meet him."

"Thanks, Destiny," Lila's lips curved into a smile as she brushed a strand of her dark hair behind her ear. "I really hope you two get along."

As they pulled up to the cafe, Destiny and Lila continued their lively conversation about Thad. The excitement between them was palpable, their laughter echoing through the van.

"Alright," Destiny said, taking a deep breath as they exited the vehicle. "Time to dive into the kitchen frenzy!"

Upon entering the kitchen, they were immediately greeted by the organized chaos of chefs and sous-chefs bustling about, preparing the delicious appetizers for the guests, who would be arriving soon.. The air was filled with a cacophony of hurried voices and people putting together ingredients to take to the hotel kitchen.

"Okay, everyone!" Destiny called out, feeling a surge of energy course through her. "We have 250 hungry guests to feed tonight, so let's make it the best meal they've ever had!"

Lila nodded in agreement, her eyes filled with determination. "We're all in this together, so let's show them what we can do!"

With that, Destiny and Lila tied on their aprons and jumped straight into the fray, joining their fellow chefs in the whirlwind of activity. Together, they were determined to make the gala an unforgettable event—a true testament to their hard work and love for their craft. When they finished, they packed up the vans and headed back to the venue to start preparing dinner.

thirteen

MILES STOOD IN FRONT OF HIS FULL-LENGTH MIRROR, adjusting his bow tie with precision. The black silk material contrasted beautifully against his crisp white dress shirt. He adjusted the collar and smoothed down his jacket, admiring himself in the mirror. Something about the touch of patriotism in his outfit made him feel proud of his country.

"Looking sharp, Mr. Huntington," he said to himself, giving a small salute in the mirror.

He grabbed his keys and walked through his spacious house, out the front door to his car. As he drove to the gala, Miles couldn't help but think about Destiny. It seemed lately she was always on his mind, her smile and kind heart, constantly making him feel warm inside.

"Destiny," he muttered, gripping the steering wheel tighter. "What am I going to do about you?"

Miles knew that his feelings for her went beyond simply friendship, but he didn't want to lose her in his life by taking things too quickly. He thought about all the beautiful things she had done, like volunteering at the soup kitchen and creating new recipes for their cafe. He thought about her talking to him about how she likes to take pictures of her beautiful creations to share with others.

"Maybe tonight's the night," he thought to himself with a smirk, turning into the hotel's grand entryway.

Miles handed his keys to the valet, a young man with a bright smile, and turned toward the entrance of the hotel. The red carpet unfurled before him like a river of crimson silk, lined with photographers, their cameras flashing like fireflies in the night. Guests in elegant gowns and sharp tuxedos posed for photos, smiles wide and laughter echoing around them. Along the carpet, special photos of veterans captured moments of bravery and camaraderie. Miles felt a swell of pride as he walked up to greet some of the honorees.

"Mr. Huntington," a reporter called out, microphone extended toward him. "How does it feel to have your company sponsor such an important event?"

"Vortex is honored to be part of this," Miles replied, adjusting the lapel of his tuxedo jacket. "Supporting our veterans and giving back to the community are core values we hold dear."

"Would you mind posing for a photo with some of our veterans?" another reporter asked, gesturing to a group of men and women dressed in their military uniforms.

"Of course," Miles agreed, joining the group for a series of pictures. He chatted with them briefly, sharing his admiration for their service and learning about their experiences. It was humbling to stand beside those who had sacrificed so much for their country.

Once the red carpet interviews were finished, Miles made his way inside the hotel. He had done a walkthrough earlier in the planning process, but seeing the venue fully decorated and alive with guests took his breath away. The ballroom sparkled with crystal chandeliers and intricate floral arrangements, each table adorned with tasteful touches of red, white, and blue.

He couldn't tear his eyes away from the reactions of the guests and honorees as they entered. Their faces lit up with delight and awe, marveling at the stunning atmosphere that had been created for them.

"Mr. Huntington," an elderly woman said, grasping his hand. "Thank you so much for all you've done to make this evening possible."

"Please, call me Miles," he replied, touched by her gratitude, clasping her hand in both of his. "It's a pleasure to be able to support such a worthy cause."

As he continued to mingle and exchange pleasantries, Miles allowed his thoughts to drift back to the woman who was gradually becoming the center of his world in the most beautiful way.He wondered how she was faring in the kitchen, and if she had a moment to appreciate the beauty of the event she had helped bring to life.

"Max, Malcolm!" Miles called out as his brothers approached with warm smiles. Vivienne elegantly accompanied him, her arm linked with his. Her gown was a masterpiece of deep navy blue and white silk, gracefully cascading to the floor in delicate folds. The bodice hugged her figure perfectly, accentuated by a tasteful silver belt at her waist. Subtle red accents along the neckline hinted at the patriotic theme of the evening.

"Isn't this place amazing?" Malcolm gushed, his eyes scanning the room in awe.

"Destiny truly outdid herself," Vivienne agreed with a proud smile.

Miles' eyes wandered across the crowd, finally landing on his mother. She was dressed in an opulent gown, a cacophony of sequins and feathers that screamed for attention. The dress was a mix of bright reds and blues, clashing violently with the otherwise elegant color palette of the event. He couldn't help but cringe at her overt attempt to steal the spotlight.

"Hey, have any of you seen Destiny yet?" Miles asked, trying not to dwell on his mother.

"Last I saw her, she was heading into the kitchen," Max said, nodding towards the door at the far end of the ballroom. Miles' heart skipped a beat as he caught a glimpse of Destiny slipping through the doorway, her chef's coat fitting her like a glove.

"Thanks," he replied, already making his way towards her. She was so beautiful, even in her all white chef's coat, that he couldn't help himself, he had to see her.

"Hey, Miles! I'm so glad I caught up to you!" a familiar voice cooed, stopping him in his tracks. He felt a hand on his arm and looked down to see perfectly manicured nails and fingers adorned with rings. Candy stood before him, her expression a mix of feigned surprise and delight. Miles plastered on a smile, doing his best to hide his disappointment at the interruption.

"Hi, Candy," he said, giving her a kiss on the cheek. "I'm so glad you could make it. I was just going to say hi to Destiny." Miles caught a glimpse of Candy's expression as she turned away. Her smile wavered, her eyes flickering with uncertainty before she composed herself and put on a cheerful facade once again.

But when he turned around, Destiny had disappeared back into the kitchen. His heart sank, and he knew he couldn't chase after her without drawing attention to himself. With a heavy sigh, he rejoined Max and Malcolm, doing his best to focus on greeting the guests and making their evening memorable.

* * *

Destiny stood in the bustling kitchen, her heart swelling with pride. The room hummed with energy as chefs and wait staff hurried about, putting the final touches on the exquisite dishes they'd prepared for the gala. She decided to take a peek at the crowd and went outside the kitchen door, scanning the sea of elegantly dressed guests mingling and laughing. She recognized some familiar faces from the breakfasts she had served at the cafe, along with high members of society she had only ever read about in magazines.

"Excuse me, Destiny?" a waiter asked tentatively, appearing behind her with a tray of canapés. "Can you just clarify the ingredients in these, please?"

"Of course!" she answered enthusiastically. "These are smoked salmon rosettes with dill cream cheese and capers, and those are bacon-wrapped dates stuffed with goat cheese."

"Thank you so much," the waiter replied, nodding gratefully before disappearing back into the crowd.

As the waiter walked away, Destiny turned back to the bustling event. Her gaze landed on Max, who stood by the entrance with a smile that seemed to light up the room. She waved at him, a genuine warmth spreading through her chest as she saw the pride in his eyes.

"Hey, Destiny!" Max called out, waving back. Malcolm appeared behind him, tapping Max on the shoulder and grinning mischievously. "Looking good, Des," he teased, nodding approvingly at her chef's coat.

"Thanks, Malcolm," she replied, rolling her eyes playfully. As they began to walk over to Miles, Vivienne joined Max, linking her arm through his. Destiny couldn't help but admire the way the couple complemented each other

—their love was evident in every gesture and shared glance.

Then, she saw Miles for the first time that night. He looked absolutely perfect—his tailored suit emphasized his strong shoulders and slim waist, his hair styled just enough to look effortlessly charming. His green eyes sparkled like emeralds, reflecting the warm glow of the chandeliers above.

Their gazes met, and Destiny noticed how Miles' eyes lit up with a mixture of surprise and delight. Her heart skipped a beat, and she gasped softly, feeling a sudden rush of emotion she couldn't quite place. Was this... attraction? Admiration? Or something deeper?

But, as Miles began to walk over, Destiny noticed a small, dainty hand with perfectly manicured nails and fingers adorned with rings encircle his arm. Miles turned and hugged the woman, smiling warmly at her. As she moved into Destiny's view, she recognized the familiar face—it was Candy Sullivan.

Destiny's heart felt like it had shattered into a million pieces. The sight of Candy brought back a flood of painful memories. This was the person who had tortured her throughout their school years and ruined her friendship with Miles.

A flashback from elementary school flickered in her mind: a young Destiny sitting alone on the playground, desperately trying to hold back tears as Candy and her group of friends taunted her relentlessly, calling her cruel names and laughing. That day, Miles hadn't witnessed the scene because he would have said something, but Destiny was all alone. Her heart clenched at the memory.

Candy's gown was stunning, no doubt—a black, form-fitting number with a touch of red and blue embroidery along the neckline, a nod to the event's patriotic theme. It clung to her curves, making her look like a sultry femme fatale. Candy's appearance was flawless, from her perfectly applied makeup to her stylish outfit. However, she seemed out of sync with the rest of the crowd. Her voice carried above all others as she laughed and inserted herself into conversations without invitation. It appeared that she wanted all the attention solely on her, with little regard for the veterans who were meant to be honored at this event.

"Of course, she has to be the center of attention," Destiny muttered under her breath.

As Destiny watched them, she wondered why Miles and Candy were still friends. He had never mentioned her before, so Destiny had assumed she wasn't a significant part of his life anymore. But seeing them together now, arm in arm and smiling at each other—they looked perfect. Like a real-life Barbie and Ken, destined to grace the covers of magazines and set unrealistic expectations for couples everywhere.

Destiny's heart felt like it had been plunged into ice water as she watched Miles and Candy together. The unbearable sight pushed her to retreat, so she turned on her heels and hurried toward the sanctuary of the kitchen.

"Stupid," she muttered under her breath, blinking back tears that threatened to spill down her cheeks. "Why would he ever choose me over her?"

Her emotions swirled like the ingredients in a blender, making it hard to focus on anything but the image of Candy's jewel-encrusted gown, perfectly complementing her immaculate figure and the glow of luxury that seemed to radiate from her every pore. Destiny couldn't help but compare herself, clad in her chef's coat, and find herself lacking.

"Hey, are you alright?" a concerned voice cut through

her thoughts. It was one of the sous-chefs, looking at her with worry etched across his face.

"Fine, I'm fine," she forced a smile, trying to regain control of her emotions. "Just...checking on the dinner set up."

"Alright, if you need anything, just let me know," he offered kindly before returning to his work.

"Thank you," she whispered, more to herself than to him. Destiny took a deep breath and reminded herself that this night wasn't about her love life—it was about honoring the veterans and ensuring the success of the gala. She had a job to do, and she needed to focus on that.

"Okay," she thought, steeling herself with determination. "No more wallowing. Time to make sure everything in here is running smoothly."

With renewed purpose, she immersed herself in the bustling energy of the kitchen, checking on each dish as it was prepared, making small adjustments where necessary, and offering encouragement to the staff. As she worked, she tried to silence the nagging voice in her head that kept whispering, "Why did you ever think you had a chance with Miles?"

"Service!" she called out, as the first course was ready to be sent out to the eager guests.

"Chef Evans, everything looks amazing," one of the servers complimented her as they whisked away the plates.

"Thank you," Destiny managed a genuine smile, feeling proud of her team's efforts. "Now let's keep this momentum going."

As the evening progressed and the kitchen ran like a well-oiled machine, Destiny allowed herself to get lost in the rhythm of her work. Her thoughts of Miles and Candy gradually faded into the background, replaced by the satisfaction of a job well done and the gratitude of the veterans they were honoring.

"Hey, Destiny," Lila peeked into the kitchen during a brief lull in service. "You're doing great out here. I just wanted to tell you that everyone is loving the food."

"Thanks, Lila," Destiny replied, her heart swelling with pride. "I needed to hear that."

"Keep up the good work," Lila smiled before disappearing back into the dining room.

With renewed determination, Destiny turned her attention back to the task at hand, knowing that she needed to focus on the people who truly appreciated her and the work she was doing. Miles would have to wait; for now, she had more important things to worry about.

fourteen

As the murmur of conversation filled the air, a sudden chime indicated that it was time for dinner. Miles, Malcolm, Max, Vivienne, Caroline, and Candy all stood and walked gracefully towards their table, situated at the front and closest to the stage. The elegantly dressed guests were bathed in the soft glow of the overhead chandeliers.

Miles couldn't help but notice that Caroline had switched the place cards as they took their seats. He glanced over and saw that she had placed Candy next to him instead of Vivienne. A flicker of suspicion crossed his mind, but he decided to let it go for now, focusing on the people who were there with him.

The first course arrived, a delicate salad that seemed to have been crafted by an artist rather than a chef. As everyone began to eat, Miles could feel the nerves building inside of him, knowing that soon he would take the stage to deliver his speech. The anticipation only grew as the night's Master of Ceremony called out his name.

"Please welcome tonight's honored speaker, Mr. Miles Huntington!"

Wiping his hands nervously on his pants, Miles stood up and made his way to the microphone. He cleared his throat before beginning his speech.

"Good evening, ladies and gentlemen. I would like to start by thanking each and every one of you for attending this special gala in support of our veterans. Your presence here tonight is not only a testament to your generosity but also to your commitment to honoring those who have so bravely served our country."

He paused for a moment, allowing his words to sink in. His green eyes scanned the room, taking in the faces of the attentive audience.

"Behind this event is a simple yet powerful idea: we must do everything in our power to ensure that our veterans receive the care and support they need upon returning home. These men and women have sacrificed so much for our freedom and security, and it is our responsibility to show them our unwavering gratitude."

The room erupted in applause, and Miles couldn't help but smile. He could feel his heart swell with pride as he continued.

"Please, enjoy the meal and the company of one another. Let us come together tonight not only to celebrate, but also to make a lasting impact on the lives of those who have given so much for us."

With that, he stepped away from the microphone and returned to his seat, allowing himself a small sigh of relief. As the clapping died down, the guests resumed their conversations, and the evening's festivities continued.

The warm glow of the chandeliers cast a romantic hue over the room as Miles quickly polished off his salad. The second course arrived, and he couldn't help but marvel at the delicious-looking soup placed before him. Destiny had truly outdone herself with the menu tonight. As the auctioneer's voice filled the air, signaling the beginning of the auction, Miles glanced over at Candy.

"Are you enjoying the meal?" he asked, trying to make polite conversation.

Candy gave him a sour look, her icy blue eyes narrowing slightly. "The salad was fine," she said, her tone dripping with disdain. "But this soup? It's absolutely fattening."

Caroline chimed in, her nose wrinkling in disapproval. "Destiny seems to have made a meal that isn't for fit people. Honestly, what was she thinking?"

Miles stifled a sigh as the mains were served. He and his brothers received a succulent meat dish, while Vivienne had a beautifully plated fish entree. Candy and Caroline, on the other hand, were presented with a vegetarian ravioli that seemed to infuriate them further.

"Can you believe this?" Candy huffed, gesturing at her plate. "All these carbs! And not even a hint of luxury. It's just, honestly, disgusting."

Malcolm, unable to contain himself any longer, slammed his fork down onto the table. "Oh, for fucks sake, just shut up and enjoy it!" he snapped. "Not everything has to be about your ridiculous diets and expensive tastes. We get it. All of us know there isn't an ounce of confidence between you."

Max rolled his eyes, shaking his head in disbelief at the childish behavior of their mother and Candy. Inside, Miles couldn't help but agree, though he kept his thoughts to himself. As they continued eating, he focused on the tantalizing flavors of his meal, wondering how Destiny managed to create such culinary masterpieces.

Candy's icy blue eyes narrowed as she turned her attention to Vivienne. "Speaking of carbs," she sneered, "I can't help but wonder why you're even here, Vivienne. We all know you couldn't afford a seat at this table on your own. Are you just mooching off of Max?"

Max bristled, his green eyes flashing with anger as he faced Candy. "Back off, Candy," he warned, his voice a growl. "Remember who you are talking to," Max added. "She is your boss."

"Please, Max," Candy scoffed, flicking her long blonde hair over her shoulder. "I'm simply looking out for the brothers and their fortune. Someone has to."

Malcolm, his messy brown hair more disheveled than ever, snorted in disbelief. "Yeah, can you do all of us a favor? You know, since you love to look out for us.'" he retorted.

Candy whips her head and narrows her eyes at Max. Miles noticed the look of triumph in her eyes, as if she just won a prize. "I guess I can," Candy says, rolling her eyes in feign annoyance.

"Fuck all the way off," Max retorted. Candy gasped in shock and Miles couldn't believe that Max said that. He is usually the level headed one of the three. Miles knew that he needed to intervene before this turned into a blowout fight.

"Alright, that's enough," Miles interjected, his tone firm yet gentle. "Let's just enjoy the evening, okay?" He looked at Malcolm, adding, "Lay off Candy, will you?" That earned him a glowing grin from Candy.

At that moment, Vivienne excused herself from the table, her face a mixture of hurt and embarrassment as she made her way to the restroom. When she disappeared from sight, Candy and Caroline were pulled away by Colter, who wanted to introduce them to someone important. With the main tension dispersed, dessert was served, and Miles tried to refocus his thoughts on the event.

"Hey, Miles," Max said quietly, his voice serious. "You

do realize that Candy insulted Vivienne, right? And you still stood up for Candy."

Miles furrowed his brow, his mind racing. "Vivienne may have misunderstood Candy's intentions," he replied. "Candy was... just looking out for us. I really just wanted to avoid making a scene."

Max frowned, clearly not satisfied with the answer. "Miles, you can't really believe that," he began, but his words were cut off as Miles' attention was suddenly captured by something else.

"Wait, Max," Miles said, his voice distant, eyes locked on an object across the room. He didn't even notice that Candy had returned to her seat, her gaze following his own.

Miles' gaze remained transfixed on the painting that had so abruptly captured his attention. The artwork was breathtaking, a vibrant explosion of colors depicting a field of sunflowers and daisies swaying gently in a warm summer breeze. The petals seemed to glow with an inner light, making them appear almost alive, while the sky above was painted in soft hues of pink and gold, giving the painting a nostalgic glow.

A sudden memory surfaced, unbidden, as Miles recalled running through fields of flowers with Destiny when they were young. Their laughter echoed through time, bringing a smile to his face despite the tension that still hung heavily in the air. He knew he needed this painting – for Destiny, for the memories it represented, and for the connection it would forge between their past and their future.

"Next up," the auctioneer announced, "is this stunning piece by renowned artist Isabella Martinez. Bidding will start at $5,000."

Without hesitation, Miles raised his paddle, heart

pounding with anticipation. The bidding quickly escalated, but he refused to be deterred, fully aware of what this painting meant to him. At last, the final bid was placed, and the gavel fell with a resounding crack.

"Sold to Mr. Huntington for $22,000!" the auctioneer declared, and the room erupted in applause. Miles couldn't help but grin. Miles was counting the moments until he could give this to Destiny, just to see the look on her face.

* * *

Destiny carefully pushed open the door to the main hall, not wanting to draw attention to herself. She leaned against the cool wall, watching as people savored the desserts she'd crafted with love. The sight warmed her heart—seeing the reactions to her creations was one of her favorite parts of being a chef.

Destiny spotted the painting displayed near the stage. It featured a vibrant field of daisies and sunflowers, with their petals reaching upward as if trying to embrace the warm sunshine. Her heart clenched at the sight, memories of her childhood days spent running through similar fields with Miles flooding her mind. The painting also evoked memories of her father, who had always loved the cheerful nature of sunflowers and daisies.

"Wow," she whispered under her breath, momentarily forgetting about where she was. As she continued to observe, she noticed Candy sitting next to Miles, their chairs practically touching. Candy leaned into Miles, her hand resting on his forearm as she whispered something in his ear. Miles gave her a polite smile, but his gaze was focused on the painting now being presented for auction.

Destiny loved that painting and could picture it in the house she could buy one day. The canvas has a sense of life and beauty that Destiny often looked at to brighten up her life. But doubt crept in, making her question whether that intimate moment she had witnessed between Candy and Miles meant they shared a connection and if the painting held significance for both of them instead.

"Get a grip, Destiny," she scolded herself internally, pulling away from the wall and taking a deep breath. "You've got work to do."

As she turned back to walk back to the kitchen, Destiny tried to shake off the nagging feeling that something significant had just happened, something that could change the course of her relationship with Miles. But for now, all she could do was focus on the present and ensure the success of the event. There would be time later to figure out the truth behind the painting and her feelings for Miles.

Destiny was about to step into the kitchen when she heard soft sniffles and the click of heels on the floor. Turning, she saw Vivienne passing by, her chestnut and auburn hair pulled into an updo that made her classic brown eyes pop. Her makeup was immaculate, but the faint smearing of mascara on her teary eyes spoke volumes.

"Vivi," Destiny called out softly, reaching for her arm. "What's wrong?"

Vivienne tried to force a smile as she blinked back tears. "Someone at the table said... some horrible things. That I'm just mooching off Max's money and taking advantage of him."

"Whoever said that is absolutely wrong," Destiny reassured her, anger simmering beneath the surface. "You don't deserve that, Vivi."

Pulling Vivienne into the kitchen, Destiny spotted Lila perched on a counter, happily munching on leftovers. Lila's eyes widened when she saw Vivienne's tear-streaked face and immediately hopped down to hug her.

"Come on, let's eat some dessert together," Lila suggested, trying to cheer Vivienne up. "We saved some corner pieces, which we all know is the best, for ourselves anyway."

As they settled in with plates of delectable desserts, Max entered the kitchen, his eyes searching. When he found Vivienne laughing with Lila, relief washed over his expression.

Max put his arm around Vivienne, and Destiny noticed her friend's tense shoulders relax under the weight of his touch. She couldn't help but smile at the warmth that radiated between them.

"Vivi, I've been looking for you," he said, his voice gentle. "I got worried when you didn't come back to the table."

Vivienne sighed, leaning into Max's embrace. "I just couldn't stand to be around them anymore, Max. But I'm okay now. Destiny and Lila have been taking care of me."

As they shared a quiet moment, Lila glanced up from her dessert and announced, "I better go pack the truck. We're gonna have a lot of cleaning to do after all this." She hopped off the counter and headed out of the kitchen.

"Right," Vivienne said, detaching herself from Max's side. "I'll grab my shawl, and then we can leave." She gave Destiny a grateful look before following Lila out of the kitchen.

Destiny turned her attention to tidying up, wiping down counters and organizing dishes. She was focused on her task when she heard her name being called softly.

"Destiny?" Max's voice made her pause and glance over her shoulder. The sincerity in his eyes warmed her heart.

"Thank you," he said earnestly. "For helping Vivi

tonight. You and Lila really made her feel better, and I'm so grateful for that."

Destiny smiled softly, touched by his gratitude. "Of course, Max. She's our friend too, and we'll always be here for her."

"Still," he insisted, "it means a lot to me. Thank you." With a final nod, Max turned and left the kitchen, leaving Destiny with a renewed sense of purpose.

As Max left the kitchen, he passed Miles in the doorway. Destiny's heart skipped a beat at the sight of him, her nerves suddenly on edge. She tried to steady her breathing as Miles entered the room, his green eyes twinkling with warmth and affection.

"Destiny," he said, grinning from ear to ear, "everything was absolutely incredible tonight. I can't thank you enough." He opened his arms wide, enveloping her in a tight embrace that made her feel safe and cherished.

"Thank you, Miles," she managed to say, her cheeks burned with a mixture of happiness and embarrassment. She could sense Candy watching them, her icy blue eyes practically boring holes through Destiny's skull.

"Didn't Destiny do a fantastic job, Candy?" Miles asked, turning towards her with an expectant smile. Candy pursed her lips, clearly unhappy about being put on the spot.

"Sure," she replied with a forced grin, "the food was... quaint and homemade. Just like Destiny herself."

Destiny bristled at the backhanded compliment but bit her tongue, reminding herself that some people never changed. Miles frowned slightly, sensing the tension between the two women but choosing not to make a scene.

"Candy," he said abruptly, "could I have a moment alone with Destiny? It's important."

"Really, Miles?" Candy huffed, crossing her arms and glaring at Destiny. "Is this necessary?"

Miles' voice was firm but gentle. "Yes, it's important. Please?"

"Fine," Candy snapped, flipping her long blonde hair over her shoulder as she stormed out of the kitchen, her heels clicking ominously against the floor.

Destiny watched her go, still feeling the sting of Candy's words. She shook her head, trying to shake off the negative energy, and turned her attention back to Miles. She had no idea what he wanted to talk about, but she couldn't let Candy's pettiness ruin her night. With a small smile, she looked up at Miles, ready to face whatever conversation they were about to have.

"Destiny, I saw this painting during the auction, and it reminded me so much of you," Miles said softly, his green eyes warm with sincerity. He carefully revealed the stunning canvas.

"Oh my god, Miles! It's beautiful!" Destiny breathed, her hazel eyes shining with awe and appreciation. She could feel her heart swelling with happiness as she took in every intricate detail of the painting. "Thank you, Miles."

"Seeing it brought back memories of when we were kids, running through fields together," Miles continued, a hint of nostalgia in his voice. He hesitated for a moment, then looked directly into Destiny's eyes. "I was wondering... would you like to go out with me properly sometime?"

"Like a date?" Destiny asked, her cheeks flushing with a mixture of surprise and excitement.

Miles nodded, smiling bashfully while rubbing the back of his neck. "Yes, a date."

"I'd love to," Destiny agreed, her heart fluttering in her chest. Her happiness bubbled up inside her, making it hard to contain her wide grin.

"Great," Miles said, his own smile broadening. "I'm looking forward to it."

At that moment, Lila appeared at the kitchen door, having finished loading the van. She raised an eyebrow at the sight of Destiny's beaming face and the intimate atmosphere between her and Miles. "Am I interrupting something?"

"Nothing at all," Destiny replied, still grinning. "We're done here."

"Perfect timing, then," Lila said, stepping aside as Miles bid Destiny farewell and walked out of the kitchen, casting her one last bashful smile before he disappeared around the corner.

"Okay, girl," Lila demanded as soon as they were in the van, "spill! Why are you grinning like the Cheshire Cat?"

"Miles asked me out! Can you believe it?!" Destiny squealed, unable to contain her excitement any longer.

"Finally!" Lila exclaimed, joining in the excited squealing as she started the van and pulled away from the venue. "I knew he'd come to his senses sooner or later."

As they drove back, Destiny couldn't help but replay the moment in her mind – the heartfelt way Miles presented the painting that reminded him of their shared past, and the sincere invitation for a date. She smiled again, feeling a warmth in her heart that had been absent for far too long.

Upon arriving back at the cafe, Destiny and Lila exchanged warm goodbyes. As Lila hopped into her car with a teasing grin, she called out, "Enjoy your evening, Desi!"

"Night, Lila," Destiny laughed, rolling her eyes play-fully. She watched as her best friend drove off before turning to head upstairs to her cozy apartment.

As she entered her living space, the stars were twinkling

through the windows. Destiny couldn't help but feel an overwhelming sense of contentment wash over her. She knew exactly how she wanted to spend her evening – a bubble bath, candles, and a good book.

With a newfound energy, she went about preparing her relaxing oasis. She filled the tub with steaming water, pouring in her favorite lavender-scented bubbles as they frothed and foamed, creating a cloud-like sanctuary. Selecting a few scented candles, she strategically placed them around the bathroom, their flickering flames casting a soothing ambiance.

"Perfect," she murmured to herself, taking a step back to admire her handiwork. But there was still something missing—music. After deliberating for a moment, she chose a playlist filled with calming acoustic melodies that she knew would perfectly complement her evening of relaxation.

Satisfied with her choices, Destiny quickly changed into a comfortable robe and applied a rejuvenating face mask before stepping into the warm embrace of the bubble-filled bathtub. The soothing scent of lavender enveloped her as the hot water eased the tension from her muscles.

"Ah, this is just what I needed," she sighed, sinking deeper into the fragrant waters. With her favorite novel in hand, she became lost in the world of its pages, allowing herself to be swept away by the story.

Is this real or am I dreaming? she wondered, feeling a mix of excitement and disbelief. "Miles Huntington actually asked me out on a date!" Her heart swelled with anticipation.

fifteen

THE BRIGHT MORNING SUN STREAMED THROUGH THE floor-to-ceiling windows of Vortex's main office, casting a warm glow on Miles as he sat at his desk, poring over the quarterly report. A satisfied smile spread across his face as he noticed the significant increase in revenue from the year before, which meant they could finally expand their operations.

Things are looking up, he thought, feeling a surge of pride for what he and his team had accomplished. He leaned back in his chair, taking a moment to soak in the sunlight and bask in the success that was laid out before him.

As he reveled in the accomplishment, the sound of the door opening caught his attention. Miles looked up just in time to see Malcolm entering the room, his usually jovial expression marred by a solemn look. The sudden shift in mood was palpable, and anxiety bubbled up inside Miles.

"Hey, Mal, what's wrong?" Miles asked, concern laced his voice as he straightened up in his chair.

Malcolm took a deep breath before speaking. "Do you remember the law enforcement algorithm we created?"

"Which one specifically are you referring to?" Miles didn't care for the tone in his brother's voice.

"The algorithm that aids them in solving past crimes, rather than preventing future ones."

"The one that assists with identifying suspects?"

"Correct." Malcolm hesitated once more, "Well, it seems like someone is solving crimes even faster than our algorithm. This has led to politicians questioning the value of our top-of-the-line system when there's an unknown entity doing it for free."

Miles sighed, rubbing his temples. "Oh that's right! It is one of our more successful programs. What's going on with it?"

"Right," Malcolm said, hesitating for a moment. "Well, someone is solving crimes even faster than our algorithm, and politicians are starting to question why they're paying so much for a supposedly top-of-the-line system when there's an unknown entity doing it for free."

"Are you serious?" Miles asked, disbelief etched on his face. "How is that even possible?"

"Your guess is as good as mine," Malcolm replied, running a hand through his messy brown hair in frustration. "But we need to figure this out, and fast."

"Alright," Miles said, tapping his fingers on the table. "Let's brainstorm. What if we reset the algorithm to focus more on making it easier for law enforcement to solve crimes instead of promising that it solves them?"

Malcolm nodded thoughtfully. "That might work. We could also look into enhancing its predictive capabilities, maybe even add a feature that allows the system to learn and adapt from successes and failures."

"Exactly." Miles grinned at his younger brother. "We still provide a valuable service, but we're not claiming to be the ultimate solution. It gives us some wiggle room and helps our clients see the value in our product despite this unknown competitor."

"Sounds like a solid plan," Malcolm agreed, relief washing over his face. "I'll get our team started on the adjustments right away."

Malcolm leaned back in his chair, calm now that they had a solution. "Now that we've got that sorted, what about your personal life? Are you excited about your date tonight?"

"Definitely," Miles replied with a grin. "I've got something really special planned. I just hope she likes it."

"Knowing Destiny, I'm sure she'll love whatever you have in store for her," Malcolm reassured him.

Miles pondered on what his brother said as he watched him get up from the chair. "I've got a meeting now, but let me know if you need any help with the algorithm stuff later."

"Will do," Miles said as he shook his brother's hand quickly. "Good luck with the meeting."

"Thanks, Miles," Malcolm said. "I can't wait to hear all about your date," Malcolm smiles, giving Miles a playful wink as he leaves the room.

Hours passed, and the sun began its slow descent in the sky. He had been working tirelessly to finish up the last of his tasks for the day, finalizing the changes they'd discussed in the meeting earlier. The satisfaction of problem-solving still lingered within him as he saved one last document and shut down his computer. Grabbing his jacket from the back of his chair, he took a deep breath and headed out to the front area where Candy was sitting at her desk.

"Leaving early today?" Candy asked, a perfectly sculpted eyebrow arching upward as she looked up from her computer screen, her blue eyes locking onto his.

"Indeed, I am," Miles replied, his excitement for the

night ahead bubbling beneath the surface. "I have some personal plans tonight."

"Interesting," Candy said, swiveling in her chair to face him fully. "I didn't see any meetings or events on your calendar."

"Actually, it's a date," Miles revealed, unable to hide the smile that spread across his face. "I'm meeting Destiny tonight."

Candy frowned, her lips pursing as she pretended to be concerned. "Are you sure that's a good idea, Miles? I mean, after everything she put you through with that goodbye message…"

Miles shrugged off Candy's thinly veiled attempt to sow doubt. "People change, Candy. We've all grown, and I want to give this a new chance. I believe in Destiny."

"Of course, it's your life," Candy relented, though the hint of a smirk played at the corners of her mouth. "I just hope you know what you're doing."

"Thank you for your concern," Miles said, choosing to ignore the subtle undertone in her voice. "I appreciate it. But for now, I'd like to focus on the present and see where this goes."

"Very well," Candy conceded, her eyes narrowed into slits as she watched him walk away. "Have a good evening, then."

"Thank you, Candy," Miles said over his shoulder, striding confidently toward the exit.

As he stepped outside, the warm breeze caressed his face, and his excitement for the date surged through him like an electric current. He couldn't wait to see Destiny's reaction to what he had planned – it was going to be a night to remember.

* * *

Destiny stood in front of her full-length mirror, scrutinizing her reflection as she put the finishing touches on her outfit for the evening. Her long, brown hair cascaded down her shoulders in loose, romantic waves that framed her heart-shaped face, and she had applied a subtle smokey eye with a touch of mascara to accentuate her hazel eyes. A hint of blush graced her cheeks, and she dabbed a soft rose hue onto her lips, which were curved into an excited smile.

Her outfit was casual yet chic—a pair of figure-hugging jeans that flattered her curves paired with a delicate lace top. She completed the look with a pair of ankle boots that gave her just enough height without sacrificing comfort.

As Destiny grabbed her purse and keys, she felt a flutter of excitement in her stomach. The anticipation of seeing Miles tonight had left her distracted at work all day, and she couldn't help but wonder what he had planned. Miles wanted it to be a special surprise, so he wouldn't tell her anything. She locked her apartment door behind her and headed to her car, her thoughts raced through the possibilities.

"Maybe he's taking me to that new Italian restaurant everyone's been raving about," she mused to herself as she started the engine. "Or perhaps we're going to see a movie or a live show… No, that seems too conventional for Miles."

As she drove toward his house, her mind continued to conjure up different scenarios. "What if it's something outdoorsy? Like a hike or a picnic in the park? That would be perfect with this beautiful weather, not so great for my shoes." She glanced out the window, noting the way the setting sun streamed through the trees and giving the road dappled patterns.

"Then again," Destiny thought as she took a deep

breath, "he could surprise me with something completely unexpected—like a hot air balloon ride or a cooking class where we make dinner together." The more she considered the endless possibilities, the more her excitement grew.

Destiny's heart raced as she parked her car outside of Miles' house. The anticipation had been building all day, and now, the moment had finally arrived. She stepped out of her car and paused to compose herself, tucking a loose strand of hair behind her ear.

"Alright, Destiny," she whispered to herself, taking a deep breath. "You've got this."

As she approached the porch, the front door suddenly swung open, revealing a beaming Miles waiting for her with a huge bouquet of daisies and sunflowers filling his arms. Destiny's heart swelled at the sight of his warm smile, feeling an instant connection between them. Her eyes were immediately drawn to the vibrant flowers adorning his front that matched what he held in his armsarms.

"Are these daisies and sunflowers?" she asked, genuinely touched by the gesture.

Miles nodded, his smile growing even wider. "I remembered how much you love them. Plus, they brighten up the place, don't you think?"

Destiny felt her cheeks flush with warmth. "They're beautiful, Miles. Thank you."

He extended his hand, and she gladly took it as they walked towards the backyard together. Destiny had seen his backyard before, but what awaited her there now was nothing short of magical. The lush green grass seemed to sparkle in the fading sunlight, and strung all around the trunks of the huge trees were delicate fairy lights, casting a soft, enchanting glow across the entire space.

In the center of it all was a picnic set up that looked

like something straight out of a romantic movie. A large, cozy blanket was spread out on the grass, adorned with plush pillows and surrounded by flickering candles. A wicker basket filled with delicious treats sat nearby, along with a bottle of wine chilling in an ice bucket.

"Miles," Destiny breathed, her eyes drinking in every detail of the scene before her. "This is absolutely breathtaking."

"Only the best for you," he replied, a hint of pride in his voice. "I wanted tonight to be special, and I thought a picnic under the stars would be the perfect way to spend our evening together."

Destiny squeezed his hand, her heart overflowing with gratitude and affection. "It's perfect. Thank you for putting so much effort into this. I can't wait to enjoy it with you."

Seated on the plush pillows, Destiny and Miles toasted to their evening together, the sound of clinking glasses echoing against the backdrop of rustling leaves. Their meal was spread out before them, an array of gourmet sandwiches, fresh fruit, and a decadent chocolate dessert that made Destiny's mouth water just looking at it.

"Everything looks so delicious," Destiny said, as she sampled a ripe strawberry. "Did you make all of this yourself?"

"Of course," Miles grinned. "I couldn't let you be the only one with culinary skills."

They laughed, and Destiny felt her chest fill with joy. As they dug into their feast, conversation flowed easily between them. They discussed everything from their favorite books to childhood memories, their words weaving together like the intricate patterns of the fairy lights above them.

"Have I ever told you how much I love astronomy?"

Destiny asked, looking up at the stars as they finished their meal.

"Really?" Miles replied, his interest piqued. "Tell me more."

Destiny's eyes sparkled with excitement as she described her fascination with the night sky. "The stars have always been a source of comfort for me. Whenever life gets difficult, I just look up and remind myself that there's something much bigger than us out there."

"Would you show me some of your favorite constellations?" Miles asked, intrigued by her passion.

"Of course!" Destiny agreed, her enthusiasm contagious.

With the picnic remnants cleared away, Destiny repositioned herself on the blanket, snuggling into the warmth of Miles' embrace. His legs stretched out on either side of her, providing a comfortable cushion as she leaned back against his chest.

"See that cluster of stars over there?" Destiny pointed, tracing an imaginary line in the sky. "That's Orion, the hunter. And if you follow that line down, you'll see Taurus, the bull."

Miles marveled at her knowledge, and the way her face lit up as she shared her passion with him. Together, they traced the constellations with their fingers, the sky becoming a canvas for their shared dreams and desires.

"Thank you for showing me this," Miles whispered, his breath warm against Destiny's ear. "I never knew how beautiful the night sky could be."

"Isn't it amazing?" Destiny replied, her voice filled with awe. "To think that we're just a tiny part of this vast universe… It's humbling, really."

Destiny turned to look at Miles and as she looked into his eyes, she saw a depth of emotion that sent shivers down her spine. The intensity of his gaze was both thrilling and terrifying, as if he was baring his soul for her to see. With an almost imperceptible nod, she granted him permission to close the distance between them.

The moment their lips met, it was as if fireworks erupted around them—brilliant bursts of color and light that left them breathless and wanting more. Their connection was powerful, electric, like two magnets drawn irrevocably together. As they pulled away, Destiny found herself lost in the warmth of Miles' green eyes, feeling his fingertips gently tracing the contours of her heart-shaped face.

"Destiny," Miles murmured, his voice low and filled with emotion. "I think I could fall for you."

Her heart swelled with happiness, and she smiled softly at him. "I think I could fall for you too."

They exchanged tender words and confessions, each revealing a piece of themselves to the other, drawing closer with every shared secret and dream. It was like they had formed a connection that was beyond the reaches of the present, a love strong enough to overcome whatever hardship it may face.

As the night grew chillier, Miles suggested they move inside to warm up by the fireplace. Hand in hand, they walked into his cozy living room, where a fire already danced merrily in the hearth. Destiny marveled at the way the dancing flames illuminated Miles' face, casting shadows that highlighted the strong lines of his jaw and cheekbones.

"Your home is gorgeous, Miles," Destiny said, her voice filled with admiration. "I love the little momentos you have. Oh look at this photo of you and young Malcolm and Max."

"Thanks! Work and my mom can really stress me out. I need an escape to relax."

"Speaking of which, how do you manage to balance

everything in your life?" Destiny asked, genuinely curious. "Running a successful company, giving back to the community, and still finding time for friends and family... It's impressive. Okay, okay, be honest. Do you ever sleep?"

Miles chuckled softly, while shrugging his shoulders, a hint of self-deprecation in his voice. "It's not always easy, but I try my best. Sometimes it feels like I'm juggling a hundred different things, but it's worth it to make a difference in the world—and to have moments like this with you."

They spent the night talking about everything. Easily transitioning from one topic to the next, there were even pauses that felt natural and content. As though reunited with her best friend, Destiny experienced a joyous evening of discussion—from small talk on their daily lives to big dreams for the upcoming years ahead. Jokes threaded in between as well.

Destiny knew about Miles' dream from when he was young. He is living his dream. Her dream of owning her own cafe is on the horizon. She tells him all about her plans and how she wants to set everything up. She wants the cafe to have even more food options and maybe set up something where people can take the food home and cook it themselves. Her dream is to use local resources to have a feel of the community coming together.

As Miles spoke, his words ignited a fire within Destiny's heart. She couldn't deny the pull she felt towards him, and as she watched his hands move with such fervor, she realized that her feelings for him went beyond admiration. With each passing second, she became more and more certain that she was in love with Miles, completely and irrevocably. How could she have not seen it before? He was not only intelligent and kind, but also fiercely dedicated to those he cared for. And now, she knew without a doubt that she was one of those people.

"Is it really that late already?" Destiny asked as she glanced at the grandfather clock against the wall, surprised to see the time. The hours had flown by in what felt like mere minutes.

"Time flies when you're having fun," Miles replied with a warm smile, his green eyes sparkling in the dim light of the room.

"True." Destiny reluctantly stood up from the cozy spot near the fireplace and stretched, feeling the warmth of the fire still lingering on her skin. "I should probably get going."

"Let me walk you out," Miles offered, taking her hand as they made their way through the house and out to her car. Miles was so close that she could feel the warmth of his body, chasing away the chill in the air.

As they reached her car, Destiny turned to face Miles, letting her eyes travel over his face. The broad brow and strong jawline were silhouetted in the hazy light of sunset, and she loved the way the orange glow caressed his features. Her eyes searched his for a moment before he leaned in, capturing her lips with his own. The kiss was soft and sweet, tender yet full of promise, and it left her breathless.

"Text me when you get home, okay?" Miles requested, his voice low.

"Of course, I will," Destiny promised, her heart brimming with affection for this man who had rapidly grown to hold significant meaning in her life. With one last smile, she climbed into her car and started the engine, pulling away from the curb and heading home. As she drove, her mind replayed the events of the evening, each memory filling her with happiness and anticipation for what lay ahead.

Upon arriving at her apartment, Destiny parked her car and hurried upstairs, eager to let Miles know she'd made it home safely. Unlocking her door, she stepped inside and pulled out her phone, typing out a message she had thought about the entire drive home.

DESTINY

Miles, I had the best time tonight! It was beyond anything I could have ever imagined. I'm so excited to see you again. Thank you for such an amazing experience. Sleep well!

Before she could even set her phone down, a reply came through.

MILES

Destiny, tonight was incredible, and I'm so glad we got to share it together. I can't wait for our next adventure. Sleep well, and know that you're in my thoughts. Until we meet again...

sixteen

MILES STOOD AT CANDY'S DESK IN VORTEX, SIGNING document after document. The pen glided across the paper with ease, but his mind was elsewhere. It had been four months since he and Destiny began dating, and with Christmas just around the corner, Miles was racking his brain to find the perfect gift for her. Their time together had been nothing short of magical.

He smiled as memories of their dates flashed through his mind—the laughter-filled evening they spent trying out different food trucks in the park, the romantic sunset picnic on the beach, and the thrilling day they spent hiking and exploring scenic trails. Each memory brought a warmth to his heart that he had never felt before.

"Focus, Miles," he muttered under his breath, shaking himself back into the present moment. This Christmas gift needed to be special; it needed to show Destiny just how much she meant to him.

Miles froze, pen hovering above the document as his eyes widened in thought. Candy looked up from her computer screen, concern etched across her face. "Are you okay, Miles?"

"Yeah, I'm fine," he replied, forcing a smile. "Just thinking about a gift for Destiny. Something to show her how much I love her."

Candy let out a gasp, her eyes filling with tears. Miles, mistaking her reaction for happiness over his newfound love, pressed on. "I want it to be something personal, something that really speaks to who she is."

"Hey, Candy," Miles began, trying to sound casual. "What kind of gift would you want for Christmas? You know, just out of curiosity."

Candy's eyes sparkled with excitement, earlier tears seeming to vanish as quickly as they came, as she sat up straighter in her chair. "Oh, well, if we're talking dream gifts here... I'd love a pair of limited edition Louboutin heels, maybe a gorgeous designer handbag—the bigger the better, of course. Oh, and tickets to that exclusive island resort where all the celebrities go."

Miles couldn't help but raise an eyebrow as Candy continued to rattle off her extravagant wish list. He knew Destiny was nothing like Candy; she valued experiences and heartfelt gestures far more than material possessions.

"Those are some great options," he said diplomatically, not wanting to offend Candy. "But I think I need to find something that's more suited to Destiny's taste."

Just then, his phone rang, and he glanced down to see Lila's name flashing on the screen. Excusing himself, he moved to a quiet corner of the office to take the call.

"Hey, Lila. What's up?"

"Hey Miles, I just wanted to let you know I found the perfect gift for Destiny," Lila replied, excitement evident in her voice. "I'll text you the details. Trust me, she'll love it."

"Perfect! Thanks, Lila. I owe you one," Miles said,

grateful for her help. He eagerly awaited her message, knowing Lila's suggestion would likely be the key to showing Destiny how much she means to him.

Miles pocketed his phone and turned to see Vivienne approaching Candy's desk. Her chestnut hair was pulled back in a loose bun, her light brown eyes sparkled with warmth.

"Hey, Viv," he greeted her happily. "Have you spoken to Destiny today?"

Vivienne smiled. "Yeah! We actually planned a girls' night at Kyle's tonight. It should be a lot of fun."

"Sounds great!" Miles said. He glanced over at Candy and noticed her shooting a spurned look at Vivienne. Miles thought she might be longing for some girlfriends of her own.

"Hey, Viv," he began hesitantly, "I was wondering if maybe Candy could join you guys tonight? She seems like she could use some girlfriends too."

Vivienne's smile faltered for a moment as she considered the request. After a long pause, she looked up at him with furrowed brows and reluctantly said, "Okay, Miles. I'll do it." Her voice was strained and he noticed the way her hands trembled slightly as she spoke.

"Really?" Miles asked, surprised by her doubt. "Is there a problem?"

"No, no problem," Vivienne assured him, masking her concerns. "Candy, we're meeting at Kyle's bar tonight at 8. You're welcome to join us."

Candy's icy blue eyes lit up as she flashed a grin. "I'll be there," she said, her voice dripping with melodramatic sweetness. Miles couldn't help but feel a swell of satisfaction at the thought of all his friends becoming closer.

"Great," Vivienne said, forcing a smile. "I'll see you

then." With that, she waved goodbye to Miles and left to continue her day.

As Miles watched her walk away, he felt a twinge of confusion over Vivienne's initial hesitation. He shook it off, however, deciding to focus on the positive outcome instead—his friends were coming together, and that was all that mattered.

* * *

Destiny's apartment was alive with music and laughter as she and Lila got ready for girls' night. The hum of excitement filled the air like electricity, as they stood side by side in front of the large, ornate mirror that hung on Destiny's bedroom wall. It had been a while since they spent an evening like this, and Destiny couldn't help but feel giddy at the thought of a carefree night with her closest friends.

"Desi, check this out," Lila announced, pulling a bright red lipstick from her makeup bag. "I just bought it today. I think it'll look fantastic on you."

"Really?" Destiny asked skeptically, eyeing the bold color. "You know I usually stick to more neutral shades."

"Exactly!" Lila exclaimed, nudging her playfully. "That's why it's perfect for tonight. You need to break free from your comfort zone every once in a while, and there's no better time than when you're surrounded by friends."

Destiny hesitated for a moment before finally giving in to Lila's persuasive grin. "Alright, fine. But if I look ridiculous, it's on you."

"Deal," Lila agreed, expertly applying the red lipstick to Destiny's lips. As she stepped back to admire her work, she couldn't help but beam with pride. "See? I knew it would look amazing on you!"

"Thanks, Lila," Destiny said appreciatively, studying

her reflection. The vibrant shade brought out the warmth in her hazel eyes, making them appear even more mesmerizing. "You always know what's best for me."

"Of course I do," Lila replied, flipping her jet-black hair over her shoulder with a dramatic flourish. "Now, let's finish getting ready. Vivi will be here any minute."

The doorbell reverberated through the apartment, startling Destiny and Lila out of their laughter-induced stupor. They exchanged excited glances before making their way to the door, anticipation bubbling beneath their grins.

"Ready for a night to remember?" Destiny asked as she swung the door open, expecting to see Vivienne with a sparkle in her eyes and an infectious smile on her face. Instead, she found her friend standing there, looking uncharacteristically nervous.

"Vivi! Are you okay?" Destiny asked, concern etching itself across her features. Lila moved closer, her electric blue eyes filled with worry.

Vivienne sighed, her chestnut hair falling around her shoulders as she looked down at her shoes. "It's Candy," she began hesitantly. "Miles sort of pressured me into inviting her tonight because she doesn't have any girl-friends."

"Of course he did," Lila grumbled, rolling her eyes. "To Miles, Cry Baby Candy can do no wrong."

"Is that really so bad?" Destiny asked, trying to remain positive. "Maybe she's realized how nasty she can be and wants to make amends?"

"Actually, it likely will be that bad," Vivienne admitted, her light brown eyes meeting Destiny's. "He even told Max at the gala that she was 'just looking out for them' when Max got upset about what Candy said to me."

"Ugh, why would Miles say that?" Destiny muttered, her hazel eyes clouded with confusion.

"Maybe he's just trying to keep the peace," Lila suggested, crossing her arms. "But honestly, I don't know if I can handle playing nice with Candy all night."

Destiny considered all of the points her friends made, aware of the potential for conflict. However, she knew that if she truly loved Miles, she needed to find a way to accept Candy's presence in his life. Her thoughts came to a screeching halt at the realization—love? Was that what she felt for Miles? She shook her head, trying to dispel the sudden emotional whirlwind. "We'll make it work," she finally said, more to herself than to her friends. "We can handle one night with Candy."

"Alright," Vivienne agreed reluctantly, stepping into the apartment. "Let's put on our battle attire and prepare to be kind." The three girls giggled and rushed back into Destiny's room to finish getting ready.

Destiny, Lila, and Vivi admired themselves in the mirror, their outfits reflecting their individual styles. Destiny chose a romantic, flowy white dress with a delicate floral pattern, cinched at the waist. She left her brown hair down in loose waves, framing her face and highlighting her hazel eyes, her red lipstick bringing the whole look together. Lila opted for a sexy look, wearing a black leather mini skirt paired with a lace camisole and chunky ankle boots. Her jet-black hair was slicked back into a high pony-tail, emphasizing her electric blue eyes. Vivi, ever the picture of timeless glamor, donned a navy blue sheath dress that clung to her curves, complemented by a string of pearls and classic red lipstick.

"Alright, ladies, we look amazing!" Destiny declared, each trying to shake off the tension from earlier. Lila was literally shaking out her muscles.

"Agreed," Lila said, flashing a confident grin. "Let's go have some fun."

The three friends left Destiny's apartment, their heels clicking on the pavement as they walked towards Kyle's. The crisp night air filled their lungs, invigorating them as they chatted happily about their plans for the evening.

Upon entering the dimly lit bar, the trio found a table with comfortable seating, grateful for the respite after their walk. They settled in, perusing the drink menu before signaling the bartender for their orders.

"Whiskey sour, please," Destiny requested, her palate craving the perfect mix of sweet and sour.

"Classic margarita for me," Lila chimed in, always a fan of tequila's bold flavor.

"Make it a gin and tonic for me," Vivi added, appreciating the simple elegance of the drink.

"Coming right up, ladies!" The bartender smiled warmly, disappearing to prepare their drinks.

Twenty minutes later, Destiny glanced up at the sound of the door opening and caught her breath as she saw Candy walk into Kyle's. She was a vision in tight, designer clothes, looking like a model that had just stepped off the runway. Her dress was form-fitting and black, ending mid-thigh, with a plunging neckline that left little to the imagination. The designer label seemed to shimmer beneath the neon lights as if taunting Destiny and her friends with its opulence.

Talk about trying too hard, Destiny thought, rolling her eyes. She couldn't help but feel that Candy was going overboard, desperate for attention in her flashy ensemble. Nonetheless, she knew it was important to make an effort for Miles' sake, so she waved to Candy with a tight smile.

Candy sauntered over, her high heels clicking on the floor, before taking a seat next to them. Not one to miss an opportunity to assert her superiority, she wiped down her seat and table with a tissue, grimacing as if the bar were beneath her.

"Martini, please, four olives," Candy called out to the waiter, "Make sure it's Clix Vodka."

"Actually, we don't have that specific brand you're asking for," the waiter replied nervously, "But we do have Belvedere."

Candy scoffed and rolled her eyes, "That's basically well liquor at the bar I go to, but fine, whatever."

The waiter scurried away quickly, visibly relieved to be out of Candy's line of fire. Destiny watched the exchange, torn between irritation and pity for the waiter. She knew she had to try and keep the peace, but it was already proving difficult as Candy continued to exude her haughty demeanor.

Sitting back in her chair, Destiny noticed Candy's eyes narrow as they swept over her and the other girls. There was something in Candy's gaze that sent a shiver down Destiny's spine, making her feel uneasy.

"Kyle's place is so...cute," Candy remarked with a half-hearted smile, taking a sip of her martini. The condescension in her tone was unmistakable.

"Isn't it?" Destiny replied, trying to keep her voice light. "Kyle puts his heart and soul into this place. We love coming here."

Candy smirked, her eyes glinting with disdain. "Well, it fits you perfectly, doesn't it?"

Destiny clenched her jaw, forcing a tight-lipped smile. She glanced at Lila, who was fidgeting with the edge of her napkin, clearly uncomfortable with Candy's presence.

"Anyway," Lila said, quickly changing the subject. "Candy, how have you been? It's been a while since we've caught up."

Candy's blue eyes met Destiny's, and she couldn't help

but flinch at the coldness in her gaze. "Well, since you haven't been around," she began, emphasizing each word. Destiny felt her chest tighten, hurt by Candy's cruel words.

"Let me fill you in," Candy continued, leaning back in her chair. "I've been traveling quite a bit—Paris, Milan, Tokyo. You know, the usual. Fashion Weeks are exhausting" She casually flips her wrist to inspect her nails and check the time on her watch. "Oh, and I just got a new handbag. It's absolutely stunning."

Destiny tried to maintain her composure, focusing on the condensation dripping down the side of her drink. She listened as Candy droned on about her lavish experiences, feeling a mixture of disbelief and sadness at little she had changed.

Vivienne hesitated for a moment, trying to insert herself into the conversation. "You know, I've heard great things about Milan. The architecture is just stunning." Her voice was tentative but hopeful, as if she could find common ground with Candy.

Candy cut her off with a dismissive wave of her hand. "I'm sorry, this conversation is for old acquaintances. That doesn't include you." Vivi frowned, hurt by the blatant exclusion.

Lila's eyes flashed with anger. "That's enough, Candy," she snapped, slamming her drink down on the table. "Don't you know what it means to be kind? Stop being such a fucking bitch every second of your life!"

"Stop it, Lila," Destiny pleaded, reaching out to place a hand on her best friend's arm. "She's not worth it."

"No, Desi, I've had enough of her bullshit," Lila retorted, her frustration evident in the set of her jaw as she turned her head towards Destiny. Lila spat out, "What she's not worth is the time and energy it takes to be nice to her. Because fuck me, it's a damn chore, Candy."

Destiny closed her eyes for a moment, taking a deep breath to calm herself. When she opened them again, Candy was standing, her eyes filled with pure hatred. Destiny felt herself shiver at the sight.

Candy's voice dripped with venom as she hissed, "You'll see, Destiny. Miles will finally realize the absolute trash you are," Her once bright eyes turned a dark blue as she went on, "Those girls that you call friends? It's no surprise that you surround yourself with people of the same low caliber. Birds of a feather flock together, after all. I'll make it my personal mission to destroy your pathetic excuse for a relationship that has been dragging on for far too long."

Destiny gasped, horrified at Candy's venomous words. Lila stared back at Candy defiantly. "You wouldn't."

"Watch me," Candy sneered, before turning on her heel and storming out of the bar.

Destiny let out a shaky breath, trying not to cry. This was exactly what had happened when she had moved away —Candy got involved and tore apart the life she had built. Vivienne reached across the table to take Destiny's hand, offering a reassuring squeeze.

"Hey, it's going to be okay," she said softly. "We won't let her ruin what you and Miles have."

"Exactly," Lila agreed, her voice wavering as she tried to smile. "We'll stick together. We always have and always will."

The girls ordered another round of drinks, attempting to salvage the rest of their night. Destiny sipped at her mojito, her mind racing with thoughts of how Candy's interference could impact her blossoming love with Miles. She couldn't deny the worry that gnawed at her heart, but she knew she had to fight for the life she wanted, no matter the obstacles thrown in her path.

seventeen

MILES SIGHED AS THE FIRST LIGHT OF DAWN STREAMED through the windows. His fingers danced across the keyboard, trying to catch up on the emails he'd left unanswered the night before. The office was quiet and serene in the early morning hours, allowing him to concentrate on his work without distractions.

As he typed out a particularly tricky response, Miles' heart jumped when his office door flew open with a loud bang. He looked up, startled by the sudden intrusion, and saw Candy standing in the doorway, tears streaming down her cheeks. Her usually immaculate clothes were disheveled, and her mascara had smeared beneath her blue eyes.

"Candy?" Miles stammered, concern flooding his voice. "What's going on?"

"Mi-Miles," she choked out between sobs, her voice trembling. "I-I just... I need your help."

Without hesitation, Miles sprang up from his chair and crossed the room, wrapping his arms around her in a comforting embrace. As he rubbed her shoulders until the tears stopped flowing, he noted how fragile she seemed, so unlike the confident, cunning woman he knew. He led her over to the plush office chairs and double-checked to make sure the dividers were closed between his office, Max's office, and Malcolm's office, ensuring they could have some privacy.

"Alright, Candy," Miles said gently, taking a seat beside her and holding her hand. "Take a deep breath and tell me what happened."

Candy wiped her eyes with the back of her hand, taking a shaky breath. "It's just... last night was supposed to be a fun girls' night, but Destiny... she was so mean to me."

Miles furrowed his brow, trying to picture the sweet and kind-hearted Destiny he knew acting cruel to anyone. "What exactly did she do?"

Candy sniffled, her voice barely audible. "She kept making these snide comments about my clothes and my job, like I wasn't good enough. And when I tried to laugh it off, she got the other girls to join in. It was like I was back in high school, being bullied all over again."

"I'm so sorry you had to go through that," Miles said, his heart ached for his friend. He couldn't understand why Destiny would act that way.

"Destiny doesn't want me to be part of your group," Candy continued, her eyes pleading. "She wants to push me out of your life, Miles. But you have to tell her that I'm your best friend, and I'm not going anywhere."

Miles squeezed her hand reassuringly. "I'll talk to her, Candy. Just give it some time. You're both important to me, and I'm sure we can find a way for everyone to get along."

Before Candy could respond, there was a knock at the door, and Max's assistant entered, his face expressionless. "Mr. Huntington, Max would like a meeting with you."

"Tell him I'll be right there," Miles replied, giving

Candy one last comforting pat on the hand. As he stood up, he noticed her narrowed eyes following the assistant, who paid her no attention. He couldn't help but wonder if there was more to the story than he was being told.

"Everything will be okay," he promised before leaving his office, his mind already racing with thoughts of how to mend the rift between Candy and Destiny.

Miles closed the door behind him, leaving Candy to gather herself in his office. As he followed Alexander, Max's assistant, to Max's office, he couldn't help but replay the conversation with Candy in his mind. Was Destiny really being unkind to her? He had always known Destiny as a compassionate and caring individual, so it was hard to imagine her treating anyone poorly. Miles took a deep breath and pushed open the door.

"Hey, Max," Miles greeted as he entered the room, finding his older brother seated at his desk, engrossed in whatever was on his computer screen.

Max looked up, his familiar green eyes meeting Miles's gaze. A smile spread across his face as he leaned back in his chair. "I thought you weren't going to make it to our meeting."

"Sorry about that," Miles apologized, rubbing the back of his neck. "Candy came into my office really upset, saying Destiny wasn't kind to her at girls night last night."

"Really?" Max raised an eyebrow, looking genuinely surprised. "That doesn't sound like Destiny. What exactly happened?"

Miles hesitated, trying to piece together what Candy had told him. "Well, she didn't give me all the details, but apparently Destiny singled her out and was pretty harsh with her. I just... I don't know, Max. It doesn't add up."

Miles studied Max's face, noting the subtle shift in his expression. It was a look he couldn't quite decipher, and it made him uneasy. "What's with that look?" he asked, curiosity getting the better of him.

Max hesitated for a moment before responding, "Vivi told me about last night. She had a different perspective on what happened."

"Really? What did she say?" Miles asked, his interest piqued.

"According to Vivi, it seemed like Candy was actually targeting Destiny, trying to stake some imaginary claim on you," Max revealed, his tone cautious.

Miles' eyes widened in shock. "What? That's... I can't believe it. She would never do that."

"Maybe she feels threatened by your relationship with Destiny," Max suggested. "Candy can be really mean and bitchy when she wants to be."

"Come on, Max. Is it possible that they're all just misinterpreting each other? Maybe they just need to talk it out instead of arguing," Miles countered, unwilling to believe that his best friend could be so manipulative. He knew people changed, but this sounded extreme.

"Look, Miles," Max said, leaning forward and locking eyes with his brother. "I know Candy is your friend, but you have to remember how she was when we were teenagers. She was the one who drove a wedge between us, and she hasn't changed since then. She's cold and calculating, and she knows how to control people like puppets. I don't want to see you become one of those puppets, especially when it comes to your relationship with Destiny."

Miles chewed on his bottom lip, mulling over Max's words. The image of Candy as a manipulative puppet master was difficult to reconcile with the girl he had grown up with. He knew his brother was trying to protect him, but the idea that Candy, his best friend since high school, would intentionally manipulate him and hurt Destiny didn't sit right. Miles chose to trust his own instincts, pushing Max's cautionary tale to the back of his mind.

"Max, I really appreciate your concern," Miles said, sincerity shining in his green eyes. "But I've known Candy for a long time. She's my best friend, and I believe she has my best interests at heart."

Max sighed, his expression a mixture of frustration and resignation. "Alright, it's your life, Miles. Just don't say I didn't warn you if things get out of hand."

"Fair enough," Miles replied, offering his brother a small smile. "Now, if you'll excuse me, I am starving. I'm going to grab lunch. "

"Sure thing, little brother," Max said, leaning back in his chair and returning to his computer screen chuckling. "You're starting to sound like Malcolm. Enjoy."

Miles left Max's office, his thoughts a tangled mess as he walked through the pristine halls of Vortex. The scent of fresh coffee floated through the air as employees hurried past, their fingers tapping away at smartphones and tablets.

Entering the elevator, Miles pressed the button for the ground floor, the doors sliding shut with a soft whoosh. As the elevator descended, Miles let out a deep breath and forced himself to focus on the task at hand: getting lunch. He needed a moment to clear his head and sort through the conflicting emotions swirling within him.

Later that afternoon, Miles found himself standing in front of Peaches, the familiar scent of freshly brewed coffee and warm pastries filled his nostrils. He pushed the door open, the bell above chiming a cheerful welcome. The cafe bustled with activity as patrons chatted animatedly and sipped their drinks. For a brief moment, all thoughts of Candy and her tearful confession vanished from his mind.

"Hey there, handsome," Destiny greeted him warmly from behind the counter, her hazel eyes sparkling. She wore a simple black apron over her blue dress, her long brown hair pulled back into a loose ponytail. Miles couldn't help but smile, reaching across the counter to brush a quick kiss on her cheek.

"Hey yourself," he replied, his heart swelling with affection. "One grilled chicken panini, please."

"Coming right up," Destiny said, while sending his order back to the kitchen. "So, what brings you here today? Besides the obvious craving for my amazing paninis, of course." She teased, throwing him a wink.

Miles hesitated, unsure of how to broach the subject of Candy's visit that morning. "Well..." he began, frowning slightly. "Candy came into my office today, quite upset."

"Really?" Destiny's expression turned serious, her brow furrowing with concern. "Yeah, she wasn't exactly the friendliest person to be around last night."

"Is that so?" Miles asked, taken aback. "That's not what I heard." He paused, considering whether he should probe further. Deciding against it, he shook his head and forced a smile. "Never mind, I probably misunderstood. Anyway, how's your day going?"

Destiny seemed relieved by the change in topic and launched into a detailed account of her latest culinary experiments. They chatted amicably as Miles waited for his sandwich to be prepared.

"Time flies when you're having fun," Miles sighed, checking his watch, as his name was called. "I should get back to work, and you clearly have your hands full here."

"True," Destiny agreed with a small chuckle. "You know where to find me if you need another panini fix."

"Always," Miles grinned, sliding off the stool. "See you later, Destiny."

"Bye, Miles!" She called after him, her voice warm and inviting.

As he walked to the door, something nagged at him. He realized suddenly that he was going to his mother's house for their monthly dinner. At that moment, he knew exactly what he had to do. He turns to ask Destiny a question that will change their relationship into something much deeper.

* * *

Destiny watched as Miles turned to leave, his broad shoulders cutting a confident silhouette against the bright sunlight streaming through the café windows. His affectionate kiss on her cheek still lingered, warming her skin and causing her heart to beat just a little bit faster. She couldn't help but smile at the thought of how amazing he was—not only a successful entrepreneur, but also a genuinely kind and caring person.

Just as she was about to turn back to her work, she heard him call out her name, halting in his tracks. Her eyebrows furrowed in confusion as he strode back towards her, an unreadable expression on his face.

"Hey," he said, hesitating for a moment. "I...uh, I wanted to ask you something."

"Sure, what's up?" Destiny asked, her hazel eyes meeting his green ones with curiosity. She absently brushed a strand of brown hair behind her ear, waiting for him to continue.

Miles shifted his weight from one foot to the other, he shuffled his feet, fidgeting with unease. Destiny couldn't fathom what could make the usually composed Miles Huntington so anxious?

"I know this might seem sudden, but would you be interested in coming over for dinner with my family sometime? I'd really like for you to get to know them better."

Destiny felt her pulse quicken at the invitation, a mixture of excitement and anxiety swirling within her. Attending a Huntington family dinner was a significant step forward in their relationship, and though the prospect was daunting, she knew it was important to both of them.

"Of course," she finally replied, offering him a tentative smile. "I'd love to come to dinner. Just let me know when."

"Great!" Miles grinned, visibly relieved by her acceptance. "I'll give you the details later."

With a final wave, he left the café, leaving Destiny with her thoughts and a flurry of butterflies in her stomach. Destiny's heart pounded in her chest as she rushed through the bustling kitchen, the savory scent of freshly cooked food filled the air. Her eyes darted around, searching for Lila amidst the controlled chaos of clanging pots and sizzling pans. She spotted her best friend by the stainless steel counter, expertly assembling a delicious-looking sandwich with quick, efficient movements.

"Lila!" Destiny called out, skidding to a stop by her side. "I need to talk to you."

"Sure thing, Des," Lila replied, plating the sandwich and wiping her hands on her apron. "What's up?"

"Remember how we talked about Miles inviting me to his family dinner one day?" Destiny asked, her hazel eyes wide with anxiety. "Well, that day is today because he just asked me! I'm so nervous! What if I make a terrible impression? What if his mother hates me?"

"Hey, hey, take a deep breath," Lila said soothingly, her eyes filled with concern. "You're going to do great. Trust me."

"Thanks, Lila, but I need some extra support tonight," Destiny admitted, wringing her hands together.

"Say no more." Lila whipped out her phone and quickly tapped out a group text to Vivi. "Girls' night at your place tonight. We'll help you prepare for this big dinner, okay?"

"Really? You'd do that for me?" Destiny asked, touched by Lila's support.

"Of course!" Lila grinned. "That's what friends are for."

A quick buzz from Lila's phone signaled Vivi's response. "She's in!" Lila announced triumphantly, clutching Destiny's arm reassuringly. "Don't worry, Des. We've got your back. Tonight's all about making sure you're ready to knock 'em dead at that dinner."

"Thank you, Lila," Destiny breathed, feeling some of the tension in her chest begin to ease. "I don't know what I'd do without you and Vivi."

"Probably show up to the Huntington family dinner wearing a clown suit and juggling pies," Lila quipped, earning a chuckle from Destiny.

"Okay, okay," Destiny said, rolling her eyes with a smile. "Let's get back to work before our customers start wondering where their food went."

* * *

"Hey, guys!" Vivi called out, shrugging off her coat and waving to Lila, who was busy tallying up the day's sales at the register. "I made it! Did I miss any of the fun?"

"Perfect timing, actually," Lila replied, grinning as she closed the register drawer. "We just finished up for the night."

"Great!" Vivi beamed, her sapphire eyes sparkling with excitement, while she chanted, "Girls night! Girls night!"

Destiny led the way up the narrow staircase to her apartment above the cafe. As they entered the cozy space, the trio slipped off their shoes and hung their coats, the familiar scents of home enveloping them like a comforting embrace.

"Alright, let me grab the cocktail and dinner ingredients, and we can start cooking!" Destiny announced, heading to the fridge. The shelves were stocked with an array of colorful produce, fragrant herbs, and succulent meats—a testament to her love for all things culinary.

"Ooh, what are we making tonight?" Vivi asked, peering over Destiny's shoulder with curiosity.

"Grilled lemon-herb chicken, garlic-parmesan roasted potatoes, and a fresh mixed greens salad for dinner," Destiny replied, her hazel eyes brightening as she described the menu. "And for cocktails, Lila's going to make her famous strawberry-basil mojitos."

"Yum," Vivi sighed in anticipation, rubbing her hands together eagerly. "I can't wait!"

As they set to work in the small but well-appointed kitchen, Destiny and Vivi teamed up to prepare the chicken and potatoes, while Lila assembled a tray of glistening strawberries, fragrant basil leaves, and frosty glasses. The sounds of laughter and friendly banter filled the room as they cooked, "Hey, Lila," Destiny called out over the sizzle of chicken hitting the grill pan. "How's the cocktail-making going?"

"Almost done," Lila replied, her nimble fingers tearing basil leaves and muddling them with strawberries in a glass. She grinned as she added the rum and a squeeze of fresh lime juice. "Just need to add some soda water and give it a good stir."

"Can't wait to try one!" Vivi chimed in, tossing the golden-brown roasted potatoes in a bowl with a generous sprinkle of garlic and parmesan.

"Here you go, ladies," Lila announced triumphantly, presenting each of them with a tall, ice-filled glass brimming with the vivid red cocktail. "To friendship, delicious food, and kicking ass at the Huntington family dinner!"

"Cheers!" Destiny and Vivi echoed, clinking their glasses together before taking a refreshing sip of the fruity concoction.

"Destiny," Lila began, her voice curious but gentle as she poured the frothy pink liquid into chilled glasses, "Tell Viv what's going on with you and Miles."

Destiny hesitated for a moment, her eyes flicking to the chicken before meeting Vivienne's gaze. "He invited me to a family dinner at Caroline's house," she admitted, feeling a hint of trepidation mingling with her excitement. "Miles wants me to spend more time with his family."

"Caroline, huh?" Vivi chimed in, her eyes narrowing slightly. "She's a tough woman to impress, Destiny. And she can be quite...catty." She paused, choosing her words carefully. "You can't let her get her claws into you. You need to be stronger than her."

Destiny considered Vivi's advice, her hazel eyes thoughtful. As she mulled it over, she heard Lila's voice cut through her reverie.

"Look, if this dinner is so important that Miles is inviting you, he must be in love with you," Lila declared confidently, her eyes sparkling with conviction.

"Destiny," she continued, her tone softening, "Do you love him?"

A blush crept up Destiny's cheeks as she pondered the question, her heart swelled with affection when she thought of Miles. "Yes," she admitted, her voice barely above a whisper.

The apartment erupted into giggles and excited chatter as the girls clinked their glasses together, toasting to love, friendship, and facing the future with courage. The table was laden with mouth-watering dishes that reflected their camaraderie—from the perfectly cooked chicken and vibrant salad to the decadent chocolate lava cake waiting for them on the counter.

They spent the evening in fits of drunken laughter, pretending that Lila was Caroline and helping Destiny prepare for any schemes the troublesome woman could come up with.

eighteen

MILES SAT AT HIS POLISHED MAHOGANY DESK AT VORTEX, his fingers tapped nervously on the desktop as he thought about the upcoming Huntington family dinner. He knew it was time to call his mother, Caroline, and inform her of his plus one—Destiny. Gathering up his courage, Miles took a deep breath and dialed his mother's number.

The phone rang for what felt like an eternity before Caroline finally answered, her voice dripping with false sweetness. "Miles, darling, to what do I owe this rare pleasure? You never call your poor mother."

"Hi Mom," Miles said, trying to keep his tone light. "I'm calling because there's going to be an extra guest at our family dinner. I've invited someone, so we'll need another place setting."

"Ah, for Candy, I hope?" Caroline asked, her voice hopeful.

"No, not for Candy. For Destiny," Miles replied firmly.

"Destiny?" Caroline scoffed. "Miles, really? She's just a cafe manager. What could she possibly bring to our family? Candy is truly remarkable. She hails from a respectable family and even volunteered to be your assistant to help your company when others wouldn't."

"Mom, Destiny is kind, strong, and genuinely cares about people. She's everything I want in a partner. I love her, and I want her to be part of our family," Miles said, his voice filled with conviction.

"I will never approve of this...person entering our family," Caroline continued, using all the ammunition she had left.

"Times have changed, Mom. Besides, it's my life. Destiny is important to me, and I'd appreciate it if you could find it in your heart to accept her," Miles insisted, his jaw clenched in determination.

"Fine," Caroline snapped, clearly defeated. "I'll set an extra place for her. But don't expect me to roll out the red carpet." With that, she hung up, leaving Miles staring at his phone in frustration.

Miles groaned, throwing his phone onto his desk and letting his face fall into his hands. The sunlight streaming through the window made the screen flicker, reflecting his tumultuous emotions. He rubbed his temples, trying to ease the tension before it turned into a full-blown headache.

"Ahem," someone cleared their throat, and Miles looked up to see Max and Malcolm standing in the doorway. Max was trying to suppress a smile, while Malcolm sported his usual shit-eating grin. Miles couldn't help but feel exposed, as if they had been eavesdropping on his conversation with Caroline.

"Alright, you two, what's so funny?" he asked, forcing a smile onto his face despite his lingering irritation.

"Nothing," Max said, attempting to stifle a chuckle. "It's just that... you must really like Destiny to put up with Mom like that."

"Like her?" Malcolm scoffed, rolling his eyes dramatically. "Come on, Max. Miles *looooves* her." He drew out the word, teasingly mimicking a love-struck teenager. Miles couldn't help but laugh at his younger brother's antics.

"Okay, okay, I admit it," he conceded, feeling a warmth spread across his chest as he thought about Destiny. "I do love her. She means a lot to me, and I want her to be part of our family."

"Whoa, big brother," Malcolm said, raising his eyebrows in exaggerated surprise. "You must be head over heels if you're willing to go toe-to-toe with the ever lovely Caroline for her." Malcolm batted his eyelashes and a lifted shoulder.

"Malcolm!" Max scolded, though he couldn't hide the amusement in his eyes.

"Hey, I'm just calling it like I see it," Malcolm defended himself, grinning unapologetically.

Miles shook his head, a genuine smile tugging at the corners of his mouth. "You two are incorrigible," he said, his heart feeling lighter as he enjoyed the back and forth with his brothers.

"Alright, you clowns, let's get to work," Miles said, sitting up in his chair and gesturing for his brothers to sit. "We've got a company to run, and I've got a wonderful woman to impress."

"Lead the way, Romeo," Malcolm teased, giving Miles a playful shove as they all took their seats.

Before any more could be said, the office door swung open, revealing Candy in all her designer glory. Her eyes flicked from one brother to another, taking in their expressions and landing on Miles' flushed cheeks.

"Am I interrupting something?" she asked innocently, though the predatory gleam in her eyes suggested otherwise.

"Destiny is joining us for family dinner," Miles explained hurriedly, hoping to diffuse any potential tension. "We were just discussing the arrangements."

Candy's eyes narrowed ever so slightly, but she quickly composed herself. "Oh, how wonderful! The more, the merrier, right?"

Miles felt a sudden sense of unease at her overenthusiastic response, but he tried to focus on what was important —Destiny's happiness. He gave Candy a tight-lipped smile, silently urging her to drop the subject.

To his surprise, Candy didn't relent. Instead, she continued, "I heard that Vivienne went to Destiny's place last night for a girls' night. Sounds like fun."

"Vivi mentioned it," Miles replied cautiously, unsure of where this was going. "Why do you ask?"

Candy's lips curled into a bitter smile. "Well, I wasn't invited. Again. I thought you were going to talk to Destiny about that."

"I did," Miles said defensively. "But maybe they just wanted a small gathering. It's not a big deal, Candy."

"Clearly, she didn't get the message that I'm going to be in your life," Candy snapped, her usually composed façade cracking. "So you'd better make sure she understands that, Miles."

A surge of defensiveness washed over Miles as he clenched his jaw. He shot a quick glance at Max and Malcolm, searching for guidance. Malcolm wore his usual smirk while Max maintained his serious demeanor.

Inhaling deeply, Miles looked up at the sky before speaking. "I'll talk to her again, but I'm sure it was just a misunderstanding." Candy crossed her arms and leveled him with a hard stare. "Why don't you come to family dinner? You two can spend more time together."

Candy studied him for a moment, her eyes flicking

between determination and frustration. With a pout on her face, she expressed, "I guess. I want to be part of your life too, Miles. I don't think I am asking too much." With those parting words, Candy turned on her heel and curtly left the room.

Miles stared at the door Candy had just exited through, his eyebrows still raised in surprise. He couldn't believe she'd just insinuated that she and Destiny are on the same level as each other. The audacity of it all left him momentarily speechless.

"Uh," he finally managed to say, turning back to face his brothers who were still lingering in the doorway with matching expressions of disbelief. "Well, that was... something."

"Something is right," Max agreed, shaking his head slowly. "You really want Candy to be at family dinner? With Destiny there?"

Miles hesitated for a moment before nodding. "Yeah. I think if they spend some time together, maybe they'll find some common ground. Or at least learn to tolerate each other for my sake. Plus, mother wants Candy there so maybe she can be a distraction."

"Are you sure that's a good idea, bro?" Malcolm chimed in, scratching his chin skeptically. "You know how those two are together. They're like oil and water. It's bound to end in disaster."

"Or fireworks," Max added with a chuckle.

"Look, I know it's not ideal," Miles admitted, running a hand through his hair in frustration. "But I'm in love with Destiny, and Candy is... well, she's important to me too. I can't just keep having them at odds with each other. Maybe this will solve everything."

Max exchanged a glance with Malcolm, who shrugged noncommittally. "If you say so, man," Malcolm said, his tone cautious but supportive. "We'll be there to back you up if things go south."

"Thanks," Miles said gratefully. "Now let's get to our daily meeting before we're late."

As they walked down the hall toward the conference room, Miles couldn't shake the nagging feeling that he might be making a huge mistake. But what choice did he have? Something had to give in this ongoing battle between Destiny and Candy, and maybe—just maybe—a family dinner was the answer.

"Oil and water," Max muttered under his breath as they entered the meeting room, and despite his apprehension, Miles couldn't help but share a small, nervous laugh with his brothers.

* * *

Destiny's breath fogged up in front of her as she carefully counted the stacks of vegetables in the walk-in fridge. The cool air nipped at her cheeks, making her nose turn a shade of pink that matched her scarf. Lost in her thoughts as she jotted down numbers on her clipboard, she didn't even notice her phone vibrating with an incoming message.

"Whoa, whoa!" Destiny exclaimed, startled and laughing as Lila burst into the fridge, nearly slipping on the icy floor. Her eyes were wide with urgency.

"Did you read the message?" Lila panted, trying to catch her breath.

"Message? No, I was just doing inventory," Destiny said, glancing at her phone lying on a nearby shelf. She could see the notification blinking, but hadn't had the chance to check it yet.

"Read it now," Lila urged, her hands on her hips. "It's important."

Destiny's fingers trembled as she unlocked her phone, the screen lighting up with the new message from Vivi. She read quickly, her breath hitching as the words sank in.

VIVI - 10:45 A.M.

You won't believe what I just overheard.

VIVI - 10:45 A.M.

The guys were in their office and Candy went in and started spewing some nonsense about not being invited to girls' night last night. Anyway Miles INVITED HER TO FAMILY DINNER.

Destiny's head snapped up, her hazel eyes meeting Lila's electric blue gaze. "He wouldn't," she whispered, the hurt evident in her voice.

"Apparently, he already did," Lila replied, her tone a mix of anger and disbelief. "You need to call him, Destiny. Get this shit sorted out now."

Taking a deep breath, Destiny nodded, her fingers flew across her phone screen as she dialed Miles' number. As much as she wanted to trust him, the thought of sharing a table with Candy sent shivers down her spine.

"Call him, and let's get to the bottom of this," Lila urged, her hand resting on Destiny's shoulder for support.

As they waited for Miles to pick up, Destiny couldn't help but replay the message in her head, the words echoing like a bad dream. She had always known that Candy was a problem, but never imagined it would come to this. The mere thought of having to be civil with her at a family dinner made her stomach churn.

"Hopefully, it's just a misunderstanding," Destiny murmured, trying to hold onto a shred of hope. But as Lila gave her a sympathetic look, she knew deep down that things were about to get even more complicated.

"Hi, sweetheart," Miles answered the phone with a warm tone that never failed to make Destiny's heart skip a beat.

"Hey, I heard you invited Candy to dinner?" Destiny blurted out, feeling her cheeks grow hot as she did so.

Miles hesitated for a moment. "How'd you find that out?"

"So, it's true then?" she replied, trying to keep her voice steady. "Vivi told me."

"Maybe Candy was right about being left out of the loop," he mumbled, making Destiny's heart race faster. "I just want you two to be friends, since you're both important to me."

"Wait, what?" Destiny's voice cracked as she tried to process this new information. "I don't even know if I can handle being in the same room with her, let alone be friends with her."

"Could you try? Just for me?" Miles asked earnestly, his voice filled with hope.

Destiny sighed, knowing she couldn't refuse him. "Fine, I'll try. But I won't tolerate her being catty."

"Thank you," Miles said gratefully.

Destiny had heard enough. "I think it's time we hang up."

Miles takes a deep breath saying, "Please, don't be upset."

Destiny took a moment to think before she replied, "Miles, I'll be nice for you, but you can't expect me to be happy about it. We'll talk later. Bye." Destiny hung up the phone leaning heavily against one of the shelves in the walk-in.

Lila raised an eyebrow. "Well, how'd it go?"

"Apparently, I'm going to try to be friends with Candy," Destiny admitted, a hint of bitterness laced her words. "Because she's important to Miles, and he's important to me."

"Are you sure about this?" Lila asked, concern etched on her face.

"Positive," Destiny replied, offering a small smile. "If it means making things easier for him, then I'll do it."

"Alright," Lila agreed, not entirely convinced but respecting Destiny's decision. "If you're sure. Just remember, I've always got your back."

"Thanks, Lila," Destiny said, touched by her friend's unwavering support.

As Lila left the walk-in, Destiny took a deep breath and tried to refocus on her task of inventorying the fridge. She couldn't help but feel a strange mix of anxiety and determination as she pondered what lay ahead for her. If trying to befriend Candy was what it took to maintain a good relationship with Miles, then she would give it her best shot —no matter how difficult it seemed.

nineteen

THE EVENING SUN WAS JUST STARTING TO SHOW AS DESTINY got ready for the night. She was so nervous thinking about the evening ahead that she felt like throwing up. The dinner was something that the Huntington's did often and not many people were ever invited. Destiny was honored that he even thought of her as part of his family, but was still terrified at the possibility of Candy pulling some stupid bullshit and ruining the night.

"Deep breaths, girl," Lila encouraged as she helped Destiny choose an outfit for the family dinner. "You've got this."

Destiny studied her reflection in the full-length mirror, smoothing the fabric of the romantic, blush pink dress that hugged her curves just right. The semi-formal attire was elegant yet understated, accentuating the soft waves cascading down her shoulders.

"Your hair looks perfect, Des," Lila said, stepping back to admire her handiwork. She had styled Destiny's chestnut locks into a half-updo, leaving a few strands to frame her face delicately.

"Thanks, Lila. I would have been a mess without you." Destiny smiled, her hazel eyes sparkled with gratitude. She then turned her attention to her makeup, applying a light touch of mascara and a swipe of nude lipstick to complete the look.

"Anytime, Destiny. You're going to knock 'em dead tonight!" Lila grinned, giving her friend a reassuring hug before heading towards the door. "Good luck!"

"Thanks, I'll need it," Destiny murmured as she watched Lila leave.

She took a moment to collect herself, looking one last time at her reflection. With a deep breath, she set her determination, ready to face the Huntington family once more.

Destiny was sliding on her white, strappy pumps, a perfect complement to her blush pink dress, when the doorbell rang. With one last deep breath, she opened the door, revealing Miles with an expectant smile on his face.

"Holy shit, you look absolutely stunning," he complimented, his green eyes sparkling with admiration as he grabbed her hand and twirled her around.

"Thank you," Destiny replied, blushing slightly. "Are you ready to go?"

"Absolutely," Miles responded, extending his arm for her to take. They stepped out of her apartment together.

As they drove towards Caroline's mansion, their conversation remained light and easy, a welcome distraction from Destiny's growing anxiety. She found herself laughing at Miles' quips and chiming in with her own, feeling the comforting familiarity between them.

However, her laughter ceased as they approached a massive, ornate gate that seemed to separate the world of the wealthy from the ordinary lives of commoners. The intricate ironwork formed an impenetrable barrier, leaving no doubt as to the exclusivity of what lay beyond.

Still as imposing as ever, Destiny thought to herself, recalling the intimidating presence of the Huntington estate from years before. She noticed the guard box stationed beside the entrance and watched as Miles pressed a button, greeting the guard and reciting a code. With a faint groan, the heavy gate began to swing open, exposing the grandeur of the mansion beyond.

As they drove up the stone driveway, Destiny couldn't help but feel overwhelmed by the sheer size of the house looming above her. It was as if the building itself was a testament to the power and influence of the Huntington family—a force to be reckoned with.

They walked up to the door hand in hand. Destiny took a deep breath, trying to steady her nerves as Miles pressed the doorbell. The sound echoed through the grand entrance, announcing their arrival. The heavy wooden doors swung open to reveal Caroline Huntington, her blue eyes narrowed and lips pursed in disapproval.

"Ah, Miles," she said with forced enthusiasm, her voice dripping with insincerity. "It's been far too long."

"Hello, Mother," Miles replied, his tone polite but distant. He stepped forward, giving her a kiss on the cheek, but Caroline barely made an effort to reciprocate. Her gaze then landed on Destiny, and her expression soured further.

"Destiny," she huffed, her voice filled with disdain as she turned her back on her without offering a greeting.

"Mrs. Huntington," Destiny responded, forcing a tight smile onto her face.

"Please, come in," Caroline said to Miles, pointedly ignoring Destiny's presence.

Miles held the door open for Destiny, who hesitated

briefly before stepping over the threshold and entering the opulent foyer. The first thing that struck her was its sheer ugliness—the ostentatious chandelier that hung from the ceiling, the garish gold accents, and the tacky marble flooring all screamed of wealth without taste.

"May I take your coat, miss?" a butler asked, appearing by her side.

"Thank you," Destiny replied, handing him her coat and watching as he disappeared down a hallway.

"Is there anything else I can do for you, Miss Evans?" another butler inquired, materializing beside her.

"Um, no thank you. I'm fine," she said, feeling slightly unnerved by the overly attentive staff.

As they stood in the front room, Destiny could hear the faint murmur of conversation coming from the nearby living room, intermingled with the sound of laughter and clinking glasses. She glanced at Miles, hoping to find comfort in his familiar presence, but he seemed lost in thought, his gaze distant. When she was about to ask him what he was thinking about, he took her hand and pulled her towards the noise.

Entering the formal living room, Destiny's gaze swept over the plush velvet couches, lit by a warm glow from an elaborate chandelier overhead. She felt her heart lift when she spotted Vivienne, Max, and Malcolm gathered around a coffee table laden with intricate crystal glasses and polished silverware. Candy was standing over by the makeshift bar in the corner of the room.

"Destiny!" Vivienne exclaimed, her chestnut hair framing her face, showcasing the beautiful auburn streaks running through it. As they embraced, Destiny felt a wave of gratitude for her friend's presence. At least she wasn't completely alone. Vivi would be there to deal with Caroline and Candy's antics with her.

"Hey Vivi," Destiny said warmly, before turning to greet Miles' brothers. "Max, Malcolm, good to see you both."

"Good to see you too, Destiny," Max replied, his green eyes sincere as he offered her a genuine smile. Malcolm nodded in agreement, his own grin slightly mischievous.

"Hey, Candy," Miles said, drawing her attention. She looked over to find him giving Candy a big hug. Destiny fought the urge to roll her eyes. While Miles greeted his brothers, she turned to Candy, who was now reluctantly detaching herself from Miles.

"Hi, Candy," Destiny said, attempting to keep any hint of animosity out of her voice. In response, Candy just huffed and rolled her eyes before making a beeline back to Miles.

"Would you like a drink, Miles?" Candy asked sweetly, batting her long lashes at him.

"Sure," Miles replied, seemingly oblivious to her flirtation. "I'll have a scotch on the rocks."

"Great choice," Candy cooed, glancing at Destiny with disdain. Destiny opened her mouth to request her own drink, but Candy deliberately ignored her, turning her back to face the bar.

"Actually, Candy," Vivienne interjected, her tone cool but polite, "I'm sure Destiny would like a drink as well."

Candy glared at Vivienne and then at Destiny, her icy blue eyes narrowing in annoyance. "Fine," she muttered under her breath, filling two glasses with an exaggerated flourish.

Just as Destiny was starting to feel the weight of Candy's cold shoulder, the butler appeared in the doorway. "Dinner is served," he announced, his voice formal and measured.

Destiny felt a sudden flutter of nerves in her stomach.

She exchanged a glance with Vivienne, who gave her an encouraging smile. Together, they followed the others out of the living room, walking towards the grand dining room. Two additional butlers held open the massive double doors, revealing a sumptuous space adorned with chandeliers, intricate crown moldings, and rich mahogany furniture. The opulence of the room took Destiny's breath away momentarily.

As they approached the table, she couldn't help but notice Miles laughing with Candy, who had slipped her arm through his. The sight stung, and she forced herself to focus on the extravagant place settings instead.

"Please, everyone, take your seats," Caroline instructed imperiously from the head of the table. Destiny spotted the name cards indicating their assigned places—Candy was next to Miles, while she was to sit across from them. Her heart sank, but she refused to let it show.

However, once they settled in their chairs, Miles glanced at the arrangement and frowned. "Candy," he said firmly, "would you mind switching seats with Destiny?"

Candy's eyes widened in surprise and annoyance, and Caroline's lips thinned into a disapproving line. But to Destiny's relief, Candy complied, albeit with a dramatic sigh.

"Of course, Miles" she replied before rising from her seat and exchanging places with Destiny.

As they switched, Destiny caught the warmth in Miles' eyes, his silent communication of support. It bolstered her spirits, and she allowed herself a small, grateful smile in response.

"Thank you," she murmured when they were seated, keeping her voice low enough that only he could hear.

"Of course," he replied, his hand briefly brushing hers under the table.

The rest of the dinner guests seemed to take no notice of the exchange, too preoccupied with their own conversations and the exquisite meal before them. But for Destiny, that one small gesture was enough to keep her afloat in the sea of tension and hostility surrounding her.

The first course arrived, a delicate arrangement of seafood and vegetables arranged with the precision of a work of art. Destiny looked down at her plate, unimpressed by the ostentatious display of opulence. The scallops were seared to a golden hue, but the smell was off-putting, a hint of decay masked by an overbearing citrus glaze. She picked up her fork and poked at the asparagus —too limp for her liking.

"Destiny," Caroline's voice cut through the air, drawing all attention to her, "what do you do for a living?"

Destiny fought the urge to roll her eyes, knowing full well that Caroline was hoping to belittle her in front of everyone. Instead, she put on her most charming smile and replied, "I'm the head chef and manager at Peaches, the local café in town."

Caroline raised an eyebrow while Candy snorted, poorly attempting to stifle a giggle behind her hand. Destiny clenched her jaw, determined not to let their petty behavior get to her.

"Ah yes, I remember now," Caroline said, her tone dripping with condescension. "When you were a child, it was quite apparent that you were destined for a life of minimum wage work and no real future."

Destiny blinked, the shock etched on her face as Caroline's cruel words rang in her ears. She glanced at Miles, who stared at his mother with narrowed eyes.

"Mother," he gritted out, his voice tense with restrained anger.

Caroline feigned innocence, raising her perfectly

groomed eyebrows as if she hadn't just insulted Destiny to her face. "What, darling? I'm only stating the truth." Her overly-sweet coated words did little to hide the venom.

Candy's laughter rang out across the table, high and shrill like nails on a chalkboard. The sound grated against Destiny's nerves, making her want to cringe away.

"Really, Candy?" Max interjected, a hint of disapproval in his voice. But his attempt at shutting down the laughter was futile, as it only spurred Candy on, her gaze locked onto Destiny with predatory glee.

Destiny clenched her hands under the table, her heart hammering in her chest. She fought the urge to lash out or storm off. Instead, she focused on her breathing, counting each inhale and exhale in an effort to regain her composure.

This is going to be such a long night, she thought to herself, steeling her nerves for the verbal battle she knew was to come.

As the evening wore on, the dining room buzzed with conversation and laughter, but Destiny couldn't shake the feeling that she was under siege. With each course that was served—delicate hors d'oeuvres, velvet-smooth soups, and succulent meats—Caroline's barbs seemed to grow sharper, her words more cutting.

"Isn't it simply divine?" Caroline gushed as she took a bite of the extravagant dessert placed before them. "Candy, dear, didn't you say one of your father's companies had a hand in catering an event for the mayor recently that you planned? Such success at such a young age."

"Indeed," Candy nodded, her eyes sparkling with pride. "We've come a long way since our humble beginnings. It's all about perseverance and ambition, isn't it?"

"Absolutely," Caroline agreed, casting a sideways glance at Destiny. "Those who aspire to greatness often achieve it. Some people, however, are content with mediocrity."

Destiny clenched her jaw, willing herself not to respond to the subtle jab. She could feel her resolve wearing thin, her armor chipping away with each thinly veiled insult. She glanced at Miles, silently pleading for him to notice what was happening and come to her defense. But his attention was focused elsewhere, engaged in a lively discussion with Max about Vortex's latest project.

"Isn't that right, Destiny?" Caroline continued, her voice dripping with false sweetness.

"Excuse me?" Destiny said, forcing a polite smile onto her face.

"Perseverance and ambition—they're important qualities, don't you think? Especially for those who want to rise above their circumstances." Caroline's eyes narrowed ever so slightly, emphasizing the challenge in her words.

"Of course," Destiny replied tightly, trying to maintain her composure. "But I also believe in being true to oneself and following one's passions. Not everyone measures success or happiness in the same way."

"Spoken like a true idealist," Caroline said dismissively, returning her attention to Candy. "Now, tell me more about that event you planned. I'm sure it was simply fabulous."

As the conversation flowed around her, Destiny's heart ached with disappointment. She had hoped that Miles would defend her, that he would see through his mother's manipulations and stand by her side. But as the night wore on, she realized that he was either completely oblivious or unwilling to intervene.

Stay strong, she told herself, swallowing the lump in her throat. *You can handle this. You've dealt with worse.*

But even as she tried to bolster her spirits, Destiny

couldn't help but feel the weight of the evening pressing down on her, suffocating her like the heavy perfume that filled the room. And she couldn't shake the nagging worry that perhaps Caroline was right—that maybe she wasn't good enough for Miles, that she would never be able to rise above the challenges life had thrown at her.

Chin up, she mentally chided herself, vowing not to let Caroline win. *This isn't over yet.*

As dessert plates were cleared, the tension in the room became almost palpable. Destiny was drained, she was ready to flee from this hostile environment. The last remnants of her patience evaporated when Caroline, with a self-satisfied smile, directed her next words at Miles.

"Darling, you know I only want what's best for you." She paused, her eyes narrowing as she looked at Destiny. "You deserve someone better than... her. Someone like Candy, who is successful and rich—everything that Destiny will never be capable of."

The whole room hushed to a quiet so profound that a pin drop would have sounded like thunder. Destiny's heart clenched painfully in her chest, and she couldn't help but glance at Miles, hoping for some semblance of support. But all she saw was his shocked expression, jaw hanging slack in disbelief.

Turning to Candy, Destiny searched for any sign of sympathy or regret. Instead, she saw Candy smirking, reveling in the drama she'd helped create. The realization that Candy was deliberately trying to tear them apart hit Destiny like a slap in the face. Tears threatened to spill from her hazel eyes, and she wanted nothing more than to escape this torturous dinner.

Destiny's gaze fell on Vivienne, who was seated nearby. The usual sparkle in her sapphire eyes was replaced with a look of despair. Destiny could see that her friend was struggling just as much as she was, trying to hold herself together in the face of Caroline's cruel tirade.

"Really, Destiny," Caroline sneered, her voice dripping with disdain, "you're nothing more than a low-life little girl living in poverty, just like your useless father was. I don't know why you ever bothered coming back."

The room seemed to close in around Destiny, the air growing heavy and suffocating. She'd reached her breaking point. The walls she had built to protect herself began to crumble, and a surge of anger rushed through her veins.

"Enough!" Destiny exclaimed, her voice shaking with emotion. She stood up abruptly, pushing her chair back so forcefully that it nearly toppled over. "I can't take this anymore!"

Her hazel eyes scanned the faces of those gathered around the table, each one wearing a different expression: pity, shock, disappointment. Miles looked stunned, as if he couldn't quite comprehend what was happening. It broke her heart to think that their relationship might be over before it had even truly begun and all because he couldn't stand up for her.

As Destiny turned away from the table, she felt the weight of her decision settling on her shoulders. She knew that walking away now might mean letting go of the love she shared with Miles, but staying meant subjecting herself to further humiliation and degradation at the hands of his family.

But before she could reach the end of the table, the harsh scrape of a chair against polished marble echoed through the room. Destiny froze, her breath hitching in her throat as she turned slowly to look at Miles. His green eyes blazed with determination, and his jaw was set in a firm line.

"Caroline, that is it!" He said with quiet intensity,

"Enough of your insulting and degrading behavior. Your immaturity and rudeness have crossed the line. If you can't speak to her with respect, then do not speak at all."

"Miles, dearest." Caroline spoke with a nauseatingly sweet tone. "This is my house; I can use whatever language I desire. Nevertheless, you could never be satisfied with somebody like her. She has such a fragile personality, just like Vivienne."

The room fell silent, the air thick with tension. Caroline's blue eyes narrowed, her lips pursed into a tight frown. "Miles, darling," she replied, her voice dripping with condescension, "How can you be happy with someone like her?"

Destiny's heart twisted painfully in her chest, but she forced herself to stand tall and face Caroline. She wanted to shout, to defend herself, but the words seemed stuck in her throat.

It was then that Miles' voice broke through her thoughts, filled with emotion. "Because I love her, Mother," he declared, the words tumbling out of him like a torrent. "I'm in love with Destiny, and I won't let you or anyone else tear us apart."

The world seemed to stop spinning for a moment as Destiny's stomach dropped to the floor and her heart leapt into her throat. She stared at Miles, her hazel eyes wide with shock, disbelief, and a flicker of hope.

Caroline's expression morphed into one of astonishment, her mouth opening and closing like a fish out of water. But Miles didn't wait for her response. He strode across the room, his hand outstretched towards Destiny.

"Come on," he said, his voice gentle yet firm as he grasped her hand, "we're leaving."

Miles led Destiny to the front door, his hand warm and reassuring in hers. As she reached for her coat, he took it from her hands and gently helped her put it on, his every movement full of care.

"Thanks," she mumbled, her cheeks flushed with a mix of embarrassment and gratitude.

"Of course," he replied, his green eyes locking onto hers. "You deserve nothing less."

Destiny's heart swelled at his words, but before they could share another moment, the sound of hurried footsteps echoed through the foyer. Turning to face the noise, Destiny's eyes narrowed as Candy approached them with purpose.

"Wait!" Candy called out, glaring at Destiny. "Miles, Caroline is just looking out for you. You know that, right?"

Destiny bristled, ready to defend herself and Miles' choice when he beat her to the punch. He looked Candy directly in the eye, his expression resolute.

"Caroline doesn't know me at all if she can't see that Destiny is perfect for me," he stated firmly, his grip on Destiny's hand tightening ever so slightly.

Candy's eyes widened momentarily, then narrowed again as she huffed and stormed back towards the dining room without another word. Destiny felt a mix of triumph and relief, knowing that Miles had stood up for their love.

"Ready?" he asked, squeezing her hand once more.

"More than ever," Destiny replied, her hazel eyes shining with determination.

The cold night air nipped at Destiny's cheeks as she and Miles made their way to his sleek black car parked on the driveway inside the gates of the Huntington mansion. Despite the chill, a warm tingle spread through her, knowing that Miles had chosen to stand by her side. The drive to his house felt like a never ending stretch of silence, as if Destiny had become a silent witness and was forcing them to apologize for Caroline's unacceptable behavior.

Every mile they drove was filled with the weight of their unsaid thoughts and emotions.

As they pulled into the driveway, Destiny took in the homey design of Miles' place, a stark contrast to the ostentatious mansion they'd just left behind. It felt more like a safe space, a place where they could be themselves without judgment. She couldn't help but feel a sense of relief wash over her.

Miles opened the door for her, and together they walked inside. The moment they crossed the threshold. Destiny's heart raced as she felt the electricity in the air—a palpable tension that crackled with unspoken words and unresolved issues. Her mind churned as she replayed every moment of the disastrous dinner, replaying every word and action from Miles and analyzing his reactions with a sense of confusion. She couldn't shake the feeling that something crucial was about to happen, and it gnawed at her insides to think about how their relationship was surely about to change forever.

Destiny stood there, her heart pounding in her chest as she took a few moments to collect herself. The silence between them was thick, heavy with unspoken emotions and thoughts that neither had dared to voice until now. She glanced at Miles, noticing the soft lighting casting shadows on his face, accentuating the intensity of his green eyes.

"Did you... really mean what you said back there?" Destiny asked, her voice barely above a whisper, as if speaking too loudly would shatter the fragile moment.

Miles frowned, tilting his head to the side slightly. "What do you mean?"

"About... loving me," she clarified, feeling the warmth rise to her cheeks. "Do you really love me, Miles?"

A smile tugged at the corners of his mouth, while he

rubbed the back of his neck. He let out a self-deprecating chuckle. "Yes, I do, Destiny. Although I must admit, I'd have preferred to tell you in a more romantic setting than my mother's dining room."

Destiny couldn't help but smile as well, momentarily imagining the scene where Miles would've confessed his love—perhaps under a sky full of stars or by the flickering light of candles. "Well, you can't always choose the perfect moment, right?" she said softly, her heart swelling with affection for him.

"True," Miles agreed, his smile growing warmer. "And I want you to know that I love you, Destiny Evans. With all my heart."

Her breath caught in her throat, and she felt tears prickling at the corners of her eyes. "I love you too, Miles Huntington. With all of my heart and soul." The words seemed to hang in the air, shimmering like fairy lights, and Destiny felt as if a thousand butterflies had taken flight inside her chest.

Miles' eyes sparkled with happiness as he closed the distance between them, wrapping his arms around her waist. Destiny felt herself being drawn towards him, their bodies meeting in an embrace that felt like coming home. As they stood there, she marveled at the warmth and strength of his arms—where she was safe and cherished.

"Promise me," Miles murmured against her hair, "that no matter what happens, we'll always fight for us."

"I promise," Destiny whispered back, her voice full of conviction. She knew that together they could face any challenge, overcome any obstacle life threw at them. They were stronger as a unit, bound together by their love and commitment to one another.

Their lips met in a tender kiss, full of unspoken emotions and promises. The passion between them grew, becoming more feverish as their hands roamed, seeking out the familiar curves and contours of each other's bodies. Miles lifted Destiny into his arms, and she willingly wrapped her legs around his waist, not wanting to be apart from him even for a second.

They moved towards the bedroom, their kisses becoming more urgent and needy as if trying to reassure each other of the depth of their love. Once inside, Miles kicked the door closed, and Destiny found herself gently laid down on the bed, with Miles hovering above her. She smiled up at him, feeling the amazing sensation of love expanding within her. They showed each other the love that was within their hearts well into twilight.

* * *

The sun streamed through the bedroom window as she stirred in her sleep. Her eyes fluttered open, and a contented smile spread across her face when she felt Miles' strong arms wrapped around her. She snuggled closer to him, reveling in the love and safety she found in his embrace.

"Good morning," Miles murmured, his voice husky from sleep. He gazed at her with a tender smile that reached his green eyes.

"Morning," Destiny replied, returning his smile. "We should probably get going soon. Work awaits."

"Unfortunately," he agreed, pressing a soft kiss to her forehead before reluctantly releasing her from his arms.

Destiny rose from the bed, feeling the cool air of the room brush against her skin. She spotted one of Miles' shirts draped over a chair and pulled it on, enjoying the warmth and scent that clung to it—a comforting reminder of him. With a quick glance back at Miles, who was beginning to dress himself, she headed to the kitchen to prepare breakfast.

"Anything you want in particular?" Destiny called out as she opened the fridge, scanning its contents for inspiration.

"Surprise me," Miles replied, his voice just audible from the bedroom.

Rummaging through the ingredients, Destiny decided on making a simple yet delicious omelet, filled with cheese, ham, and fresh herbs. As they sat down to eat, their conversation flowed effortlessly, punctuated by laughter and shared glances.

"Thank you for breakfast," Miles said, placing his fork down after finishing the last bite. "It was perfect, as always."

"Anytime," Destiny responded, feeling her cheeks flush from his compliment.

After clearing the table, they got ready to leave— Destiny still wearing last night's clothes, and Miles looking dapper in his suit. As they drove towards Destiny's apartment, the car was filled with comfortable silence, both of them lost in their own thoughts.

Upon arrival, Destiny stepped out of the car and spotted Lila waiting for her with a serious expression. "We'll talk about why you're doing the walk of shame later," Lila said, her eyes flicked pointedly to Destiny's attire. "Right now, go up and change. The owners are here needing to talk to you."

twenty

Miles felt the warmth of the sun on his face as he stepped out of his car, parked in front of Vortex headquarters. The morning light glittered off the glass windows of the tall building. Opening his eyes to see Destiny this morning was the most wonderful way for him to start his day.

Ah, what a beautiful day, he thought, taking a deep breath and letting the crisp air fill his lungs. His mind wandered to the previous night's events—the laughter, the intimacy, the promise of a future together with Destiny. A contented smile spread across his face.

As he entered the building and stepped onto the elevator, he couldn't help but whistle a happy tune, his heart overflowing with joy. It was as if Destiny had brought a newfound sense of purpose and happiness to his life that had been missing before. The elevator chimed, announcing its arrival to his floor, and Miles stepped out, still whistling merrily.

"Morning, Miles!" a coworker greeted him enthusiastically. "You seem to be in a great mood today!"

"Morning, and yes, I am, thanks! How are you?" he replied, giving a friendly nod. He was about to share the reason for his happiness when he caught sight of Candy standing near his office door. She looked distraught, her blue eyes filled with tears and her usually immaculate blonde hair slightly disheveled.

The sight of her in such a state brought Miles' whistling to an abrupt halt. He knew that whatever had happened must be serious for Candy, who thrived on control and perfection, to appear so vulnerable.

"What's wrong?" Miles asked Candy, his heart rate increasing as he saw the look of distress on her face. He could hardly believe that only moments ago, he was whistling with joy, thinking about Destiny and their blossoming relationship. But now, his attention was solely focused on the woman standing before him, clutching a tablet in her trembling hands.

"Y-yes," Candy stammered, tears welling up in her icy blue eyes. "There's been a massive data breach at Vortex. Client information has been stolen and posted online." Her voice cracked as she continued, "Most of the leaked data...it's my father's and mine."

"Let me see the tablet," he said, extending his hand.

Candy handed it over, her fingers brushing against his momentarily. As Miles scanned the screen, he took note of how vulnerable she seemed. It was as if all of her defenses had crumbled, leaving her raw and exposed.

"Alright," he said, taking a deep breath. "First things first, I need to call Max and get him on this. Then we're going to Malcolm's office—he'll know what to do."

Without waiting for a response, he pulled out his phone and quickly dialed Max's number. "Max, meet us in Malcolm's office immediately. We've got a major data breach on our hands."

"Got it," Max replied, his voice tense. "I'm on my way."

Upon reaching Malcolm's office, Miles pushed open the door to find his younger brother hunched over his computer, typing furiously. Dark bags hung under Malcolm's eyes, a testament to his dedication.

"Malcolm," Miles said, his voice serious. "I assume you're already aware of the breach."

The tech genius glanced up from his screen, his messy brown hair falling across his forehead. "Yeah, I've been working on it since I found out. It's bad, Miles. Real bad."

"Can we trace it?" Miles asked, trying to make sense of the chaos unfolding before him.

"Working on it," Malcolm replied, his fingers flying across the keyboard like lightning. "This bastard won't get away with it."

As they waited for Max to arrive, Miles leaned against the wall, a mix of anger and concern swirling within him. Destiny's number flashed on his phone screen as she tried to call him. Although he wanted nothing more than to hear her soothing voice, he knew that he needed to stay focused. He sent the call to voicemail and turned his attention back to Malcolm typing away.

Twenty minutes later, the sound of hurried footsteps echoed down the hallway outside Malcolm's office. The door burst open, revealing a disheveled Max, his brown hair sticking out in all directions as if he had just rolled out of bed.

"Malcolm, what have you got?" Max asked, panting slightly from his sprint to the office.

"Take a look at this," Malcolm said, gesturing to the computer screen. Miles joined them, his green eyes widening in shock as he took in the information displayed before him.

"Someone used one of our personal codes to gain access to the system," Malcolm explained solemnly, his voice heavy with the weight of the situation.

"Whose code was it?" Miles asked, his stomach twisting into knots as he braced himself for the answer.

Malcolm hesitated for a moment, the tension in the room growing palpable. Then, slowly, he turned to face Miles, his gaze filled with equal parts sympathy and disbelief. "It was your code, Miles." His words hung in the air like a dense fog, suffocating the room.

Miles felt as though the wind had been knocked out of him. How could this be? He had never shared his code with anyone.

"Is there any way someone could have hacked my code?" Miles asked, desperation lacing his voice.

"It's possible, but unlikely," Malcolm answered, his fingers resuming their rapid dance across the keyboard, filling the room with a thunderous clatter. "I'll keep digging. We'll get to the bottom of this."

Miles clenched his fists, determination burning in his chest. He had built Vortex from the ground up, pouring his heart and soul into this company. He would not let it be destroyed by some unknown saboteur—especially not when the people he cared about most were caught in the crossfire.

"Find them, Malcolm," Miles said firmly, his voice laced with anger. "No matter what it takes."

"Count on it," Malcolm replied, his eyes focused intently on the screen before him. "We'll figure this out."

A soft knock on the door drew everyone's attention away from Malcolm's computer screen. The door creaked open, and Candy appeared in the doorway, her eyes red-rimmed and brimming with tears.

"Have you found anything new?" she asked, her voice

shaky. "My father is so upset. He trusted Vortex to protect his information, and now it's all out there for anyone to see."

Miles' heart clenched at the sight of her distress. He had never seen Candy this inconsolable before, and it was a stark reminder of just how much was at stake. He stepped forward, placing a comforting hand on her arm.

"We're working on it, Candy," he assured her, trying to sound confident despite the turmoil churning inside him. "We'll find out who did this and make it right. I promise."

Candy sobbed, her shoulders shook as she buried her face in her hands. "Someone must really hate me to do this," she choked out between sobs. "To hurt me and my father like this... they're putting us in danger, and I'm terrified. I don't even want to go home, I'm scared something might happen there."

Miles hesitated for a moment, considering his options. It wasn't an ideal situation, but he couldn't bear the thought of Candy feeling unsafe. "You can stay with me for a bit if that would make you feel better," he offered gently.

At his words, Candy's tear-streaked face lifted, and her eyes brightened with gratitude. "Really, Miles? You'd do that for me?"

"Of course," he replied, giving her a reassuring smile. "I want to make sure everyone feels safe."

Candy threw her arms around him, hugging him tightly. "Thank you, Miles. I don't know what I'd do without you."

Max cleared his throat from behind them, breaking the emotional moment. "As touching as this is, we still have work to do. We need to find out who used Miles' code and figure out how to stop them before they cause any more damage."

Miles nodded, extricating himself from Candy's embrace. "Right," he said, his voice firm and resolute. "Let's get back to work and solve this mess."

As everyone returned to their tasks, Miles paused to catch his breath. He knew Destiny was expecting him to call, but he couldn't leave the chaos they were dealing with. She would surely understand—this company was his passion and he had to save it. Not only that, but there were also dedicated employees who relied on him and he needed to protect them.

* * *

Destiny hurriedly changed out of her evening attire. She needed to be in control and prepared for whatever the day held, so she quickly donned her usual work outfit. Taking a deep breath, she ran downstairs, her heart pounding with anticipation.

"Hey, Lila," Destiny greeted her best friend as she entered the café. "What's going on?"

"Destiny, the owners are in your office," Lila informed her, concern evident in her blue eyes. "I led them there when I noticed you weren't home."

"Thanks, Lila." Destiny nodded, appreciating her friend's support. She paused for a moment, taking another deep breath to steady herself. The uncertainty gnawed at her insides, but she knew she couldn't let it show.

As she walked quickly towards her office, a feeling of intense dread washed over her. What could the owners possibly want? Were they unhappy with her performance? Had something gone wrong with one of the catering events? Her mind raced through countless possibilities, each more distressing than the last.

"Okay, Destiny," she murmured to herself, trying to

quell her anxiety. "You can do this. You've faced worse before, and you'll face worse again. Just stay strong and keep it together."

Destiny took a deep breath, her heart pounding in her chest as she braced herself for the confrontation ahead. The moment she entered her office, she saw the two owners seated in chairs on the opposite side of her desk, each cradling a steaming cup of coffee between their hands. Their expressions were stern yet weary, clearly troubled by the information they had received.

"Hi Mr. Mitchell, Mrs. Mitchell," Destiny spoke up hesitantly, her voice wavering slightly. "How are you both doing?"

"Frankly, we've been better," one of the owners, David, replied, his brow furrowing with concern. "We received a message through the cafe's contact page that has us very worried."

"Someone claims that after a recent catering event, they were charged significantly more than what was initially agreed upon," Emma, the other owner added, her tone somber. "We looked into it and found that the amount in the register matched the original agreed-upon sum, but there's still $2,500 unaccounted for."

"Wait, what event are you talking about?" Destiny asked, her mind racing as she tried to piece together the situation.

"The veterans gala," David answered, watching Destiny closely for any sign of guilt or recognition.

Shock washed over Destiny's face, her hazel eyes widening in disbelief. "Do you think I stole that money?" she asked incredulously, feeling her heart twist painfully at the mere suggestion.

"We don't want to believe it," Emma said gently, "but

the evidence points to something amiss, and we need to get to the bottom of it."

"Please, let me call the person who runs the company," Destiny pleaded, her voice shaking with emotion. "There must be some mistake. I would never do anything like that."

"Go ahead and make the call," David agreed, his expression softening slightly. "We'll wait."

"Thank you," Destiny whispered, her hand trembling as she reached for her phone. She dialed Miles' number, praying he would pick up and help clear up the misunderstanding.

As the call went to voicemail, Destiny's heart sank with despair. How could she prove her innocence without Miles' help? Biting her lip, she fought back tears, determined to find a way to set things right.

Destiny stared at the floor, feeling as if the ground beneath her was crumbling away. Her heart raced, and she barely registered the owners conversing in hushed tones. She just wanted to disappear.

"We can't take a chance of this happening again," David finally spoke up, his voice firm but not unkind. Destiny glanced up, her hazel eyes shimmering with unshed tears. "Given the circumstances, we have no choice but to demote you to baker. You won't be handling money in that position."

The words struck Destiny like a slap across the face. A baker? After all her hard work and dedication, she was being relegated to a position far beneath her capabilities. But what could she do? With Miles unreachable and no other witnesses to vouch for her, she was cornered.

"Okay," she choked out, struggling to maintain her composure. The Mitchells exchanged sympathetic glances, clearly not enjoying the situation any more than she was.

One of them stepped forward and opened the office door, calling for Lila. Destiny's best friend entered the room, her eyes wide with concern. David addressed Lila, explaining the predicament and promoting her to manager in Destiny's stead.

"Congratulations, Lila," Emma said, trying to inject some enthusiasm into the announcement. "We trust you'll handle your new responsibilities well."

"Th-thank you," Lila stammered, her gaze never leaving Destiny's devastated expression. The weight of the moment hung heavy on everyone in the room.

"Destiny," David started, his voice gentler than before, "we promise to investigate this matter thoroughly. If it turns out there was a mistake or someone else is responsible, we'll make things right."

"Thank you," Destiny whispered, her voice barely audible. She watched as the Mitchells left the room, leaving her and Lila in a deafening silence. She got up and ran to her apartment with Lila hot on her heels.

Destiny's sobs echoed in the empty apartment as she slammed the door behind her, her legs gave out under the weight of her anguish. She crumpled onto her bed, burying her face in the softness of the duvet to stifle her cries.

"Desi, I'm here," Lila said breathlessly, having followed her best friend up the stairs. "We'll figure this out, together." Determination laced her voice as she sat down next to Destiny, rubbing soothing circles on her back.

"I can't be here, Lila," Destiny choked out between sobs. "I just... I need to get away from this place for a while."

"Stay at my place, then," Lila offered without hesitation. "As long as you need."

"Thank you," Destiny whispered, wiping her tear-streaked cheeks with the back of her hand. "You're the best friend I could ever ask for."

"Always, Des." Lila smiled sadly, squeezing Destiny's shoulder before rising to her feet. "I'll go downstairs and put the assistant manager in charge for now. You pack some things and we'll head to my place when you're ready."

"Okay," Destiny agreed, already feeling a tiny bit lighter knowing she wouldn't have to face the cafe and its accusing whispers for the time being.

While Lila headed back down, Destiny quickly gathered her necessities—clothes, toiletries, and a few treasured keepsakes—tossing them hastily into a duffel bag. Her movements were frantic, fueled by the desperate need to escape and find solace in Lila's comforting presence. As she zipped the bag closed, Destiny took one look around her small apartment, the space that had once been her haven now tainted by betrayal and heartache.

The sound of the front door creaking open pulled Destiny's attention from her tightly packed bag. Lila stood in the doorway, a determined expression set on her face. Without a word, she reached out and grabbed Destiny's hand, giving it a reassuring squeeze.

"Come on," Lila said softly, guiding Destiny through the back door of the cafe. Together, they climbed into Lila's car, the familiar scent of leather seats and lavender air freshener enveloping them. As the engine hummed to life, the weight of the day's events crashed down upon Destiny like a tidal wave, and she finally let the tears fall unchecked, her shoulders shaking with quiet sobs.

Lila reached over, placing a comforting hand on Destiny's knee. "It's all going to be alright, Des."

Destiny nodded, wiping fresh tears from her cheeks as they drove through the city streets, eventually pulling up to

Lila's apartment building. The two women got out of the car, Destinyslung her duffel bag over her shoulder, and followed Lila up the stairs to her apartment. The soft click of the lock disengaging filled the air as Lila opened the door and ushered Destiny inside.

Stepping into Lila's apartment was like walking into a puzzle master's paradise. Crime novels lined the pristine bookshelves, nestled among stacks of brain-teasing puzzles and logic games. The space was clean and organized, reflecting the sharp mind of its owner. The living room housed a cozy pull-out couch, which Destiny gratefully sank onto, her body feeling heavy with exhaustion.

"Welcome to my humble abode," Lila joked, bringing out a set of sheets for Destiny to use on the couch. "Make yourself at home."

"Thank you, Lila," Destiny murmured, her voice cracking slightly. They began unpacking her duffel bag, the silence between them filled with unspoken worry and determination.

"Any ideas on what we should do next?" Lila asked as they neatly folded Destiny's clothes.

"Until I can talk to Miles and clear this up, I think I'll just… bake," Destiny admitted, her eyes welling up with fresh tears. "It's the only thing that makes sense right now."

"Sounds like a plan," Lila agreed, her electric blue eyes flashing with steely resolve. "And while you're baking, I'll do some digging. Maybe Thad can help, too! Let me reach out and ask him. We'll find out who did this, Des. We won't let them get away with it."

A small smile tugged at the corners of Destiny's lips. It was in moments like these that she truly understood the depth of Lila's loyalty and friendship. She knew, without a doubt, that together they would weather this storm and come out stronger on the other side.

twenty-one

Miles' eyes burned with exhaustion, the fluorescent lights of Vortex's office casting an unforgiving glare on his face. He rubbed his temples, trying to stave off the headache that threatened to consume him. Every day for the last week, he and his brothers had been coming in early and staying late, desperately trying to figure out how the breach happened.

"Can this get any worse?" Miles muttered, as he scanned through the latest information that had been released. At first, it seemed like Candy and her father Colter were the main targets, but now there was an even more troubling development.

"Looks like someone really hates Candy," Max remarked, leaning over his shoulder to look at the screen. "Never thought I'd say this, but I almost feel sorry for her."

"Almost," Malcolm chimed in, amusement tugged at the corners of his mouth despite the severity of their situation.

"Guys, we need to focus," Miles said, shaking his head. "We have to find out who's behind this and stop them.

Candy and Colter trusted us and we let them down. Now they're struggling."

"Right," Malcolm agreed, straightening up and returning to his computer. "At least we've managed to put a temporary halt to the information leak."

Miles glanced at his brothers, taking in their haggard appearances. Max's normally well-groomed brown hair was disheveled, and deep shadows lurked beneath Malcolm's usually bright green eyes. They were all running on empty, fueled only by determination and copious amounts of coffee.

"Great job on that, by the way, Malcolm," Miles said sincerely, clasping his younger brother's shoulder.

"Thanks, but it's just a band-aid solution," Malcolm replied, adjusting his glasses. "We need to find the root cause and fix it."

"Any ideas?" Max asked, looking between the two of them.

"None yet," Miles admitted, his brow furrowed with frustration. "But I have a feeling that whoever is behind this knows us... knows me very well."

"Let's not jump to conclusions," Max cautioned, ever the voice of reason. "We'll figure it out. We always do."

Miles nodded but couldn't shake the nagging suspicion that the answer was right in front of them, just out of reach. He knew they needed to work fast before more damage was done, and with every passing moment, he felt the weight of responsibility bearing down on him.

"Let's keep digging," he said, determination hardening his features. "We're not stopping until we find the person responsible for this mess."

And as Miles delved back into the digital labyrinth, he couldn't help but stop the nagging feeling that their enemy might be closer than they thought.

The fluorescent lights overhead cast a harsh glare on the trio of exhausted brothers. Miles, Max, and Malcolm each held a cup of coffee in their hands, taking alternating sips and grimaces between analyzing data and discussing strategy. The dark liquid was a far cry from the rich, velvety brew that Peaches usually served. This tasted like burnt rubber mixed with sludge, but it was the only thing keeping them awake at this point.

"Ugh, I can't believe we're drinking this swill," Malcolm muttered, making a face as he forced down another mouthful.

"Desperate times call for desperate measures," Max replied wryly, his eyes bloodshot from lack of sleep.

Miles nodded in agreement, his own eyelids heavy as they threatened to close. He couldn't remember the last time he had slept properly, but there was no time for rest. They needed answers, and they needed them now.

Just as Miles was about to take another sip of the bitter concoction, Malcolm's computer chimed, signaling the completion of the tracking program. The brothers exchanged hopeful glances before turning their attention to the screen.

"Alright, let's see what we've got," Malcolm said, tapping a few keys to bring up the results.

As the information loaded, Miles felt a knot of dread form in his stomach. It was much worse than he'd anticipated. Not only was it his personal code that had been used to access the system, but the perpetrator had also logged in using his personal password. It was as if someone had reached inside his brain and pulled out the one piece of information that could cause the most damage.

His hand shook slightly, causing the coffee to slosh over the side of the cup and onto the table. "This... this can't be right," he stammered, his voice barely above a whisper.

"Unfortunately, it is," Max confirmed, his tone somber. "Someone got a hold of your personal information and used it against us."

"Against Candy," Miles corrected, the guilt crashing over him like a tidal wave. This was his fault. Someone had targeted Candy, and it was because of him.

"Hey, don't do that to yourself," Malcolm interjected, concern etched onto his features. "We'll figure this out, and we'll make it right. We're in this together."

"Mal's right," Max agreed, placing a reassuring hand on Miles' shoulder. "We're going to find whoever did this, and they will pay for what they've done."

Miles took a deep breath, trying to steady himself. He knew his brothers were right; they would get through this together. But he couldn't shake the feeling that he'd let everyone down, especially his best friend.

"Let's keep digging," he said finally, determination hardening his features. "We're not stopping until we find the person responsible for this mess."

And with that, they dove back into their investigation, each man silently vowing to bring justice to those who had been wronged.

Miles stared at the computer screen, his mind raced with thoughts and possibilities. Destiny was there when he logged in that day, and she was the only one who could have known his personal password. He couldn't think of anyone else who would risk their job or hate Candy enough to do something like this. It had to be her.

"Guys," Miles said, his voice tight with tension. "I think it's Destiny."

Max raised an eyebrow, clearly surprised by the accusation. "Why do you say that?"

"Isn't it obvious?" Miles argued, feeling a surge of

anger bubble up inside him. "She hates Candy. She's said as much."

"Did she really say that, or are you interpreting that?" Malcolm chimed in, narrowing his eyes as he studied Miles' face.

"Whose side are you on?" Miles snapped, his frustration boiling over. "Do you even want to be part of this company?"

"Of course we do, Miles," Max replied, his voice level and calm. "But we need to be sure before we start accusing people. Remember, we're all in this together."

Miles rubbed his temples, taking a deep breath as he tried to gather his thoughts. He knew his brothers were right, but the weight of guilt still hung heavy on him. Was he just looking for someone to blame to ease his own conscience?

"Fine," he conceded, forcing himself to look away from the computer screen. "Let's keep digging until we find concrete evidence."

"Agreed," Malcolm said, nodding firmly. "We'll get to the bottom of this, and we'll do it as a team."

"Right," Max added, offering a reassuring smile. "We'll figure this out, Miles. We always do."

As they continued their search for answers, Miles couldn't help but feel a nagging doubt in the back of his mind. Was he really doing the right thing by accusing Destiny? Or was he simply jumping to conclusions out of fear and desperation?

With each passing moment, the pressure to find the truth grew heavier on his shoulders. But one thing was certain: he wouldn't stop until justice had been served, no matter who was responsible for the breach.

Max's eyes flashed with indignation, and Malcolm crossed his arms defensively. "How could you even ask that?" Max shot back. "We're trying to help you, Miles. But accusing Destiny without any solid evidence isn't the answer."

"Maybe you're right," Miles admitted through gritted teeth. "But I need to talk to her. I need to know the truth."

With that, he turned on his heel and stormed out of the office, leaving his brothers behind. As he walked towards Peaches, he tried to steady his breathing and calm himself down. This conversation would be crucial, and he couldn't afford to let his emotions get the better of him.

The sound of laughter and the scent of freshly brewed coffee greeted him as he entered the warm, inviting cafe. He scanned the room, searching for Destiny among the bustling crowd. His heart ached at the thought of confronting her, but he needed answers—the sooner, the better.

* * *

Destiny's fingertips were dusted with flour as she expertly rolled out the dough, her focused gaze on the task at hand. The warmth of the kitchen enveloped her, a comforting embrace that reminded her of afternoons spent baking with her father. The delightful aroma of freshly baked pastries permeated the air, mingling with the cheerful hum of conversation among the other cooks who bustled around with trays and mixing bowls.

"Hey, Destiny," Lila's voice cut through the noise, accompanied by the click-clack of her heels on the tile floor. She stepped into the kitchen, her eyes narrowing in annoyance. "Miles is out front."

Destiny looked up from her work, surprise etched on her features as she processed the information. Wiping her hands on her apron, she frowned in confusion. "Miles? What's he doing here?"

"Your guess is as good as mine." Lila shrugged, her jet-black hair swinging with the motion. "But I have a feeling it has something to do with that data breach thing he's been dealing with."

It had been a week since she'd last seen Miles, and their conversations had dwindled down to near nonexistence. The data breach had consumed his every waking moment, leaving little room for anything else. Despite the distance between them, Destiny couldn't help but talk to him because she was worried. She knew how much his company meant to him, and if there was even a sliver of a chance she could offer support, she'd take it. He was dealing with a huge company meltdown. She didn't want to bother him by asking about the missing money.

"Okay, I'll go see what he wants," Destiny said, determination settling in her chest. She removed her apron and hung it on its usual hook, preparing herself for whatever awaited her outside of the kitchen.

Destiny emerged from the kitchen, her hazel eyes scanning the bustling cafe for Miles. She spotted him leaning against a pillar, his tall frame tense and his jaw clenched. Her heart skipped a beat at the sight of him, but she couldn't shake the concern that weighed heavily on her chest.

"Hey," she called out softly as she approached him, trying to infuse some warmth into the strained atmosphere. He looked up, his green eyes meeting hers with an intensity that took her aback.

"Hi, Destiny," he replied curtly, his voice devoid of any warmth or familiarity. He gestured to an empty table nearby, and Destiny nodded, her unease grew with each step they took.

As they settled into their seats, she attempted to break the ice with a smile, reaching over to take his hand in hers. "Miles, it's been so long since we've talked. Are you okay?"

He pulled away from her touch abruptly, like her hand was a live wire shocking him. The motion stung more than she'd anticipated, and she found herself folding her hands in her lap, a protective barrier constructing itself around her heart.

"Yeah, I'm fine. We just need to talk about something important," he said, his tone heavy with unspoken implications. Destiny felt a chill run down her spine, her stomach knotting in apprehension.

"Okay," she replied, steeling herself for whatever was about to come. "I'm here to listen, Miles. Whatever's bothering you, we can work through it together."

He hesitated for a moment, seemingly gathering his thoughts before finally speaking. "Destiny, I don't want to believe this, but I have to ask you... do you know anything about the data breach? Anything at all?"

Her heart dropped like a stone, the shock and hurt swirling within her like a tornado. "Miles, why would you think that?" she whispered, her voice barely audible over the sound of the cafe around them.

"Because," Miles continued, his voice strained, "my personal password was used to carry out the breach, and I can't help but think... Did you have something to do with it? After all, you hate Candy, and she's at the center of this mess."

Destiny couldn't believe what she was hearing. The accusation hit her like a physical blow, and her heart ached in agony. She sat up straighter in her chair, stealing her spine as she prepared to defend herself. Her hazel eyes blazed with hurt and anger, no longer reflecting the warm light of Peaches.

"First of all," Destiny said angrily, her voice trembling with emotion, "I did not have anything to do with that breach. Yes, I was there when you logged in, but I wasn't watching you type your password, Miles! I trusted and respected your privacy!"

She gripped the edge of the table, her knuckles turning white from the force. "And secondly, I would never come between your relationship with Candy, even though she so easily came between us. I'm not that kind of person, Miles, and it hurts that you would even think that of me."

Her chest heaved as she tried to catch her breath, her anger leaving her momentarily winded. But she refused to let her guard down, unwilling to give Miles any more power over her emotions.

Destiny took a deep breath, her anger momentarily subsiding as she prepared to reveal her own struggles. She stared at Miles, her voice firm and steady. "You know, if you had bothered to speak to me during this past week, you would have known that I'm dealing with my own issues right now."

Miles looked puzzled, which only irritated Destiny more. "What do you mean?"

"*Your* company contacted the Mitchells," Destiny explained, her eyes never leaving his, "claiming that I charged them more on the day of the event than what I had billed them. But that's not true. The Mitchells never received any extra money, and now they're investigating me for stealing it."

She leaned in slightly, closing the gap between them. "I've given you the benefit of the doubt, Miles, even though your company is accusing me of something I didn't do. Don't you think I deserve the same consideration?"

Miles' eyes widened, and he opened his mouth as if to say something but closed it again, at a loss for words. He was clearly taken aback by her revelation, and confusion began to replace the suspicion in his gaze.

"Unbelievable," Destiny muttered under her breath, shaking her head. She pushed back her chair, the screeching noise of metal against the floor echoing throughout the cafe. "I have to get back to work, Miles. If you want to continue playing detective, then maybe you should be looking for the real criminal instead of pointing fingers at someone who would never betray you."

With that, she got up and walked away, her steps purposeful and determined. The anger inside her continued to simmer, fueling her every movement. As she reached the entrance to the kitchen, she blinked back the tears threatening to fall, refusing to let him see how much his accusations had hurt and frustrated her. But as she pushed open the swinging door, a single tear escaped, trailing down her cheek like a silent indictment of his actions.

Destiny clenched her jaw as she stepped back into the kitchen, her hands shaking with suppressed rage. The familiar scent of fresh dough and baking bread enveloped her, offering a small comfort as she tried to regain her composure. Her coworkers bustled around her, oblivious to the emotional turmoil bubbling beneath her calm exterior.

"Hey, Des, you okay?" Lila asked, raising an eyebrow as she noticed Destiny's reddened eyes.

"Fine," she snapped before catching herself. "Sorry, Lila. Just... dealing with something."

"Got it," Lila replied gently, giving Destiny a knowing look filled with empathy.

"Alright, let's get back to work," Destiny muttered, wiping her hands on her apron and turning her attention to the dough waiting for her on the counter. She slammed her fists down onto it, kneading the mixture with purposeful force. Every push and pull was a release of the anger that had built up during the confrontation with Miles.

"Des, just so you know, I'm always here if you need to talk," Lila offered quietly, her words barely audible over the hum of mixers and ovens.

As Destiny continued kneading, she couldn't stop constantly replaying the conversation with Miles in her head. She couldn't believe he'd accused her, of all people, of being involved in the data breach. She thought they'd developed a bond, a mutual respect and understanding, but apparently, she had been mistaken.

"Asshole," she muttered under her breath, rolling out another sheet of dough with a bit more force than necessary. "Think you know me, huh? Well, you don't."

"Preach," Lila whispered with a smirk, having overheard Destiny's comment. The small gesture of solidarity brought a fleeting smile to Destiny's lips.

Maybe he'll realize how wrong he is, Destiny thought, trying to cling to a sense of hope. *He's smart, right? He'll figure it out.*

"Damn straight he will," she told herself, allowing the anger to subside just enough for her to focus on the task at hand. She channeled her frustration into creating the flakiest croissants and the most tender cinnamon rolls the cafe had ever seen.

Come on, Miles, she silently urged as she slid a tray of pastries into the oven. *Get your shit together, and see the truth.*

Before long, the kitchen was filled with the tantalizing aroma of baked goods fresh from the oven. As Destiny pulled the last tray from the oven, she allowed herself a moment of satisfaction in a job well done. Whatever Miles chose to believe or do next, she knew that she would keep moving forward, one perfect pastry at a time.

twenty-two

MILES WALKED BACK TO THE OFFICE, HIS MIND SWIRLING with thoughts of Destiny. The breeze ruffled through his brown hair as he strolled along the busy sidewalk, barely noticing the bustling foot traffic surrounding him. The sun cast long shadows across the pavement, but all he could see was Destiny's face—her hazel eyes full of concern, her lips forming words he wished he had paid more attention to.

He was surprised when Destiny had said that she had her own issues going on. The guilt of not reaching out or even thinking of her during this last week gnawed at his insides. How could he have been so wrapped up in his own problems that he failed to notice hers? As much as he valued honesty and loyalty, he couldn't help but feel that he hadn't been the best boyfriend she deserved lately.

"Get it together, Miles," he muttered under his breath, shaking his head as if trying to reorder his jumbled thoughts.

He was so wrapped up in his thoughts, that he didn't even realize he'd made it back to the office until the elevator door opened on his floor. Another pang of guilt hit him, as he realized that while he was responsible for keeping this place running smoothly, he had let Destiny down by not being there for her. She was always so considerate of him. She would check in and never bring up the theft because she knew what he was dealing with.

Miles walked out of the elevator, his polished shoes clicking against the immaculate marble floor. The office was abuzz with activity—phones ringing, fingers clattering on keyboards, and hushed conversations between colleagues. As he made his way to his glass-walled office, he noticed Candy sitting at her desk, frowning as she glanced up from her computer screen. Her eyes met his, and he did all he could to push all sense of unease to the side to give his friend a reassuring smile.

Heading into his office and sitting down, he made the decision to look into everything Destiny had told him. "Okay, let's see what this is all about," he murmured to himself, pulling up the invoice Destiny had mentioned. His green eyes scanned the document, finally landing on the total: $52,500. It seemed reasonable enough, but then he noticed Candy's note in the corner—she claimed to have paid Destiny $55,000 after being asked for an extra $2,500. Frowning, he rose from his chair, feeling a mix of confusion and concern.

Miles steeled himself before leaving the sanctuary of his office, tablet in hand. He took a deep breath and approached Candy's desk, trying to keep any suspicion from his expression. "Candy, do you have a minute?"

"Of course," she replied, her smile wide and seemingly genuine as she looked up at him. "I always have time for you, Miles."

"Thanks." He handed her the tablet, displaying the invoice in question. "Destiny mentioned that someone complained about being charged an extra $2,500. She says she didn't do it. Can you help me understand what happened?"

Candy's eyes flicked to the screen, studying it intently. Her playful demeanor vanished, replaced by a mask of professionalism. "Yes, I remember this. I reached out to the owners because it wasn't right for Destiny to charge us more than the agreed-upon amount."

As she spoke, Miles' mind raced with questions. Did Candy really believe Destiny was capable of theft? Or was there something else going on? He couldn't help but glance at her perfectly manicured nails tapping on the keyboard, searching for answers.

"Here, look." Candy turned the computer screen towards him. "The records show that $55,000 was paid—$52,500 initially, then another $2,500 later."

"Thank you, Candy." Miles tried to suppress the unease churning inside him as he retreated back to his office, his thoughts consumed by Destiny's predicament. If she truly hadn't taken the money, who had?

Miles sat at his desk, the dark mahogany wood reflecting the afternoon sunlight. He stared blankly at the screen of his computer, Destiny's face dominating his thoughts.

"Could she have really done that?" he muttered to himself, the idea of Destiny stealing money that had him sick to his stomach. He knew her life wasn't extravagant; she lived simply and worked hard for every dollar she earned. And yet, perhaps desperation had driven her to steal. The thought unsettled him.

For the next hour, Miles was contemplating if Destiny could have really done what she'd been accused of. Could she have stolen? If she did, why? Yes, she lives on basic means and could possibly use the money. Miles put his head in his hands to think. Destiny hates Candy. That is obvious and Candy was the target of the breach—but would Destiny do something like this out of spite? She isn't normally one for such rash behavior. Miles sat for a while longer questioning everything and everyone. He didn't know who he should believe.

* * *

Destiny glanced up at the clock on the cafe wall, watching the hands tick away the hours since Miles had left. The conversation they'd had weighed heavily on her mind, and she couldn't shake the feeling that their relationship was hanging in the balance.

"Hey, you okay?" Lila asked, concern etched into her features as she placed a comforting hand on Destiny's shoulder.

"Yeah, just... thinking," Destiny replied, her hazel eyes distant.

"About Miles?" Lila guessed, her voice gentle. Destiny nodded slowly, biting her lip as she contemplated what she needed to say to him. Lila was totally fed up with him and his thoughtless behavior.

"Then go talk to him. I can handle things here," Lila encouraged, giving Destiny a soft smile.

"Thanks, Lila," Destiny said, returning the smile with gratitude. She took a deep breath, gathering her courage. "Okay, I'm going to do it."

"Good," Lila responded, giving Destiny a gentle push towards the door. "Now go tell that man what's up!"

As Destiny walked towards Vortex, she felt a whirlwind of emotions coursing through her. Anxiety, determination, and love all fought for dominance in her heart. She knew she had to stand up for herself while also hearing Miles out—it was the only way they could move forward together.

She rode the elevator up to the executive floor, clutching the access card Miles had given her like a lifeline. As soon as the doors slid open, she stepped out, her eyes fixed on the path to Miles' office, determination coursed through her. She was ready to face the conversation head on.

"Okay, Destiny," she whispered to herself, "you're strong, you're resilient, and you're going to stand up for yourself." With a determined nod, she stepped out onto the plush carpet and made her way toward Miles' office.

She barely made it halfway before Candy appeared as if summoned by some twisted fate. Her eyes narrowed as she approached Destiny, an insidious smile playing at the corner of her lips.

"Destiny, what a surprise," Candy purred, her voice dripping with fake sweetness. Her blonde hair fell over her shoulder as she cocked her head to the side like a predator. "What brings you up here?"

"I'm here to talk to Miles," Destiny replied, trying to keep her voice steady. "Candy, please move."

Candy's smile widened as she reached out and grabbed Destiny's arm, her grip like a vise. Destiny gasped in pain and tried to pull away, but Candy held on tight.

"Really? Well, I'm afraid Miles is rather busy right now," Candy said, her voice cold and menacing. "I don't think he has time for you."

"Let go of me," Destiny demanded, her voice shaking slightly. She yanked her arm away with a burst of resolve as she looked at Candy with nothing but disgust on her face. The spot where Candy's nails had dug into her arm hurt, but she wasn't going to show Candy that she'd gotten under her skin, either physically or emotionally

Destiny's heartbeat quickened as she watched Candy's

eyes darken with malice. Her icy blue eyes were cold and calculating, and her full lips twisted into a sneer.

"Liars and thieves aren't welcome here," Candy spat, her voice dripping with contempt. "You really think Miles would want someone like you after everything you've done?"

"What are you talking about?" Destiny rolled her eyes. She could feel her anger boiling under the surface. She was so tired of Candy's manipulative bullshit.

"Playing innocent won't work anymore," Candy snapped, getting closer and invading Destiny's personal space. "I know what you did, and so does Miles. He deserves better than you. But don't worry, I'll show him better." At the last sentence her voice turned into the sickeningly sweet tone she so often showed.

"Better than me? That's rich coming from you," Destiny shot back. "Miles and I are together, and there's nothing you can do about it. Just give up, it's getting pathetic, Candy."

Candy laughed, a cruel, chilling sound that sent shivers down Destiny's spine. "Are you sure about that? If you're so important to him, then why did he me to move in with him?" she taunted.

"What?" Destiny gasped, feeling as if she'd been punched in the gut. Her eyes stung with unshed tears, but she tried to maintain her composure. She was getting more and more frustrated at the situation and Miles' lack of communication. He had made her look like a fool.

"Aw, poor little girl," Candy cooed mockingly, her wicked grin growing wider. "He didn't tell you? It was fun while it lasted, but he'll be mine for the rest of his life. You were just a temporary distraction. Now give this to me," Candy spits out while ripping the key card out of her hands. "You don't deserve direct access. You know, considering you're a security risk and all."

Destiny spun on her heel and stormed out of the office, Candy's malicious laughter echoed in her ears like nails on a chalkboard. Her heart pounded in her chest as she stomped down the hallway, holding back the tears that threatened to start streaming down her face. The elevator seemed to take an eternity to arrive, and when it finally did, she dashed inside and frantically stabbed at the button for the ground floor.

"Pull yourself together," she muttered under her breath, taking a deep breath. But the tears finally fell, blurring her vision as she stumbled out of the elevator and into the lobby. No one paid her any mind as she ran through the revolving doors and out onto the bustling sidewalk, her world crumbling around her.

The journey back to her apartment passed in a blur, her thoughts consumed by the devastating words Candy had hurled at her. When she finally reached her doorstep, she fumbled with her keys before throwing the door open and slamming it shut behind her with a loud bang.

Without pausing for breath, Destiny raced to her bedroom and came to a halt in front of the full-length mirror that hung on the wall. Her reflection stared back at her—a girl with red-rimmed eyes, tear-streaked cheeks, and a broken heart. Her curly brown hair was pulled back into a messy ponytail, the frizz causing stray strands to fall and frame her makeup-free face. She wore jeans and a casual shirt.

Destiny tilted her head to the side and began to compare herself to Candy, who always looked like she'd just stepped off the runway. Candy's perfectly curled blonde hair, expertly applied makeup, and trendy office outfits were effortlessly chic, while her sky-high heels only added to her air of unattainable perfection.

"Is that what Miles wants?" Destiny whispered, burying her face in her hands. Her heart ached at the thought that she could never compete with someone like Candy, who seemed to hold all the cards in their twisted game of love and deceit.

"Maybe I'm not enough for him," she sobbed, collapsing onto her bed as the enormity of everything that had transpired finally hit her. "How the hell did he not tell me about her *moving in*?" The frustrated tears flowed freely now, each one a testament to the heartache and betrayal that threatened to suffocate her.

As the minutes dragged on, Destiny's thoughts raced, cycling between anger, confusion, and despair. It was clear that there were so many conversations that needed to be had—with Miles, with Candy, with herself. But where would she even start?

Her eyes drifted back to her reflection in the mirror, the girl looked so lost and uncertain. In that moment, Destiny resolved to face the truth head-on, no matter how painful it might be. She would not let Candy win without a fight, and she would not let her own insecurities dictate her future with Miles.

twenty-three

WALKING INTO VORTEX, MILES LOOKED AS THOUGH HE had been through a battle with an army of nightmares. His brown hair was tousled, sticking up in odd angles, and the dark circles under his green eyes spoke of his sleepless night. With a heavy sigh, Miles flicked on the lights.

"Maybe some peace and quiet will help me clear my head," he muttered to himself, rubbing his temples.

It was still early, the usually bustling workspace was empty, providing Miles with the solitude he so desperately needed. He decided to take advantage of the quiet by diving into the seemingly endless sea of emails he had been ignoring.

"Focus, Miles," he scolded himself, forcing his attention back to the task at hand—answering emails.

His fingers flew across the keyboard, rapidly typing responses to clients and colleagues alike. Despite his exhaustion, there was a sense of satisfaction in finally tackling the neglected messages. The silence in the office allowed him to focus, the only sound being the rhythmic tapping of the keys.

About an hour later, the distinct sound of heels clicking against the polished floor echoed through the empty office. Miles glanced up from his computer screen, surprised to hear someone arriving at this early hour. He knew without a doubt that it had to be Candy. Her unmistakable strut was as familiar to him as the rhythmic tick-tock of the clock on his wall.

"Seven in the morning? She's never here this early," he thought, brow furrowing in confusion. Curiosity piqued, he pushed back from his desk and stepped out of his office, ready for whatever fresh chaos Candy would undoubtedly bring.

When he caught sight of her, Miles couldn't help but do a double take. The always impeccably dressed Candy looked like she'd just rolled out of bed. Her usually sleek blonde hair was tousled and disheveled, and the designer clothes she wore hung off her frame as though they were hastily thrown on. It was such a stark contrast to her normal poised self that Miles momentarily wondered if he was still dreaming.

"Good morning, Candy," he said cautiously, trying not to let his shock show too much on his face. "I didn't know you were awake when I left this morning."

Candy's eyes darted toward him, and she offered a weak smile that didn't quite reach them. "Morning, Miles," she replied, her voice subdued, lacking its usual confidence. "I couldn't sleep."

"Is everything... okay?" he asked, genuinely concerned for her well-being. It wasn't like Candy to let her guard down like this, especially around him. Something must have rattled her to her core.

She hesitated for a moment, biting her lip and avoiding his gaze. Finally, she sighed and said, "Not really, no. But we should probably talk about it later. You have enough on your plate right now with the breach and all."

"Okay, Candy, seriously, what's going on?" Miles asked, his brow furrowing with concern. "I've never seen you like this before."

Candy took a deep breath and wiped her eyes before meeting Miles' gaze. "Destiny," she whispered, her voice cracking. "She came to the office yesterday, and she was...she was just horrible to me, Miles."

Miles frowned. "Destiny? What did she say?"

"She accused me of trying to come between you two," Candy choked out, tears streaming down her cheeks. "And that I was only pretending to be your friend for ulterior motives." She sniffled and added, "That's not true, Miles. You know it isn't."

"Of course I know that," he said firmly, his heart ached for Candy. "What else?"

"Something about my father," she continued, her voice trembling. "She said his business must not be doing well if they had to take out a mortgage on his house. That it was proof he was failing."

Miles froze, his blood running cold. That information had been in the breached file, but it had never been posted publicly. How could Destiny have possibly known?

"Destiny must have been behind the breach," Candy sobbed. "No one else would know that, Miles."

Fury coursed through him as the pieces fell into place. He couldn't believe that he'd been so blinded by Destiny. He let their history and her, clearly fake, kindness and it hurt Candy in the proce.. It was too much.

"Stay here," Miles told Candy, his voice low and dangerous. "I'm going to deal with this."

Without waiting for a response, Miles stormed out of

the office, his mind racing with disbelief and anger. How could Destiny have betrayed him like this? And more importantly, how could he have been so blind to it all this time?

Destiny, he thought bitterly, *you've got some serious explaining to do.*

* * *

Destiny hummed softly to herself, her fingers deftly arranging the pastries in the display case with practiced ease. The morning sun streamed through the cafe's windows, casting a warm golden glow across the room. It was early, still hours before their usual rush of customers filled the space, but Destiny liked to get a head start on her day.

Lost in her thoughts, Destiny didn't hear the bell above the door chime, signaling the entrance of a customer—or rather, an unexpected visitor. She continued to work, her mind preoccupied with the events of the previous day. She had confronted Candy at Miles' office, unable to keep her emotions in check any longer.

Destiny always felt bad when she said something hurtful. *Oh, snap out of it Destiny!* She thought. Feeling regret is the old Destiny. The new Destiny is a strong badass chick that doesn't take this shit anymore.

As she placed the final pastry on the shelf, Destiny straightened up and glanced around the cafe. It was then that her gaze fell upon Miles, standing by the door with a thunderous expression on his face. A jolt of panic shot through her, and she momentarily froze, unsure of how to react.

"Good morning, Miles," she managed to say, her voice

tight with forced cheerfulness. "What brings you here so early?"

Deep down, Destiny knew exactly why he was there. And she braced herself for the storm that was about to come.

Miles stormed towards the counter, his green eyes blazing with fury. The veins in his neck stood out, a clear indication of the anger boiling within him. Destiny swallowed nervously, her heart pounding as she instinctively took a step back.

"Is it true?" he growled, leaning across the counter to invade her personal space. "Did you tell Candy those things about Colter's mortgage? I know you were the cause of the security breach."

Destiny's hazel eyes widened in shock, her hands trembling slightly. How could he think that she would do something so despicable? She searched for the right words, desperate to make him see reason.

"Of course not! What—How the hell would I even know about Colter's mortgage? !" she protested, her voice shaking with indignation. "Why would you believe Candy over me, Miles?"

"Because she said you told her," he replied quietly, his tone laced with hurt. "And if only a select few people knew about it, how else would you find out?"

Destiny bit her lip, her thoughts racing. She needed to convince Miles of her innocence, but how could she do that without any concrete evidence? She racked her brain for a way to prove that she hadn't betrayed his trust. Then it hit her. Why is she trying to convince him of anything? He obviously believes he has all of the answers.

Destiny's heart thundered in her chest as she clenched her fists at her sides, pure anger arising within her. "Well, if you believe perfect fucking Candy, then go ahead and be with her!" she yelled, her eyes blazing with fury. She jabbed a finger in his direction, emphasizing each word. "You came here to tell me all the shit you know, but you really don't fucking know anything!"

Miles flinched, clearly taken aback by her outburst. He opened his mouth to speak, but Destiny wasn't done.

"Jesus, Miles," she continued, her voice shaking with indignation. "You never respect my boundaries or this damn café! You're always barging in here, yelling at me like I'm some kind of criminal. I never storm into Vortex and scream at you!"

She took a deep breath, trying to steady herself. Her thoughts swirled like an angry tempest, making it difficult to focus. But she knew she had to say this. It was now or never.

"You know how I feel about Candy," she said quietly, her resolve hardening. "You hid that she moved in with you because you knew I wouldn't like it. Did you ever stop to think about how that would make me feel? To find out like this?"

Her voice broke, tears pooling in her eyes. "This is the ultimate betrayal, Miles." With a heavy sigh, she added, "I can't do this anymore. We're done. Go fuck yourself, Miles."

The words hung in the air between them, thick and suffocating. The finality of it all made Destiny's stomach churn, but she knew in her heart that it was the right decision.

Without waiting for a response, she turned on her heel and walked away, slipping through the swinging door that led to the kitchen. Leaning against the cool metal surface, she let out a frustrated growl.

As her frustration echoed through the empty kitchen, it seemed like the earth itself was mourning the loss of something beautiful, torn apart by forces beyond their control.

Destiny's breath hitched as she pressed her ear closer to the door, trying to catch every word between Lila and Miles. It was hard to focus on their conversation when her heart was being crushed under the weight of betrayal, but she couldn't walk away now"You think you're so damn smart, Miles. But you're just a fucking idiot," Lila snarled.ed.Destiny could easily imagine the electric blue fire in her friend's eyes as she defended her.

"Look at this," Lila continued, and Destiny heard a rustling sound. She knew what it was without seeing it—the poster that had been taped to the front door of the café earlier that day. It was a cruel, photoshopped image of Destiny made to look like a mugshot, with the word "thief" plastered in big, bold letters underneath. The caption below it read, "If she's willing to steal from a charity, would she steal from you too?"

Destiny crumpled the paper, shoving it deep into her apron pocket as if she could bury the hurtful words and the vicious intent behind them. Her hands shook, rage and sorrow battling for dominance within her.

She continued eavesdropping, straining to hear more of the conversation between Lila and Miles. The anger in Lila's voice was palpable as she said, "You know what, Miles? I'm banning you from the café."

"Are you serious?" Miles' disbelief was clear, even if his voice was muffled by the door. But Destiny didn't need to hear his response, not after everything that had happened.

"Dead serious," Lila shot back. "I'm the manager now, and I can do that. Get out."

Unable to take any more, Destiny sunk to the cold tiled floor, tears streaming down her face. The strength she'd once prided herself on seemed to have evaporated, leaving her feeling more vulnerable than ever before. A sob escaped her lips, and she quickly pressed her hand over her mouth to muffle the sound.

She barely noticed Lila sliding up next to her on the floor, the door clicking shut behind her. Her best friend's presence was a balm to her aching heart, but even that couldn't erase the pain of Miles' betrayal.

twenty-four

MILES STORMED INTO HIS OFFICE, RAGE PULSATING through every vein. He slammed the door behind him with such force that it shook the frosted glass pane. His hand darted to the control panel and he pressed the button harshly, closing the dividers for privacy. He needed space— space from the break up that had shaken him to his core.

As Miles turned around, taking in the familiar surroundings of his office, he couldn't help but notice how much of Destiny's personality had infiltrated his life. From photos of them laughing together at Lila's birthday party to the quirky little owl mug she had gifted him after discovering his love for the nocturnal creatures, her presence was everywhere. She had nestled herself snugly into his heart, and now, all of it felt like a lie.

"God damnit!" Miles roared as he picked up the framed photo on his desk and slammed it down on the desk. The sound of shattering glass filled his ears as the frame hit the desk , leaving a spider web of cracks in its wake. His breathing was heavy, a mix of anger and suffo- cating betrayal constricting his chest.

"Everything I thought we were building..." he trailed off, gripping the edge of the desk so hard his knuckles turned white. His mind raced, replaying every moment, every touch, every whispered promise. Had it all been an act?

"Enough!" he yelled, his voice echoing through the room. But was it ever going to be enough? How could he erase her from his life as easily as she had seemingly betrayed him?

His heart ached like never before, and Miles found himself struggling to keep the tears at bay. He allowed his back to slide down the wall, collapsing onto the floor amidst the remnants of happier times. He buried his face in his hands, trying to take deep breaths in a futile attempt to regain control over his emotions.

"Destiny," he whispered, the name tasting bitter on his tongue, "why did you do this to me?"

* * *

Max glanced up from his computer as a loud crash echoed through the office. Frowning, he pushed back from his desk and hurried toward the source of the noise. Malcolm was just jogging over, his wide eyes meeting those of his oldest brother..

"Something's going on in Miles' office," Max said, his voice tense.

"We should… we should see if he needs help, right?" Malcolm replied, nodding resolutely. "It sounds… emotional." Malcolm tried to don his usual grin and humor despite the unsettling feeling that settled in his gut at his brother's emotional outburst.

"Let's just be gentle." Max chuckled and rolled his eyes at Malcolm.

With a shared look of determination, they approached the frosted glass door of Miles' office. Max reached out and opened it, revealing a scene of chaos—papers scattered across the floor, a shattered snow globe in one corner, and Miles sitting against the wall, his face buried in his hands.

"Jesus, Miles, what happened?" Max asked, taking in the destruction with a mixture of shock and confusion.

Miles lifted his head, his green eyes filled with anger and betrayal. "Candy told me everything, Max." His voice cracked as he struggled to control his emotions. "Destiny is behind the breach."

"What?" Malcolm blurted out, disbelief etched on his face. "You can't seriously believe Candy, right? You know she's never been known for being the most trustworthy of people."

"Apparently more so than Destiny," Miles spat. "Why else would she tell me about this?"

"Because she wants you, dude!" Max exclaimed, trying to reason with his brother. "Don't you see that?"

"Destiny wouldn't do this, Miles. You have to know that deep down," Malcolm urged.

"Deep down?" Miles laughed bitterly. "What I know deep down is that people lie and betray you when you least expect it."

"Please, just think about this rationally," Max pleaded as Malcolm rolled his eyes. "Candy has always had an ulterior motive. Can't you see that she's manipulating you?"

Miles' jaw clenched, his green eyes narrowing as he stared at Max and Malcolm. Their words echoed in his head, but the stubborn side of him refused to accept it. He couldn't—wouldn't—believe that Candy had orchestrated this entire situation.

"Enough!" Miles roared, standing up suddenly. "I can't trust any of you!" With that, he stormed out of the office, leaving Max and Malcolm in stunned silence, surrounded by the remnants of his broken trust.

As much as he wanted to trust Max and Malcolm's instincts, he couldn't shake the feeling that there was more to the story. And until he knew for certain, he needed to distance himself from everything—and everyone.

"Hey, Candy," Miles called out as he spotted her at her desk, her fingers flying over the keyboard with practiced ease. "I'm heading home early today. You want to come with me?"

Candy looked up, her eyes meeting his as a slow smile spread across her face. "Of course, Miles," she replied, her voice dripping with honeyed sweetness. "Just give me a minute to grab my things."

As she rifled through her drawers, gathering her belongings, Miles leaned against the wall, his arms crossed over his chest. With each passing second, that little seed of doubt grew larger, threatening to crush him under its weight. But he pushed the thoughts aside, focusing instead on the familiar comfort of Candy's presence.

"Ready when you are," she announced, stepping towards him with her designer handbag slung over her shoulder.

Miles offered his arm, which she gladly took, and they walked out of the building together. Despite the turmoil roiling inside him, he managed a tight smile, a thin semblance of normalcy amidst the chaos thanks to having his best friend by his side.

* * *

As the elevator shut behind Miles and Candy, Max turned to Malcolm, his green eyes filled with concern. "This is so wrong," he muttered, running a hand through his brown hair in frustration.

"Tell me about it," Malcolm replied, crossing his arms over his chest. "But you know how stubborn our brother can be."

Max sighed, leaning against the wall. "Yeah, but he's had enough time to figure this shit out. He's making the wrong choice here, and we need to help him see that."

"Agreed. But how?" Malcolm asked, raising an eyebrow.

"Let's put our heads together and find some concrete evidence. If we can prove Destiny's innocence, maybe he'll finally listen." Max straightened up, determination set in his features.

"Sounds like a plan," Malcolm said, nodding in agreement. "Even if they don't get back together, at least Candy will be out of our lives, finally."

He knew they needed to step in and do something about the situation between Miles and Destiny. They couldn't let their brother continue down this path with Candy. He pulled out his phone and crafted a group text, hoping everyone would be on board.

"Alright," Max said aloud, hitting send.

MAX - 2:05 P.M.

SOS!! We need to discuss Miles and Destiny. Kyle's at 8.

Malcolm glanced up from his computer, a hint of worry in his eyes. "You think they'll be on board?"

"Only one way to find out," Max replied, trying to sound confident.

VIVIENNE - 2:10 P.M.

heart emoji

LILA - 2:11 P.M.

got it.

"Looks like we're a go," Malcolm said, relief evident in his voice.

"Let's just hope we can get through to him," Max muttered, taking one last look at the town before turning away. The brothers shared a determined glance before heading off to their respective offices, preparing for what was sure to be an emotional night ahead.

"Ready?" Malcolm asked, knocking on Max's office door.

"Let's do this," Max replied, steeling himself for the conversation to come.

* * *

As 8 o'clock rolled around, Lila rushed into Kyle's. The moment the door opened, they were greeted with the comforting aroma of hearty pub fare and the low hum of friendly conversation. She headed over to the bar and pulled out a seat next to Vivi.

"Ah, there she is," Vivi said, her sapphire eyes twinkling with determination. "Let's get to work."

"Agreed," Lila replied, her electric blue eyes flicking over the cozy pub before settling on their friends. "Operation: Save Destiny is a go."

"Hey, guys," Lila greeted cheerfully, trying to ease the tension she could sense in the air. "What's the plan?"

"First things first," Malcolm interjected, raising a finger for emphasis, "we all need a drink."

"As always, Malcolm, you're a genius.," Lila chimed in, signaling the bartender with a casual wave. "I'll have a glass of red wine, please."

As the bartender prepared their drinks, the four friends exchanged glances, each keenly aware of the gravity of the situation. They knew that they ne and right into Candy's arms presenting the evidence they had collected; one wrong move could push Miles further away from Destiny and right into Candy's arms.

"Destiny was absolutely inconsolable," Lila began, her eyes meeting Max and Malcolm's gaze. "She kept saying she never thought Miles could do something like this. He's being such a jackass." She paused, glancing sheepishly at the brothers. "Sorry."

Malcolm shook his head, his messy brown hair falling into his eyes. "No, don't be. We agree with you. Miles has really screwed up this time."

"Big time," Vivi chimed in, sipping her wine thoughtfully. "I mean, I can't imagine how hurt Destiny must be right now."

"Speaking of hurt," Lila started, leaning forward and fixing her intense gaze on Max and Malcolm. "There's no doubt in my mind that Candy is behind this whole atrocity. She's the one who manipulated Miles into believing Destiny betrayed him."

Max raised an eyebrow, swirling the amber liquid in his beer glass. "Yeah. We thought that too. I just can't get out of my head Colter Sullivan. I mean I don't know about you, but I find it hard to believe she would leak his information that could destroy his business."

"Candy's always had it out for Destiny. And we all know she's wanted Miles for herself for years," Malcolm chimed in, his own eyes narrowing. "It isn't a far stretch to think she would be vindictive and selfish enough to hurt anyone else if she could get her way."

Vivi's expression turned steely. "Well, then it's settled. We need to prove to Miles that Candy's the one who orchestrated this entire mess and help him make things right with Destiny."

As the four of them sat there, united in purpose, the atmosphere in the bar seemed to shift. The low hum of conversations around them faded into the background, replaced by the fire of determination that burned within each of them. They knew the path ahead wouldn't be easy, but they were more than ready to fight for the happiness of their friends.

"Here's to setting things right," Lila declared, raising her glass in a toast.

"May love conquer all," Vivienne added with a small smile.

"Cheers," Max and Malcolm echoed, clinking their glasses together, sealing their pact.

Just then, Kyle, the bar owner and an old friend of the group, approached their table with a tray of refills. Lila looked at him gratefully as he set down the drinks. "Thanks, Kyle."

"No problem," he replied, leaning against the bar with a casual air. "Couldn't help but overhear you guys talking. Were you talking about Candy? Candy Sullivan?"

Lila exchanged a glance with the others before nodding. "Yes, why?"

Kyle shook hiead, a grim expression on his face. "I thought so. You should know that she's trouble. She's a snake getting ready to strike. I banned her from this place after the night the girls came. She came back and she caused so much chaos that my bartender threatened to quit. It's no secret she has eyes for Miles."

"Really?" Vivi asked, her eyes widening in surprise. "What exactly did she do here?"

"Let's just say she tried turning my staff against each other, spreading lies and causing a lot of unnecessary drama," Kyle explained, frustration evident in his voice. "It took weeks to clean up the mess and regain everyone's trust. I don't want her stepping foot in here again."

Lila clenched her fists, anger bubbling inside her. If Candy could cause that kind of chaos in a bar, what more damage could she do to Miles and Destiny's relationship?

"Thanks for the heads-up, Kyle," Max said, his voice tight. "We'll be careful."

"Good luck," Kyle replied, offering them a sympathetic smile. "You're gonna need it." With that, he straightened up and headed toward another customer who was waving him over.

Vivi stretched out her arms, stifling a yawn. "I think it's time for Max and me to call it a night," she said, looking over at her husband. He nodded in agreement, his green eyes filled with concern. "Are you guys going to head to Lila's place to keep working on this?" Vivi asked.

"Yeah. I want to take this bitch down," Lila said, giving them both tight hugs. "Keep us updated if you hear anything else about Candy."

"Will do," Max replied, his voice firm. "Now go kick some ass."

"Count on it," Malcolm chimed in, a mischievous glint in his eyes.

As Vivi and Max left the bar, Lila turned to Malcolm, resolve etched on her face. "Let's get to work."

"Lead the way," he said, following her out of the dimly lit bar and into the cool night air.

They walked side by side, their footsteps echoing on the empty streets as they made their way to Lila's apartment.

As he stepped inside Malcolm couldn't help but marvel at the array of gadgets and gizmos scattered across her spare bedroom, dubbed by Lila as her "tech lair." It was a testament to her brilliance, with multiple computers, monitors, and various pieces of equipment that only someone like Lila could decipher. It looked so much like the office in his own house that he instantly smiled.

"Alright," Malcolm said, hopping onto one of the swivel chairs and turning on her main computer. "Where should I start?"

Lila tapped her chin, lost in thought for a moment before snapping her fingers. "I remember Destiny mentioning how excited she was when Miles gave her a keycard for the executive floor. It's needed to access anything up there. Maybe we can find something related to that?"

"Good idea," Malcolm replied, his fingers flying across the keyboard as he brought up the security system for Vortex. "Let's see if we can pinpoint any strange activity involving Destiny's keycard."

Lila watched him work, her eyes filled with admiration for his skill and dedication. It was moments like these that made her believe that they could be an unstoppable team.

"Malcolm," she said softly, resting a hand on his shoulder. "Is that what I think it is?"

He looked up at her, his brown eyes warm and understanding. "We've got her. Look!"

* * *

The next day, Miles' office was filled with tension as Lila, Malcolm, Max, and Vivienne stood in front of his large mahogany desk. The usually calm and collected billionaire was visibly furious, the veins in his neck throbbing as he clenched his fists by his side.

"What the hell are you all doing here?" he barked, his green eyes blazing.

Max stepped forward, his tone firm but gentle. "We're

here for you, Miles. Lila and Malcolm found evidence last night that proves Destiny wasn't behind the breach."

Malcolm turned his laptop around to show Miles the keycard access the night of the breach. Miles was looking closely at the time stamps and noticed the number matching Destiny's.

Miles scoffed, his anger unabated. "Evidence? It shows on Malcolm's laptop that it was Destiny's keycard used to access the executive floor! How does that not prove she did it?"

"Wait," Malcolm interjected, holding up a hand. He turned his laptop back to Miles, revealing the security footage he and Lila had uncovered. "Just watch this, Miles."

The room fell silent as they watched Candy, dressed in black and moving stealthily, sneak onto the executive floor using Destiny's keycard. She slipped into Miles' office and opened his laptop, her fingers tapping away at the keys. Just a few seconds later, the timestamp on the footage lined up perfectly with when the breach occurred.

Miles stared at the screen, his face a mixture of disbelief and horror. His heart pounded in his chest as the realization sank in. Candy, not Destiny, had been the one to betray him. How could he have been so blind?

"See?" Lila said softly, her voice full of empathy. "Destiny wasn't the one who betrayed you. It was Candy."

Miles shook his head, trying to process the information. His mind raced, thoughts tumbling over themselves like a torrential downpour. He couldn't believe he'd let his emotions get the better of him and accused Destiny without any concrete proof. Miles turned to the people supporting him and said, "Why would she do this? Against herself," Miles' anger climbs as he yells, "Her own father?! Who does that?!"

twenty-five

MILES SLAMMED HIS FIST AGAINST THE WALL, THE FORCE OF his anger reverberating through his body. His face twisted into a mask of rage and disbelief, his knuckles turning white as he clenched them tight. The room spun around him and his stomach roiled with nausea. "FUCK!" he bellowed, unleashing all of his pent-up frustration and pain.

As the gravity of his mistake hit him, Miles was hit with l an overwhelming sense of regret and guilt. He knew he had made a grave error, but now he couldn't ignore the consequences that were sure to follow. How could he make things right? Was it even possible? He knew he needed to make things right with Destiny, and there wasn't a moment to lose. As he bolted towards his office door, Lila's voice stopped him in his tracks.

"Hey, Miles! Destiny has the day off. She should be at her apartment," she called out, her eyes filled with concern.

"Thanks, Lila!" he shouted back, not breaking stride as

he burst through the office doors and into the hallway. His green eyes locked onto his destination, his focus unyielding.

As he rounded the corner, he collided with Candy, who stumbled back from the impact. Her eyes narrowed, and she asked accusingly, "Why are you in such a rush, Miles?"

He glared at her, disgust filling every inch of his expression. He didn't have time for her games, not when Destiny needed him. Without a word, he pushed past her and continued sprinting down the hallway.

Miles ran all the way to Peaches. He dashed up the back staircase, taking the stairs two at a time, his lungs burning with exertion. He knew that trust was invaluable to Destiny and that he had broken hers. He couldn't help but berate himself as he climbed, wondering how he could have been so blind.

Reaching Destiny's apartment door, he knocked urgently, his breath coming in ragged gasps. He stood there, waiting, his heart pounding in his ears like a desperate plea.

The click of the locks echoed through the hallway, and as the door creaked open, Miles' heart caught in his throat. Destiny stood before him, her usually radiant hazel eyes now dull and lifeless, framed by the dark circles that marred her pale skin. Her brown hair hung limply around her face, a stark contrast to the vibrant waves he remembered.

"Des," he whispered, anguish etched across his features. "Please, let me explain."

Destiny stared at him, her expression cold and guarded. She hesitated for a moment before nodding sharply, wordlessly telling him to continue. Miles breathed a sigh of relief, knowing this might be his only chance to make things right.

"Thank you," he said softly. He could feel the weight of

her skepticism, but it only fueled his determination to set things straight.

"Destiny," he began, his green eyes searching hers for any sign of forgiveness. "I should have trusted you, or at least looked for evidence before accusing you. I'm so sorry. You were right about everything."

"Go on," she urged, her voice barely audible.

Miles took a deep breath, his desperation growing. "Candy was the one spreading lies, manipulating everyone around her—including me. I can't believe I fell for it. I should have known better, especially when it came to you."

"Then why didn't you?" Destiny asked, her voice cracking with emotion. "Why did you choose to believe her over me?"

"I don't know, her father has done so much for me. She's been with me since high school, we even went to the same college. She was my best friend. only now, I realize that i never actually knew her." Miles admitted, shame washing over him. "But I promise you, I'll spend the rest of my life making it up to you if you'll let me."

Destiny's eyes pooled with tears, but her voice was strong. "Miles, I can't forget the hurt you caused me. You should have asked me what was wrong when she accused me of stealing from your company. You were so quick to believe her! It felt like a blow to my heart when you stopped talking to me while all this was going on. And then you moved Candy into your house, as if it didn't matter how we felt about each other. I can't forget that."

"Destiny, I know I messed up," he pleaded, his heart aching with the pain he had caused her. "But please, give me a chance to show you how much I love you and that I can be the man you deserve."

For a long moment, they stood there in silence.

Destiny's gaze never wavered from his, as if she were searching for the truth hidden within his soul.

He reached out to her, desperation clearly written on his face. "Destiny, please, give me another chance. I swear, I'll spend every day showing you just how much I love you."

The hurt in Destiny's eyes was a tangible ache in his chest, but she shook her head slowly. "No, Miles. You lost that chance. We both know that I deserve to be treated better." Her voice was barely above a whisper, but it cut him like a knife.

"Destiny, I—" he started, but she held up a hand to silence him.

"Can I ever trust you to choose me over her? No, I don't think so. Have a good day, Miles," she said with a sad finality. She closed the door gently, leaving Miles standing in the dimly lit hallway, the pain of rejection settling heavily within him.

He leaned against the wall, devastated by her words, and buried his face in his hands. Was he being selfish in wanting a second chance? The thought gnawed at him, but he knew he couldn't just walk away without trying to make amends, not only for himself but for Destiny too. And he had to start by fixing what Candy had destroyed.

Determined, Miles pulled out his phone and dialed the number of the owners of the cafe. His heart raced as he waited for someone to answer.

"Hello, David and Emma Mitchell's office, this is Gianna speaking," came the cheerful greeting.

"Hi Gianna. My name is Miles. I am the CEO of Vortex and I was wondering if David and Emma have a moment to speak with me" His voice was urgent, filled with purpose. He needed to right some wrongs, starting with the cafe.

* * *

Destiny leaned against the door, listening as Miles' footsteps faded away down the hall. She closed her eyes, feeling a mix of pain and relief wash over her. As she stood there, gathering her thoughts, determination stirred within her.

"Enough," she whispered to herself, straightening up. "I am not a doormat. Not anymore."

She stared at her reflection in a nearby mirror, her hazel eyes resolute. Gone was the woman who allowed others to walk all over her. In her place stood someone strong, fierce, and ready to take control of her own life.

"Okay, Destiny," she said, psyching herself up. "Let's make some changes."

With her new determination and a steely glint in her hazel eyes, Destiny strode to the bathroom, discarding her worn-out clothes on the floor. The warm water of the shower washed over her like a baptism, soothing her aching muscles and rinsing away the pain that had clung to her for far too long. She meticulously shaved her legs, savoring the smoothness that followed, and massaged fragrant lotion into her skin.

"Time for a fresh start," she murmured, studying her reflection in the steamy mirror. "New beginnings, new me."

Destiny blew out her hair in big, luxurious waves, feeling a sense of pride as they cascaded down her back. With a light touch, she applied a layer of makeup, enhancing her natural beauty while allowing her inner strength to shine through. Never again would she allow anyone to make her feel small or unimportant.

"Alright, Destiny, you've got this," she told herself, striking a confident pose. "This is your time to shine."

Just as she finished dressing, her phone rang. It was

Rebecca, one of the cafe's waitresses. "Hey, Des," she said, slightly out of breath. "Sorry to bother you, but Jenny called in sick, and we're swamped. Can you please come down and help?"

"Of course," Destiny replied, her voice steady and strong. "I'll be right there."

As she descended the stairs, Destiny felt her sense of purpose return. This wasn't just about helping out at the cafe; it was about stepping up and showing the world who she truly was—a woman who refused to be walked over ever again. With each step, her resolve grew stronger, and by the time she reached the cafe floor, she was ready to face whatever and whoever crossed her path.

"Alright, team!" she announced, clapping her hands together. "Let's get to work!"

The staff rallied around her, and together they tackled the busy day with enthusiasm, laughter, and determination. Destiny's heart swelled with pride as she watched her team work in harmony, their laughter and camaraderie filling the cafe with a warm, infectious energy.

"Wow, Des, you're killing it today!" Rebecca remarked during a brief lull.

"Thanks," Destiny replied with a smile, feeling a surge of pride. "I've finally realized my worth. It's amazing what that will do for you."

"About time!" Lila chimed in, clapping her on the back. "You always were a force to be reckoned with—you just needed to see it for yourself."

Stepping into the kitchen, Destiny inhaled deeply, allowing the comforting scents of baking bread and fresh coffee to rejuvenate her senses. She noticed the Mitchells standing by the door, their expressions a mixture of unease and determination. Destiny's hazel eyes met theirs, and she strode over with purposeful steps.

"Destiny, could we have a word with you in the office?" David asked, his voice tinged with an apologetic tone.

"Of course," she replied, curiosity piquing as she led them into the small but cozy office. The walls were lined with shelves overflowing with cookbooks and binders, and a large window offered a picturesque view of the bustling cafe.

Once they had settled into their chairs, David cleared his throat and began. "We received a call from the owner of the company that sent us the complaint about you."

Emma chimed in, her voice soft yet firm. "The CEO, Miles, told us it was actually another employee who stole the money, not you. He'll be holding them accountable. Destiny, he said you've been nothing but professional."

David nodded solemnly. "We're so sorry for doubting you and demoting you. You really didn't deserve any of this."

"You did what you had to do. I'm thankful that you kept me on." Destiny gave each of them a kind smile, they really had been nothing but kind to her from the moment they met. "I love this place."

"Would you be willing to take the manager position back?" Emma asked hesitantly, wringing her hands.

Destiny felt a surge of emotion, a whirlwind of relief, gratitude, and disbelief. All those sleepless nights, worrying about her future, finally seemed to be fading away. But she couldn't help wondering if taking the job back would be wise, considering everything she'd gone through.

She paused for a moment, gathering her thoughts before speaking. "I appreciate your apology and the offer to come back as manager." She met their gaze, her expression resolute. "But I need to know that you'll trust me going forward. I can't work in an environment where I'm constantly looking over my shoulder."

"Absolutely," David agreed, nodding fervently. "We should have trusted you from the start, and we won't make that mistake again."

"Then I'd be happy to take the job back," Destiny replied, her voice strong and steady. The relief that washed over the Mitchells' faces was palpable.

"Thank you, Destiny," Emma whispered, tears of gratitude welling in her eyes. "And again, we're truly sorry for all the pain this caused you."

Destiny's heart pounded in her chest as she walked out of the office, a smile lighting up her face. Her hazel eyes sparkled with renewed hope and determination. The Mitchells offered a final apologetic wave before exiting the cafe, leaving Destiny to share the good news.

She spotted Lila by the counter, tinkering with the cash register. Her jet-black hair was pulled back into a messy bun, her eyes gleamed with curiosity as Destiny approached.

"Guess what?" Destiny exclaimed, barely containing her excitement. "They offered me my job back as manager!"

Lila's eyes widened. "No way!" She jumped up, practically tackling Destiny in a hug. "That's amazing! I knew they'd come around!"

"Apparently, Miles made a call and cleared everything up for me," Destiny confessed, her voice softening as she thought of his actions.

"Of course he did," Lila said knowingly, a grin tugging at her lips. "Now come on, let's celebrate!"

With laughter bubbling from their throats, Destiny and Lila performed an impromptu happy dance, their arms flailing wildly as they spun around. The other staff members observed their celebration with bemused expressions.

"Alright, everyone!" Lila called out, clapping her hands together. "Gather 'round, I've got an announcement to make!"

The employees quickly huddled together. Destiny felt a warmth spread through her chest as she looked at the faces of her colleagues, knowing she had their support.

"Destiny is officially our manager again!" Lila announced proudly, beaming at her best friend.

A cheer erupted from the staff, accompanied by claps and whistles. Their enthusiasm was infectious, and Destiny couldn't help but laugh along with them.

"Alright, alright," she said, raising her hands to quiet the crowd. "Thank you all so much, but we've got a cafe to run! Let's get back to work!"

With that, the staff dispersed, their spirits lifted and decided to put their best foot forward. Destiny glanced over at Lila, who gave her a knowing nod.

"Things are finally looking up, huh?" Lila said softly, her eyes filled with pride.

Destiny smiled, feeling a sense of hope and belonging. "Yes, they are," she agreed, her heart swelling with gratitude. And as she looked around the bustling cafe, she knew things really were finally starting to look up.

twenty-six

MILES SHUT THE DOOR OF HIS CAR AND TRUDGED ACROSS the parking lot towards his office. His face was haggard as he approached the front doors of the building. It was early, and only the night guard was present. Miles forced a smile as the guard glanced at him with concern. He knew he looked terrible; he had been working tirelessly for the past two weeks. It had been exactly that long since he had last seen Destiny.

He glanced at the clock; it was early and he was exhausted, but sleep seemed like a distant luxury he couldn't afford. Instead, he buried himself in work, hoping that somehow, it would numb the pain. Miles, Max, and Malcolm had successfully closed the breach, and everything was back to normal—or as normal as it could be without Destiny by his side.

"Miles? Do you want to head home?" Candy's voice pierced through his thoughts, her heels clicking against the floor as she entered his office. Miles looked up, his eyes weary and devoid of their usual spark.

Miles hated that Candy felt his house was now her

home. He was getting agitated and said in a clipped tone, "It's safe now for you to go to your own house. Just pack up your things and make sure you're not there when I get home." His words were harsh, but he couldn't bring himself to care.

"Miles? Where are you going?!" Candy whispered loudly as Miles strode through the house and out the front door, a determined look in his green eyes.

"None of your concern," he replied curtly, remembering the promise he and his brothers had made to keep their knowledge about Candy to themselves until they had proof.

Candy frowned, clearly unhappy with his response. "Fine," she spat out, turning on her heel and leaving him alone once more.

Sighing, Miles leaned back in his chair, his gaze drifting to the framed photo on his desk—a happier time, when Destiny's laughter filled his world and her hazel eyes held nothing but love for him. A sudden pang of determination surged through him. He was going to fight for the woman who had captured his heart so completely, the woman he'd completely destroyed.

"Destiny, I won't give up on us," he whispered, his voice cracking with emotion. "I'll do whatever it takes to make you see how much I love you."

With that promise lingering in the air, Miles shut down his computer and left the office, resolve fueled his every step. He knew it wouldn't be easy, but he was willing to face any challenge if it meant having Destiny back in his life

As the sun sank low in the sky, Miles hammered the last nail into the new gazebo. It was a beautiful white structure that gleamed against the backdrop of the sunset. The spot where he and Destiny had shared their first kiss now transferred into a sanctuary for stargazing. As he stepped back to admire his handiwork, he imagined her warm in his embrace as they sat under the stars with a bottle of wine and whatever hors d'oeuvres Destiny concocted.

"She's going to love this," he murmured to himself. "As long as I can get her to come back here, that is." He gave himself a self depreciating chuckle.

"Earth to Miles," a voice jolted him from his thoughts. Max stood in the doorway, his brow furrowed with concern. "Are you okay?"

"Absolutely not." Miles said as he took a swig of his beer. "I mean.. I've never been worse than I am right now. I mean, I've survived a childhood with fucking Caroline. But what's going on now and how I feel about losing Destiny? It's so much worse."

Max crossed the yard and sat down on the bench opposite Miles. He studied his younger brother for a moment before speaking. "Anything is possible, Miles. Don't give up hope."

"Easy for you to say," Miles muttered, bitterness creeping into his voice. "You didn't lose the love of your life because of your own stupidity."

"Hey," Max said gently, leaning forward. "You made a mistake. It happens to the best of us. The important thing is to learn from it and move forward."

"Move forward?" Miles echoed, his green eyes filled with despair. "How can I do that when all I want is to go back in time and fix everything?"

"We can't change the past," Max replied, rising from his seat. "But we *can* shape our future. You need to show Destiny how much you love her, not just tell her."

"Show her?" Miles frowned, the gears in his mind turning as he considered Max's words. "You're right. I've been trying to tell her in texts and voicemails, but maybe... maybe showing her would be better."

"Exactly," Max agreed, placing a hand on his brother's shoulder. "You built this beautiful gazebo for her. Now it's time to let it speak for you."

"Thanks, Max," Miles said softly, grateful for the support of his older brother. "I'll do whatever it takes to make this right."

"Good," Max replied, giving Miles' shoulder a reassuring squeeze. "Now go get ready. The night is young, and who knows what it might bring?"

As Max went back into the house, Miles allowed himself a small smile, hope flickering like a candle flame in the darkness. Determined to win back Destiny's heart, he was resolved to show her just how much she truly meant to him.

Miles stared at the door as it clicked shut behind Max, his words echoing in his mind. Show her, not tell her. He needed to do something more than just send texts that fell on deaf ears. He would show Destiny what she meant to him by sharing the beautiful space he'd created for her.

The scent of fresh flowers filled the air as Miles entered the local flower shop. "Do you have daisies?" he asked the florist, who nodded with a warm smile and led him to a display of the delicate white blooms. They reminded him of his childhood, when Destiny taught him to weave flower chains and they spent hours trying to get his right. He purchased a bouquet and headed to the park, searching for inspiration.

Sitting on a quiet bench under an old oak tree, Miles began to weave the daisies into a chain, each reminding him of a time where he'd seen Destiny smile or laugh in his direction. The sun shone high in the sky as he worked, the world around him fading away with each intricate twist and turn.

Finally, the chain was complete, and Miles penned a note to accompany it. His heart pounded in his chest as he wrote, the weight of his emotions spilling onto the paper. He knew he couldn't take back the mistakes he'd made, but he could show Destiny how much he had learned from his mistake. He just hoped that would be enough.

With a deep breath, Miles approached Destiny's apartment, clutching the gift and note tightly in his hand. He hung them on her door without knocking, his fingers lingering for a moment before he forced himself to let go. As he turned and walked away, he held onto the hope that this simple gesture would be the first step in mending their fractured love story.

"Please, Destiny," he whispered to himself as he walked towards Vortex. "Give me a chance."

* * *

Destiny stood at the threshold of her apartment, her eyes glued to the daisy chain that hung on her door. She couldn't believe it—Miles had remembered their connection to these simple flowers. Carefully, she removed the chain and unfolded the note tucked beneath its delicate petals.

Destiny I love you. You are my everything. I made this chain, yes it took far too long. Just like it used to. I know I don't deserve a chance, but can you meet me at my house? I want to show you something. Tonight at 8. All my love, Miles.

A flood of emotions washed over her as she read. She knew that Miles was trying to make amends, and even though she was still hurt by his actions, she couldn't deny the small glimmer of happiness that flickered inside her.

"Alright, Miles," she whispered, clutching the daisy chain to her chest. "Let's see what you got."

Destiny stood in front of her full-length mirror, carefully applying a soft pink lip gloss to complete her look. She chose an outfit that matched her new feeling of empowerment. A flowy, off-the-shoulder white blouse tucked into high-waisted, dark denim jeans and a pair of strappy black heels completed the look.

Her brown hair fell in loose waves around her shoulders, framing her face beautifully. She had opted for a natural makeup look, with just enough definition in her eyes to make them stand out. As she looked at her reflection, Destiny felt a surge of pride in the woman she had become.

"Okay," she whispered to herself, "let's do this."

As the clock struck eight, Destiny took a deep breath and headed towards Miles' house, her heart pounding with a mix of excitement and trepidation. The daisy chain wrapped around her wrist, a reminder of the love they once shared and the possibility that maybe, just maybe, it could be rekindled.

Upon arriving at Miles' house, she saw a trail of rose petals leading from the driveway to the front door. A note accompanied the petals:

Follow the flowers. I'll see you soon. Miles.

Her curiosity piqued, Destiny carefully stepped onto the rose petal path, feeling a sense of enchantment as she followed the fragrant trail.

"Whatever you're up to, Miles, you certainly know how to make an entrance," she mused, her spirits lifting despite the uncertainty that filled her heart.

Following the rose petals, Destiny stepped into Miles' backyard and noticed a line of candles surrounding a pathway that led to something magical. Her heart began to race with anticipation as she smiled at the romance of it all. As she turned the corner of the side of the porch, her eyes widened at the sight before her.

Miles was standing in the exact spot of their first kiss, but now, in its place was a beautiful white gazebo. The structure was intricate and delicate, with ornate carvings that seemed to tell a story of love and devotion. Its wooden pillars were wrapped in elegant ivy, adding an ethereal touch to the scene. A glass-domed roof allowed the stars to shine through, creating an intimate and enchanting atmosphere.

"Wow," Destiny whispered under her breath as she continued towards the gazebo.

As she got closer, she realized that the gazebo was surrounded by what looked like a thousand flowers of all kinds—roses, lilies, daisies, and more. The vibrant colors only added to the enchantment of the moment.

"Surprise," Miles said softly, his voice tinged with a mix of excitement and trepidation. Destiny stepped onto the gazebo, the sweet aroma of countless flowers enveloping her as she took in the scene before her.

Twinkling lights adorned the entire structure, reminiscent of their first date when the trees had been illuminated by the same magical glow. As she looked around, the memories of that night came flooding back, and she couldn't help but smile at how their love story had begun.

"Are you ready?" Miles asked, biting his lip nervously. Destiny nodded, feeling her heart race in anticipation.

With the press of a button, the projector came to life, casting images onto a makeshift screen set up on one side of the gazebo. Destiny watched as photos from their childhood played across the screen—innocent moments of laughter, shared secrets, and the foundation of a bond that would eventually grow into something much deeper.

The slideshow continued, showcasing pictures from when they reconnected and started dating. Destiny felt tears prick the corners of her eyes as she relived the moments spent with Lila, Malcolm, Max, and Vivi during the holidays. She marveled at the thought and effort that went into pulling off such a gesture. She didn't even know that a lot of the pictures had been taken.

"Wow, Miles, this is...incredible," Destiny murmured, smiling widely and wiping away a stray tear as the video neared its end.

The final frame displayed Miles, looking directly into the camera, a vulnerable expression etched across his face as he spoke. "Destiny, I know I've made mistakes, and I can't change the past. But I can promise you that I will do everything in my power to make our future together the best it can be. All I'm asking is for another chance to prove my love to you."

The darkness that enveloped the projector seemed to reflect Destiny's own tangled emotions, a mix of pain and joy that threatened to overwhelm her. As she processed the memories displayed before her, she couldn't help but feel an ache in her heart for what they had lost.

"Destiny?" Miles' voice cut through her thoughts, tinged with both hope and vulnerability. "What are you thinking?"

She turned to face him, her hazel eyes glistening with unshed tears. "I...I just need time, Miles," she admitted softly. "There's so much I need to process. You've shown me how much you care about me, but I have to figure things out for myself. A lot has happened between us."

Disappointment flickered across his face, but he nodded in understanding. "Alright. Whatever you need, Destiny. I'll be here, waiting. Let me know if there's anything that you need from me, no matter how small."

"Thank you," she whispered, her lips curving into a sad smile.

Without another word, Destiny turned away from him and made her way back down the path lined with rose petals. The scent of the flowers mingled with the crisp night air, carrying with it a bittersweet feeling of longing. As she reached her car, she paused, taking a deep breath to steady herself before climbing in and starting the engine.

The drive home was filled with contemplation as Destiny weighed the pros and cons of giving Miles another chance. Her mind played in a loop the video he prepared, his heartfelt plea, and every tender moment they shared together.

They had shared so many amazing moments. He suspected her of stealing from his company, which he knew she would never do. He moved in a girl who treated her with utter contempt. It was too much for Destiny, she knew that Miles felt deeply for Candy, if not then why would he invite her into his home? How could she ever forgive him, even though deep down she still loved him?

Pulling into her driveway, Destiny sighed heavily, feeling the weight of her decision bearing down on her. She entered her apartment, the familiar surroundings offering little solace as she ascended the stairs to her bedroom. With each step, she felt the ghost of Miles' touch, the memory of his warmth, and the taste of their love lingering on her lips.

In the sanctuary of her room, Destiny prepared for bed, her thoughts still a whirlwind of emotion. As she slipped beneath the covers, she clung to a small sliver of hope that with time, her heart would heal and find its way back to Miles. But for now, she would allow herself to be embraced by the night, her dreams awash in a sea of daisies and starlight.

twenty-seven

DESTINY DRAGGED HER TIRED FEET DOWN THE STAIRS, EACH step feeling heavier than the last. Her hazel eyes were rimmed with dark circles, speaking volumes about her sleepless night.

"Ugh," Destiny muttered under her breath as she pushed open the kitchen door. "I need something to take my mind off things." Determined to find solace in her passion for cooking, she decided to try making a new soup recipe that had been dancing around in her head for weeks. She began rummaging through the well-stocked pantry, reaching for the ingredients that would soon coalesce into a comforting bowl of goodness.

"Let's see," she murmured, ticking off items on her mental checklist. "Butternut squash, sweet potatoes, carrots... ah, there they are." She gathered the vibrant orange vegetables in her arms and brought them over to the counter. Destiny carefully washed and peeled them, revealing their hidden depths of color and fragrance.

It wasn't long before the kitchen was filled with the rich aroma of roasting vegetables. The warmth from the oven seeped into Destiny's weary bones, providing temporary respite from her emotional turmoil. As she started to blend the roasted ingredients with a mix of vegetable broth and coconut milk, Destiny couldn't help but be drawn into the mesmerizing whirlpool of colors—the deep orange and creamy white swirling together like an edible work of art.

"Maybe a hint of spice would do wonders," she thought, selecting a jar of curry powder from the spice rack. A pinch of the fragrant powder sent tendrils of steam curling up into the air, adding another layer of complexity to the already heavenly scent filling the kitchen. Destiny tasted the soup, closing her eyes in satisfaction as the warm, velvety liquid filled her mouth with a burst of flavor —sweet and earthy, with just a touch of heat.

"Perfect," she whispered, feeling a small sense of accomplishment in creating something so delicious. For a brief moment, Destiny was able to forget about her heartache and lose herself in the art of cooking.

Before Destiny knew it, hours had passed. The rhythmic sounds of knives slicing through vegetables and the bubbling of her soup on the stove were interrupted by the familiar chime of the cafe door opening. Employees began clocking in, chatting about their weekends and plans for the day. A sudden burst of cool air brushed against Destiny's face as Lila walked into the kitchen, her eyes scanning the room before landing on Destiny.

"Well, don't you look like shit?" Lila remarked, her tone a mix of concern and amusement. "What's wrong?"

Destiny sighed and leaned against the counter, feeling the cold stainless steel press against her back.

"Last night was...unexpected," Destiny began, her voice faltering a bit. "Miles surprised me with memories of our relationship through time, as in starting when we were kids. The rose petals, the candles, the gazebo in the spot of our first kiss with all those flowers adorning it. He asked for another chance."

Lila raised an eyebrow, her curiosity piqued. "Wow, that's…intense. So, what's the problem? You still not sure about him because of the whole Candy situation?"

Destiny nodded, her hazel eyes clouded with uncertainty. "I just don't know if I can trust him. He was so blind and uncaring of my feelings about Candy. It feels like I'm setting myself up to get hurt again. Not to mention that he didn't even check on me when I got demoted." Destiny finished speaking and looked up at Lila, whose eyes seemed to be sizing her up. "What do you think I should do, Lila?"

Lila leaned against the cafe's kitchen counter, crossing her arms and giving Destiny a thoughtful look. "Sounds like Miles is trying to fight for something he wants," she began, tapping her finger on her chin. "But a relationship isn't just one person fighting, Des. If he's someone you see in your life, even a little bit, you need to fight for him too."

Destiny mulled over Lila's words, memories of times spent with Miles flooding her brain. Their first kiss under a sky filled with stars, holding hands while stargazing on a chilly winter night, and the warmth shared during the holidays together. She recalled the Christmas gift he had given her—a locket containing a picture of them in kindergarten on one side, and a silhouette photo of them looking at the stars that Lila had taken during a family picnic they all had attended.

With renewed purpose, Destiny untied her apron and draped it over the back of a chair before making her way towards the front door of the cafe. The smell of freshly brewed coffee and warm pastries lingered in the air as she hurried through the cozy space, her footsteps echoing off the hardwood floors.

"Where are you going?" Lila shouted after her, following close behind with a grin.

"Vortex!" Destiny called back, pushing open the door and stepping out onto the sidewalk.

"Ooh wait. I'm going, too!" Lila called behind her, rushing out the door as well.

The morning sun was a beacon to her intended destination as Destiny ran avoiding people as they hurried about, going to work or running errands. But Destiny had only one destination in mind—and it was time she fought for what she wanted.

The moment Destiny and Lila burst through the sleek glass doors of Vortex, the corporate world felt a million miles away from the cozy warmth of the cafe.

"Come on," Lila urged, grabbing Destiny's hand and pulling her towards the elevator. Their footsteps echoed across the vast lobby as they raced past receptionists and suited executives, who raised their eyebrows at the pair but said nothing.

"Shit ," Destiny muttered under her breath, suddenly realizing something. "Candy took my access card. I can't get up there."

"Let me," Lila said, unflinching. She whipped out her own access card and swiped it against the elevator's scanner. The familiar ding signaled their success.

Destiny laughed, her eyes wide with disbelief. "Where did you get that?" she asked, her curiosity piqued.

Lila smirked, leaning against the elevator wall. "Miles destroyed my best friend," she stated matter-of-factly. "He owes me." With a conspiratorial wink, she pressed the button for Miles' floor, and the elevator began its ascent.

As the elevator doors slid open, Destiny's heart hammered in her chest, anticipation coursed through her veins. They stepped out onto the polished floors, and

Destiny spotted Candy sitting at her desk outside Miles' office. At the sight of them, Candy's icy blue eyes narrowed into a glare, and she began to rise from her seat.

"Too slow, Cry Baby Candy" Lila whispered, her electric blue eyes twinkling with mischief as they dashed past Candy, who struggled to keep up in her stiletto heels.

Destiny threw open the door to Miles' office, her breath catching in her throat. The large room was filled with floor-to-ceiling windows that bathed everything in a soft, golden light. Max and Malcolm stood near the window, immersed in hushed discussion, but there was no sign of Miles.

"Where is he?" Destiny asked, her voice quivering with uncertainty as she scanned the room.

Just then, the sound of the door opening behind her made her heart skip a beat. She turned, and there he was: Miles, his brown hair tousled and his green eyes searching hers. As their gazes locked, Destiny felt all her love for him flooding back to her like a tidal wave, leaving her breathless and rooted to the spot.

Destiny's heart raced as she took in the tense atmosphere of Miles' office. Max, Malcolm, and Miles all stood with clenched jaws and furrowed brows, their anger palpable in the air. Miles walked behind his desk, while Max and Malcolm exchanged heated glances between them.

"Is everything okay?" Destiny asked hesitantly, her voice barely a whisper. She felt a sudden pang of uncertainty, wondering if she should have stayed away.

"Everything's fine," Miles replied curtly, not meeting her gaze. He looked to Max and Malcolm, who both nodded in agreement, but their expressions remained tight and troubled.

Before Destiny could question them further, Candy

barged into the office, her face flushed with fury. "I'm so sorry!" she exclaimed, feigning concern. "I tried to stop them, but they just pushed right past me!" The force of her entrance knocked Destiny and Lila off balance, sending them stumbling.

Just as Destiny was about to speak, Candy stepped forward with a wicked smile. "Allow me to handle this," she said, reaching out and gripping Destiny's arm with surprising strength. Her sharp nails dug into Destiny's flesh, making her yelp in pain.

"Let go of me!" Destiny growled through gritted teeth, trying to free herself from Candy's grasp.

Candy merely sneered at her, oblivious to the anger that radiated off the boys in the room. They seemed poised to intervene, but Lila beat them to it. With a fierce determination in her eyes, she slapped Candy's hand away hard, finally freeing Destiny.

"Ow!" Candy cried, rubbing her hand and giving Lila a venomous glare. "You didn't have to be so rough!"

"Really?" Destiny stared at her in disbelief, nursing her own injured arm. "You practically drew blood, and you're complaining about Lila being too rough?"

"Are you okay?" Miles asked, walking over to Destiny with concern in his eyes.

"Fine," Candy replied quickly, batting her eyelashes at him. "Thanks for asking."

Miles cleared his throat, and when he spoke, there was a cold edge to his voice. "Actually, I was talking to Destiny."

Destiny's heart fluttered at the concern in his eyes, and she couldn't help but feel grateful that he had her back. She knew she needed to focus on the situation at hand, but part of her thought about how Miles didn't defend her at his mother's dinner until she got up and walked away.

"Thanks, Miles," Destiny murmured softly, meeting his gaze. "I'm okay. Just a little shocked."

As she spoke, the office door cracked open and Vivienne slipped inside, her chestnut hair pulled back in a sleek bun and her sapphire eyes filled with seriousness. Destiny managed a smile, but anxiety bubbled under the surface as Vivi's stern expression seemed to hint at something wildly out of place.

"Vivienne?" Candy sneered, crossing her arms over her designer blouse. "What are you doing here? Don't you ever give the gossip tree a rest?"

Destiny bristled at the insult, her protective instincts flaring up for her friend. She opened her mouth to snap a retort when Miles stepped forward, his green eyes flashing dangerously as he got into Candy's personal space.

"Enough, Candy," he growled, his voice low and controlled. "Max, Malcolm, and I have been investigating everything that's happened."

Destiny's heart raced, and confusion swirled within her as she tried to grasp what Miles was getting at. She glanced between him and her friends, hoping for some clarity. Her thoughts were racing, trying to piece together the puzzle laid out before her.

"Everything?" she echoed, her hazel eyes wide with surprise. "What do you mean? What have you found?"

The office was tense, the atmosphere thick with anticipation as everyone waited for answers.

"Let's just say we've uncovered some truths," Max chimed in, his voice was steady and reassuring, though the situation was anything but.

"Truths?" Destiny repeated, overwhelmed by the unknown. She wished she knew what was going on, but it seemed like everyone else had a piece of the puzzle that she didn't.

Destiny's heart raced as she tried to process the information, her hazel eyes darting between Miles and Candy. She wondered if they had finally figured out who was behind the breach—it certainly wasn't her.

Her thoughts were interrupted by Miles' gentle touch as he turned towards her, holding her hands.

"Destiny," he said softly, his green eyes filled with regret. "Candy has been behind everything. And I mean everything. Down to you having to move away in high school.. Candy made Colter fire your father. I'm so sorry, Des."

The weight of his words hit her like a ton of bricks, and her hands trembled within his grasp. A mix of anger and sorrow surged through her veins, and hot tears began streaming down her pale cheeks. Destiny whipped her head in Candy's direction, her voice shaking as she screamed, "You killed my father!"

Miles held her back, concern etched on his face as he asked, "What do you mean, Destiny?"

"Remember when I told you my father had cancer?" she said, swallowing the lump in her throat. "He was getting tested regularly because it ran in our family, and because he lost his job, we couldn't afford it. He missed one year of testing, and he died five years later… all because of her." The memories of her father, once so vivid, now seemed to be slipping away from her grasp like sand through her fingers. "We could've caught it sooner, and he might still be alive today."

Destiny's chest heaved with every breath, her emotions threatening to spill over. The pain of losing her father cut deep, and the knowledge that Candy played a part in his death felt like a betrayal she'd never recover from. As she stared at Candy, her eyes glinted with defiance, offering not a shred of remorse for her role.

The tense atmosphere in the office was palpable, as if a storm was brewing just outside the windows. Everyone's eyes were fixed on Candy, their expressions a mixture of disbelief and disgust. Even Max and Malcolm, who had always been somewhat neutral when it came to Candy, couldn't hide their disdain. Destiny felt Miles' strong arms wrap around her, cocooning her in his warmth and protection, as she continued to glare at the woman who had caused what felt like every ounce of pain in her life.

"Isn't it funny?" Candy wore a sinister grin, sauntering over to them as if she were walking down a runway. "You all think you know everything." Her eyes flicked across the room before landing on Miles. "You see, dearest Miles... Caroline, your precious mother, was the mastermind behind it all." The words dripped from her lips like venom, a twisted smile playing across her face as she reveled in the shock of her revelation. "That's right, you asshole. Your mother was the one who came up with everything. I was just her little soldier."

Destiny's heart clenched in her chest, the implications of Candy's words sending a shiver down her spine. Could it be true? Did Miles' mother play a part? Destiny knew his mother was a bitch, but would she have gone that far? She searched for answers in his eyes, trying to gauge his reaction to the news. Miles' expression was unreadable, but the tick of his jaw betrayed the turmoil raging within him. He held her tighter, his grip conveying his silent promise that he wouldn't let her go through this alone.

"Are you seriously trying to shift the blame onto someone else right now?" Lila spat, her voice laced with contempt. "Just because you had a partner in crime doesn't make you any less guilty, Candy."

"Guilty?" Candy sneered, her gaze flicking dismissively

over Lila. "I never claimed innocence, darling. I merely stated a fact."

Destiny could feel the anger bubbling beneath her skin, threatening to erupt like a volcano. She took a deep breath, trying to steady herself as she focused on the gentle pressure of Miles' arms around her. It was in moments like these that she remembered all the reasons why she had fallen in love with him in the first place—his unwavering support, his fierce loyalty, and his ability to make her feel safe even in the darkest of times.

"Regardless of who came up with the plan," Destiny said quietly, her voice shaking with raw emotion, "you both have blood on your hands. And nothing you say will ever change that fact."

Destiny turned to Miles and waited for him to say something. The seconds ticked by and it felt like hours by the time he spoke.

"Candy," Miles started, pausing as if fighting back the pain and anger at this revelation. "Tell me everything. What you have done and my mother."

Destiny watched as Candy took a seat on one of the chairs. As she sits, she says, "Well let's just start from the beginning. Shall we."

Destiny and Miles looked at Candy with their arms crossed over their chests knowing that their lives are going to be forever changed by what Candy has to say.

twenty-eight

CANDY COULDN'T HELP BUT REVEL IN THE ATTENTION SHE was receiving from everyone in the room. It was as if she were the star of her own show, and she couldn't help but think about how interesting this was going to get. The way Destiny's eyes bore into hers, filled with a mix of pain and disbelief, only fueled Candy's desire to take center stage.

"Are you all comfortable?" Candy asked with a sly grin, taking a seat in the plush leather chair positioned behind Miles' desk. "Because I am." She crossed her legs, showing off her perfectly toned calves, and took a moment to admire her Christian Louboutin heels. The red soles seemed to taunt those present. They were almost proof of the fact that she could do as she pleased and the universe will still give her all that she wanted.

"Well let's just start from the beginning. Shall we." she said, flicking an imaginary speck of lint from her immaculate designer dress. Though Destiny looked like she wanted nothing more than to lunge across the desk and strangle her, Candy knew that Miles' protective presence would keep her safe—for now, at least.

"It all began when we were just five years old," Candy said with a smirk, uncrossing her legs and leaning forward on the desk.

The room seemed to darken as she spun the tale, recalling the first time she had eavesdropped on Daddy and Miss Caroline. She could still remember the way the afternoon sun streamed through the curtains in her father's study, casting long shadows that danced across the floor as they spoke in hushed tones.

"Destiny, you may not know this, but your precious Miles was quite the little heartbreaker back then," Candy said, her eyes flickering with amusement. "All the girls wanted to play house with him—even me." She paused for a moment, letting the words hang heavy in the air before continuing. "But there was one person who didn't think much of you, Destiny. And that person was none other than Miss Caroline."

The room seemed to collectively hold its breath as Candy recounted how she had hidden behind the door, listening intently as her father implored Miss Caroline to leave her wealthy husband for him. The desperation in his voice was palpable, and it fueled Candy's determination to find a way to use the information against them later.

"Miss Caroline, however, was not so easily swayed," Candy continued, her voice dripping with disdain. "She didn't want to give up her lavish lifestyle, so she rebuffed Daddy's advances and insisted that they keep their relationship a secret."

Candy glanced around the room, reveling in the shock etched on everyone's faces. She knew that this revelation would send ripples through their tight-knit group, and the thought of the chaos that would ensue made her giddy with anticipation.

"Of course, Destiny, it wasn't just about money for

Miss Caroline," Candy added, her voice taking on a mocking tone. "She always hated that Miles chose you. There were so many others that wanted his attention, yet he only had eyes for you."

With a flourish, Candy thought about how she skipped away from the scene of her childhood eavesdropping, her laughter echoing through the room like the tinkling of shattered glass.

"Ah, those were the days," she sighed, leaning back in her chair as she prepared to launch into the next part of her tale. "But little did I know just how useful that knowledge would be in the years to come..."

As the words poured from her lips, Candy could see the doubt and hurt growing in Destiny's eyes—and it only made her want to push the knife in deeper. After all, she had waited years for this moment, and she wouldn't let it slip through her fingers now.

Candy's cold blue eyes flickered over the faces of her captive audience, drinking in their shock and disbelief like a potent elixir. The power she felt coursing through her veins as she held them enthralled with her tale was intoxicating, and it only fueled her desire to reveal more.

"Shall I continue?" she purred, absently twirling a strand of her blonde hair around her finger.

With a wicked grin, Candy launched into the next part of her story, her voice soft and seductive as she wove a web of betrayal and intrigue. As her words painted vivid images of their shared past, she could feel the tension in the room building, and she relished in the knowledge that she was the one pulling the strings.

"Fast forward a few years," she began, "to when we were all 14. Destiny was still a thorn in my side, always getting in the way of what I wanted most—Miles."

In her mind's eye, Candy could see it all unfolding

again: Caroline, her father's secret lover, speaking urgently with Colter, trying to convince him to fire Destiny's father. Colter had refused, praising the man's work ethic and insisting that he couldn't let him go. Candy remembered the frustration that had bubbled up inside her as she watched the scene from a distance, knowing that something needed to be done if she were ever to have a chance with Miles.

"Caroline knew that Destiny needed to be out of the picture, so she came up with a plan," Candy continued, her voice dripping with glee. "She told me to convince my father that it was in his best interest to fire Destiny's dad. So I did what any teenage girl in love would do—I put on my best 'daddy's girl' act and went to see him in his office."

Candy paused for a moment, savoring the memory of her manipulative performance. She had been so convincing, tears streaming down her cheeks as she lied about Destiny bullying her and mocking her wealth. Her father had fallen for it hook, line, and sinker—and she had walked out of his office triumphant, sharing a wicked grin with Caroline as they sealed their alliance.

"Of course, Daddy did what I asked. After all, his sweet daughter was being relentlessly bullied," Candy said, her voice cold and unfeeling. "Destiny's father lost his job, and she was forced to move away."

Candy's eyes shifted from the horrified faces around her, landing on Destiny as she is pressed against Miles giving Candy a glare that shows a confidence she has never seen out of Destiny. Seeing them together like that—so close and loving—sent a surge of anger through her veins. She clenched her fists at her sides, nails digging into her palms as she imagined herself in Destiny's place, wrapped in Miles' strong arms.

"Hey, Candy," Destiny choked out between sobs.

"What about that Ken and Barbie message? Who came up with that?"

Candy couldn't help but throw her head back and release an evil, throaty cackle. The sound echoed through Miles' office, bouncing off the walls and making everyone else flinch. "Oh, that was me," she admitted without shame, smirking at the memory. "I sent it to everyone on my phone, but I made sure to send it to you from Miles' phone. And then, of course, I deleted the message right after, so all he would see is your pathetic little goodbye."

She watched as Destiny's face paled even further, her hazel eyes wide with disbelief. "Caroline's the one who thought it'd be fun to dress up like Ken and Barbie, though. You know, make it look like a couples costume and really drive the point home." With every word, Candy's voice dripped with venom, soaking in the happiness of all of the pain she inflicted upon her rival.

Destiny clung to Miles tighter, seeking solace in his embrace. Candy could almost taste the sweet satisfaction of watching her crumble, and yet, her hunger for victory had not been satiated. She wanted more. She needed to ensure that Miles would never choose Destiny over her.

"There has to be more," Destiny choked out between sobs, her hazel eyes searching Candy's for any sign of humanity. "Why do you even work here, Candy? You have so much money already."

Candy leaned back in her chair, crossing her legs and admiring her shoes again as if they held the answers to all of life's questions. She smiled, feeling the weight of all eyes on her—just as she had always wanted. "Oh, honey," she purred, her voice dripping with condescension. "I'm just getting started."

She let the words hang in the air for a moment before continuing, her mind drifted back to when Miles had first needed an assistant. Caroline, ever the opportunist, had been the one to suggest that Candy apply for the position. At first, Candy had been hesitant—after all, why would someone like her need to work?

But then, she saw the potential benefits. If she could get close to Miles, maybe she could finally have him for herself. It was a tantalizing possibility, one she couldn't resist pursuing.

"Fine," she had told Caroline, her voice steady with determination. "I'll do it, but only if you promise to try and push my relationship with Miles. I want him, Caroline, and I won't take no for an answer."

Caroline had hesitated, her blue eyes narrowing as she considered the proposition. Finally, she sighed and agreed —but only on the condition that Candy would keep her mouth shut about her ongoing affair with Candy's father. Candy knows Caroline's husband is rich and she doesn't want to lose that. It was a small price to pay for the chance at true love, and Candy had accepted without a second thought.

Candy's laughter filled the room, her icy blue eyes glittering with devious delight. "Oh, wait," she said, smirking at the stunned faces before her. "Now the story is getting good."

As Destiny stared at her in disbelief, Candy allowed herself to drift back to another memory—one that showcased just how far she'd go to secure Miles for herself.

The morning sun had barely risen when Caroline called her in a panic. Candy, still wrapped in her silk sheets, answered the phone with a yawn. "Caroline, this better be good. I was having the most wonderful dream. Let me tell you, Miles and I on one of Daddy's yachts in Greece. Can't you just see, Caroline?"

"Shut up and listen!" Caroline hissed through the

receiver. "Miles invited Destiny to the family dinner tonight!"

Candy bolted upright in bed, her heart pounding with anger. "What? How dare he?" Her voice seethed with disdain as she imagined Destiny cozying up to Miles over a lavish meal, their relationship progressing right under her nose.

"Exactly," Caroline agreed. "Which is why you need to get yourself invited too. We can't let that little nobody ruin our plans."

Candy gripped the phone tightly, anger flooding her veins. "Fine. I'll do it. Just make sure you're ready for whatever might happen."

"Of course, darling," Caroline replied with a wicked chuckle. "We'll talk some sense into my son together. Heaven knows we can't let another low life into the family. I couldn't stop Max from marrying that horrid girl, but we can stop Miles at least.."

Back in the present, Candy's eyes flashed with malicious glee as she recounted the tale. She could practically see the wheels turning in Destiny's head, the realization of just how deep Candy's manipulation went dawning on her.

"Did you really think I'd let you waltz into Miles' life without a fight?" Candy taunted, enthralled in the power she held over everyone in the room. "You never stood a chance."

Destiny's hazel eyes burned with a mixture of hurt and defiance, but she remained silent. The others, however, couldn't contain their shock and disbelief at Candy's revelation.

Candy basked in the gasps and chuckles that filled the room, her eyes sparkling with a cruel satisfaction. She knew she had them all hooked on her every word, and the thought made her icy heart race. If only they knew what else she had up her sleeve.

"How about we move on to the night of the dinner," Candy mused in a sing-song voice. "You know? Where Miles blurts his love for you?"

Candy thinks back to that night. Miles and Destiny left, with the others following not too long after. Candy stayed so that Caroline could comfort her since she was upset about Miles' large declaration.

"We still have some options, Candy," Caroline said while awkwardly patting her shoulder to try to calm her down.

"Like what?" Candy hiccupped, looking up at Caroline with despair-filled eyes. "You fucked this up by making the little bitch cry!"

"Easy," Caroline replied, a wicked grin spreading across her face as an idea took shape in her mind. "We spread a rumor that Destiny's been stealing money from the café."

"Brilliant!" Candy exclaimed, her spirits lifting instantly. "And since I'm handling the invoices, I can doctor them as needed. We could even use the extra cash!"

"Exactly," Caroline agreed, pleased by Candy's enthusiasm. And then she added, "But what if we took it a step further? What if we made Miles doubt the security of his precious company?"

Candy's eyebrows shot up, clearly intrigued. "Go on..."

"Make it look like Destiny is somehow involved. Also, make you the center of the information leak. We can add Colter in too so it isn't suspicious. That way, Miles will have no choice but to stand up for you and your family."

"Pure genius," Candy whispered, admiration shining in her eyes. "Caroline, I don't know how you do it."

"Neither do I," Caroline confessed with a shrug, a smug smile playing on her lips. "But I'm damn good at it."

As she snapped back to the present, the weight of her words settled over the room like a shroud, leaving everyone speechless. But for Candy, there was still so much more to say—and she couldn't wait to watch the pieces fall into place.

Miles' eyes blazed with fury, his hands clenched into fists at his sides. "We caught you on camera that night, Candy," he growled, his voice barely controlled. "But how the hell did you get my password?"

Candy leaned back in her chair, crossing her legs as if she didn't have a care in the world. With a smug grin, she met Miles' gaze head-on. "Oh, that was the easiest part," she purred. "Your precious nerd, Malcolm's little tech genius, Dave? A couple of nights together, and he was more than willing to spill your secrets."

"Wait. You slept with him?!" Destiny's face contorted with outrage, her hazel eyes flashing with anger.

"Please, don't be so naive," Candy scoffed, rolling her eyes. "It's just business, sweetheart. And it worked like a charm, didn't it?"

As Destiny stared at her in disbelief, Candy celebrated the chaos she'd created. The room felt electric, charged with tension, and she took the chance to bask in the attention. Her own heart might have been made of stone, but there was something intoxicating about watching others crumble under the weight of her secrets.

"Anyway," Candy continued, her voice dripping with false sweetness, "when Caroline's plan fell through, I went to her house to regroup. I knew the boys had figured out that it was me behind the breach and not Destiny, but I also knew we could still turn things around." She flicked a strand of her blonde hair over her shoulder and reminisced on the day she looked at Caroline, who had gone pale.

"Caroline told me something quite interesting then," she said, leaning forward in her chair, her eyes locked on Miles. "She said, 'Sweetheart, no one would dare assume you're smart enough to pull this off.' Can you believe that?

"Of course, I was furious. But in a way, I'm grateful for what she said. It made me realize that I'm just like you all —a victim in this twisted game. I might have been the one pulling the strings, but Caroline was the puppet master."

With that, Candy rose from her chair, smoothing her new dress as she prepared to leave the room. She felt a swell of pride, certain that she'd managed to shift the blame onto Caroline and position herself as nothing more than a lovestruck fool.

As she reached the door, Miles called out her name in a low, dangerous tone. She turned, her heart skipping a beat as she saw the look in his green eyes. It was a promise— there would be repercussions for her actions.

"Remember, Candy," he said quietly, his voice tight with anger, "every action has an equal and opposite reaction. You might think you've won today, but you won't always be this lucky."

Candy's eyes met his for a moment before she forced a smile onto her face. "We'll see about that, Miles," she replied airily, refusing to let him have the last word. As she swept out of the room, she hid the small shiver of fear that ran down her spine.

Candy stepped out of the office, closing the door behind her with a soft click. The sound seemed to echo through the empty hallway, amplifying her sense of isolation. She leaned against the wall, her carefully constructed facade crumbling as she allowed herself to feel her fear.

"Get it together, Candy," she whispered to herself,

taking slow, deep breaths. As she did, she glanced down at her shoes, the heels clicking on the polished floor as she shifted her weight from one foot to the other. For once, their beauty failed to comfort her.

"Didn't realize you were the sensitive type," came Lila's voice from behind her, dripping with sarcasm. Startled, Candy spun around to find Lila leaning against the opposite wall, her arms crossed and a knowing smirk on her face.

"Save your pity for someone who cares," Candy snapped, her fear momentarily replaced by irritation. Lila was the last person she wanted to deal with at this moment.

"Trust me, I have none to spare for you," Lila retorted, pushing off the wall and walking towards her. "Just thought you might want some advice."

"From you? I'd rather take fashion tips from Destiny."

"Ouch," Lila said, feigning hurt. "But seriously, Candy, Miles isn't one to make idle threats. If he says there will be consequences, you can bet he means it."

"Thanks for the warning," Candy replied icily, her heart pounding in her chest. "Now if you'll excuse me, I have better things to do than stand here and listen to you."

"Suit yourself," Lila shrugged, stepping aside to let her pass. As Candy strode past her, she could sense Lila's eyes boring into her back, studying her every move. It made her skin crawl.

Candy gave Caroline a quick call, tipping her off that Miles is aware of everything. "They know it all," Candy said before chortling, "Good luck," abruptly ending the call on a stunned Caroline. For the first time in her life, she found herself on shaky ground, unsure of what the future held and whether she'd be able to regain control.

twenty-nine

MILES' EYES REMAINED FIXED ON THE DOOR AS IT CLICKED shut with finality, his heart thudding heavily in his chest. The air in the room seemed to grow thicker, suffocating him with the weight of betrayal. He had always known that Caroline was capable of cruelty, but never in his wildest dreams did he think she would conspire with Candy to hurt Destiny for no other reason than to "save" him. His mother had crossed a line he never thought she would.

He registered Lila's departure as she followed Candy out, her blue eyes narrowed and jaw set with determination. But he couldn't bring himself to care about their confrontation, not when Destiny stood before him, tears brimming in her hazel eyes, threatening to spill over. Miles felt as if he were drowning in regret, grasping for a lifeline that didn't exist.

"I'm so sorry," he croaked, barely recognizing the raw pain in his own voice. "All of this... it's my fault."

"Hey," Destiny said softly, reaching up to touch his arm. Her skin felt like a soothing balm against his turmoil.

"You can't control other people, Miles. You didn't do this."

But Miles couldn't shake the feeling that he had failed her. He had let the most important woman in his life down—one by not seeing through Candy's lies, and the other by not protecting Destiny from the storm that raged around them.

Miles clenched his fists and took a deep breath, the fire of determination igniting in his green eyes. Without another word, he strode out of the office, each step firm and resolute. The elevator doors opened with a soft chime, and Miles stepped inside, followed closely by Max, Malcolm, Lila, Vivienne, and Destiny.

"Where are you going?" Lila asked, her eyes filled with concern.

"Time to have a conversation with my mother," Miles said, his voice as cold as steel.

"Are you sure that's a good idea?" Max chimed in, his brow furrowed. "You're pretty worked up."

"Damn right I am," Miles growled, punching the ground floor button. "Mother dearest has gone too far this time."

The elevator doors slid open, revealing the sleek, modern lobby of Vortex headquarters. Miles led the way across the polished marble floors, his steps echoing through the vast space. He grabbed the keys to the large company SUV from the security desk and motioned for everyone to follow him.

"Let's go," he said, his voice steady and determined.

They piled into the SUV, and Miles started the engine, its purr reassuring him. He glanced at Destiny sitting beside him, her hazel eyes filled with quiet strength. As they drove towards his mother's house, the world outside blurred into a landscape of green lawns and pristine houses, each one a testament to the wealth and power of their occupants.

"Wait," Miles said, his brows drawing together as he spotted his mother's car in the Sullivan's driveway. "She's at Colter's."

"Of course she is," Lila muttered darkly, her disdain for Candy's father evident in her tone.

Miles took the turn down the Sullivan's street, his grip on the steering wheel tightening. As they approached, he saw his mother sitting on Colter's porch, sipping tea with an air of smug satisfaction. It was time to confront the truth – and the woman who had betrayed him.

Miles skidded the SUV to a stop. Before anyone else could react, he flung open the driver's door and stormed towards the porch, his face flushed with anger. The rest of the group scrambled out of the car, trying to keep up with him.

"Hey, Miles," Max called out as he caught up to his brother, grabbing his shoulder in an attempt to slow him down. "Calm down, man. You don't want to make things worse."

Miles pulled away, his green eyes blazing. "I'm done letting her get away with this, Max. It ends now."

Caroline looked up from her tea, her blue eyes widening in mock surprise as she took in the scene before her. "Hi, dear," she cooed, attempting to feign innocence. "What brings you here?"

"Save it, Mother," Miles spat, his voice dripping with disdain. He folded his arms across his chest, his posture rigid. "We know everything. Candy told us how you two planned to ruin Destiny and destroy my relationship with her. You've betrayed me and hurt innocent people for your own selfish gain."

Caroline scoffed, lifting her chin haughtily. "You

wouldn't believe that little tramp over your own mother, would you? She's obviously lying."

Miles clenched his fists, fighting the urge to yell. He knew his mother was manipulative, but to hear her deny her actions so brazenly only fueled his anger further. The thought of what she had done to Destiny—and to him—made his stomach churn.

Miles stared at his mother, the disbelief sinking in at how evil the woman sitting in front of him now. It was like looking into the eyes of a cold and heartless human being.

He felt a gentle touch on his arm and glanced down to see Destiny standing beside him, her eyes bright with determination despite the tears that lingered on her lashes. Miles squeezed her hand as he turned back to face Caroline, drawing strength from her presence.

Caroline's gaze flicked over to Destiny, her nostrils flaring with disdain. "This neighborhood is a little out of your price point, dear," she sneered. "You should just leave before you embarrass yourself further."

"Shut the fuck up, Caroline!" Miles snapped, his voice echoing through the large garden. The air around them seemed to crackle with tension. "What Candy said matches the evidence we found. You both were involved, and you, Colter" - he looked pointedly at the man who had been silently standing beside his mother - "are just a weak-ass bastard who's being led by his dick rather than making your own choices."

Caroline's eyes flashed with venom as she spat out, "I knew that girl was a little bitch." With one last glare at Destiny, she whirled around and stomped off to her car, the sound of her heels clicking angrily against the pavement.

"Caroline, wait!" Colter called after her, but she didn't even pause, she simply slammed her car door shut and raced away. He sighed heavily, rubbing a hand over his face in frustration.

Miles watched her go, his green eyes dark with anger and disappointment. In that moment, he realized that no matter how much he wanted it to be otherwise, this was the woman his mother truly was—and there was nothing he could do to change it. He had to let her go, for his own sake and for Destiny's.

Miles' heart thundered in his chest as his gaze fell to Destiny. The scent of fresh rain and honeysuckle lingered in the air around them, creating a surreal atmosphere amidst the chaos that had just unfolded. He reached out, hesitating for a moment, before holding out his hands towards her.

"Destiny..." he whispered, praying she would take them.

Her delicate fingers intertwined with his, her touch warm and reassuring. Miles let out a breath he didn't realize he was holding, relief washing over him like a wave crashing onto the shore.

"Why did you come to Vortex earlier?" he asked, his voice barely audible above the sounds of the world around them.

She looked into his eyes, a determined glint reflecting within her own. "Miles, you need to be open to trusting others... but so do I."

The simple honesty in her words struck a chord deep within him. For too long, they had both been hiding behind emotional walls, too afraid to let each other in completely.

"Will you give me another chance?" he implored, his heart pounding as he awaited her answer.

Time seemed to slow as Destiny's gaze searched his face, looking for any hint of insincerity. When she finally spoke, her words carried the weight of a thousand unspoken promises. "Yes, Miles. I will."

In that instant, it felt as if the entire universe had faded away, leaving only the two of them locked in this moment of pure connection. Unable to contain himself any longer, Miles pulled Destiny in and kissed her with a passion that spoke volumes about the love he held for her.

As they broke apart, Miles couldn't help but smile at the sight of her flushed cheeks and the way her eyes sparkled with happiness. It was then that he became aware of the hoots and hollers from his brothers, Vivi, and Lila as they celebrated the love that is exploding like fireworks high in the sky.

"Hey!" Lila called out, a mischievous grin plastered across her face. "Get a room, you two!"

Miles chuckled, feeling his cheeks grow warm. Pulling Destiny in close, he whispered into her ear, "I'm gonna marry you one day."

Her angelic laughter filled the air as she replied, "I'll hold you to that."

Hand in hand, Miles and Destiny descended Colter's porch steps, their hearts filled with renewed hope and love for each other. The warm sunlight bathed them in a golden glow, reflecting the happiness that radiated from their intertwined fingers.

"Thank you all for being here," Miles said sincerely to his brothers, Vivi, and Lila, who had gathered at the bottom of the steps. They exchanged heartfelt hugs, the collective strength of their bond grounding them in this moment.

"Of course we'd be here," Max replied, giving Miles a firm pat on the back. "We're family."

"Besides," Lila chimed in, her eyes twinkling with

mischief, "we wouldn't miss this for the world, did you see the look on their faces?!"

Miles couldn't help but laugh, feeling lighter than he had in ages. He turned to Destiny, his emerald eyes sparkling with affection. "You know," he murmured, a smile playing at the corners of his lips, "I always imagined our love story would be full of sunflowers and daisies, just like your favorite bouquet."

Destiny's hazel eyes lit up with delight as she looked back at him. "And happiness that will span a lifetime?"

"Absolutely," Miles confirmed, his voice filled with conviction. In one fluid motion, he swept Destiny off her feet, eliciting a surprised squeal from her. As he twirled her around, her laughter rang out like music, filling the air with infectious joy.

"Promise?" Destiny asked breathlessly when they finally stopped spinning, her eyes searching his for sincerity.

"Promise," Miles vowed, sealing his words with a tender kiss.

As they stood there, surrounded by their friends and family, it was clear that no matter what life threw at them, they would face it together. For theirs was a love that could weather any storm, bound by unbreakable ties of loyalty, trust, and the promise of a lifetime full of sunflowers, daisies, and endless happiness.

epilogue

SIX MONTHS LATER, THE SUN STREAMED THROUGH THE windows of Miles' house, shining the moving boxes that filled their living room in bright light. Destiny looked around, taking in the sight of her life, neatly packed away in cardboard containers. She felt a surge of happiness at the thought of finally creating a home with the man she loved.

"Hey, Dest! I didn't know you had so many kitchen tools!" Miles called out from the kitchen, his voice tinged with amusement.

Destiny laughed, picturing him surrounded by an army of spatulas and whisks. "Well, I love to cook," she replied playfully. "Did you expect me to survive on microwave meals when I'm not at work?"

"Of course not, but this is quite the impressive collection," he said as he emerged from the kitchen, holding up a spiralizer with mock reverence. "I didn't even know these existed!"

"Are you happy that we're moving in together?"

Destiny asked, searching his eyes for any hint of doubt or hesitation.

His green eyes sparkled as he smiled warmly at her. "I couldn't be happier, Destiny. This is the beginning of our life together, and I can't wait to see what adventures await us."

"Me too," she murmured, feeling her heart swell with contentment.

Destiny pulled another box towards her, the cardboard edges slightly worn from being moved around. She carefully pried open the flaps to reveal an assortment of photo albums and loose photographs—their memories captured in snapshots.

"Ah, here's our pictures," she announced with a glint in her hazel eyes. Picking up the first photo, she smiled as she recognized the day Miles had asked her to move in with him. "Miles, look at this," she called out, waving the photo in his direction.

"Let me see," he said, walking over and taking the photo from her hand. A smile spread across his face as he remembered that day.

The memory came back to her in vivid detail.

They were sitting on a picnic blanket in the lush green park, surrounded by blooming flowers and the laughter of children playing nearby. The sun was shining brightly on everything it touched. Destiny had been happily nibbling on a sandwich as Miles fidgeted beside her, seemingly lost in thought.

"Hey, you okay?" Destiny asked, placing a hand on his arm.

"Actually, I have something I want to ask you," he began, his voice uncharacteristically nervous. He took a deep breath, his green eyes locking onto hers with a serious intensity. "Destiny, every day I'm more and more certain that I want to spend the rest of my life with you."

Destiny felt her heart pound in her chest, anticipation building inside her.

"Would you consider moving in with me?" he asked, worry etched into the lines on his forehead.

She didn't hesitate. "Of course, Miles. I'd love to," she replied, her voice filled with genuine happiness. Miles let out a relieved sigh and pulled her into a tight embrace.

"Thank you," he whispered into her ear. "You have no idea how much this means to me."

"Actually, I think I do," she said softly, resting her head on his shoulder.

As the memory faded away, Destiny was filled with a sense of warmth and contentment. That day had marked the beginning of a new chapter in their lives—one that had led them to where they were now, unpacking boxes in their new home together. She glanced over at Miles, who was still holding the photo, a smile tugging at the corners of his lips.

"The day we met seems like a lifetime ago, doesn't it?" she mused.

"Feels more like yesterday to me," he replied, placing the photo back in the box. "We've come so far since then, haven't we?"

Destiny carefully pulled out the second photo from the box, her eyes immediately lighting up with recognition. The picture captured the night of their engagement, a moment frozen in time that she would never forget. Her heart swelled as the memory came rushing back to her.

Miles had planned everything down to the smallest detail. He'd transformed Max and Vivi's backyard into a romantic wonderland, with twinkling fairy lights strung overhead and soft music playing in the background.

Destiny remembered stepping through the French doors and feeling as if she'd walked right into a dream.

"Surprise!" Max, Malcolm, Vivi, and Lila had shouted in unison as she entered the enchanted space. They were all there, dressed to the nines and ready to celebrate the love she and Miles had found together.

"Is this...?" Destiny had begun, her voice trailing off as her eyes landed on Miles. He stood before her, looking dashing in his suit, an air of nervous excitement radiating from him.

"Destiny, I've spent my entire life searching for something that was missing," Miles began, his voice filled with emotion. "But it wasn't until you came waltzing back into my life that I realized what it was."

He paused, taking a deep breath as he reached into his pocket and produced a small velvet box. As he opened it, the ring inside sparkled under the fairy lights, capturing Destiny's gaze.

Miles dropped to one knee, his expression alight with longing, and opened the box. The round brilliant diamond winked up at me, its fire dancing in my eyes. His voice filled with passion, he asked me a single question that held my heart's desire: "Destiny Evans, will you do me the greatest honor of my life and marry me – so I can love you for eternity?" yes.

Destiny felt an overwhelming sense of joy, warmth, and belonging. She knew, without a doubt, that she wanted to spend the rest of her life by Miles' side.

"Of course, I will," she replied, her voice thick with emotion. "I love you, Miles."

Miles slid the beautiful ring onto her finger before pulling her in for a passionate kiss. The moment their lips met, the world around them seemed to fall away, leaving only the two of them and the love they shared.

"Congratulations!" their friends cheered as they broke apart, surrounding the newly engaged couple with hugs and well-wishes. The rest of the evening had been filled with laughter, dancing, and heartfelt toasts to the future Destiny and Miles would share together.

As the memory faded, Destiny found herself back in their new home, the engagement photo clutched in her hand. She looked over at Miles, who was watching her with a tender smile on his face.

"Remember how perfect that night was?" she asked softly, her voice infused with gratitude and love.

"I'll never forget it," he replied, taking her hand and giving it a gentle squeeze. "It was the night I promised myself to you, and you to me. And I intend to keep that promise for the rest of our lives."

Destiny's heart swelled as she leaned in to give him a sweet, lingering kiss. Their past was filled with beautiful memories, but what awaited them in the future was even more promising. Together, they would continue to build a life full of love, joy, and endless possibilities.

Destiny pulled out another photo. This one was taken by Lila on wine night, all the girls in fluffy robes and face masks making goofy faces into the camera. She couldn't help but remember that was the day she learned about the consequences Candy and Colter faced for their actions, the shock she felt then still lingering in her mind.

The memory of that particular day came flooding back —the day when Miles had called her, his voice heavy with the weight of the news he was about to share. He had asked her to come over to his house for dinner, and she could sense the urgency in his tone. Worried, Destiny agreed without hesitation.

As she arrived at his home, she found him finishing up dinner, his brow furrowed with concentration. Miles looked up from the stove and motioned for her to sit on one of the barstools at the counter.

"Destiny, I need to talk to you about something," he began, his voice serious yet gentle. "It's about Candy and Colter."

"Okay, what happened?" she asked, concern etched across her face.

Miles took a deep breath before continuing. "I confronted Colter today, told him that his daughter was behind the breach and released all of his information. I also told him how Caroline and Candy manipulated him." His hands clenched into fists, anger simmering beneath the surface. "But don't worry, he promised to do something about it."

Destiny's thoughts shifted as she remembered the day she saw Candy shopping at the local Goodwill. It was a far cry from her days dripping in designer clothes, like a fallen queen forced to mingle with her subjects. The image of Candy, disheveled and wearing ill-fitting clothes, brought an ironic smirk to Destiny's face.

Miles ran a hand through his brown hair the day he fired her. He had made sure she was blackballed, exacting justice just like Colter had done to Destiny's father. After Miles made it clear she was a thief, the manager at the diner in the next town over hired her as a dishwasher, since she couldn't be trusted around money. Destiny couldn't help but be reminded of how karma really caught up with her.

Destiny's thoughts shifted over to the ringleader of the whole plan to destroy her family. The last thing she wanted to go to was dinner at Caroline's house. The atmosphere had been stifling, and Destiny could still feel the weight of her reluctance to attend. But she trusted Miles when he promised it would be the last time.

"Baby, we need to make an appearance," Miles had whispered into her ear, his breath warm and reassuring. "Just one more time."

"Fine," Destiny had sighed, knowing that if Miles was asking, it was important.

As they entered the lavish home, hand in hand, Destiny's steps were heavy with dread, but she held her head high. The dinner table was set with fine china, silverware gleaming under the soft light. All eyes turned toward them as they made their grand entrance, fashionably late.

"Ah, finally, the guests of honor!" Caroline announced, forcing a smile that didn't quite reach her eyes.

Dinner was an exercise in strained conversation and forced laughter. Destiny found herself picking at her food, unable to shake the tension gripping the room. When the plates were cleared away, Vivienne stood up, holding a folded piece of paper.

"Before we go, I have a little gift for our gracious hostess," Vivi said, her sapphire eyes sparkling with mischief.

Curiosity piqued, Destiny glanced at Miles who smirked knowingly. As Vivi handed the paper to Caroline, the room went silent, anticipation hanging thick in the air.

"Family woman? Or gold digger?" Destiny read aloud from her own copy of the paper, her voice dripping with disbelief and amusement. She scanned through the pages detailing Caroline's exploits, each revelation more shocking than the last. The one that caught her eye was the ongoing torrid affair with Colter Sullivan. Destiny glanced at Caroline whose mouth was open like a fish out of water to Lawrence, who looked like the world was ending right in front of him. She felt no remorse for Caroline, but she felt a tinge of sadness for Lawrence being caught in the middle.

"I...I can explain," Caroline stammered, face flushed crimson with embarrassment.

"Save it, Caroline," Lawrence snapped, his anger evident. "I thought our relationship would last. I knew you had been married plenty of times before, but I thought I could change you. Now I see that the only person you love is yourself. You and Colter enjoy yourselves. I'm done."

Lawrence got up and excused himself. With one final glare at them, Caroline followed, her heels clicking as she screamed for Lawrence to wait while tripping over her ridiculous gown.

"Vivi," Destiny turned to her future sister-in-law, laughter bubbling up within her. "When did you send this?"

"Wine night, of course!" Vivi replied with a wink.

The group erupted into laughter as they made their way out of Caroline's house, leaving the woman to face the consequences of her actions. The cool night air brought relief, and Destiny felt lighter than she had in months.

Destiny's thoughts snapped back to the present as Miles approached her, a glass of wine in his hand. His green eyes twinkled with warmth and love as he handed her the wine. She took it gratefully, feeling a sense of comfort wash over her.

"Thanks, Miles," she said softly, sipping the velvety red liquid.

"Of course," he replied, sitting down next to her and wrapping an arm around her shoulders. "So, I have some news for you. Caroline's house finally sold."

"Really?" Destiny asked, raising an eyebrow. "Who bought it?"

"Doesn't matter," Miles shrugged. "What's important is that she's out of our lives for good. She's been begging

Colter to take her back, but he won't. Can you believe that?"

A memory flashed in Destiny's mind—the high-pitched scream of Candy echoing through the café when Colter revealed his plans to sell his house and business, pack up, and leave town to escape further embarrassment. The look on Candy's face had been priceless, and Destiny couldn't help but feel a small sense of satisfaction knowing that both Candy and Caroline were getting what they deserved.

Destiny took another sip of her wine, enjoying the rich taste that filled her mouth. She glanced around the room, taking in the chaos of moving boxes and the comforting presence of Miles beside her. As her gaze fell on an old, worn cardboard box tucked in a corner, she felt a pang of emotion.

"Hey, what's that box over there?" Miles asked, following her line of sight.

Destiny hesitated before replying, "That's my dad's box. I just couldn't bring myself to open it when he passed."

Miles reached out and squeezed her hand gently. "Do you want to go through it together?"

Nodding, Destiny took a deep breath and pulled the box closer. The flaps were sealed with yellowed tape, and she carefully slid a pair of scissors under it, cutting through the silence of the room. As she opened the box, the scent of her father's cologne wafted into the air, instantly transporting her back to her childhood.

Inside the box, she found various memorabilia from her father's time in the military—medals, ribbons, and a well-worn, leather-bound journal with faded pages filled with his handwriting. A collection of dog tags jingled softly as she picked them up, running her fingers over the embossed names and numbers.

"Wow," Miles whispered in awe, looking at the items spread across the floor.

"Every year, we would exchange letters on our birthdays," Destiny explained as she gingerly lifted a stack of envelopes tied together with a ribbon. "We'd leave them on each other's pillow for one of us to open first thing in the morning."

"Sounds like a beautiful tradition," Miles said, a soft smile on his face.

"Here, it looks like this letter is unopened," Miles said, handing her the letter.

"He wrote me another one," Destiny said in awe, pulling out an envelope from the bottom of the stack. The date on the front wasn't Destiny's birthday, but rather the day her father had passed.

With trembling hands, Destiny opened the letter and began to read:

Dear Destiny,

As I write this letter, I know that my time here is limited. But I wanted to leave you with a few words of wisdom and love that you can carry with you for the rest of your life.

First, always remember how proud I am of you. You have grown into a strong, resilient, and compassionate woman—qualities that will serve you well in whatever path you choose.

Second, never be afraid to ask for help or lean on those who care for you. Life can be challenging, but you don't have to face it alone.

Cherish the relationships you've built and hold them close.

Lastly, my sweet girl, never forget that you are loved. Even when I'm no longer around, my love for you will remain an eternal force. Remember that I'll always be there for you, watching over you and cheering you on from above.

I will love you forever, my sweetie pie.
Dad

Once Destiny composed herself after the emotional letter, she wiped away her tears and looked back at the box. She reached in and pulled out the last photo, a smile spreading across her face. It was a picture of her and Miles standing in front of the café, their arms around each other, grinning from ear to ear. A large banner hung above them, proclaiming "Sweetie Pie Café" in bold letters. Destiny's heart swelled with pride as she remembered that moment.

"Perfect," she murmured, getting up from the couch. She carefully arranged the pictures on the mantel, placing the one of her and Miles right in the center. Taking a step back, she admired her handiwork—a visual representation of the happiness and love she'd found with him.

Miles came up behind her, wrapping his arm around her waist and pulling her close. "You did a great job with these," he said softly, admiring the photos along with her.

"Thank you," Destiny replied, leaning into his embrace. She felt safe, secure, and loved in his arms—everything she'd ever wanted in life.

"Are you glad the Mitchells decided to sell the café?" Miles asked, his breath warm against her ear.

Destiny smiled up at him, her eyes shining with happiness. "My dreams have all come true. My own café and you." She glanced back at the photo of them in front of the Sweetie Pie Café, remembering the joy she felt knowing it was finally hers and how far they had come together.

The sound of people on the porch opening the door broke Destiny out of her reverie. She looked over at Miles, who squeezed her hand reassuringly before releasing it to answer the door.

"Got it," he said with a grin and moved toward the entrance, his strong frame casting a shadow on the wooden floor.

As Destiny heard the door opening and familiar voices making their way inside, a smile lit up her face. Her friends and family had come to help them unpack and settle into their new life together. The warm afternoon sun filtered through the windows, casting a golden glow on the room filled with boxes waiting to be opened.

"Let's get this party started, shall we?" Vivi chimed in with her trademark enthusiasm, Max followed closely behind, grinning at each other as they carried more boxes inside.

"Please tell me you brought some of your brownies, Vivi," Miles teased as he joined the group, placing a gentle hand on Destiny's lower back.

"Of course! And don't think I forgot about your love for jalapeno poppers, Mr. Huntington," Vivi replied with a wink.

Destiny watched her friends and family laugh and joke with one another, the atmosphere light and full of joy. It felt like home—something she'd been searching for her entire life. In that moment, surrounded by love and laughter, Destiny looked up and gave a silent thank you to her father for guiding her on this journey.

"Everything okay?" Miles asked, concern written on his handsome face.

"Better than okay," Destiny replied with a warm smile, her hazel eyes shining with happiness. "I finally feel like I've found my way home."

Miles' green eyes sparkled as his lips curved into a loving smile, clearly understanding the depth of her words. He leaned down to press a tender kiss on her forehead before turning back to their friends and joining in their lively banter.

As she watched him interact with their loved ones, Destiny's heart swelled with gratitude for all they had been through together and the life they were building side by side. She knew without a doubt that they were truly destined for love.

If you've reached the end of the story, thank you! I hope Miles and Destiny's story warmed your heart as much as it did mine.

Before you close the book, could you do me a tiny favor? Leaving a review would mean the world to me. Your thoughts help me, as the author, by giving me invaluable feedback to craft even better stories in the future.

So, if this book stole a piece of your heart, please consider sharing your thoughts with the world.

afterword

Dear Reader,

As I sit down to write this afterword, I find myself overwhelmed with emotions. First and foremost, I want to extend my deepest gratitude to you. Yes, you, the one holding this book in your hands, the one who has just embarked on a journey through the pages of my debut novel.

When I first started jotting down the ideas that eventually became this book, I had no clue where it would take me. It's been a wild ride, filled with tons of writing, editing, and late-night brainstorming sessions (and let's not forget the endless cups of tea to keep me going). But above all, it's led me to Miles and Destiny.

Knowing that you're taking the time to step into the world I've created, to hang out with the characters I've come to love, means the world to me. Seriously, your decision to give my book a shot is beyond words.

Putting this novel together has been a labor of love, something I've dreamed about for years. Seeing it in your hands, knowing it's made a little impact in your life, brings me so much joy. Whether you laughed, cried, or just found a moment of peace within these pages, it's everything to me.

As a debut author, every reader who picks up my book is a gift, a validation of my passion and dedication to storytelling. So, from the bottom of my heart, thank you. Thank you for believing in me, for joining me on this journey, and for allowing my words to be a part of your life, if only for a little while.

As you close the final pages of this book, I hope you feel a sense of contentment, knowing your support has meant the world to me. And as you go about your day, may the characters and their love story stick with you, a gentle reminder that love is always worth the journey, whether in fiction or real life.

With love and gratitude,

Sara

Sara McClaflin, a dedicated author of romance, crafts tales that are not only heart-melting but also delve into the delicate facets of humanity. Having spent the past few years as an avid reader, Sara transitioned from writing book reviews to creating her own narratives. Her passion for romance, in all its diverse forms, shines through as she weaves stories that resonate with readers.

Residing on the vibrant west coast with her husband and beloved dog, Sara McClaflin is surrounded by the inspiration of nature and the love of her family. In her world, there is no such thing as too many books or an over-filled "want to read" list, as each story unfolds new possibilities and adventures.

- **Amazon Author Page:** https://www.amazon.com/stores/author/B0CR8VHBHJ/about
- **Instagram:** https://www.instagram.com/authorsaramcclaflin/
- **Facebook:** https://www.facebook.com/profile.php?id=61551822185090
- **Twitter (X):** https://twitter.com/authorsaramcc
- **TikTok:** https://www.tiktok.com/@sara.mcclaflin
- **Goodreads:** https://www.goodreads.com/author/show/47632250.Sara_McClaflin

- **Newsletter Signup:** https://subscribepage.io/SaraMcClaflin